FALKIRK COMMUNITY TRUST

30124 02667642 1

CANCELLED

Lizzie's Daughters

D1438493

FALKIRK COMMUNITY TRUST LIBRARIES	

ALSO BY ROSIE CLARKE
FROM CLIPPER LARGE PRINT

Lizzie's Secret
Lizzie's War

Lizzie's Daughters

Rosie Clarke

W F HOWES LTD

This large print edition published in 2017 by
W F Howes Ltd
Unit 5, St George's House, Rearsby Business Park,
Gaddesby Lane, Rearsby, Leicester LE7 4YH

1 3 5 7 9 10 8 6 4 2

First published in the United Kingdom in 2017
by Aria

Copyright © Rosie Clarke, 2017

The right of Rosie Clarke to be identified as
the author of this work has been asserted by her
in accordance with the Copyright, Designs and
Patents Act, 1988.

All rights reserved

A CIP catalogue record for this book is available
from the British Library

ISBN 978 1 51007 763 8

Typeset by Palimpsest Book Production Limited,
Falkirk, Stirlingshire

Printed and bound by
T J International in the UK
Printforce Nederland b.v. in the Netherlands
Ligare in Australia

MIX
Paper from
responsible sources
FSC
www.fsc.org   FSC® C013056

PROLOGUE

Sobbing, gasping for breath, she ran into the dark night, terror lending her the strength to escape him. He'd tried to drug her, to use her for his foul purposes, but she was neither as naïve nor as stupid as he believed her and in the seconds he'd turned his back on her to answer his phone, she'd switched drinks and sipped one before emptying the rest beneath the bed and falling back against the pillows in what she hoped looked like a drugged stupor.

'He comes, ma cherie . . .' the hateful voice, a voice she'd thought she loved, said close to her ear, the smell of wine and cigarettes thick on his breath, 'and then he will give me what I want for you, ma petite. He likes a *ménage à trois,* so we'll share you and then each other . . . it's time you learned what it's all about, my English prude . . .'

Even as the revulsion and fear trailed through her, she'd lain without protest, giving a faint moan, and she'd heard him pick up his wine glass and known he was drinking the wine meant for her. He must have drunk it all, just as he believed she had, because she heard him swear and then felt his weight as he suddenly slumped on the bed next to her. Pushing his bulk away from her, she'd scrambled over his body and out of the bed. He made an attempt to grab her ankle, cursing in a blurred voice as he couldn't hold her; it told her clearly what effect that foul drug would've had on her if she'd been as drunk as he thought and taken the glass he'd intended for her.

Evading his grasp as he fell back useless against the pillows, she'd grabbed her clothes and run, down the wooden staircase to the alley below. She hid in the shadows and hurriedly pulled on her clothes as she saw the man who had paid for her walking eagerly towards the wooden steps that zig-zagged up the outside of the wall to the small garret studio. As soon as he opened the door and went in, she ran and ran . . . the fear of being caught making her unaware that her feet were bare on the sharp cobbles. Until she paused for breath, believing that she was safe for now, though for the moment lost in the maze of dark alleys of Montmartre, an area of cobbled streets known for its seedy nightlife and busy cafés, where the music flowed as easily as the rich wine and her friends met to smoke and drink and laugh. She'd come to know the sights and sounds well in the few weeks she'd spent in Paris, visiting the beautiful churches and art galleries whenever she had the time alone. Although it was October, the evening was warmer than it would be at home in England, and now that she'd stopped running she could breathe more easily.

Gradually, she recovered her breath and became calm enough to recognise her surroundings. She didn't know what kind of drug he'd tried to give her, but she suspected some kind of opiate, the drugs so often used to bring wilful girls into line in houses of disrepute, and she shuddered as she realised what fate he'd had in store for her had she not tricked him into drinking the wine himself. Her feet were cut and sore, but, unconsciously, she'd been running in the right direction to find a safe harbour, though it would only be safe until he came looking for her again, which she feared he would. Once, she'd thought she loved him, but now the very thought of his touch made her sick with shame and she wished a thousand times that she'd never met him. In that moment she knew she must get away from this place. She'd believed she'd found a way to live and find happiness, to put him out of her mind, but what he'd done tonight had convinced her that he would never let her go free while she was of use to him.

She must go back to England, though she could never go home. Yet in her own country she could find a place to hide and perhaps in time she would find a new life. It was no longer a matter of choice, but perhaps the only avenue left open to her . . .

CHAPTER 1

'I wish you'd let me take you home,' Frank Hadley said as he saw the way Betty's eyes were sparkling dangerously. 'You shouldn't drink so much, Betty – and I don't like this crowd here tonight. What would your father say if he knew the company you keep?'

'Why would he care?' Betty Oliver tossed her long reddish blonde hair. She was gradually having it lightened to what she hoped would be a fabulous strawberry-blonde, but it was taking ages, because she didn't dare to have it done all over and was adding streaks a few at a time. Her greenish-blue eyes snapped with temper. 'If you think my father loves me, Frank, you're wrong. I'm not really his and he only cares about my sister . . . and Mum, of course.'

'That's ridiculous,' Frank said and took hold of her arm. 'Come on, Betty love, you've had enough wine. I'm getting you out of here . . .'

The jukebox was playing an Everly Brothers song in the background and Betty swayed dreamily to the romantic music. 'Dance with me, Frank,' she said and looked up at him enticingly, her full skirts swishing about her hips. The skirt was made fuller by layers of net petticoats and she had flat red shoes on her feet so that she could dance to the fast numbers, because she loved to jive and twist to the popular songs. 'Hold me . . .'

'Come on, we're leaving . . .' Frank said, but Betty pulled away from him, her smile gone as she refused to leave.

'You go,' she said petulantly. 'I want some fun and I'd like another Babycham . . .'

'I'm leaving now,' Frank said, suddenly angry. 'You can come or you can stay here – but this isn't a place I want to be, Betty . . .'

'I'm staying.' Betty flounced away from him, her neatly cut hair tossing as she lifted her head in defiance.

Frank watched her walk across the room, feeling angry and frustrated. Betty wasn't his girl yet but he'd had hopes. When she'd asked him to bring her to this club this evening, he'd been pleased, but when he discovered what was going on he felt let down and disappointed. He frowned as he saw her start dancing with a man he'd seen around in the cafés and dances they all went to. Frank knew he was French and he'd heard rumours about the man Betty was snuggling up to. There was nothing substantial, but Frank's instincts told him that he meant to seduce Betty if he could. That sort who would think nothing of getting an innocent girl drunk and taking advantage. It would serve her right if he stuck to his word and went off and left her – but Frank wasn't the sort to abandon a girl if he took her out.

He would stay on and watch over Betty, try to stop her drinking too much and eventually take her home in his car. Even if she was behaving foolishly, he couldn't help the way he felt. Frank had been attracted to the lively girl the first time he'd met Betty at Matt's home. She was wilful, sometimes sulky, but her smile lit up the room and he hadn't been able to take his eyes off her. He and Matt Court had been at college together, and bonded because of their love of sport, though Frank was three years older; he hadn't been able to take up his place for a couple of years due to his father's death and his mother's collapse.

'How yer doin', Frank?' Matt's voice made him spin round and he smiled as he saw the tall hand-some younger man. They were much the same build and height, but if anything Frank was a little heavier, and both were good at all the strenuous sports like rowing, rugby and boxing. 'Has our Betty gone off and deserted you then?'

'She didn't like it because I wouldn't get her another drink and tried to make her let me drive her home.'

'She's headstrong sometimes,' Matt frowned over it. 'She thinks Sebastian loves Francie more than her and that's so wrong. He spoils her rotten and always has – but I know how she feels, because I was in the same boat. My mother had Jenny and me before she married . . .'

Frank nodded, anxious about the girl he felt so protective of. 'She won't listen to me but that man she's dancing with . . . I know him, Matt, and I don't like him. He'll get her drunk and then you know what will happen . . . I wish you'd talk to her.'

'Betty has always been a bit of a handful – but I'll see if I can rescue her.' Matt grinned. 'Maybe, I'll just give him a look and scare him off . . .'

Matt was the college champion in all things sporting – and his size made him rather terrifying, especially when he was angry. Although of a similar build and almost as successful at sport, Frank had a quieter personality and people often mistook him for a country bumpkin, which was far from the truth.

'You do that,' he said, watching as Matt strode across the room, unconsciously clearing a path as people moved out of his way. Betty argued for a moment, but then put her arms about Matt's waist affectionately and let him bring her away. The Frenchman stared after them, a glint of anger or even menace in his eyes as he met Frank's gaze, but turned aside and then moved off. Frank saw him speak to another girl and leave the club with her and breathed a sigh of relief. He'd been worried, because what he knew about that particular man had made him anxious for Betty's safety and he was glad Matt had managed what he couldn't . . .

Frank couldn't always be around to watch over

her. If she'd given him her promise to be his girl-friend, he believed she would keep it, because underneath the stubborn and sometimes sulky girl he knew there was a sweet nature. However, Betty saw him as Matt's boring friend and at the moment she hardly noticed him at all, except when she could use him to bring her somewhere like this . . .

Betty groaned as she opened her eyes and felt the light strike them She'd drunk too much Babycham the previous evening and been more than a little tipsy when Matt and Frank had insisted on driving her home. She'd wanted Pierre to take her in his car, as he had a couple of times before, but after Matt had intervened he'd gone off in a mood, because he was annoyed with her.

Pierre was like that, charming, handsome and exciting, smelling of exotic Turkish cigarettes and expensive hair oil, but he could get angry if thwarted. Betty liked the hint of danger about him, and the things he whispered in her ear. His compliments sounded so much nicer in his mixture of French and broken English, making her toes tingle and her stomach clench with a need she hardly recognised as desire. Their relationship had been exciting and Betty knew she was a little out of her depth, but she couldn't resist his smile or the sexy purr of his voice, even though she'd known him only a few weeks.

A few weeks before her eighteenth birthday,

Betty was still immature enough to be thrilled by the knowledge that neither of her parents would approve of her seeing the Frenchman, which she had been doing throughout the summer holidays.

Francie, her younger sister, had been home from her art college earlier in the summer and Betty had given her a hint that she'd met someone she liked, but she hadn't told even her how far things had gone . . . about the night Pierre had made love to her in the back of his car. Betty hadn't meant for her affair to go that far so quickly, but she'd been a little drunk and somehow she'd found herself giving into his persuasion. It was a secret she had to keep, because her family would be shocked by what she'd done, and Betty had been a little anxious about whether she would fall for a child. She'd avoided meeting him for a while after that night, but then they'd met at the club.

Pierre had asked her to dance, telling her he loved her and wanted her to meet him in the café they all used, the next morning. With his arms around her, Betty had felt the pull of his charm and longed for him to kiss her and love her again.

'We'll go for a drive,' he'd whispered in her ear. 'My time 'ere is almost over, Betty. I finish my studies and must go 'ome – but I stay for you . . . you're so beautiful and I want you . . .'

'Oh, Pierre . . .' Betty had pressed into his lean, hard body, melting into him and wanting to be alone with him so that she could show him how much she loved him. They'd made love only once so far, but she knew it was just a matter of time before it happened again. 'I'd love to come with you . . .'

Matt had interfered then and Pierre had left the club soon after, but she knew where to meet him and she'd made up her mind she would. Her rebellious feelings surfaced as she heard her mother calling to her and knew she had to make the effort to get up. Betty was sick of being told what to do and expected to excel at school the way her younger sister did. She had no intention of going back there and had her own ideas about the future – or she had until Pierre came along and now all she really wanted was to be with him . . .

'What sort of a report is this to show your father when he comes home?' Lizzie Winters looked at her eldest daughter's school report in dismay. '*Betty could do better but is lazy and inclined to mock the advice of her teachers . . .*' she read the first few lines of the Headmistress' summary to her daughter, who sat at the kitchen table drinking fizzy Vimto through a straw. 'You've got a C-grade in everything but art and for that you've got a B+ . . . do you think that's good enough?'

Betty shrugged and sent her a look of defiance. 'We can't all be as brainy as Francie, can we?' she replied, but though the words were meant to pierce there was no real malice behind them. Because Betty adored her younger sister and had protected her from everyone when they were

11

small. But she had not been able to keep up with her clever sibling and, when Francie had been accepted at a prestigious boarding school that specialised in art, they'd parted with floods of tears from both girls – more from Betty than Francie if the truth were known. 'I don't need higher maths and sciences for what I want to do, Mum. You didn't pass a load of exams at school but you've done all right for yourself . . .'

'I never had the chance . . . but then I got taken on at Bert's workshop and that was my lucky day,' Lizzie said defensively, because sometimes when Betty looked at her she saw Harry's eyes gazing back at her and she felt guilty. Was it her fault that Betty was so defiant and so determined to disappoint Sebastian? Did she feel that her parents loved her less than her sister because she was Harry's daughter and not Sebastian's? Harry had been Lizzie's first husband, but their marriage had broken down during the war and he'd died in a terrible accident, only hours before his daughter was born. Betty had never known her true father, and although Sebastian had always loved her and treated her as if she were his, perhaps she'd felt shut out or deprived of a father's love? 'I had good friends and then I met Sebastian and he believed in me and my talent . . . you have the opportunity to do so much more . . .'

'Maybe I'm not as talented as you or Francie,' Betty said, 'but you can't deny that I'm good at making and trimming hats – and clothes. Why won't you give me a job in your workshops, Mum? It's all I want to do, for now anyway – and my arithmetic is good enough to work out the cost of a range and the correct mark-up . . .'

Perhaps Lizzie ought not to be surprised that Betty loved hats and wanted to be involved in the business. Betty had been in and out of the workrooms all her young life, watching the various steps towards making the beautiful hats her mother was now famous for. It was August 1958 and Betty's eighteenth birthday was in September. She'd had enough of school and exams and wanted to experience life – and Lizzie could hardly blame her. She'd chafed at the bonds that held her back when her aunt had kept her dressed like a schoolgirl long after she'd left school to work in a canteen on the Docks.

'It's not what your father wants for you . . .' Sebastian had hoped that Betty would learn something useful and find a good job that would take her out into the world and give her the freedom their generation had never had. He didn't want her to be a workshop girl, because life was different now and Sebastian saw his daughters living fuller more exciting lives. Air travel and foreign holidays were gradually becoming available to anyone with a decent job, and the new motorways made it easier to get from London and the rest of the country. Although they'd had a short period of petrol rationing after the crisis in the Suez canal – that had finished the previous year and the severe shortages had ceased completely in the early fifties making it possible to buy so many lovely things in the shops these days, goods that had been imported from all over the world. It was a different world, an exciting world, and Sebastian intended that his daughters should be free to enjoy all the benefits education could give them. Lizzie half agreed with him, because she knew that running your own business was a hard life, even if you loved it and were talented enough to be successful, but mostly she just wanted her daughters to be happy in their lives. 'He thought you might be a secretary with extra languages and find exciting jobs here or abroad . . . or perhaps work in his West End shop, learn to be the manageress and eventually take over . . . unless you wanted to travel. What happened to your flair for French and German? You seemed to enjoy other languages when you were younger . . .'

'Boring . . .' Betty yawned and twirled the end of the exquisitely cut hair that made her look like a model out of *Vogue*. Her hair was much lighter in colour these days and Lizzie suspected she rinsed it with a hairdressing product to take some of the redness out of it, because it was more blonde than the sandy red it had been once she'd lost her baby blonde. 'Besides, much as I adore Sebastian, he isn't my father and I don't see why I have to do what he wants. You wouldn't mind me working with Ed and Romany, would you?'

Lizzie smiled at the mention of Ed's name. He'd

taught her the basics of her craft when she'd first joined Bert Oliver's workforce, though all the ideas for the hats women still loved to wear had come from inside Lizzie's head – and it wasn't right or fair of her to deny her much-loved daughter the chance to fulfil her own talent. Romany, was a younger woman Lizzie had taken on five years ago when Ed had started talking about the business being too much for him. After Bert had left Lizzie his business, Ed had taken over the running of it and become her partner, but he couldn't manage to run both that and Lizzie's own workshops when she cut her own hours, and so she'd advertised for an experienced milliner to take over the second workshop. Romany had been the first and only person she'd needed to interview.

Ed was now into his early sixties, but still young in outlook and very fit, perhaps because he walked and played tennis and cricket in the summer and football in the winter. It had taken him a long time to recover from the death of his wife Madge during the war, though more than once Lizzie had had hopes that he'd found someone else. He'd taken several women out and towards the end of the war she'd thought there was someone special, but for some reason nothing had come of it. He was devoted to his work running the workshops and producing the wonderful hats that Lizzie designed, and it had made him a comparatively wealthy man – much better off than he'd ever been working for Bert. Lizzie did little of the actual work these days, though she always made up samples of her latest designs to take into the workshops and often made hats for her friends as gifts.

It was hardly surprising that some of her love for millinery should rub off on her daughters. Seeing Betty's sulky face, she sighed, knowing that she was going to give in. Sebastian would say she was spoiling her – and perhaps there was some truth in that, because she always felt as if she had to make up for what her daughter had lost.

'I'll talk to your father,' she said, and saw the green eyes light up, reminding her so much of Harry when they were courting and he was happy and careless, before his jealousy destroyed their marriage and his life. 'And Sebastian *is* your father, Betty. He's always loved you as much as Francie – and you know that's true. He spoiled you rotten right from the moment he met you . . .'

'I know . . .' Betty got up and went to put her arms about Lizzie and hug her. 'I'm a little beast sometimes. I can't help it, Mum. It comes from inside – makes me restless and dissatisfied and when I'm like that I say things I don't mean. Dad is my father in every way but one, and I'm a mean bitch . . .'

'Language, my love, please don't say such things. Your father would be angry and I don't like them,' Lizzie frowned, wondering where Betty's expressions had come from because she'd gone to a private school until she won a scholarship for the Grammar School and decided that she would prefer that to continuing at the exclusive school Sebastian had chosen for her. That was when she'd seemed bright, intelligent and eager, but somewhere along the way that eagerness to do well had gone and Lizzie didn't understand why. Was it because Francie had done so much better? She knew the sisters loved each other, but was Betty torn by jealousy, because Francie was so very talented, already a wonderful artist? Francie had been accepted by a prestigious college that only took the most promising candidates. 'I haven't ever done or said anything to make you think I didn't love you, have I?' she asked, feeling a little upset. 'You must know that I adore both my girls equally?'

Betty's laugh was sheer joy to hear and her face lit up, making her so beautiful that it almost hurt to look at her. 'Oh, Mum – as if I didn't know!' she cried and kissed Lizzie's cheek. 'You've spoiled us both rotten. I've had the best childhood any girl could have – but don't you see? That's just it. I've been given everything and I feel like one of those little rich kids you see in American movies. I want to prove myself . . . the way you did . . .'

How could Lizzie argue with that? Betty's restlessness came from Harry of course. He'd always had that certain something inside that she couldn't touch, something that drove him away from all that was safe and good. He'd wanted so much to be a pilot, but then he'd found the constant flying through flak terrifying, risking his life every day, and he'd ended up becoming a nervous wreck.

His accidental death had robbed Betty of ever knowing her father and Lizzie couldn't give her that back. But even though Lizzie worried about her daughter, she knew she wouldn't refuse her request. She couldn't even though when Sebastian came home at the weekend she would need to spend hours arguing with him until he gave in. He would give her and Betty their own way, because he always did, though whether it was for the sake of a quiet life or because he could refuse them nothing, Lizzie wasn't sure. In this instance she just hoped he wouldn't get too upset, because she knew he had his own plans for both his daughters . . .

CHAPTER 2

Sebastian looked tired when he arrived home that Friday evening. He'd been on one of his long business trips, which seemed to take up more and more of his time these days. Lizzie had never been quite sure of the extent of her husband's business, because he said he didn't want to talk about work when he was with his family. He always seemed to be travelling and she wasn't sure whether it was for the factory, his exclusive dress shop, or some other business that he never discussed.

Lizzie sometimes felt that he went away more because of her – because she'd had three miscarriages in four years and the doctors had told Sebastian that she mustn't try to have more children.

'If you suffer as you did last time, you could die,' Sebastian had explained gently after she came home from the expensive nursing home to which she'd gone for a rest and treatment after the last miscarriage. 'I know you want a son, Lizzie. I'd like that too – we'd hoped for a bigger family, my darling, but we have two delightful daughters and

19

that's sufficient for me. A hundred sons wouldn't make up for losing you, Lizzie Larch . . .'

He'd used her maiden name to make her smile, because all through her marriage to Harry he'd refused to call her Lizzie Oliver. She'd thought then that he was just flirting with her and it had taken her a long time to believe that someone as special as Sebastian could really be in love with her.

Lizzie had been so lucky. She had a husband she adored and two lovely daughters.

Francie was passing all her exams, and progressing just as they'd hoped. A beautiful girl with long shining hair, that was even blacker than Seb's, she had eyes that were a softer shade of blue than his and a sweet, loving nature. At just over a couple of months away from her fifteenth birthday at the end of October, she was a talented artist, proficient both in watercolour and oils. Last term, they'd sent her to a special college in Cambridgeshire that educated pupils who had an artistic bent, and Francie had justified their decision. Her latest work had left Lizzie in awe of her daughter, moved by the passion and skill in her paintings of the bleak fen landscape and the awesome skies. She knew that she could never have produced anything approaching the brilliance of Francie's work, and she'd always known that Sebastian was so very proud of his daughter. Yet he still treated her no differently to Betty, expecting equally high stand- ards of both of them, and although generous in his gifts, both girls understood they had to work hard and do well.

She waited until the next morning. Betty had gone out to meet a friend and Sebastian had been working in the garden. He employed a full-time gardener, but still liked to potter when he was at home. When Sebastian entered and sat down at the table, she put steaming coffee laced with cream and a plate of his favourite homemade biscuits in front of him.

'Betty wants to leave school and start work with Ed and Romany,' she said and sipped her coffee. 'Her school report isn't encouraging and it's what she really wants to do so I thought . . .'

'No! Definitely not,' Sebastian was firm. 'We've talked about this before, Lizzie. She either goes to college or takes a secretarial course now that she's old enough to leave school – I'd prefer she had one more term at school so that we have time to look for somewhere right for her – perhaps abroad . . . I've made some inquiries about a place in Switzerland, which I was going to talk to her about . . .'

'She won't be happy at college, wherever it is. She hates academic work and she isn't particularly good at it; if she has to stay another year or more I think she might resent us both for making her do it and the workshops will be hers and Francie's one day. It makes sense for her to learn the trade, and I think she does have strong artistic talent, even if not for designing hats . . .'

'Yes, I know she has. I'm not blind, Lizzie, and

21

I've seen the clothes she makes for all of you – but she needs proper training, to learn from the bottom up – and I know Ed. If she works with him, he'll spoil her, make things too easy for her, and she'll never knuckle down to any real work. Besides, it's not the right place for her . . .'

'Ed has told me he intends to leave his shares in the business to Betty . . . . . . so perhaps it would be sensible for her to learn the business from him . . .'

'If she wants to take the workshop over one day, that's fine, but not yet, Lizzie. I want her to keep learning for a while. She needs to have a broader outlook on life and not be stuck at a workbench for years . . . without your talent the business would just become ordinary, and in time it will fail, just as Bert's business was failing until you breathed new life into it – and Betty could do so much more . . .'

'But it's what she's set her heart on . . .'

'Let me talk to her, Lizzie. She's too young to know what she's doing and she'll regret it later when she's stuck in a dead-end job . . .'

'I've made a success of myself,' Lizzie retorted without stopping to think. 'Making hats is a good life in my opinion.'

'She doesn't have your talent, Lizzie. If I thought for one minute she could do what you did I'd give her the money to start her own workshops right now – but I've looked at her sketchbook and most of the hats she's done are just variations on things you've made in the past . . . she doesn't have your talent for designing hats, but . . .'

'Sebastian, that's not fair!' Lizzie said, cutting off what he was about to say. 'Betty doesn't claim to have my flair for designing hats. She simply wants to learn to make them and perhaps take over Ed's job when he retires . . .' Lizzie frowned as she saw he was annoyed because she was taking Betty's side. 'I think we should let her do what she wants . . . give her the chance to be happy doing a job she loves . . . after all, she may marry in a few years and have children . . .'

'And what sort of men will she meet working in Bert Oliver's old place, tell me that? I don't want her stuck in some council flat with half a dozen kids and a husband that drinks all the time . . . She's too highly strung, too much like Harry . . .' Sebastian's voice rose angrily. 'I've given way over things that didn't matter because I wanted you all to be happy – but this does matter, Lizzie. My daughter's future is at stake and I'm not prepared to stand by and let her ruin her chances . . .'

'I've told her I'll talk to you,' Lizzie said, feeling uncertain. She'd never seen her husband in this mood before. He seemed made of iron and there was an underlying anger she didn't recognise in him. 'I think if you refuse her now she will resent you, Sebastian. Are you sure you want to make her do something she hates so much?'

'I'll talk to her. She'll understand when I explain what I have in mind for her . . .'

Suddenly, the door burst open and Betty rushed in, her lovely face red with temper. 'Oh, I understand all right,' she shouted rudely. 'If it was Francie it would be different wouldn't it? She's so clever and you think the sun shines out of her arse! But because it's untalented me, who couldn't produce a Lizzie Larch original, but only a copy; I'm not to be trusted – I'm too much like my real father. Well, perhaps that's why I want to be what he was before the war . . . a working milliner not a pampered designer who just sits at home and draws pretty pictures and leaves all the real work to her minions . . .'

'Betty, that is rude and ridiculous,' Sebastian said in a tightly controlled manner. 'You will apologise to your mother immediately. She has worked hard all her life, as you know very well, and I will not stand for you speaking to her or about her in such a manner.'

'I'll say what I damned well please . . .'

'As long as you live in our house you'll behave in a proper manner. You've not been taught to swear at your mother. I think it's time we discovered what kind of company you've been keeping recently . . .'

'Why the hell should I listen to you?' Betty cried, still too hurt and too angry to retract the cruel words she'd flung at her parents. 'You're not my father and you're hardly ever here. How would you know what I want to do with my life or what sort of person I am?'

'I'm your father whether you like it or not and you'll do as I tell you until you're twenty-one and old enough to look after yourself . . . though at the moment I can't see that ever being the case . . .'

'I hate you! You're not my father and I shan't do what you tell me . . . I don't care if you are married to Mum. My father's dead and you said horrible things about him . . .'

'You know nothing about the way he treated your mother . . .'

'Seb, don't!' Lizzie cried. 'Betty, stop this please . . .'

'I shan't because he's a liar and he doesn't care about any of us or he wouldn't go off the way . . .' Betty was shouting, too far gone to realise what she was saying.

Sebastian took a step towards her, raised his hand and slapped her once across the face.

'Sebastian, no!' Lizzie cried but was silenced by his angry glare.

Betty was shocked, because never in all her life, despite several tantrums as she was growing up, had he hit her. The colour drained from her cheeks and her eyes were wide with pain, which was more mental than physical. 'Please apologise and then go to your room,' Sebastian said quietly and Betty stared at him, the tears clearly hovering. She looked at Lizzie then, brushing a defiant hand over her eyes.

'I'm sorry, Mum, I do know how hard it was for you in the war,' she said clearly. 'I shouldn't have said that to you, because I know you had to work when I was small . . . but I'm not sorry about what I said to *him*. He isn't anything to do with me and I shan't take any notice of him. I'll go and live with Aunt Miriam. She said I could . . .' She looked daggers at Sebastian.

'Your Aunt Miriam is not your guardian,' Sebastian said still in that controlled tone, though a muscle flicked in his cheek. 'I am your legal guardian, Betty. You are my child, under my jurisdiction until you turn twenty-one; just remember that. If you run away I'll have you fetched back . . .'

'And I'll run away again,' Betty said, her eyes as cold and angry as his as she stared at him. In that moment they looked so alike in their fury, so determined not to give in, that a stranger would find it impossible to believe that Sebastian was not her blood father . . . but, of course, Harry had had a violent temper too.

'Please, don't,' Lizzie cried, unable to keep silent any longer. 'You're tearing each other apart and I know that neither of you means what you're saying. Betty, please go to your room for now and I'll talk to your father some more . . .'

'You would be wasting your time,' Sebastian told her coldly. 'This time I mean what I say so you'd both better get used to the idea – and now I have someone to see . . . I'll be home for dinner, Lizzie, but don't expect me before that . . .'

Lizzie gasped in distress, stunned and disbelieving. Sebastian was never violent and she could scarcely believe he would slap Betty. It wasn't the first time they'd disagreed but never before had he let his temper overcome him. Harry, Betty's natural father, had had a violent temper, but Sebastian was always calm and in control, no matter how far he was provoked. She stared after him as he picked up his jacket and walked out. They had never quarrelled like this and it hurt her terribly. Why was Sebastian so very angry? He'd seemed quiet the previous evening, though they'd made love and it had been as good as it always was between them. The long trips away and the moods he'd had recently would've made Lizzie wonder if he'd found someone else, except that he had spoken of how much she meant to him when they lay together after making love, and the emotion in his voice had told her that he meant it – and yet she was just as certain that something was troubling him. Something deep and disturbing that he couldn't bring himself to share with her . . .

Alone in her room, Betty turned her transistor radio up so that the music of Bill Haley blasted out, reverberating against the walls. In a burst of fury, she flung the expensive Box Brownie camera Sebastian had bought for her last birthday at the wall; following quickly on its heels went the silver compact and the René Lalique glass figure of a swan that had been two of his Christmas presents to her. As the beautiful glass swan shattered, her tears fell in an angry torrent and she flung herself

27

on her knees and tenderly picked up the pieces of the delicate glass figure she'd loved so much. Damn him! Why had he made her do it? She hated him. She hated him! He was always away and she knew that hurt her mother – but she'd hurt her too, and she hadn't meant to. It was Sebastian saying that she had no talent and was too vulnerable to be trusted – too much like her real father, as if that was something bad . . .

She'd come in from meeting Pierre in time to hear her father telling her mother that she didn't have her talent and was too like her real father, not capable of producing original work, and her anger had mounted so that she hardly heard the rest of his words. Why did he think so little of her? Sebastian had often given her more expensive presents than he gave his own daughter, which made her suspect that he was doing it to make up for the fact that he couldn't love her as he did Francie. Why would anyone love her with her quick temper and her selfish ways when her sister was everything she was not?

Who would ever truly love her? She couldn't see why anyone would want her – except that Pierre said he did and when he smiled at her and caressed her bare arm, she'd believed him. Pierre wanted her to go back to Paris with him. He'd told her that this morning when they met at the coffee bar as arranged. He'd come to England on an exchange visit of mature students, because he was twenty-five and studying to be an architect, but his course

28

had finished, his visa had run out, and he was due to return to France any day now – and Betty adored him.

She'd known she was being foolish to let him go all the way that night in the back of his car, but she'd done it in a mood of recklessness. She'd been unsure after that, because she didn't know if Pierre truly cared for her, but he'd told her that morning when they met at the café, that he couldn't bear to part with her and begged her to go to France with him. Betty had been uncertain, afraid of making such a reckless move – but now rebellion flared in her heart. Why shouldn't she go? Pierre loved her and her parents didn't care . . .

Betty suddenly made up her mind. Why should she stay here and be told what she could and couldn't do? Pierre wanted her and she loved him. She was old enough to live her own life with someone who cared for her. She would leave now, while her mother had gone to visit Romany and discuss some new designs for the workshops. Had her father not told her he would fetch her back, she would've gone to Aunt Miriam and worked on her mother to let her start at the workshops. Mum wasn't against it – it was only him and he didn't care about her, because she wasn't his daughter. So, since she couldn't go to her real father's aunt, she would go with Pierre. He had begged her to leave with him that night, and told her he'd bought a ticket for her on the late flight to Paris.

Betty hadn't confirmed that she would go, because it was such a huge step and she rather enjoyed living in her parents' house and she'd wanted to work with Ed, because he was always so kind to her – but now things were different. She was going to be made to go to a college she would hate and be a secretary or something equally boring. So why shouldn't she go with Pierre?

It was shocking of course, and Mum and Aunt Miriam would be upset – but her father would be angry and that would give Betty pleasure, because she wanted to hurt Sebastian.

Betty threw some of her favourite jeans and tops and long skirts into a suitcase then added her sketch pad and box of pencils and took her passport from the chest of drawers that contained her undies. She'd had the passport for a school trip to Austria when she'd first gone to the grammar school.

Betty's excitement grew as she thought about the future. In Paris she might find work for one of the famous designers of haute couture clothes. She might not be as good at designing hats as her mother, but she'd made some lovely clothes for both her and Francie.

Taking her savings from the drawer, she counted all fifty pound notes with glee. She had a small fortune of her own, so she wouldn't be dependent on Pierre and her grasp of the French language was sufficient to enable her to find work.

In the kitchen, Betty hesitated about leaving her

mother a note to explain where she'd gone, because she didn't want her to worry too much – but if she gave them too big a clue, Sebastian would fetch her back.

She tore a page off of one of Lizzie's sketch pads and scribbled a few words.

I'm going to someone who wants me. Don't look for me because you won't find me. When I'm rich and famous I'll come back and say hello. Love you, Mum. Betty.

She added a couple of kisses at the end so that her mother would know she loved her and it was just Sebastian she resented.

She tucked the note inside her mother's sketch pad, because she was sure to find it as soon as she opened it, but Betty would be with Pierre by then and on her way to France. She picked up her case and ran to catch a bus that would take her to Oxford Street, knowing that Pierre would be waiting for her at the café they liked . . .

CHAPTER 3

Sebastian looked at Marianne Gutiere and felt the pain of his failure strike him. He'd promised he would find Gretchen for his friend's wife, but although he'd visited ten orphanages in West Germany, that they had thought might have some knowledge of the girl, he'd drawn a blank.

'She wasn't there?' Marianne asked, tears glistening in her eyes. 'It's a hopeless task, isn't it? She would be eighteen now and I'm not sure I would know her, because she was only six years old when I left. When I escaped from Eastern Germany after the war, Karl promised he would follow with her the next day . . . but they arrested him and she was taken somewhere to a children's home; he was told she would be quite safe. Karl was able to send only one letter, but he was sure that she would be cared for . . .' her voice caught on a sob.

'I'm so sorry,' Sebastian said and touched her hand in sympathy. 'You know that Karl and I were very close before the war. I wanted him to get out before it started but he had a good job at the University in Berlin and he didn't believe that

32

Hitler would kill the Jews, even though he was stripping them of money, property and dignity . . .'

'Did anyone believe it?' Marianne asked sadly. 'We none of us expected what happened, but Karl was right; his work was necessary to our masters and they kept us as hostages to ensure he worked for them – and so we lived, but when the war was over Karl sent me away. I was carrying another child. I begged to take Gretchen with me, but he said if we all went it might arouse suspicions and we weren't sure about the Russians then. We thought they might be our friends. Neither of us thought they would accuse him of war crimes and execute him . . .'

'Karl was a decent man and a brilliant physicist. Whatever the Nazis made him do I know he wasn't a criminal by choice, Marianne. Whatever he did was to keep you safe and I shall not condemn him – but you were innocent of any crime and so is Gretchen, and I promise I will find her, Marianne.'

'But you've been searching for three years, ever since I first spoke to you – just before I got that letter to say that she was in an orphanage and alive . . .'

'It was a such a pity that whoever sent it didn't sign it,' Sebastian said. 'Had they done so we might have got more information – as it is, we just have to keep looking.'

'I know there were so many displaced children after the war,' Marianne said regretfully. 'I wrote to everyone I could contact; some replied but no one knew where Gretchen had been taken. I should've come to you sooner, but I might never have had the courage had we not met by chance on that railway station in Western Germany and you recognised me . . .'

'It was meant to be,' he said. 'I'm glad you asked for my help. I intend to do all I can for you, and not just for Karl's sake.'

'I'm not the only one you've helped, am I?'

'It's something I can't talk about, even to you,' he said and frowned. 'We have a different kind of enemy these days. Lives depend on secrecy, and not even my wife knows what I do when I'm away . . . you should understand the political situation out there better than anyone.'

'I do, of course, and I shan't ask. I know you love your wife very much and sometimes I feel guilty for taking up so much of your time.'

'Lizzie knows I love her.' Sebastian stood up and glanced at his watch. 'I must leave I'm afraid. I'm so sorry not to have better news, but I have many friends who have contacts both in Germany and in other countries where Gretchen might have gone and I shall go on looking until we discover something . . . one way or the other . . .'

'You are so kind, but your family need you. I must not ask too much of you . . .'

'Karl would have done the same in my place. I could not leave you alone in Germany, Marianne. It took a while to arrange passports and permissions, but I got you here to London and I'll find you a better job than waitressing – and I'll do my best to find Gretchen.' He frowned. 'You need some decent clothes – no, I know you can't afford them, but I can. I'm going to take you to the shop of a friend of mine. She will give me a discount and I'll make sure you have what you need to look the part when you apply for a job.'

'You've done so much already. I can't let you do this . . .'

'I want to help – and I feel bad that I let you down again. Let me do this one small thing, please?'

'Thank you,' she said with quiet dignity and Sebastian left the flat he'd rented for her when she first came to England two years earlier. He'd hoped then that she would soon have her daughter with her, but his efforts had so far been in vain. He might have to talk to someone who could help, though he was reluctant to involve Jack and the department, because it would only draw him deeper into their arms when he knew it was time for him to think of his own life and his family . . .

As he walked from the building and hailed a passing taxi, Sebastian thought about what he'd learned from his inquiries in Western Germany – the things he hadn't told Marianne. He believed that if Gretchen was still alive she was in East Berlin and it was notoriously difficult to trace children who'd been separated from their parents during the troubled time just after the end of the war; some were placed in orphanages in the

Russian sector, others had simply disappeared. The child would be a young woman now. If she'd imbibed the anti-West doctrine that had undoubtedly been fed her these past years since the Cold War had started to escalate, she might not want to come to England to meet her mother and if she hadn't . . . it would still be very difficult to get her out. The Russians had no intention of letting the East Germans escape to the West in large numbers – and there were unbelievable rumours about what they were planning to prevent it.

Sebastian wasn't sure whether his informants were just talking to earn the money he paid them on behalf of the service, or if there were really people who were considering building a wall between East and West Berlin. Or was it just rumour and the tit for tat politics that went on continuously; a part of the Cold War that was affecting relations between Russia and the USA and its allies? It seemed ridiculous to Sebastian that anyone would even consider dividing Berlin by a wall, but with Russia demanding the withdrawal of all foreign troops from the city, it was entirely possible they might step up measures to prevent people escaping to the West. He'd heard whispers of a recent flurry of Russian activity, which meant if they wanted to get a few important people out, it ought to be set in motion sooner than later.

The situation was more dangerous in Sebastian's opinion than the general public was aware. It was communism versus capitalism, and with the threat of the Atomic bomb hanging over the world it was deadly, because if one country decided to use it there would be so much destruction the world would never be the same again. Marches against the nuclear threat had taken place in London and other capital cities, but it was a shadow that many people considered with growing concern.

Sebastian frowned as he pushed Marianne's troubles to the back of his mind and thought of the quarrel with Betty and Lizzie earlier that day. He shouldn't have slapped his daughter, even though she'd been very rude and insulting to both him and her mother, but she'd made him angry, causing so much fuss about another few terms at school or college, when he'd so recently returned from searching for the daughter of the woman he'd just left. Marianne had had so much to bear: fleeing from East Germany in fear of her life, losing the child she carried and living in deserted ruins or on the streets until a Catholic nun had taken her in. She'd found a way to live, working as a waitress and waiting for her husband and child to join her, but it had never happened. So much suffering – and Betty was creating hell because he'd told her she must go to college. When he thought of Gretchen's likely childhood, as the daughter of a disgraced Jew who had been executed for crimes the Nazis forced him to commit . . . well it had made him feel sick and impatient with his impetuous daughter. Yet he knew he'd had a hand in indulging Betty and he wished the harsh words unsaid.

Sebastian shook his head. He would apologise to Lizzie and explain to Betty that he thought she would do better at an art college where she could learn to draw the things she was good at, and perhaps to learn the craft of dressmaking. He'd been looking for the right place but wasn't sure yet that he'd found it. Perhaps her hats didn't have the style of Lizzie's, but her clothes certainly did . . . and he should not allow his own worries to cloud his judgement. Betty had always been a little vulnerable. She needed his love, which was why he'd tended to spoil her, and by letting her hear those awful things he'd said in anger, he knew he'd hurt her badly – and if she did something reckless because of it he would never forgive himself.

Lizzie entered the kitchen carrying flowers and a basket of fresh food. She loaded the meat, cheese and vegetables into the refrigerator and cupboards and then filled the kettle. The house seemed very quiet and she went to the foot of the stairs and called out.

'Come down, darling, I've got an idea we'll put to your father . . .'

Lizzie waited but there was no answer. She frowned and went upstairs, knowing that some-times Betty was prone to sulks, but when she opened the bedroom door she was shocked. Her wardrobe was open and drawers had been pulled out. She went to the wardrobe and saw that Betty's suitcase had gone. Surely she wouldn't have gone to Miriam's after what Sebastian had said?

Seeing the broken glass swan, Lizzie frowned. Betty must have been really upset if she'd deliberately smashed something she loved so much.

It didn't enter Lizzie's head to look for her daughter's passport immediately. Betty had been angry and upset, but she wouldn't have gone far – and she would probably come back when she cooled down.

Sebastian would be furious, of course. Lizzie was still a little upset that he had been so cold with her earlier, wondering what she'd done to deserve it except try to calm the situation and point out that Betty was better at doing things than at the schoolwork she hated.

Returning to the kitchen, she made tea. Should she ring Miriam and ask if Betty was there? Sebastian probably wouldn't believe her even if Miriam said no – he would go round and look for her himself. Besides, it might be best to give Betty a chance to calm down and talk it over with her aunt.

Sipping her tea, Lizzie opened her sketchbook and Betty's note fell out. What was this? Recognising Betty's handwriting, she felt relieved at first but when she read the scribbled message, she began to feel worried. It didn't sound as though she'd run off to her aunt's as she had once or twice in the past in a childish fit. Lizzie felt a flicker of anxiety as she realised this was different. Betty was no longer a child and this note seemed to suggest she'd gone with a friend – who? As far as Lizzie knew Betty didn't have a boyfriend but the tone of this note was almost like a challenge, as if her daughter was going to a close friend – or a lover?

Surely that couldn't be right! She was too young . . . and yet in a month or so she would be eighteen and Beth had fallen in love at that age . . . she'd had her twins soon after her nineteenth birthday. Oh no, it couldn't happen to her Betty! Lizzie's eyes stung with tears and for a moment she was tempted to telephone her best friend and pour it all into her ears, but she couldn't trust herself not to burst into tears.

Dropping the note and the pad, she ran from the kitchen and back upstairs, hunting for Betty's passport. She searched every drawer, all the pretty bags she'd bought her daughter and all her coat pockets. It wasn't there . . . Betty was planning on going further afield . . .

As she dashed back down the stairs, the thoughts were whirling in Lizzie's head. Where could Betty have gone? She didn't have much money, although she'd been saving up for a better record player, because she wanted one of the new high fidelity sets and liked to collect records. She surely hadn't saved enough to go very far? If she was alone . . . but supposing she wasn't? A ripple of fear trickled down her spine, because her impulsive daughter could be in trouble . . . As she went into the kitchen, she saw that Sebastian was back and he'd found the note. He looked annoyed as he glanced at her across the table.

'I suppose she's gone to Miriam's?'

'I don't think so, not this time,' Lizzie said and the fear rushed through her. 'Sebastian, I think she has taken her passport . . .'

'The silly girl,' he said but looked stricken. 'I shouldn't have lost my temper with her, Lizzie. I was angry and worried about something, exhausted too if I tell the truth – and I thought she was making too much fuss over a small thing, but I never thought she would run away . . .'

'It may have seemed a small thing but it meant a lot to her,' Lizzie said, 'but where would she go? I don't think she has enough money to go abroad . . . unless she's staying with someone she knows . . . She doesn't have any foreign friends, does she?'

'Not to my knowledge,' he said, 'but I'm going to find out. This is my fault, Lizzie, and I'll find her. I promise you I will find her, however long it takes me . . .'

'Matt . . . can we meet?' Frank asked over the telephone. 'Look, I don't want to worry you but I've got something to tell you about that damned Frenchie Betty was hanging around with . . .'

'Where are you?' Matt asked. 'I'm a bit busy at the moment. Tony wants me to help him with some bookwork. I hate doing his boring shop accounts but he's my stepfather and he's been good to us since Mum married him . . . a hell of a lot better than the one she had before . . .'

'I'm working at Marshall's airport in Cambridge for a few days,' Frank said, 'but I was briefly at Gatwick yesterday. It's so much bigger since they spent seven million on it and I've been asked to do an efficiency report and I was having a first look round – but, never mind that, what matters is that I think I saw Betty with Saint-Jacquez . . .'

'What would she be doing at an airport? You must be mistaken, Frank. I'm sure she's at home . . . Mum would've told me . . .'

'It's just that I've discovered something about him . . . something worrying . . .' Frank hesitated then, 'I don't want to say on the phone. I could get the train up in the morning – can we meet?'

'Sure, come round and we'll have a drink and then go to the cricket match at Lords . . .'

'Fine, but just go round and make sure Betty is OK, will you? I shan't rest until I know for sure. I'll see you tomorrow lunchtime . . .'

Frank put down the phone, frowning, because he couldn't get the picture of a girl's face out of his mind. He'd only caught a fleeting glance of her as the couple passed through the gate in the departures lounge at Gatwick. Frank was certain the man was Pierre Saint-Jacquez but the girl's face had been turned from him. He'd hesitated, uncertain of what he'd seen and then his attention was drawn by the man who had commissioned his report and when he looked again the couple had disappeared.

Frank frowned, because if it was Betty, if she had gone off with that devil, he would never forgive himself. He'd made a phone call that evening to a colleague who was working in Amsterdam, but hadn't been able to reach him until this morning. Ahmed had mentioned Saint-Jacquez a couple of times before, but Frank hadn't been interested until he discovered that Betty was getting involved with him. Ahmed had told him that he had no proof but believed that Pierre might be involved with a man of Turkish descent who was known in certain circles for abducting girls who were never seen nor heard of again.

'You're joking!' Frank had been horrified. 'How does Saint-Jacquez come into it?'

'I don't know that he does,' Frank's informant admitted. 'I only know that he has a reputation for picking up girls and dropping them when he's had enough of them, bit of a lothario if you ask me . . . but someone told me that he'd been seen with this other chap in London at an illegal gambling club . . . and . . . a girl I liked disappeared after going off with him . . .' He hesitated, then, 'It's a racket, my friend. They get the girls hooked on heroin or cocaine and then they imprison them somewhere, make them have sex for money with the men they bring to the house, until they're no longer fit to work . . .'

'My God,' Frank groaned. 'I asked because he's been hanging round a girl I know . . .'

'Then you'd better make her aware of what he's like and fast . . .'

Frank closed his eyes as he heard the office door open behind him and his manager's voice asking if he'd finished with the phone. If that devil had taken Betty somewhere he would never forgive himself . . .

CHAPTER 4

'It's lovely to see you,' Lizzie said and gave Beth a hug as she welcomed her into the kitchen. Her friend was wearing a smart new navy blue dress with short sleeves, a flared skirt and a large white collar that stood up at the back, pairing it with a navy and white hat that perched on the back of her head and complemented the flicking curls around it. 'How are you?'

'Really well,' Beth said, smiling. 'Tony took me to see *My Fair Lady* at Drury Lane last night. I've wanted to see it ever since it came out in April, but it was such a sell-out that it was impossible to get tickets before now. It was wonderful . . .'

'How lovely,' Lizzie said and smothered a sigh. All she could think about right now was what had happened to Betty! Yet she didn't want to spoil her friend's pleasure. 'I knew it had been given rave reviews, but sometimes it's a disappointment when you actually get to see it . . .'

'Not this time. I loved it,' Beth said and then frowned as she sensed Lizzie's mood. 'What is it, love? I know something's wrong . . . is it Betty? Only when Matt rang and asked to talk to her,

Sebastian was a bit short with him and said she was out . . .'

Lizzie took a deep breath, because she couldn't hide it from her best friend any longer. Sebastian had stressed they must keep it to themselves, because he was certain Betty would come home when she got over her temper.

'Betty ran away. She and Sebastian had a row and he banished her to her bedroom. When I came back she'd smashed things he'd given her, left me a note and gone off.'

'You've no idea where? She hasn't gone to stay with Miriam for a while?'

'Not this time,' Lizzie said and shook her head. 'It's been four days now, Beth, and I'm worried to death . . .'

'Four days and you didn't tell me?'

'I kept thinking she would be back – and I suppose I thought if I didn't talk about it maybe it would all be all right . . .' She caught back a sob. 'Sebastian says she's just playing up and will come back when she's ready but . . .'

'She's a naughty girl to upset you like this,' Beth said. 'After all you went through in the war years, you're entitled to be happy and secure these days . . .'

'I can't help worrying, Beth, though I know she does get moody . . .' Lizzie said. Betty took after Harry for her ability to sulk, but Lizzie was hopeful that she would come home soon and apologise to her father for upsetting them all. 'I wish she would just phone or send us a card – anything to let us know she's all right . . .'

'She's spoilt that's her trouble,' Beth said. 'You've let her run rings round you, Lizzie.'

Lizzie shook her head, because she knew Beth thought she spoiled Betty too much but she didn't want to argue about it when she was so on edge. Turning the subject, she asked, 'How are all your family?'

'Lizzie, don't change the subject. What happened between Sebastian and Betty and what made her go off . . . it isn't like her. I know she sulks some-times, but she always gets over it. Matt says you just have to know how to handle her . . . he's a bit worried about her for some reason, though he wouldn't tell me why . . .'

'It just blew up out of nowhere . . .' Lizzie held back a sob. 'I've been so worried, Beth. I know it's just a few days, but apart from that school trip to Austria, she's never been away from home without me and she's only seventeen . . .'

'Nearly eighteen – haven't you noticed how grown-up she's getting lately? Sebastian should stop trying to treat her as if she's still a schoolgirl . . .'

'Beth, he doesn't . . . does he?'

'He's not quite as bad as your aunt was with you,' Beth said. 'But he does tend to come the heavy father a bit too much, and that's why you give in to her all the time. She's a rebel, a bit like you were when you married Harry. Lizzie, don't look like that, because you were as impulsive as she is. I shouldn't worry too much. I imagine she'll come home when she runs out of money.'

'I've never seen Sebastian as angry with her . . . though he's regretting it now.'

'He's not the only one, Lizzie. Matt and Tony are arguing again,' Beth said and pulled a wry face. 'It's strange how they can bond over some things, like in February; mourning together when the Munich disaster happened and all those Manchester United footballers were killed, and then going mad with delight when Brazil won the World Cup – but then they fall out over whose turn it is to put out the dustbins . . .'

'Oh, fathers and sons always argue . . .' Lizzie laughed. 'At least so I've heard. I haven't been lucky enough to have a son yet . . .'

'You're not brooding about that, are you?' Beth said and shook her head. 'You know what the doctor said, love. Besides, children are often more trouble than they're worth if you ask me.'

'You know you don't mean that,' Lizzie said and gave her a teasing look. 'Who's as proud as punch because she'll soon be a grandmother then?'

'Oh, my Jenny is no trouble, and nor is Tom,' Beth agreed. 'It's just Matt I'm worried about – I keep thinking he and Tony will come to blows . . . he got so cross because Matt cut college to go on that CND march to Aldermaston, even though he passed his exams with flying colours . . .'

'I'm sure you're wrong,' Lizzie said and poured deliciously fragrant coffee into large earthenware cups. 'You tell me not to worry about Betty but you're just as bad about your three . . . come on, let's enjoy our coffee and cake and then we'll go shopping and forget all about errant children.

Except that she wouldn't, because neither she nor Sebastian had done anything but worry about Betty since she left. She might be nearly eighteen and grown up, but it was natural to worry over a girl who'd just run off on a whim. If she'd said where she was going or who with it wouldn't have been so bad. As it was they were both frantic with worry. Sebastian had been out every night searching the cafes and coffee bars looking for her, but so far he was no nearer to finding her than he had been at the start . . .

Paris was all Betty could ever have hoped for and particularly the older quarters around Montmartre; once the very centre of the bohemian life led by artists, their models and those who came to experience the gaiety of the thriving nightlife, it was fascinating to a girl who had never before experienced such a heady mixture of beauty and faded decadence. The white dome of the Basilica of the Sacré-Cœur presided over the crowded hill and its maze of little streets, nightclubs and cafés, and the majestic river that wound through the city. The Left Bank where she wandered when Pierre was busy working and the artists sketched your portrait in seconds and then offered to paint you properly for a few francs had become a favourite haunt for Betty since she'd been here, and more than one had drawn her face and asked if she would model for them, to be answered by a smile and a shake of the head. Betty didn't mind spending most of her days alone, because there was always something new to see and explore. She loved the little boats that seemed to skim up and down the Seine; the narrow alleys that twisted and turned endlessly and where you could get lost for an afternoon looking through dusty windows into tiny shops that smelled of spices and herbs and sold everything and anything; the beautiful soft cream stone of graceful but ancient buildings and unbelievably blue skies; the magnificent cathedral of Notre Dame and the flower sellers who called out to Pierre when he took her out in the early evening, and persuaded him to buy her a rose or a tiny bunch of violets. She adored the little cafés and the dark soft nights, the taste of the wine and the fresh crusty bread, delicious food with lots of garlic; coffee in bowls with no handles, tables without cloths, waiters who babbled at her in French so rapidly that they might have been speaking in Chinese, and the girls who all looked so well dressed that they made her feel like a tramp in her jeans and tight jumpers. And most of all she loved Pierre and the way he loved her.

Pierre had taken her to his apartment, a tiny old-fashioned garret that they entered by means of a wooden staircase built on the outside walls that looked ancient enough to give way under their weight, but he'd laughed at her when she'd looked dubious and threatened to carry her up if she was too scared to walk. Inside, it consisted of a small kitchen, and an even smaller toilet with a wash-basin, and a long studio, with a nook at one end hidden only by a thick curtain in which Pierre had his bed. His clothes were stored in a large very battered chest of drawers or scattered over the chairs and slung on hooks from the wall. Betty didn't know where to put hers, so she left them in her suitcase and thrust it under the bed.

If she occasionally felt a pang for her lovely spacious bedroom at home and the wardrobe filled with her things, it was forgotten as Pierre kissed her, then pulled her down on the unmade bed and loved her with a passion that took her breath away and left her weeping in his arms. For two weeks Betty lived in a delirium of happiness. Pierre was gentle and loving, taking her to see all the things she'd only read of in guidebooks, laughing at her as she blossomed in the freedom and the warm sunshine, feeding her delicious patisseries and forcing her to eat escargot in garlic, which she found so delicious she ate all of his portion as well as her own. They walked, went on the river, explored, drank wine and made love and it was paradise, beyond her dreams and more. As a young girl, she'd fantasised about being in love and living somewhere exciting but also of being famous like

51

her mum was for making hats. Sebastian's dismissal of her talent had hurt her and she was glad she'd run away. Perhaps he was sorry now!

It was one Saturday afternoon at the end of those wonderful two weeks that Betty realised there was a serpent in paradise. It was after they'd lunched with some of Pierre's friends at one of their favourite cafés by the river. Pierre had been drinking steadily, laughing with Michele and especially Janine, a beautiful girl who worked as a mannequin for one of the many fashion houses. When they got home, he immediately drew Betty into their bedroom and made love to her. It was so good that she wept for sheer happiness.

'Why do you weep, my little one?' he asked in that soft voice that turned her knees to butter and made her ready to die in his arms. 'Did I hurt you?'

'Oh no,' she sobbed and buried her face in his shoulder, inhaling the salty scent of his sweat and the musk of their mingled sex. 'It was so gorgeous . . . I never knew making love could be so satisfying, Pierre.'

'That's because you were just a child when you came to me and now you are my woman – no?' He smiled confidently down into her eyes and Betty glowed. He'd told her how beautiful she was as he kissed every little inch of her body, caressing it with his tongue and bringing her to a state of tingling need, and now he was starting to do it again. 'Perhaps you are still half-child, half-woman

. . .' he suggested, teasing her with his tongue and lips until she was gasping with longing. 'No, no, my darling, I shall not give you what you want just yet. You must earn it . . . you must learn to please me as I please you . . .'

Betty opened her eyes in surprise. She had no idea what he meant and as he began to explain what he wanted she was shocked and a little repulsed at some of the things he demanded, but she reached for him with her hand tentatively and touched with one finger as he said, growing bolder as she saw his reaction, and then she bent her head and licked the length of his shaft, feeling the leap of excitement that went through him.

'Oh yes,' Pierre said and encouraged her in his soft seductive voice. 'I think you will be a good learner, my sweet, and you will repay me for all I've given you, believe me . . . and now take me into your mouth and . . .'

Betty had moved on to kissing his smooth flat stomach as she stroked his sex with her hand, but she jerked back and stared at him, not sure she'd heard right and somehow not ready for such an act. She was like a little puppy in her desire to please and yet a little afraid; she wasn't ready to go so fast and she hesitated.

'Must I?' she asked plaintively. 'I don't think I want to . . .'

'You do not want to please me?' There was a new note in his voice that worried Betty. Did he think she was an immature child? Of course she was compared to some of the women he knew. 'Surely you are not so selfish . . .?'

Not wanting to spoil their lovely adventure, she did as he asked, at first licking the softly rounded tip of his sex and then, as he approved and made a guttural sound in his throat, she opened her mouth and took just the first part of his large shaft inside the moist warmth of her mouth. She moved her head back and forth not trying to take more than a little of him in, but Pierre grabbed her head and pushed her forward as he thrust so that suddenly he was filling her mouth, thrusting back and forth against the back of her throat and making her feel as if she would gag. Perhaps it was fortunate for her that he came very quickly and moved away to spill his seed over her long hair as he withdrew.

Betty drew back, tears on her face, but this time they were not tears of joy. She felt for the first time that he didn't really care what she wanted, otherwise he wouldn't force her to do something that she didn't like. It was all so different to anything she'd ever experienced or imagined. She'd never even had a proper kiss until she met Pierre and she'd thought it so romantic when he declared he loved her, couldn't live without her and wanted her to go to Paris with him. Betty hadn't thought about the future at all. She'd just wanted to leave home and make her parents sorry for doubting her, but she'd believed Pierre loved her and she supposed she'd thought he would take care of her and marry her one day, but now it seemed that he wanted something more than the sweet lovemaking she'd so enjoyed. The force he'd used made her angry and distressed but she didn't want him to leave her or stop loving her, so when he bent over and kissed her lips, licking at her and teasing his tongue into her mouth she allowed him to do as he liked, and when he grew tired of her unresponsiveness he began to kiss her breasts and then moved slowly down her body until he reached her sex. His assault on the citadel of her femininity with his lips and tongue made her gasp with pleasure and her body writhed, responding to him even though she'd been angry with him for forcing her to do something she hadn't been comfortable with. She cried out at last, unable to hold back as the waves of pleasure burst over her and something unexpected happened inside; it was a feeling of such exquisite pleasure that seemed to ripple through her in a wave and she dug her nails into his bare shoulders as hard as she could.

'Yes, my little tigress,' Pierre purred like a big cat and slid away from her, but still leaning towards her, watching her. 'Now you begin to learn – but if you want such pleasure you must give back . . .'

Betty sat up and then quickly slid out of bed, dashing for the small toilet, where she relieved herself. She filled the washbasin with cold water and splashed her face and dipped her hair, scrubbing at it with a flannel and then washing herself all over, as if to restore some kind of balance.

Staring at herself in the small spotted mirror on the wall, she saw that her eyes looked dark and her face pale. In that moment Betty knew that she was still a child in many ways. Pierre wanted a woman and she hadn't been ready for that . . . she was used to being spoiled, pampered and given what she wanted. She wasn't sure whether she would ever want to do some of the things Pierre demanded from her . . . and yet she knew that if she didn't he would soon tire of her and then . . .

She could go back to London, throw herself on Aunt Miriam's mercy. No one would ever have to know what had happened here. Betty thought of her money safely tucked inside her suitcase. It was her way of escape if she found life too demanding with Pierre – but he was so good at lovemaking when he set out to please her, and she was enjoying her life here. Perhaps he was right and she was just a selfish little girl – and she should learn to please him as he wanted . . .

Rubbing herself dry, Betty went back to the cubbyhole that Pierre called his bedroom. To her surprise he was dressed and on the point of leaving.

'Where are we going?' she asked.

'You're staying here,' he said in that harsh voice she'd first heard earlier. 'Where I'm going isn't for little girls . . . I'll see you later, and if you're good I'll take you to the café and we'll watch the cabaret . . .'

Betty didn't answer nor did she try to stop him. She was beginning to realise that she didn't know him very well. She'd fallen for his charm, his good looks and his sexy voice, but she hadn't given herself time to know him.

As soon as she was alone, she got dressed and, taking a few francs of the money she'd changed when they first arrived, went out. She would explore Paris alone and look for the workshops that she'd heard about from some of Pierre's friends.

The important names of Dior, Chanel and others of equal fame wouldn't look at a young and inexperienced girl like her, but according to Helene, one of Pierre's many friends they met in the evenings, there were lots of small workshops making clothes and they might take on an English girl who spoke reasonable French and teach her how to cut and machine to professional standards. She could only try, because she would need to find work of some kind if she wanted to stay in Paris . . . Besides, there were many places in Paris she wanted to see that Pierre had no interest in showing her . . . and perhaps it was time she showed a little bit of independence, reminded him that she had a right to her own decisions . . .

'I may have to go away for a few days,' Sebastian said as they sat over dinner that evening and savoured the fine wine he'd bought to accompany their meal. 'But I've set things in motion, Lizzie. I've got people looking for her . . . a private detective. I didn't want to bring the police in on this and I still don't, because she's a minor and I don't want her name to get in the papers; mud always sticks and it could ruin her chances of a good life. Besides, I've employed an agent who has more time and resources than the police . . .'

'Oh, Sebastian, do you have to go?' Lizzie said, feeling hurt and angry that he could still put his business first when she needed him here – and she was hardly sleeping because she was so worried about Betty. 'I need you here with me . . .'

'It's just to the factory,' he replied frowning. 'I'm not going abroad again just yet. I don't think there's a lot of sense in my visiting all the coffee houses myself, Lizzie. I've tried but no one has seen her – or if they have they aren't saying. I think a private detective might have more luck . . .'

'I suppose you're right . . .' Lizzie didn't want another argument with her husband. He was on edge the whole time recently and she didn't think it was just because of Betty, although she knew he was blaming himself bitterly for what had happened. 'Is anything wrong, Sebastian? Anything you haven't told me?'

'I have a few business problems,' he admitted and smiled wryly. 'I'm sorry if I've been short with you, Lizzie darling – but I'm as anxious about Betty as you are. I could've done without this at the moment . . .'

'Is there anything I can do to help you?'

'No, except just trust me. I promised I'd find

her, Lizzie, and I shall – but I do have other things on my mind . . .' He stood up and kissed her on the brow. 'I need to do some work, darling. You're looking tired. No need to wait up for me. I'll probably sleep on the sofa . . .'

Lizzie turned her head as he left the room. She carried the used dishes through to the kitchen and put them in a bowl of hot water to soak. Tonight she was just too tired to bother with washing up, and all she felt like doing was having a good cry . . .

'Why didn't you say something before?' Beth asked, looking at her eldest son in annoyance. 'Lizzie and Sebastian are worried to death . . .'

'I wasn't sure that anything was wrong,' Matt said. 'Frank told me he'd seen a girl that might have been Betty at Gatwick. He'd been there on business and just caught a fleeting glance as this couple went through departures. I thought he was probably imagining it and Betty would just turn up. You know what she can be . . .' He hesitated, wondering whether to tell his mother what else Frank had told him in confidence – yet what was the point? They had no proof and it would just make things worse for her parents. 'Frank has no idea which plane they were catching – it could have been anywhere in the world, although . . . he thinks she might have been with a French bloke she's been seeing at the club, if it was her . . . and as I keep telling you, we don't know for sure . . .'

Beth looked at her son in exasperation. He was so casual about it. Didn't he know how serious it was?

'What French bloke? Why haven't you said anything about this? Betty is only seventeen, Matt – if she's been getting into bad behaviour you should have given us a hint.'

'I didn't want to make things worse for her if she just turned up and said she'd been staying with a friend, but it's been a couple of weeks now . . .' Matt looked guilty. 'I scared him off at the club and had a few words with Betty when we brought her home later – but she insisted he was just a friend and it wasn't my business, and it isn't, Mum. Betty is old enough to get married if she wants and . . .' he faltered. 'Look, Frank said he'll ask around a bit, see what he can find out. He's a good bloke and will do what he can . . .'

'Well, I'm going round to Lizzie right now to tell her what I know – and if Sebastian comes after you, he'll want the whole truth, Matt – not just the bits you've told me . . . I shouldn't want to be in your shoes when he hears what you've just revealed . . .'

Matt stared after his mother. Sebastian would probably tear him off a strip and he felt guilty now, because Frank had wanted him to tell her parents, but Matt couldn't believe that Betty would've have been daft enough to go off with a man like that . . .

* * *

'You haven't heard anything more?' Beth asked as she sat in Lizzie's kitchen an hour or so later. She looked concerned as Lizzie shook her head, because they were still so close that they felt each other's sorrows. Beth was the sister Lizzie had never had and they'd shared so much during the war years, and since: the children's illnesses, their triumphs and failures. 'I thought she might send you a postcard or something . . . or even telephone you and let you know she's all right.'

'Betty was so angry when she left,' Lizzie said. 'I told you that she'd thrown things that Sebastian had given her at the wall and smashed them? I know she loved that glass swan; she must have really hated him to do that . . .'

'Just for a moment she probably did,' Beth agreed. 'Look, Lizzie, I don't know for certain, but Matt thinks that his friend might have seen Betty at Gatwick with a man. He only caught a fleeting glimpse but he thought it might be her . . .'

'Oh no! Sebastian has been hunting all over London, ringing all her friends, but I don't know if he has checked the airports . . . I knew she'd taken her passport but I didn't really think she would leave the country on her own . . .'

'Betty is old enough in law to fly unaccompanied, Lizzie. Your daughter is a young woman, as I've said before, even if she seems like a child to you – and according to Matt, she'd been hanging around with a Frenchman. He came here as a student of architecture some months ago and his visa ran out last month . . .'

'You think he might have gone back home and taken Betty with him?' Lizzie was horrified. 'But that means she's probably living with him . . .'

'Yes, I think it probably does,' Beth agreed. 'I know it's a shock, love, but I wasn't so much older when I fell in love with Mark; it happens and as long as she's happy and being taken care of . . .'

'I know she looks grown-up, Beth; Betty is still young in many ways,' Lizzie said. 'We all had to grow up fast and face the reality of life when we were young – our kids have had it easy.'

'Yes, I know,' Beth sighed. 'Children can be so difficult, especially when there's a stepfather involved. I told you Matt and Tony argue like crazy all the time and it has got worse just lately – Yet they went off down the pub together last night and came back the best of pals. They were laughing over something they'd seen – one of those peculiar bubble cars. Matt said he was going to get one for Tom for Christmas, but of course he wouldn't be allowed to drive it. Even if they do look like a kid's toy, they're actually cars of a sort . . .'

'I haven't seen one yet, but they look fun. Matt was probably teasing; he'll get him a toy one.' Lizzie smiled, her anxiety about Betty forgotten for a moment, because there had always been a certain amount of friction between Beth's eldest boy and his stepfather.

'Jenny always adored Tony,' Beth said now. Beth's only daughter Jenny was married to a soldier and no longer lived in London. She'd been all over the place with her husband, living in married quarters – in Cyprus for a while, which she'd raved about in her long letters home, until all the trouble between the Turks and Greeks escalated out there, and they'd been transferred to Germany. Jenny was now pregnant for the first time and was saying that they were coming home in the autumn and would be based near Aldershot and would probably stay with her mother around the time of the birth, especially if her husband was away on manoeuvres. 'Tony wasn't keen on her getting married at seventeen, but she cried and he gave in, of course – and it's worked out well. She's really happy . . .' Beth saw the pain in Lizzie's eyes. 'I wish it could be the same for Betty . . .'

'We don't know she isn't happy,' Lizzie said, determined to be brave and not give way to despair. 'Sebastian has been telephoning round her friends, trying to find out where she might have gone – if there was anyone she might have arranged to stay with, but so far he's drawn a blank.'

'Tell him to talk to Matt,' Beth said. 'I think he knows more about this man than he's telling me and he doesn't like him . . .'

'What is his name, where did he come from?'

'I don't know. Matt only told me today . . .'

Lizzie felt a cold trickle of fear down her spine.

'If we knew who he was we might be able to find him – and if Betty is with him . . .'

'Matt will want to help as much as he can. He's always been fond of Betty, as you know . . .'

Lizzie nodded. Betty and Beth's twins, Matt and Jenny, had been brought up almost as brother and sisters during the war and she'd known Matt kept a brotherly eye on her daughter.

'I'd noticed that Betty was doing things to her hair and wearing make-up more often, but that didn't worry me. I was determined I wouldn't try to stop her growing up the way my aunt did me . . .'

'Betty has Harry's reckless nature. And you're one of the most stubborn people I know, Lizzie. You can't blame Betty for being the way she is . . . and she's nearly eighteen. A lot of girls are married by that age . . .'

'If she was here and we could help her it wouldn't be so bad but she's too young to be off on her own somewhere, Beth. She's still an innocent – a child embarking on life. She should be here where we can all look after her . . .'

'Some girls grow up sooner and perhaps she met a man she thought she loved . . .'

'Oh Beth,' Lizzie said, her distress almost over-whelming her. 'I've hardly slept since she went. I can't stop thinking about where she is and if she's safe . . .'

'Of course you can't,' Beth said sympathetically. 'I can't believe Sebastian actually hit her. He's never struck you – has he?'

'Never!' Lizzie shook her head emphatically. 'He's never hit either of the girls before. I know he regrets it dreadfully. He was upset about something that day – and since then he's like a bear with a sore head. He's blaming himself for her going off like that and he's out all hours trying to find her. I don't sleep but he hardly comes to bed at all . . . and he doesn't eat much either. I've tried telling him it isn't his fault, but he knows it is . . .'

'I always thought Betty adored him, Lizzie . . .'

'I think that's the trouble. She did and he made such a fuss of her when she was little – and then I got pregnant with Francie. Sebastian says he loves them both equally, but how can he? Betty isn't easy. She's got a temper and she acts without thinking, says things she shouldn't – and Sebastian tries to keep her right, but he's away so often and perhaps he's lost touch with her . . . perhaps neither of us realised that she needed to move on in her life.'

Beth wrinkled her brow. 'Do you think she's jealous of Francie – of her talent, and because Sebastian is her father?'

'Matt and Jenny aren't jealous of Tom, are they?'

'They spoil him silly,' Beth assured her. 'When he was born they hardly ever let me do a thing for him . . . Jenny was a little mother to him and as soon as he could walk and talk, Matt took him over. Tony and I hardly got a look in . . .' Beth laughed because she was in a good place and knew she was lucky. The dark days when she'd given birth to illegitimate twins after their father's ship was sunk and the even blacker days when she'd been married to Bernie Wright for a brief time were far behind her. Then she'd married Tony after he was badly wounded and sent home from the war and she'd never been happier. Tony's little shop had become three thriving businesses, selling sweets, cigarettes, tobacco and newspapers. His false arm had gradually become a useful tool, even though he was always conscious of it, but it didn't stop him becoming a successful man – or a loving husband. 'I've been really lucky, Lizzie. We both have – but I know some things could have gone better for you, love . . .'

They both understood that she was talking about the unfortunate miscarriages that Lizzie had endured. She'd visited several doctors and in the end been advised to take precautions so that she did not fall pregnant again.

Her doctor had told her, 'If you continue to miscarry, Mrs Winters, you could seriously endanger your own health. You have two lovely daughters – why not settle for that? I can make it quite easy for you . . .'

'I don't want a hysterectomy,' Lizzie had said, fearing that he would ask her to have an operation to make certain she could not fall for a child again.

He'd smiled kindly at her. 'I wouldn't dream of suggesting it. Perhaps one day you might have the son you so desire, but you need to heal inside and get strong again.'

He'd given Lizzie a cap that fitted inside her and which was very easy and discreet to use. It had caused her no trouble and been successful in preventing her falling for another child . . . but she'd torn it accidentally and thrown it out some while back, neglecting to have a new one fitted. Sebastian would scold her if he knew and tell her to go back to the doctor to have a new one fitted – but Lizzie didn't want that: she wanted one last chance to give her husband the son she knew he craved, even though he'd never put it into words.

'Oh, I'm over all that now,' Lizzie told Beth, because she wasn't ready to tell her or anyone else something she couldn't quite believe herself. It was much too soon and she couldn't be sure that she'd fallen for a baby again. 'I'm going to see Ed this afternoon. Would you like to come and see the new machinery we've installed in the workshops?'

Beth gave her an odd look, as if she'd guessed that Lizzie had deliberately turned the conversation, but she got up and retrieved her shopping bag from the back of a chair. 'I'd better get home,' she said. 'Tony has a dinner on this evening – a businessmen's thing, Chamber of Commerce annual shindig, and he wants me to go with him, though he knows I hate them. I've got an appointment at three to have my hair done . . . and I've no idea what I'm going to wear . . .'

'You'd better tell me everything,' Sebastian said grimly when he and Matt met in the public bar the younger man had suggested. 'You know more than you told your mother – don't deny it . . .'

'I couldn't tell her what Frank told me,' Matt agreed. 'I didn't want her or Betty's mother to worry too much until we know a bit more – but this chap Betty may have gone off with is a nasty character by all accounts . . .'

'In what way?'

'The general opinion is that he's a bit of a lothario, getting girls into trouble and then dropping them – that's one rumour, but Frank's made inquiries at the college Saint-Jacquez was attending and they asked him to leave before his course was finished. He'd been gambling heavily at some club and they sent the heavies in after him, causing a rumpus at the college campus . . .'

'Gambling, women,' Sebastian said and his gaze narrowed. 'That isn't the worst of it – is it?'

'I'm not certain of any of it . . . but Frank was told Saint-Jacquez has been seen associating with a man of Turkish descent, or Middle-Eastern. No one knows much about him, but the rumours say he's been associated with the disappearance of a lot of beautiful girls . . . apparently he particularly admires blondes . . .'

'Betty's hair is reddish . . .'

'But she's been trying to make it lighter for ages . . .' Matt sighed. 'Betty is headstrong and sulky at times, but I think a lot of her – and if there's anything I can do, I'm happy to help.'

'Thanks. You've already helped a lot. I'll put the

word out with some friends of mine and see what I can come up with.' Sebastian smiled at him. 'Why couldn't my daughter have fallen for a chap like you?'

Matt's colour heightened and he grinned. 'Betty still thinks of me as her brother . . .'

'Yes – but you don't see her that way, do you?'

'Not sure what I think,' Matt replied honestly. 'I'm only a few months older than Betty, and not ready to settle down. I didn't think she was – and I hope to God she gets a chance to get married to a decent bloke and be happy . . .'

'Thanks,' Sebastian said and stood up. 'I'll be in touch if you can help me again. Take care of your-self, lad – and good luck . . .'

Sebastian sat in the hotel lounge and drank his coffee. He massaged his temples with his finger-tips, because his head was pounding and he felt physically sick. It was mid-September and Betty's birthday. Lizzie's red eyes at breakfast that morning had told him that she'd been crying. He felt like hell himself, because although it was only a few weeks since she'd run off he was beginning to think it was an impossible task to find her, and he hardly knew how to face his wife on their daughter's eighteenth birthday. It should have been a wonderful day for all of them. He would have been taking her and Lizzie out to a special lunch and there would have been presents and cards and a beautiful cake for tea. Francie had sent both a card and a present and they were lying on the bed in Betty's room, together with other cards that had come from friends and Lizzie's gift to her. Sebastian hadn't bought her a present, because he was too angry with her for running away, and too upset to carry on as if she were just away on holiday and would soon be back. Yet he felt his guilt resting like a hard lump in his chest and sometimes he felt so tired. There was so much weighing him down . . .

He hadn't told Lizzie what Matt had confided in secret. There was no point in distressing her more than she already was and he was praying that Matt and his friend had it all wrong, because if they were right his daughter was heading for heartbreak at the very least and the thought of what might happen to her made him sick with fear. He blamed himself for not paying more attention to what was going on – but he'd had more than he could cope with just recently . . .

It had all crept up on him so fast that he hadn't seen it coming and it made him feel such a fool. How could he have neglected his business to such an extent that it had come to this? The factory that had made boots so successfully and profitably during the war had been losing money for the last couple of years. After the war he'd switched to making beautiful hand-crafted leather shoes that had once been the hallmark of British quality. Their shoes were still admired and bought by those who understood that their quality made them keep their shape and last for years, but lately the market had been flooded with cheap imports that made it impossible to make a decent profit at home.

Sebastian had been searching for markets abroad for the past three years, and he'd been successful up to a point. They were exporting to America, where the quality of the hand stitching was still appreciated, and in smaller quantities to other countries – but not, so his accountant told him, in sufficient amounts to pull them out of the red.

'It's a case of letting the factory go while the fashion shop is still making money or draining yourself and ending up with nothing . . . my advice is to sell the factory. You could cover your debts and reinvest the residue in your shop or property.'

Sebastian knew it was good advice but he hated to let down the men and women who worked in the factory. It wouldn't be easy to find a buyer who would keep it going in its present form – which meant highly skilled men and women would be out of a job. Of course he'd see they got redundancy money, but he knew the pride that went into making a good product and he was reluctant to take that away from people he'd known and appreciated for years.

Sighing, he paid for his coffee and left, pulling up his coat collar as he went out into the chill of a wet September afternoon. Why did troubles never come singly? He'd tried everywhere he knew in London and he thought that Matt was probably right to suspect that Betty had gone to France with that man – but it was a big country and he wasn't sure where to start. There was only one man he could ask for help . . . and Jack would expect favours in return. It was the way it worked. Jack had the huge resources of the secret service at his disposal, but they'd asked a lot of Sebastian over the years; even after the war was over, they'd expected him to carry on with work they considered vital to the nation's security. Now he felt he'd given enough and had been hoping to extricate himself sooner rather than later. Asking for Jack's help in a personal matter would draw him right in again.

Sebastian's secret work was such that Lizzie could unexpectedly find herself a widow at any time. How Marianne knew what he did while ostensibly travelling for his business he had no idea; she certainly hadn't learned it from him: he'd been roped in a few years back when it had been realised what was going on and he'd been asked to help get important people back from East Germany to the West – or sometimes the families of those already here who were afraid to speak about what they knew, because their loved ones would suffer.

Sebastian had at first refused. Lizzie wanted a quiet life, working and bringing up their children, and so did he, but he'd been shown photographs by his former colleagues, documents that turned his stomach and he'd been drawn in against his better judgement . . . and then Marianne had asked him for help. He hadn't hesitated, because he knew Karl would've done the same for him. In fact, he'd saved Sebastian's life when they were both still in college. It wasn't a conscious choice, he'd just given his word – but perhaps it had cost Sebastian more than he'd bargained for. Too much time spent away from home – and that had led to a financial loss with the factory and perhaps to the rift between Betty and himself. If he'd been home more, he would have noticed what was going on, but he'd only recently become aware of the resentment on his daughter's part – because Betty was his daughter in every way, and he ought to have made sure she knew it.

She'd gone with that man, Sebastian was certain of it, and it made him fearful for his daughter, because she was far too innocent. She had no idea how much evil was in the world and it broke his heart to think of her alone and vulnerable . . . Betty had been protected and loved and she wasn't ready for a world that could be dangerous and cruel . . .

CHAPTER 5

'Look, I've got three days off this weekend,' Frank said into the mouthpiece of the telephone. 'Can you get away – come to Paris with me?'

'I'm not sure . . .' Matt sounded wary. 'Tony wanted me to work this weekend . . .'

'We owe it to Betty to look for her,' Frank was urgent. 'If you can't get away I'll go on my own, but I'd rather you were there. If we find that bastard we'll make him tell us where she is – we'll beat it out of him . . .'

'We don't know she's in Paris . . .'

'I've been thinking it over and that's where I think he would take her . . .'

'Perhaps I should tell Sebastian? See what he wants to do . . .' Matt was cautious but Frank was impatient, because he felt Betty had been gone too long.

'I don't know what her parents are doing about it, but I've made up my mind I'm going to give it a try . . . are you coming?'

'All right,' Matt agreed. 'I'll tell them I'm meeting you but I shan't say what we're going to do –

there's no point in raising their hopes until we're sure we can do something. I'm not even certain she'll come home if we do find her . . .'

'She'll come for you, Matt, that's why I asked. I can't rest until I at least try to find her. I feel so guilty. I should've warned her, made her realise what a devil that rotter is . . .'

'We did try,' Matt reminded him, 'but she wouldn't listen. Maybe she will now – if she's realised what sort of a pig he really is . . .'

'I'll book the flights and pay the expenses . . . don't argue, Matt. I earn more than you, and you'll be doing me a favour . . .'

'Betty was a bloody fool,' Matt said. 'She didn't know what a good bloke she had in you, Frank. A lot of men wouldn't bother with her after what she's done . . .'

'You *would* if you loved her,' Frank said gruffly. 'Right, Gatwick at twelve-thirty – OK?'

Frank replaced the receiver and left the office. He wasn't supposed to use the office phone too often, but at the moment he couldn't think straight. It was driving him mad worrying about what might have happened to Betty. Matt had told him that her father was keeping things quiet, because he didn't want it to get into the papers, but Frank wasn't prepared to just sit around and do nothing. If Saint-Jacquez had got her hidden away somewhere he would tear the place apart – and him . . .

★　★　★

Wake up,' Pierre's voice cut through her sleep bringing her sharply from her dream. Betty stared at him, blinking as she saw that he was wearing a business suit and looked different, as if he were someone she didn't know. 'I must work and you must leave now . . .'

'W-what do you mean?' Betty was wide awake now with shock. Pierre normally worked a few hours every day at his architectural plans in the apartment, but she had learned to leave him to get on with it and he'd never ordered her out before. She sat up and swung her legs over the side of the bed, dragging the sheet with her to cover her nakedness. 'When can I come back?'

'You leave now,' Pierre said in that harsh voice he'd used more and more towards her of late, his English broken as it was sometimes when he was angry or emotional. 'We 'ave fun while it last, but I must bring clients 'ere and you must not be 'ere. I 'ave a large commission pending, a job that will make my fortune and my reputation as an architect, and he comes 'ere this afternoon . . .'

'But I can come back this evening . . .' Betty was bewildered. 'You're not throwing me out? Pierre . . . I thought you loved me? I left everything to be with you . . .'

'Better for you we finish now . . . If you stay it will be too late . . .'

What was he talking about? She stared at him, shocked and numbed for a moment as she struggled to realise what had happened. Betty had thrown her life away for this man and after a few short weeks together in Paris, he was telling her it was over.

'But where will I go . . . what will I do?

'I give you good time,' Pierre said and pulled her to her feet, kissing her briefly on the lips. His hand slid down her back, briefly caressing the soft roundness of her limbs and then his hands gripped the soft part of her arm hard. 'I am not a good man, ma petite . . . and there are others even worse. You would not like them . . . go now before is too late . . . go home to your family . . .'

'How can I go home now?' Betty demanded, her temper rising, chasing away the numbness. 'You're a cheat and a selfish pig. You set out to seduce me and now you're throwing me out . . .'

'You, ma cherie, are spoiled baby,' Pierre replied scornfully. 'You behave like little virgin and expect me to be satisfied – well, let me tell you there are women who know how to please in ways you haven't the faintest clue about, and they do it willingly, eagerly for a fraction of what I've spent on you.' He took a few francs from his pocket and threw them at her. 'That's more than you're worth – and it's the price of the fare home. Take it and run back to Mummy like the good little English girl you are . . .'

'Pierre . . . you can't mean it's over just like that?' Betty flung herself at him desperately as he started to walk away. 'I love you . . . I'll do anything you want . . .'

'Too late,' he said and thrust her away. 'I don't want you 'ere when I get back . . . take warning and go. Stay and you will regret . . .'

Betty felt as if he'd poured a bucket of cold water over her. She was still in shock as she went to the tiny toilet and had a wash in the hand basin, a storm of tears overcoming her as she realised her world had just ended.

Why, oh, why had she run off with him? She'd been so angry with her parents and in Sebastian's case she'd been hurt, because he thought she wasn't fit to work in her mother's workshops . . . Betty had just wanted someone to love her and she'd been taken in by Pierre's sweet talk and the money he'd spent on her. Now she felt as if she'd been punched in the stomach and left gasping for breath.

Pierre didn't want her anymore. She'd been a novelty for him, an innocent he could seduce and mould as he thought fit – only she'd resisted and refused some of the things he'd asked her to do . . . things she just didn't feel comfortable with. He'd been angry sometimes, sometimes laughing at her and teasing her into agreement – and some-times walking out . . . Taking her suitcase from under the bed, she started packing the few items that she'd left lying about. It was only as she was about to close it that she realised her money wasn't there. She pulled everything out and hunted in the little pockets inside, but there was no sign of her money. Repacking every item after shaking each one, Betty realised that it had gone. She'd changed ten pounds into francs but that had left forty English notes that she'd deliberated kept as her emergency money – and it had gone.

There was only one person who could've taken it. Pierre must have helped himself when he was short. She saw the money he'd thrown at her lying on the bed and counted it – ten francs. Hardly enough to buy the cheapest passage back to England, and far less than he'd taken from her.

It wasn't enough that he'd taken her innocence, he'd stolen her savings as well. Angry tears filled her eyes but she knuckled them away, because she wouldn't give him the satisfaction of her crying over him. She'd been going to leave his money on the bed, but now she scooped it up, knowing it was all she had to keep her off the streets and it wouldn't last long.

'Francie says she'll come home for a week in October, so she'll be here for her birthday,' Lizzie said, looking up from her letter as Sebastian pushed his chair back from the table. 'Do you want to read it?' She offered their daughter's letter.

'I thought she was coming this weekend . . . haven't they all got a few days off to concentrate on their course work?'

'She's going to stay with a friend instead, Jilly and her grandmother. . . . That's where she was when . . . Betty ran off . . .' Lizzie's voice caught and she shook her head, blinking back the tears.

Every day her daughter was missing seemed like an eternity. 'If Francie had been home, perhaps she would have talked some sense into her and Betty might not have gone, because they've always been close . . .'

'You haven't told Francie about Betty?' Sebastian frowned as if he disapproved.

'No . . . we agreed it was best not to, you know we did. She'll be home soon . . . and I'd rather not do it by letter . . .'

'She ought to know,' Sebastian said. 'We don't want her to resent us for not telling her . . . Betty hasn't contacted us, but she might have written to her sister . . .'

'Francie would tell us . . .'

'Unless Betty swore her to secrecy . . .'

'She wouldn't!' Lizzie looked at him anxiously. 'Francie would know we were worried. I keep thinking Betty will come home any day and then Francie won't need to know . . .'

'It's more than four weeks now since she ran off and she hasn't sent a card or phoned. I can't see her coming back unless I find her. She has too much pride, rather like her mother . . .' Sebastian said grimly. He looked at his watch. 'I'm sorry, love. I have a meeting at the factory again. I have to go.'

'Will you be back this evening?'

'I doubt it,' he said and dropped a kiss on the top of her head. 'I'm really sorry I haven't found Betty . . . I know you must blame me for all this . . .'

'It isn't your fault,' Lizzie denied loyally. 'Neither of us thought she would go off the way she did . . .'

'Tell Francie,' Sebastian said. 'Write to her or phone her, Lizzie. I know we tend to think of her as a child, but she really isn't – and I don't want to lose her too . . .'

Francie looked round the large hall excitedly. They were in Manchester and she'd acquired the tickets to this prestige fashion show by sending a picture of herself in a bathing costume to the young women's magazine. The competition was to win a contract as a photographic model and the second prize had been three tickets to this show by *Styled*, the new fashion magazine that catered for modern young women. Like most girls of her age, Francie loved new clothes and she particularly loved the magazine that seemed to be talking to girls like her rather than to older women. Her mother often had one of the big glossy magazines like *Vogue* or *Woman & Home* on her coffee tables as well as trade magazines showing stylish hats and clothes, but this magazine was aimed at younger women – perhaps teenagers, though it didn't actually pitch it as a teenage interest.

Francie had been over the moon when she won the second prize. As well as the tickets to the show, she'd been given vouchers for twenty-five pounds so that she and two friends could pay the necessary travelling expenses from Cambridge to Manchester, and stay at a hotel overnight, all courtesy of the magazine. She'd chosen her closest friends, Jilly and Averil. Averil was already sixteen, a quiet studious girl who wore her long dark hair back in a thick plait. Her mother was a widow and couldn't have afforded the fees for the small but well-respected art school they both attended in Cambridge. However, her uncle had paid for his niece, persuading Mrs Bassett that her daughter had a worthwhile talent. Like most mothers, Averil's wanted her daughter well married and settled, but Averil had set her mind on a career in commercial art. She was a modern young lady and didn't see why she had to get married at seventeen, just because it was what her mother had done.

Jilly was different; she would have liked to spend more time in Cornwall with her grandmother on the farm. It was her gran who had forced Jilly's parents to let her have a year at the expensive college.

'Gran has all the money,' Jilly told Francie when they were talking over a bottle of pop and some biscuits they'd smuggled up to the dorm for a midnight feast. 'Mum wanted me in secretarial college so that I could start earning a living, but Gran wouldn't hear of it. I know Mum expects that Gran will leave the farm and her money to her and my stepfather, but I don't think she will . . . I know I could go and live with her when my year is up, but I want to be independent for a few years, find myself a job and make something of my life, though I shall spend all my holidays with Gran because she's a darling . . .' Her face was alight with enthusiasm and she looked pretty, fairer than either Francie or Averil, with bright blue eyes.

'I'm not sure what I want,' Francie had told her friends. Her long black hair was swept up in a ponytail because it was easy to control that way, her eyes blue but a softer colour than her father's, though her colouring was very like Sebastian's. 'Dad is convinced I can be a great artist and I don't want to let him down, but I'm not sure I'm good enough and I'd like to have some fun before I settle down . . .'

Francie knew she was lucky. Her parents were loving and generous and she was given most things she wanted, but in return she was expected to work hard and she knew her father was expecting her to pass all her exams and reward his faith in her. She wanted that too, but there was a bit of a rebel inside her and that girl wanted to kick over the traces and have fun. It was the feeling that she needed a break from the intensity of her art rather than any real desire to be a model that had made her send in pictures of herself. She'd been delighted to win the tickets for the show, especially as she was allowed to bring two friends with her.

She, Jilly and Averil had booked into the hotel, which had been paid for in advance, and was pleasant, quiet and respectable and close to the venue for the show, and then headed straight to the fashion show. None of the girls had asked permission from their parents for the visit and all of them had told the school they were going to stay with Jilly's family for the weekend. None of them felt guilty, because it was an adventure and all three had decided that after working hard for months, mostly at their art, but also at the normal curriculum lessons they were expected to attend, they were entitled to some fun.

'Gosh this is great,' Jilly said, grabbing at Francie's arm. 'Look at all the clothes on those rails! Do you think we're allowed to go through them? I'd love to try some of them on . . .'

'It said in the magazine that there would be loads of things to see, some available to buy, others just to look at, and if we're lucky we might get some free samples. I think they're giving away Elizabeth Arden samples over there . . .'

'I love Elizabeth Arden's perfume and make-up, but it's so expensive,' Averil said and pulled at Francie's other arm. 'Let's get in the queue and see if we can get some samples . . .'

'I've got to present myself to *Styled* first,' Francie said. She fished in her handbag for the tickets for the show. 'Look I'll give you your tickets and I'll meet you there when the show starts if not before . . .'

'Oh, I thought you would be with us,' Jilly objected. 'Can't we come with you and then look round the stands afterwards?'

'Yes, why not?' Francie said and laughed, flicking

84

back her long straight dark hair. Her eyes were a soft greenish brown that some people called hazel, and she had a generous mouth that smiled easily. 'I probably shan't be long and we don't want to get separated in this crowd.'

'It's over there!' Averil cried, pointing doubtfully at the large stand, which was surrounded by girls of a similar age. 'They seem to be very busy . . .'

'Well, it's their show,' Francie said. 'They organised the competition and I'll bet there were thousands of girls of our age who went in for it, because the lucky one got a contract to be a model . . .'

'I wish I'd sent my picture,' Jilly said, 'but my mother would kill me if I left college to become a model. Even though Gran paid I should never hear the last of the money I'd wasted . . .'

Francie smiled sympathetically. They'd all heard about Jilly's mother before. Francie knew she was lucky, because her parents never questioned what she wanted, they just gave her everything. Sometimes, she thought it wasn't fair that she had so much when others struggled to buy the paints and brushes they needed. Francie was always passing on tubes of paint she'd half used on the pretext that she didn't like them. Jilly didn't have a lot of spending money but gave her friends holidays to her grandmother's home in the country. It was lovely there and all the girls liked staying at half term. It was where they were supposed to be now. A flicker of unease went through Francie, because her father would be angry if he knew she'd allowed her mother to think she was in the country with friends when she was in Manchester. Francie shook her head, she wouldn't let herself worry about that now.

She pushed her way to the head of the queue, Jilly and Averil following close behind, and ignoring the angry looks and remarks of the girls who didn't want to give up their place.

'Sorry, but I have to report in,' Francie apologised to one pretty girl who just refused to let her past. 'I've got a pass . . . see.' She held it so that the girl couldn't mistake it and she reluctantly moved aside. Francie mounted the steps and went up to one of the desks. 'I'm Francie Winters . . .' she said and handed over her pass.

The woman glanced at it, snatched it from her hand, and looked relieved. 'Thank God, you've turned up,' she said. 'Come with me. We're behind with the shoot now . . .'

'The shoot?' Francie looked at her in surprise. 'I was the runner-up not the winner . . .'

'And that makes you our reserve if the winner defaults,' the woman said. 'My name is Kathy and I'm the commissioning editor. We're here to do a big spread for the magazine – and you'll be modelling some of the clothes for us . . .' She looked over Francie's shoulder. 'Who are these girls?'

'My friends. I got three tickets to see the show as my prize.'

'Yes, well, you'll be getting rather more now.' Her eyes went over Francie's friends, then she smiled and invited them with a gesture of her hand, 'Do you want to come and watch – we might take photos of you just for fun if you like . . .?'

'Can we try on some of the clothes?' Jilly asked and Kathy smiled at her.

'Why shouldn't you? We're selecting a few girls to model clothes – as well as our winner. You two will get a free hairdo, make-up and the chance to try some designer clothes . . .'

Jilly and Averil giggled and looked at each other and they all trooped behind Kathy as she led them behind the screens at the back of the stand, down a narrow hall and into a large room. Cameras on stands were set up with lots of lighting pointing towards a large white screen.

'The dressing rooms are over here,' Kathy said, leading the way. 'I'll show you what we want you to wear, Francie – and there are some spare rails your friends can pick from . . . what are your names, by the way?'

'Jilly . . .'

'Averil . . .'

'Well you two pick something you like and then go over to that lady there. Mabel will do your make-up and Roger will style your hair . . .' She fingered Averil's frizzy red hair and frowned. 'A wig to cover this mop, I think . . . Come along, Francie. Your friends will be fine . . .'

Francie felt as if she were being swept along on a rushing tide. She couldn't believe this was happening. When she'd entered the competition she'd vaguely hoped she might win the tickets and when it happened she hadn't been able to believe her luck. Now she felt as if she were caught in a dream . . . they couldn't really be saying that she was to take the place of the winner and have a modelling contract? No, this was just for today and the real winner would claim her prize as soon as she could . . .

Francie didn't have much time to think about what was happening to her, because she was asked to try on a succession of clothes until the styling team were satisfied they'd got the right colours and sizes for her. A few adjustments were made with pins and while she was having her hair styled and her face painted with what felt like heavy make-up, the seamstress got to work.

Francie caught sight of her friends; they seemed to be having a great time. She saw them both wearing fabulous dresses and posing for the camera, giggling and enjoying the fun. Then Kathy was telling her how to walk down the catwalk and how to hold herself.

'You're not a professional model, but that's the whole point of today and it's our pictures that matter most. You go on, pause to let the audience look at you, and then walk down the catwalk, turn and walk back, keeping a faint smile on your face – do you think you can manage that without falling over?'

Francie looked down at her very high heels. 'I think so, though I'd rather have bare feet than these . . .'

'You have to wear them; they're part of the ensemble . . .' Kathy said, but a man came over to look and he disagreed, his assessing gaze making Francie feel a little like a filly in the show ring being put up for sale.

'I think that's a wonderful idea, Francie,' he said. 'Let her carry the shoes, Kathy – it could cause a sensation. I'll do a shoot of her with the shoes – and without.'

'Well . . . if you think so, Roger . . .' Kathy looked doubtful, but Roger led her across to the set and told her how he wanted her to hold the shoes and then set a wind machine going; it lifted her full skirt and swirled it around her legs, and her hair blew across her face. He showed Kathy how it looked through the viewer and she nodded, a big smile spreading across her face.

'Yes, I see what you mean . . . Stylist . . .' she summoned the make-up girl.

The hair stylist and the make-up artist came over and smoothed Francie's hair into place and a powder puff was dabbed at her cheeks. Roger then shot a variety of pictures with Francie wearing the shoes and Kathy checked the stills with him, nodding.

'Time, Kathy . . .' Someone called and Kathy sped into action, propelling Francie towards some curtains and giving her last minute instructions. 'Remember what I told you about keeping a confident smile, and hold the shoes as Roger showed you . . . imagine you're on a beach with the man of your dreams . . .'

'OK,' Francie said, though she didn't have a man she idolised or fantasised over, as some of her friends did, but she remembered a wonderful holiday with her parents and Betty in Cornwall when they'd spent ages riding ponies along a deserted beach, so she decided to think about that holiday, which had been the best of her life, because it had been one of the rare times her father had been with them.

As the curtain was drawn to one side and Kathy gave her a little push forward and an encouraging smile, Francie stepped into the bright lights of the stage and walked down the red carpet, swinging her beautiful but impossible shoes from her right hand with a casual air, as if she owned dozens of pairs of designer shoes and couldn't care less about them. She was thinking of one particularly lovely day in Cornwall when they'd galloped across the deserted beach and then dismounted, taking off their boots, rolling up their jodhpurs and walking in the sea, leading the ponies. It had been such a perfect day and she couldn't ever recall being happier.

Francie posed at the end of the runway, giving a little twirl so that the full pleated silk skirt fanned out about her legs as it had when the wind machine was playing, then turned, glanced back mischievously over her shoulder as she had at her father that day on the beach and walked back with an unconsciously sexy sway that the audience appeared to find appealing because there was a burst of clapping as she reached the curtains. The clapping made Francie aware of the audience and she half ran through the curtains as she was suddenly covered in confusion, because for a moment she'd forgotten where she was and had been lost in her memories.

'Ooh, you clever thing,' Jilly said. 'You looked like a professional out there. We were peeping from the side of the stage . . .'

'Well done,' Kathy congratulated her with a warm smile. 'I think it was a lucky day for us when the winner defaulted. After that little display I think you're going a long way in the business, Francie. Now, there's no time to lose, you've got two more outfits to model and then Roger wants some pictures of you and your friends together . . .'

'What do you mean – a long way in this business?' Francie asked, suddenly apprehensive. Never for one moment had she expected to win the contract, even though it was an exciting idea, and yet there was her scholarship for a year studying art in Paris and she really wanted that . . . and what would her father say? 'I only won second prize . . .'

'Didn't you read the small print?' Kathy asked slightly annoyed. 'When you signed that form and entered our competition you agreed to work for us as a model for a year if you won – and you have, which means the contract is legally binding . . .' Kathy pushed her towards the changing rooms with a smile. 'It's going to be wonderful,

Francie. You'll earn a fortune . . . hurry up and get changed, you've got ten minutes and you're on again . . .'

Francie went through the motions as if she were in a gorgeous dream for the rest of the day. Her next visits to the catwalk were greeted with spontaneous applause and she repeated her little pause to look back on each occasion and was aware of lots of cameras popping in her face. After the fashion show, of which she'd seen only the briefest glimpse as the other models got changed and walked past her, Francie and her friends were given a fizzy drink and cream cake – though Kathy warned her not to eat too much, and then Roger took some pictures of them in their own clothes, looking like the schoolgirls they were.

'Thanks a lot, girls,' Kathy said to Averil and Jilly. 'You can both pick something you like from the rails there, as a thank you for today – and you too, Francie, but you'll be getting paid, of course.' She whisked a form under Francie's nose. 'Sign this and we'll post your cheque on Monday . . .'

Francie scribbled her name hastily, not bothering to read what it said. According to Kathy, she'd already signed to work for them for the next year, but Kathy's assurance that she would only be needed when there was a specific contract from a clothing store had reassured her. She could still take up her art scholarship, which wasn't due to start until next spring anyway, and it was easy enough to come back for a short visit from France these days.

Her arms tucked blithely through her friends' arms, she went out into the pleasant autumn afternoon, clutching the bags with free samples of clothing and make-up and giggling at how much fun they'd had . . .

CHAPTER 6

It's no use,' Matt said as they left perhaps the fortieth bar they'd visited over the past evening. 'We'll never find Betty like this . . . no one seems to have seen or heard of her.'

'I thought someone might have noticed her, perhaps her hair – and the fact that she's English . . .' Frank sighed. 'I'm bushed. Let's go back to the hotel and get some sleep, we'll start again tomorrow.'

'You do know it's useless,' Matt frowned. 'They could've gone anywhere in the world. We have no proof that they came to Paris . . .'

'I was told he lives here,' Frank said stubbornly. 'I'm going to ask round the cafés tomorrow . . .' He broke off as he saw a man leave a café and stand on the pavement opposite. Clutching at Matt's arm, he directed his gaze. 'That's him – I'm sure it is . . .'

Matt looked but, before he could answer his friend had gone charging across the road, narrowly avoiding a collision with a passing cycle. 'Frank – wait a minute . . .' he said, but Frank had grabbed the man by the arm and was haranguing him. As he approached, he caught part of what was being said . . .

'I 'ave no knowledge of this girl . . .' Pierre protested. 'You madman . . . let go my arm . . .'

'I'm damned well not going to let you go until you tell me what happened to Betty Oliver,' Frank snarled and twisted the Frenchman's arm behind his back, making him yell out in pain. He slammed him up against the wall, making the man's nose bleed. 'I know she was with you, you bastard – I saw you at Gatwick . . .' He jerked Pierre's arm up again. 'If you've harmed Betty I'll kill you . . .'

For a moment Matt thought he saw panic in the man's eyes but then it had gone and he was sneering at Frank. 'If your lover leave you it not my fault . . .' he said and broke free of Frank's grasp. 'I know not this girl . . . she not with me . . .'

'I'll make you sorry you laid a finger on her . . .' Frank threw himself at Saint-Jacquez again but he surprised him by punching him in the stomach and then dashing into a nearby café as Frank doubled over, winded. 'Bastard . . . why didn't you stop him?' Frank demanded as Matt reached him.

Matt helped him to stand upright. 'Sorry, but I don't see where this gets us . . . he'll never tell us anything now . . . we should've tried to talk to him, asked where she is and if she's all right . . .'

'I'm going after him . . .' Frank said and rushed off, disappearing into the café.

Matt followed reluctantly. Frank seemed to have

lost his reason. Searching for Betty was one thing, but attacking a man they didn't even know had taken Betty anywhere was another. Being a large strong man, Matt had always been careful to use his strength in the right way, but Frank had lost his temper because he was so upset over Betty.

Standing just inside the door, Matt scanned the café. Pierre Saint-Jacquez was not there. He'd probably gone straight through and out the back door and would be miles away by now. Because of Frank's impetuous attack on him they'd lost their chance to reason with the man and perhaps persuade him to tell them where Betty was.

Frank came back to him. 'I let the bastard slip away . . .'

'Not your fault,' Matt said. 'We'll start again in the morning, ask for Betty – and him, though I doubt he'll tell us anything now if we find him . . .'

'You think I went in too hard . . .' Frank looked uncertain.

'You're angry and I am too, but violence doesn't help much. He'll go to ground for a few days now . . . but we might find her if we're lucky . . .'

Frank shook his head. 'I should have been on my guard. It's my fault he got away. Damn the man . . . I'll make sure he doesn't slip away next time . . .'

'Forget him,' Matt said. 'We've made him aware people are looking for her. With any luck he'll realise the game is over and send her home . . .'

'I wish I thought so,' Frank said, 'but you're right. We can't do anything more tonight. We just have to hope we'll find her tomorrow . . .'

Matt nodded and shivered, suddenly chilly. He knew it was an almost impossible task in a city this size – even if she was here. They had a couple of days and without help it could take months to find her . . . if she could be found . . .

'You English,' the man behind the wine bar said with a faint sneer. 'You, of no use to me. You no speak our language . . .'

Betty protested volubly in French, using some words that Pierre had taught her and the man looked surprised, laughed and then leered at her. 'Little whore,' he said. 'You speak the language of the gutter . . . maybe I find use for you in my bed, no?'

Betty told him what he could do with that offer in the language he'd accused of her using and he laughed as she flounced out of the bar, seething inside. Why would none of them give her a chance, just because she was English? The excuses varied, but it was usually because she didn't understand French well enough or she was too young. One plump sour-faced woman had told her she did not employ whores in her café and shouted at her rudely until she left, the tears burning inside but unshed. Why did people keep saying horrid things to her? She wasn't a whore even if she had been stupid enough to fall for a man that treated her like one.

Leaving the wine bar, Betty lifted her head, determined not to give up. She would go back to her daily round of trying all the fashion workshops and retailers, looking for a job and if she got too down-hearted, she'd try some more cafés later.

She wasn't sure why she didn't just book a passage back to England, except that she'd spent the few francs Pierre had given her on food long since and anything she'd managed to earn, washing up for a few hours or cleaning the windows of an inn, went on food and the poky little room she'd managed to find. She'd been forced to sell Aunt Miriam's heavy silver bracelet and she might just manage to get home with what she had left, and yet a part of her didn't want to give in. It had been such fun living in Paris when she was with Pierre, but it wouldn't be fun sleeping on a park bench and she might be forced to do that unless she found regular work soon. Her only other alternative would be to go to one of the friends she made in her first weeks in Paris and she wasn't sure whether any of them would take her in, because although they'd welcomed her to Paris, they were really his friends not hers. She might bump into Pierre and she was trying to avoid him. Even if he didn't want her, he needn't have thrust her out at a moment's notice! Besides, she didn't like to beg and was determined to earn a living. She couldn't go home until she had enough money to do so without throwing herself on her family's mercy.

Several times Betty had thought about ringing home; she'd even tried once, but as soon as she heard her mother's voice she'd put the phone down, unable to speak, though she'd since phoned Francie's school and asked for her – it had been the day before Betty's birthday and she was feeling homesick. Francie had been out when she rang and Betty had replaced the receiver without leaving her name. At this moment she felt so miserable she just wished she was dead . . . or at home with Aunt Miriam. Her aunt had always taken her side . . .

'You haven't heard from Betty at all?' Aunt Miriam frowned as she sat drinking coffee at Lizzie's kitchen table that October morning. 'Oh, my dear, I'm so sorry. I thought . . .' she hesitated for a moment and then opened her small leather bag and took out a postcard. 'I had this, a couple of weeks ago, but I wasn't sure . . . I thought you must have had something too . . . Betty said she was going to ring you.'

'Why on earth didn't you tell us at once? We've been worried to death . . .'

Lizzie almost snatched the postcard from her hand; it was of the Eiffel Tower and she turned it over eagerly, her heart thumping. On the back was scribbled a brief message:

I'm all right, Aunt Miriam. One day I'll come and see you. Don't worry about me . . . I'll try to phone Mum but I can't talk to him!

'There was an odd call about ten days ago . . . it was sort of crackly and when I asked who it was, the receiver suddenly went down . . .'

'Perhaps Betty tried to ring and couldn't get through . . .'

'Or couldn't face talking to me, the silly girl. Doesn't she know how much we love her and want her back?'

The relief surged through Lizzie and she sat back feeling a torrent of emotions. She'd been imagining all sorts of things when there hadn't been a word from Betty, picturing her dead or injured or simply alone and frightened. 'Thank God she's still alive. I've been half out of my mind with worry.'

'Oh, Lizzie . . . I thought you must have heard. I feel awful now . . .'

'No, only that odd phone call. You're the only one to get a card from Paris. At least I think that's where your postcard came from, though I can't read the postmark . . .'

'It's a French stamp,' Aunt Miriam said and frowned. 'I thought she must be all right and I was sure she would ring you . . .' She shook her head. 'What did Sebastian do to make her run off?'

'Nothing much,' Lizzie said, sensing disapproval of her husband and immediately rising to his defence. 'Sebastian wanted her to stay on at school or take a college course, but she overheard him say she wasn't talented enough to design hats and she was upset, angry . . . it led to a row and he slapped her . . .

'Oh dear . . .' Aunt Miriam frowned. 'She's such a hothead . . . just like her great-uncle and Harry . . .'

'Sebastian is usually so calm but she said things that really hurt me and he lashed out without thinking. I know he has bitterly regretted it since and blames himself.'

'Well, in a way it is his fault . . .'

'I think he has a lot on his mind, but he won't tell me . . .'

'Yes, I dare say . . .' Aunt Miriam faltered and picked up her gloves. 'I don't want to fall out with you, Lizzie – but are you certain Sebastian is the devoted husband you've always believed him?'

'Quite sure,' Lizzie said firmly. 'What makes you doubt it?'

'Well, he goes away so often, sometimes for weeks at a time . . . I mean is that really necessary for his business? And . . .' she paused and then shook her head. 'No, it isn't my place and it might have been perfectly harmless . . .'

'What are you talking about? What might have been harmless?'

'I suppose it will nag at me unless I tell you . . .' Aunt Miriam frowned and then cleared her throat. 'I saw Sebastian and . . . a woman in a dress shop in Knightsbridge a month or so ago. He was paying for her purchases and she thanked him with a kiss on the cheek . . .'

'You must have been mistaken . . .' Lizzie felt chilled but disbelieving. 'Were you in the shop yourself?'

'Oh no, it would be too expensive for me, but I know you deal with them and I dare say Sebastian gets a good discount there . . .' the older woman faltered. 'I was there to see my doctor. You know that I go privately every six months to Mr Sawbridge. He has his office in an exclusive building near there and I went for a consultation about my skin condition. My local doctor advised specialist treatment . . . they say it is a nervous complaint, but Mr Sawbridge gave me a cream which helps the symptoms.'

'Yes, it has seemed a little better since you started using the cream,' Lizzie said 'but how did you see Sebastian and this woman?'

'I stopped to look in the shop window, because they sell hats as well as clothes and I thought some of them looked like your designs, Lizzie – and they were. There was a little ticket saying they were exclusive to *Miss Margaret Modes* and designed by Lizzie Larch. I was going to tell you . . . and then I saw Sebastian with this woman . . . buying a lot of clothes . . .'

'Yes, we do have an exclusive line for that shop, and if Sebastian wanted to buy some clothes for a gift he would probably go there, because he knows the owner well. They've been business friends for years . . .' Lizzie said. 'I sell them a particular line . . . very small hats to be worn on the side of the head . . .' She sighed and then shook her head. 'I'm sure you made a mistake about Sebastian and this woman . . . it's easy

102

enough if you just catch a glimpse of someone through a window to think it's someone you know . . .'

'Well, I may have been mistaken,' Aunt Miriam said and stood up, pulling on the gloves she always wore outside the house, because she didn't like anyone to see the unsightly rash on her hands. 'Please don't think I'm being spiteful, Lizzie. I like your husband – but men do tend to stray when they reach a certain age . . .'

'Surely Bert was never unfaithful to you?'

'Oh no,' Aunt Miriam laughed. 'Bert was only ever interested in his business and making money – but you see it everywhere these days. The papers are full of it and . . .' She shook her head. 'I expect I'm just a silly old woman, but I'm so fond of you and Betty – Francie too, of course . . .'

'I know,' Lizzie rose to kiss her cheek. 'Francie is coming home for her half-term break soon. You must come to tea next Sunday and see her. I know she would love that . . .'

'Does Francie know that Betty has run off?'

'We haven't told her. I don't know if she's heard anything. I didn't want to ask in case it upset her . . . I know she has exams soon . . .'

'Is it wise to keep it from her? You will have to tell her when she comes home, Lizzie. It would be wrong to lie to her.'

'You're perfectly right and I shall tell her as soon as she comes home. I've wanted to but she's had a lot of work on and I didn't want to do anything that might put her off . . .'

'You know best,' Aunt Miriam said and touched her arm in concern. 'You're looking a bit peaky yourself, my dear. You're not ill – are you?'

'No, of course not,' Lizzie reassured her. 'I suppose I haven't slept too well lately . . .'

'Understandable, my dear, in the circumstances, but you must take care of yourself. You are very precious to us all . . .'

Lizzie smiled and shook her head as she saw her visitor out. How could she worry about herself when Betty was still missing?

'You know why you're here, of course?' Miss Honiton looked at her severely over the heavy horn-framed glasses she wore perched on the end of her nose. 'Your work has not been what I expected from you, Francie – since the summer you've missed several days of lectures and work days and your interim exam results reflect that. You've always achieved A or A+ but this last series of work only merits a B. Can you explain that?'

Francie couldn't meet that piercing stare and her heart was racing so fast that she thought she might faint. She'd been on two weekend photo-shoots and one of them had lasted until Tuesday night, which meant she'd had to miss two days of college. She'd told her tutor she'd been off sick, but her friends knew she'd been away with the magazine crew, and earlier that morning Jilly had refused to cover for her again.

'I can't keep lying to everyone,' Jilly said. 'If I got thrown out of art school my mother would murder me for wasting the money Gran spent on the fees. Besides, I need to pass my exams. I want to go into commercial art and I need good grades if I'm going to find a job when I leave school . . .'

'Oh please,' Francie begged. 'I don't want my parents to know. Dad will kill me if he sees some of the pictures they've made me do recently . . .'

'You shouldn't have signed that contract,' Jilly said and put an arm round her waist. 'Surely you looked at what you were signing?'

'She told me I signed a contract when I entered the contest, and I thought I was just signing a work chit until I got my copy in the post saying she was my agent with my first cheque for fifty pounds . . .'

'That's such a lot of money,' Jilly said enviously. 'I wish they'd picked me. I could really do with the money.'

'I'll give it to you if you'll pretend that I'm sick this weekend,' Francie said. 'Mum is expecting me home but the magazine says I've got to do a shoot in Devon on Friday and Saturday, and they're arranging a flight for me from Marshall's airfield. It will be a small private plane and they will fly me back as well. If I get back on Monday, I can go home for the rest of the week and say I feel better . . .'

'It's lying, Francie,' Jilly looked upset. 'You're

my best friend and I'd do anything for you – and I don't want your money, but I can't tell your mum such awful lies. She's been lovely to me and I love staying at your house. Your dad is super – please don't ask me to lie. Can't you just ring her and tell her you've got to put in some extra work?'

'Are you listening to me, Francie?'

Francie blinked as the anger in Miss Honiton's voice brought her back to the present. 'I'm sorry, Miss Honiton. I-I haven't been feeling too well recently. I promise I'll do better next month . . .'

'Painting is a vocation, Francie,' her principal said gravely. 'It consumes your life, your passion and your time. You have to live it, breathe it, taste it and feed on it, otherwise it becomes soulless and dull. I do not feel that you've been giving your art your full attention.' She looked at Francie above her thick glasses. 'Is there something you haven't told me? Something that is bothering you perhaps? I'm here to help if you're anxious about your work or there is something else on your mind . . .'

Francie had the uneasy feeling that Miss Honiton knew the truth. How could she? Kathy had told her that the magazine with her latest pictures wouldn't be out for another two months . . . but of course the pictures they'd taken of her and her friends at the fashion show had been out for a couple of weeks now . . . and if her mother happened to buy a copy of the magazine . . . She wouldn't, of course, because it was for younger women and Mum liked *Vogue* and *Woman's Own*.

'Did you see the photos of us in Manchester?' Francie said and saw the flicker of a smile on Miss Honiton's face. 'I won a competition – well, actually, I won second place, which was three tickets and an all-expenses-paid trip to the show. I didn't think they would take my picture, but the winner didn't turn up so they said I had to do it instead . . .'

'She was a sensible girl . . .' the principal looked stern. 'It was a foolish thing to do, Francie, but surely you haven't got yourself into a tangle over this, have you? Oh, Francie, why didn't you come to me at once?'

'I didn't know what to do . . .' Francie bit her lip. 'They say I'm contracted for a year, but I only have to work for about three days every so often. I thought I could do the shoots and my work here . . .'

'Well, it must be clear to you by now that you can't,' Miss Honiton said seriously. 'I suggest that you go home this weekend and talk to your father and mother about this. If I know Mr Winters he will have something to say about firms who ensnare underage girls into signing contracts they don't understand . . .'

'Yes, Miss Honiton . . .' Francie hung her head. 'I know it was foolish . . . but it is rather exciting and they pay me a lot of money . . .'

'Well, it is your choice,' the principal replied in a cold tone. 'You were offered a scholarship in Paris, which most girls would think was a dream come true. If you want to sacrifice that for a tawdry little job posing in scanty clothes that is up to you – but I can assure you that you cannot have both. Unless your work improves next month the offer of the scholarship will be withdrawn . . .'

Francie's eyes filled with tears. She wanted that scholarship and she truly wanted to paint, but she also liked the fun and excitement of being a photographic model, trying on all the new clothes and having lovely make up and shoes. If she was lucky, it would involve travel to other countries and she might be famous one day. Kathy had told her that she was putting her wage up to two hundred pounds plus all her expenses for every day she was used for the magazine.

'We've had lots of inquiries about you, Francie,' she'd told her last time they'd met for coffee after a shoot. 'You're going to be in big demand and you'll have agents queuing to sign you up – but remember you've signed with us for a year . . .' Kathy had had the grace to look a bit awkward, because she knew she'd pulled a fast one, but she tried to bluff through it. 'I couldn't pay you unless you were contracted to us . . .'

In her heart Francie knew that it was just a weak excuse and her father would tear holes in it. He could probably get her out if the contract in seconds, but did she really want him to? Francie knew that once she was properly launched, she could be working every week for three or four days, living out of a suitcase, because it meant travelling all over the world. These days, magazines were just as likely to ask for a shoot in the African jungle as a studio in London, and Francie couldn't help being carried away by the excitement of it all, although she wasn't sure whether she would be able to fly without her parents' permission. She would have to find out what she needed to do . . .

Miss Honiton was waiting for an answer. Francie brushed a hand over her eyes, refusing to cry. 'I'll talk to him this weekend,' she promised, crossing her fingers behind her back, because she knew she wasn't going to.

'Very well. Use your holiday wisely, Francie. I want to see fresh ideas in your work for the rest of the term – otherwise I shall have to think twice about that scholarship . . .'

'But I won it . . .'

'Because you were the most promising student, but it was given on merit and can be rescinded if your work fails to show improvement. You really must learn to read the small print before you sign contracts . . .' Miss Honiton gave her a severe look and told her she was free to go.

As Francie walked back to the room she shared with other students, she was deep in thought. It wasn't fair that she couldn't have both her scholarship and the contract with *Styled*.

CHAPTER 7

Sebastian walked into the kitchen and sniffed the air. It reeked of Yardley's Lavender Water and that meant that Aunt Miriam had been here; she had a habit of soaking her handkerchief with the stuff and he found it rather cloying. He opened a window and then put the kettle on. It was as he was looking for the teapot that he saw the postcard lying on the table. Flicking it over, he read it and frowned. Betty had written to her Aunt Miriam telling her not to worry, but she hadn't bothered to tell her own parents.

For a moment he wanted to grab the girl by the shoulders and shake her, but then he remembered the quarrel and that it was his fault that his daughter had run off. He'd slapped her and she'd been frightened of him and bolted – and that made him feel sick with remorse. After his talk to Matt, he'd telephoned Jack and asked for his help.

'We can make a check on whether she flew from Gatwick and that should tell us where she went, Seb – and once we know that our network should be able to trace her within a few weeks . . .'

'I was wondering if I ought to fly over myself . . .'

'Wait until I give you the word. This Frenchman may not have been returning to France; he could have taken her anywhere . . . I'll do what I can to help, Seb. We have a job coming up for you soon – it's going to be dangerous . . .'

'When isn't it?' Sebastian remarked wryly. 'Just find my daughter or at least where she was headed – and I'll keep my part of the bargain . . .'

'Of course. You always do – and I'll wangle a bit of cash for you, though they don't like paying. Our masters consider we should be honoured to work for the country . . .'

'That was in the war but I need the money for a particular cause – but finding Betty is more important, and Gretchen, of course.'

'Finding Gretchen is harder. It isn't as easy to get information out from Eastern Germany, as you well know.'

'Yes, I do . . .'

'Right, be in touch then . . .'

Jack hadn't been in touch yet, but now Sebastian knew his daughter was in Paris. At least he had a starting point . . .

Sebastian's mind had run riot since his chat with Matt; Betty might be locked up in an Eastern harem by now or even dead . . . because some of these men girls met in cafés were evil. But if Betty was in Paris with this man she was at least safer than if she'd been shipped off to an Eastern destination. He'd been worrying that she might have

111

been abducted but it looked as if his daughter had gone willingly and was perfectly fine, which perversely made him angry again.

He wondered where Lizzie was, because she was usually at home at this hour of the day. About to go upstairs in search of her before making his tea, he heard the phone ring and went into the hall to answer it.

'Seb?' Jack's voice spoke and Seb's breath caught in his throat, making it impossible to answer for a moment as hope surged. 'Are you there?'

'Jack, I was just about to ring you – have you any news of Betty for me?'

'She flew to Paris with a man named Pierre Saint-Jacquez, as you suspected. I've checked, and he has a bad reputation for gambling and women – and it's possible he's in league with some rogues, but that's all I can tell you so far.'

'I've just seen a card from her to her aunt. She is in Paris but I was hoping you could tell me where.'

'We're still working on it – but there's more, about Gretchen. Daughter of your friend Karl, who was shot as a war criminal by the Russians?'

'You've heard something? Thank goodness!'

'The Intelligence Service comes in useful sometimes; we have a slender lead, but nothing concrete as yet,' Jack said. 'You know it takes time, Seb. You've done enough digging for us in the past. We might have won the war but the bloody Russians think they're winning the peace.'

'So what do you know? Is Gretchen still in the Eastern sector?'

'Yes, that much we are sure of. She was at a house we've heard of until a short time ago, but she disappeared . . . as a good many others have. We think we might know who she is with but we're waiting for confirmation . . .'

'I'll be grateful for anything specific you can give me . . .'

'Just whispers at the moment – and there's always plenty of those, as you reported yourself. The boss was pleased with what you had to say about the plans the Russians have for Berlin.'

'I thought it was just propaganda . . .'

'No, they really are mad enough to do it, Seb. They're already making plans to build a damned wall right across Berlin to keep their lot in and ours out . . .'

'It's plain ridiculous. It will just make people more determined to escape to a better life.'

'And it will be so much harder to do. The poor devils that try will probably get shot . . .'

'Yes, I imagine so.'

'If you want this girl over here you're going to have to go in and fetch her before it's too late . . .'

'I realise that, but I haven't a clue where to start. I've been searching for three years . . .'

'I'm on to something, Seb, but I'm waiting for more information. Stay in touch and I'll let you know. You're not planning on leaving London for a while I hope?'

'I may be going to France quite soon – Paris . . .'

'Well, that could be handy, but stay in touch and leave your number with us as soon as you arrive . . .'

'I'll check in as normal – the same number?'

'I'll be waiting . . .'

The line went dead and Sebastian replaced the receiver. For a moment he stood staring into space, and then he became aware that someone was looking down at him. He glanced up and saw Lizzie. She appeared a little odd and he instinctively moved towards her just as she gave a little sigh and started to crumple up. Instinct had him rushing towards her and he caught her, taking the full force of the impact as she fell towards him. Her weight as she collapsed into his arms rocked him and it needed all his strength to save them both from crashing backwards to the bottom of the stairs. He held her tightly, steadying her as she recovered from her faint and started to apologise. Holding her tight to his body, Sebastian half led and half carried her into their comfortable sitting room and sat her down in a large wing chair, kneeling at her feet as she looked at him and he could see how pale she was.

'You're ill, my love,' he said gently. 'It's all this worry and the sleepless nights you've had over Betty . . .'

'No . . .' Lizzie passed a hand over her eyes. 'I haven't been sleeping well, but that isn't it . . . I think I may be pregnant, Sebastian . . . just a few weeks, but I'm sure I'm right . . .'

'Lizzie!' Sebastian stared at her in sheer terror. 'You know what the doctor said, Lizzie. Oh, my darling. Why didn't you tell me? What happened – did you forget the cap or . . .?'

'It tore and I threw it away,' she said and met his eyes tearfully. 'I wasn't sure at first and then we've had all this upset over . . . and I want to have this baby, Sebastian. I don't want them to take it away . . . whether it's a boy or a girl, I want our baby . . .'

'Lizzie . . .' Sebastian groaned, because the longing in her eyes and the pleading in her voice told him how much she wanted a son, just as he did – but he wasn't willing to risk her life, and it seemed that she was. 'My love, don't you know how I feel about this?'

'Yes, and that's why I haven't told you,' Lizzie said, looking a little guilty. 'I knew if I told you, you would call the doctor and he'd say I'd have to have it terminated – and I won't. I'll rest more . . . I've been sleeping this afternoon because I felt so tired, and then as I came downstairs I felt faint . . . but you caught me . . .' Tears trickled down her cheeks and Sebastian put his arms about her, holding her close. 'I love you, Sebastian, but I can't lose my chance to have our son . . .'

'Oh Lizzie . . .' He felt his heart being squeezed with remorse and pain, because he thought he'd hidden his disappointment so well, but he couldn't have done, because she knew how much it hurt and she was willing to give her life to give him a son – but she meant so much more than he could ever tell her. 'I'm going to get the doctor, Lizzie, and you must promise me that if he says it's you or the baby you will let me save you.'

'I want my baby,' Lizzie said stubbornly and caught his arm. 'If I have to go into a nursing home for a while – or in hospital as the time comes nearer, I'm going to have my child.'

'Let's talk to the doctor first,' Sebastian said. 'Sit there and don't even try to move. I'll make you a cup of tea as soon as I've made my call . . .'

Lizzie promised and closed her eyes. She looked so weary that Sebastian's heart caught with fear. It might already be too late for the doctors to safely terminate, and she looked fragile. He wondered that he hadn't noticed it sooner, but he'd put it down to sleepless nights and worry over Betty. The wretched girl ought to be here with her mother! Lizzie needed her family about her during the next months if she was to carry the baby full term and even then it would be touch-and-go whether she survived the birth.

The doctor had been and given his opinion that Lizzie was about two months gone, which meant her baby was due in April the following year. He'd told them that she would be all right if she was sensible and rested more, and had gone back to his surgery, leaving her lying in bed, smiling at Sebastian as he sat on the edge of her bed and watched her drink her tea. She hadn't wanted anything to eat, but he'd made her some dainty and very tasty salmon sandwiches with the crusts off and she'd managed a few.

'Will you have some ice cream and tinned strawberries?' he asked, eyeing the remainder of the sandwiches critically. 'Doctor Everett says you have to eat regular meals and rest every afternoon – and you're to stay in bed for at least three days. He'll be monitoring you regularly from now on, and if your blood pressure goes up sharply he'll have you in hospital and then a nursing home until the birth. However, if you're sensible and agree to a nurse coming in you may be able to stay here . . .'

Lizzie smiled. 'I don't mind that; you know he said I'll need a caesarean birth because I might not be able to give birth naturally . . .'

'He thinks it would be too much for you, Lizzie,' Sebastian said. 'I'll wait a couple of days until the doctor says you're over the worst and then I shall have to go. If Betty is in Paris I must look for her, even though it seems she's fine – but I don't want to leave you alone. Perhaps Francie could do her work at home for a while . . .'

'No, I won't ask Francie to give up her studies,' Lizzie said firmly. 'I'll ask Beth to come over as often as she can . . . she'll do my shopping and take my designs to the workshops . . .'

'No designs,' Sebastian said firmly. 'You're in bed for a rest. Until you've had that rest and you're out of danger you will be banned from lifting a pencil . . . or a pen . . .'

117

'Too much fuss for a little faint . . .' Lizzie complained and then laughed as she saw his face. 'All right, no work. I'm sure the nurse won't allow me to do anything.'

'It's that or risk your own health and the baby. Unless you do exactly as he says, you could lose the child – and you might die . . .' Sebastian gripped her hand. 'Please don't do that to me, Lizzie. I'm not sure I could bear it . . .'

'I promise I won't stir from this bed until I'm allowed up,' she said a little shakily, 'even though it's embarrassing when I want the toilet.'

'You will use the bedpan,' he said and laughed. 'I know what it's like. I had some of it when I was in the hospital during the war – and I was in a ward with a dozen other men. At least you have the privacy of your own room.'

'OK, OK, you win,' Lizzie said, but mentally hoped the nurse would arrive sooner than later. She took his hand and held it tightly. 'Francie will be home tomorrow. We have to tell Francie about her sister – and then you must go and look for Betty in Paris. I shan't rest properly until I know she's really safe and home with us, Sebastian . . .'

'I want her home as much as you do,' Sebastian replied. 'And if Francie is here I shan't worry so much, even though I know you'll have the nurse and I'm sure Beth and Miriam will come over all the time.'

'I've got good friends,' Lizzie said, 'but my family means the world to me, Sebastian. You and the

118

girls – and now our son . . .' She touched her belly, which was just faintly rounded, with loving hands.

'Sure it's going to be a boy this time?' he said with a laugh.

'Yes, because it feels different,' she said and looked at him with love. 'It's silly I know, but I'm sure . . .'

'I've left you too much recently,' Sebastian said and looked regretful. 'It has been for a good reason, Lizzie, but I don't want to talk about it just at the moment – I promise I will tell you soon. Perhaps when I get back from France . . .'

'Yes, I know you have things you can't always tell me, I'm not sure what it is you do, but I suspect it has something to do with the people you worked for in the war. No, I'm not asking you to tell me,' Lizzie said. She remembered what Miriam had said to her about another woman and dismissed it from her mind. Sebastian loved her. He wouldn't do anything to hurt her and his daughters. If he'd been in that shop with a woman there was a perfectly good reason. 'Don't worry too much about me, Sebastian. It's true I'm upset about Betty and I want her home, but I'm all right. I'm stronger than everyone thinks . . .'

'Frank . . .' Matt said over the phone. 'I just wanted to let you know that Betty sent her Aunt Miriam a postcard from Paris . . .'

'Thank God!' Frank shouted his relief. 'I knew that bastard had taken her despite what he said that night . . . I wish I'd held on to him tighter. We might have found her that weekend . . .'

'I'm not sure she would've come with us if we had,' Matt said. 'Anyway, she was able to send a card so it seems he hasn't hurt her – which is a relief. I don't think I would ever have forgiven myself if she'd disappeared for good.'

'I still don't trust that devil,' Frank said. 'I've a good mind to fly over and have another go at finding her . . .'

'Her father is going quite soon now,' Matt told him. 'Knowing Sebastian he'll bring her back so you can stop worrying . . .'

'You're more confident than I am, Matt – but thanks for letting me know.'

'Frank . . .' Matt hesitated. 'I think she was with Saint-Jacquez for a while even if she isn't now . . . what difference does that make to your feelings for her?'

'I love her, Matt. I was pretty sure the first time we met but after she disappeared . . . I knew if anything happened to her I'd want to die. Why do you ask?'

'Oh, no reason,' Matt said. 'Betty . . . she's like my own sister. I would hate to think this had ruined her life . . .'

'I would marry her if she would have me. Why do you ask?'

'Just wondered . . .' Matt said. 'I'll let you know if Sebastian brings her home.'

'Thanks. I'll be back in London soon . . .'

'Fine, we'll meet up then . . .'

Matt replaced the receiver and frowned. Frank was a decent chap and ready to forgive. Matt wasn't sure how he felt; he was relieved that Betty was alive and able to send a card but bloody angry that she'd gone off with that damned Frenchie in the first place . . . he'd thought she would talk to him before she did something like that . . . and it hurt that she hadn't . . .

Betty winced as she rubbed the cream in between her sore fingers. Her hands were red from all the washing up she'd been doing since Pierre threw her out. It was the only job she'd been able to find and it paid a pittance, hardly enough to pay for her board and food.

There was never any money to spend on clothes or going out for fun. She no longer went to the trendy cafés she'd frequented with Pierre and so seldom saw any of the friends she'd made in Paris and she was fed up with her life here. She regretted the way Pierre had thrown her out, because she'd thought she was in love with him and still couldn't understand why he'd changed so suddenly. She'd been full of hope when she started to try for a job in one of the fashion workshops but they'd all dismissed her as an ignorant English girl with no sense of style.

Betty had given her sketchbook to one small fashion house and the vendeuse had asked her to leave it and call back in two days, because Madame

Vennier was very busy but would have a look when she had time. However, when Betty returned two days later, one of the assistants gave her the book and told her Madame Vennier said there was nothing of any merit. It was only after several days that Betty discovered three of her sketches had been torn out of the book. Someone had removed them very carefully, but she knew exactly which designs had been taken, because she had earlier versions in another book.

She'd gone back to the fashion house that afternoon and demanded to see Madame Vennier or the vendeuse who had accepted her sketchbook. At first they'd just tried to deny her, but Betty refused to leave, and in the end the senior saleswoman came down looking sulky.

'What is this about?' she demanded.

Betty opened her book, pointing to where the pages had been removed. 'What happened to the drawings of three evening dresses I gave you?'

'I have no idea what you're talking about,' the woman said, looking angry. 'Please do not waste any more of our time. Madame Vennier says you have no talent worth speaking of and should go home and find yourself a job as a typist or something more suited to your capabilities . . .'

Betty felt as if she'd been slapped in the face, but she knew there was no point in complaining further because they would only deny all knowledge of her designs. She'd been cheated and felt angry and dispirited as she walked away. What was the point of asking for work she wanted to do when everyone laughed at her and told her that only the French truly understood style?

So she'd started asking at the wine bars and cafés again, looking for work as a waitress, but no one seemed interested in taking her on other than for a few hours washing up; though more than one man had leered at her and made unpleasant suggestions.

Eventually, Betty had decided she would have one more try for a decent job and if she still couldn't find anything, she would go back to England once she had enough money saved. Aunt Miriam would give her a bed for a while until she found the kind of work she wanted. She didn't think she would ask anyone else if they were interested in her designs, because it hurt too much being told that she had no talent – but she could make hats, or she could trim them, and with a bit of help she could make a good life for herself. Ed had volunteered to teach her, but he'd told her she must ask her parents for permission first.

'Lizzie would skin me alive if I took you on without her knowing,' he'd told Betty with a laugh when she'd asked him for a holiday job the previous summer, but her mother had said she could go in a couple of days a week during her holiday if she liked and she did. Ed fussed over her as if she was his own and she loved him like the uncle she felt he was to her.

Yes, she would enjoy making hats for her a living

and she would forget designing anything, because she was now convinced that she had no talent for drawing at all.

After another three days of walking all over Paris, asking at the various wine bars and cafés if there was work, Betty finally found a job serving coffee and wine in a café-bar on the Boulevard de Rochouart. It was a wide street with open-air cafés, shops, hotels and an area of leafy trees dividing one side from the other. Madame Rousseau was a plump, friendly woman who smiled as she took Betty on and asked her lots of questions about why she was in France and where she was living. Her English was better than Betty's French, and she told her that she had been married to an Englishman when she was very young.

'It very hard in Paris after the war,' she told Betty as she showed her what her duties would be. 'I go to live in London with my aunt who was seamstress and I meet my Andre and marry him. His name Andrew but I call him Andre; 'e was a kind, lovely man but older than me and 'e die too soon. Afterwards, I take what 'e left me and return to Paris and open my own café.'

Betty was happier once she started working at *Madame Marie's* bar, as it was called, but since the pay wasn't very much more than she'd been earning, she continued washing up for a week in the evenings until Madame Rousseau noticed her hands and made her give up the second job.

'I can pay you no more,' she said sorrowfully,

'but I give you a room in my house and you pay nothing . . .'

So Betty accepted the offer. She'd settled in quickly, enjoying her life again now that she worked in a pleasant atmosphere. The cream that Madame Rousseau gave her was gradually taking the soreness from her hands and she was getting to know the customers and look forward to serving them. Now she discovered that most people were friendly and smiled at her when she brought their food to table, and several of the men left her generous tips. She soon found that she loved her work, because they got all sorts of people in the café; French girls on their way to work; tourists and businessmen, who flashed their money; and artists who came because Madame Marie let them sit for hours over a coffee and pastry – and sometimes offered them brandy just because she felt sympathy for them. Madame had a back room filled with paintings that the artists had given her to pay for their coffees and their brandy.

'One day they become famous and I am rich,' she'd told Betty, throwing up her hands in the air with a twinkle in her eyes and a little twist of her mouth. 'What do you do, my little one? My nose, 'e tells me that you are more than just waitress . . . you not brought up to this work, this I know . . .' she tapped the side of her nose.

Betty shook her head, because she knew she had no talent and it would only make Madame feel pity for her if she told her sorry tale of the stolen sketches. However, ten days after she moved into her employer's home, Madame found her sketchbook while changing the sheets of her bed, and brought it to her, pointing to one of the dresses Betty had illustrated.

'This charming,' she said. 'Now I know why you come to Paris – but no one buys your designs, no? They pigs . . . do these imbeciles not know talent, ma petite?'

'Madame, you are too kind,' Betty said and flushed, trying to take the book away, but somehow she found herself telling the tale of the stolen designs and Madame shook her head sadly.

'She cheat you, Betty,' she said. 'I feel anger and sadness that my countrywoman did this thing to you . . . but you have no proof that she take them. Even if you 'ave copy you can never prove that she took your sketches . . .'

'She said I have no talent,' Betty said and Madame threw her hands in the air and shouted rude things in French so rapidly that Betty could only guess at their meaning.

'You make a dress for me, yes?' she asked. 'I buy the materials and I pay for your time – and I wear it when I go to visit my cousin. Will you do this for me, ma enfant?'

'Yes, of course, but I will take no payment for the work,' Betty said firmly. 'You've been so kind to me, Madame, and I should like to do this for you.'

'Bon, we are both 'appy,' Madame said and smiled, 'and now you will call me Marie, yes?'

'Of course, Marie,' Betty said and hugged her. 'You are so kind . . . I am glad I came here for work . . .'

'You like daughter to me,' Marie said and hugged her back so tightly that Betty could hardly breathe for the fumes of garlic, coffee and brandy that wafted from her.

Marie thought she had talent, but that was because she was fond of her. Neither of her husbands had given her children and Betty sensed Marie was lonely. She'd taken Betty to her heart and for the first time since Pierre had turned against her, Betty felt truly at home and comfortable . . .

Sometimes she thought wistfully of her home in London and all her friends and her mother, and then it was hard not to cry, but she couldn't go back . . . even if she wanted to, she would be too ashamed . . .

CHAPTER 8

Francie felt guilty as she walked into the kitchen and saw Aunt Miriam preparing a tray of tea. She'd telephoned to say she was on her way and her father's tone when he demanded to know where she'd been since Friday had been ominous.

'Your mother is ill and she needs you,' he'd growled. 'Just get here and be prepared to stay with her for a while . . . I'll square it with the college . . .'

'How is Mum?' Francie asked her throat tight with fear now. 'Can I go up please?'

'Your mother is resting and of course you can see her,' Aunt Miriam said and presented her cheek for a kiss. 'Are you feeling better now? Did you have that tummy bug that's going around?'

'Just a bilious attack after a dodgy meal out,' Francie lied, beginning to feel awful and understand why Jilly had refused to lie for her. 'I want to see Mum . . .'

She ran out of the room and up the stairs, wanting to escape before her great-aunt pried too deeply. The door to her mother's room was open and she could see her sitting propped up against a pile of pillows. Her eyes were closed and she looked very pale.

'Mum . . .' Francie moved forward anxiously, unaware that her father was standing by the windowsill until he turned and looked at her.

'Francie, my darling,' her mother said and smiled as she opened her eyes and looked at her. She held out her hands and Francie went to her, bent to kiss her cheek and hold her hands as she sat on the edge of the bed. 'Are you all right? We got your note to say you had a little bug and wouldn't come home until you were sure you were not infectious. You are all right now?'

'Yes, I wouldn't have come to you if I'd been infectious,' Francie said. 'What about you, Mum? Dad said you were ill and needed me with you for a while. You know I've only got until Monday . . . there are exams coming up soon and I have to do well . . .'

'Francie, think of us for once,' her father said, sounding angry. She looked at him, feeling puzzled, because he never used that kind of tone to her or her sister. He must be very worried about her mother. 'I have to go somewhere and I want you here with your mother until I get back . . . you can do your work here. I'll speak to your principal and she'll allow you a little leeway I'm sure . . .'

Francie nodded but didn't answer. She could see that her father had made up his mind and knew that on the rare occasions he put his foot down there was no point in arguing, even if her mother was shaking her head at him. If Miss Honiton told him she was thinking of rescinding Francie's scholarship because her work wasn't up to standard – and if she told him why . . . he would be so angry. She didn't like the way he was looking at her now and he'd be even worse if she were expelled from Art College, which she might be . . . because Kathy was putting pressure on her to do more and more work for the magazine. Only it wasn't just for them now. She was doing shoots for all sorts of magazines and she was booked for a fashion show in Birmingham next month. Kathy was acting as her agent, taking on work without consulting her and keeping fifty per cent of the fees Francie was earning. The cheques she was getting were mounting up in the bank, but she had the feeling that she was being taken advantage of, although she loved the fun and excitement.

Robbie, the grip, as they called him, who looked after all the travel arrangements, including her train tickets, met her with a car, fixed up her hotel and generally did all the odd jobs for the magazine when they were on location, had told her that she was being ripped off.

'They should pay you at least seventy-five per cent of all fees,' he'd told Francie when she'd asked him about things she didn't understand in the contracts she was asked to sign. 'All these extra fees are just rip-offs, Francie. You want to get yourself a lawyer – or an agent.'

'Kathy says she is my agent. It's in the contract I signed on the day of the fashion show. I didn't know what it was, but it authorises her to handle all my work and to take a twenty-five per cent fee – and the other twenty-five per cent goes to the magazine, because they discovered me . . . at least that's what she said . . .'

'She took advantage of your innocence,' Robbie said, shaking his head. 'It can't be legal, Francie. I wouldn't put up with it if I were you.'

Francie knew he was right but she was frightened of all the legal jargon in the contract. Kathy said the magazine would sue her for lost fees if she refused to work and that could amount to a lot of money. Francie didn't have the money to pay and she couldn't ask her father for it, especially at a time like this . . .

'Your father thinks you should be here,' Lizzie said breaking her thoughts. 'I'll be fine if you need to be at college, my love . . .'

'Of course I'll stay if you need me. What's wrong with you, Mum?' she asked, fighting her tears. It hurt to see her mother looking so ill and to have her father angry with her. He thought she was selfish and uncaring and it wasn't true. Of course she wanted to be with her mother when she was ill, but she was already being pulled two ways and she didn't know what to do. 'It's not something horrid, is it?'

'Of course it isn't,' her mother said and squeezed her hand. 'I'm just having a baby and it's making me very tired. The doctor says I have to stop in bed and . . . your father wants you to be here, because he has to go to Paris to fetch Betty home . . .'

'A baby?' Francie was shocked and then laughed and clapped her hands. 'That's wonderful – isn't it? I thought you might be really ill when Miriam told me . . .'

'Yes, it is wonderful,' Lizzie said and touched her hand. 'But I'm thirty-nine and that's a little old for having babies so I've got to rest and be careful . . .'

'You're not old,' Francie declared stoutly. 'You don't look much more than twenty-eight or thirty at most. My friends always think you're my sister.'

'Thank you, darling . . .' Lizzie laughed softly. 'I certainly don't feel old.'

'Your mother still has to take care and this business of Betty running off to Paris has upset her,' her father said.

'Betty is in Paris?' Francie stared at him in surprise, because her mother's news had driven everything else from her mind. 'What is she doing there?'

'We had an argument,' Francie's father said, looking stern. 'It was my fault, Francie – but Betty ran off without waiting for me to make it right . . .'

'And you didn't tell me?' Francie looked at him and then her mother in disbelief. 'How could you not tell me? Is she all right? Where is she staying?'

'We don't know; she hasn't been in touch, though she may have tried to phone us once. Aunt Miriam had a card with a Paris scene and a French stamp, so your father is going to look for her,' Francie's mother said and looked anxiously at her. 'Please don't be cross with us, darling. We thought she would come back and we didn't want to upset you for nothing . . . we knew this term was very important for your college work . . .'

'I'm not a child, even though you both seem to think I am,' Francie said, feeling hurt and angry. 'I should've been told that Betty had disappeared . . . she could be ill or . . . How long has she been missing?'

'Since late August, when you were staying with Jilly . . .'

'So that's why she hasn't phoned, or written to me, for ages; there was one call to the school for me in mid-September, the day before her birthday, but she didn't leave a name and I wasn't there . . .' Francie felt cold all over. 'I think it was Betty, Mum . . .' She bit her lip. 'I sent her card and present here, but of course she didn't get them. It's my birthday this week. I wonder if she'll try to get in touch with me?'

'She might try to ring you again at college . . . perhaps they will tell her you're not there and she'll ring here . . .' Lizzie said hopefully.

'You haven't heard a word from her – not even a phone call . . .?'

Her mother looked sad. 'Aunt Miriam's card came recently, but that's all . . . Betty says she's all right . . .'

Francie's mother held her hand tightly and looked so upset that Francie's anger faded, leaving her close to tears. 'Oh, Mum,' she said and the tears wouldn't be held, dripping down her cheeks as she hung her head. All this time she'd been so stupid, thinking it was clever to be the centre of attention as the lights flashed and cameras rolled, knowing that her behaviour would shock and upset her parents – and they already had so much to worry them.

'I'm sorry,' she said and leaned forward to hug her mother gently. 'I know how upset you are, Mum. I love you so much – and I want you to be well, and I think it's lovely that we're having a baby.' She looked up at her father. 'I'll stop here while you go and look for Betty, Dad. When you find her, tell her I love her and I want her to come home to us . . .'

'Yes, I will,' her father said gruffly. 'Perhaps she'll come for you – but I have to find her first and that could take a while. I'll square it with your principal, Francie.'

'Yes . . .' Francie took a deep breath, then, 'Can I talk to you first, Dad – before you telephone Miss Honiton?'

'Fire away . . .' His gaze narrowed as she glanced at her mother anxiously. 'Ah, it's confidential is it? You don't want to upset your mum?'

'I'm in a bit of trouble with my work,' Francie said. 'It's nothing for you to worry about, Mum, but Dad needs to know before he telephones Miss Honiton.'

134

'As you wish, darling . . .' Francie saw her mother's gaze go to her father and he nodded. He would give her his version of events afterwards.

'I need to show you something. I'll bring it down to your study, Dad.

Francie left her mother's room, her heart racing wildly. She felt as if the world were about to impact about her, because when she showed her father the magazine with the pictures taken at the fashion show he would be displeased, but if he saw the more recent ones he'd forbid her to leave the house!

'Francie! My God, what did you think you were doing?' Sebastian looked upset as he turned the pages of the fashion magazine, shaking his head over the more provocative pictures of his youngest daughter looking back over her shoulder and pouting. 'I don't know what your mother and I have done to deserve this – Betty running off and worrying us to death and you keeping this from us . . .'

'I'm sorry, Dad. It was just a bit of fun and it got out of hand. That expression – I didn't know what it would look like . . .'

'Well, I suppose it would be all right if you were older . . . but you're my little girl, Francie. I don't want you to grow up too fast . . .'

'I know. Kathy told me to stop and smile and I did . . . I didn't realise how sexy it would look in a photograph . . .'

'How many more shoots have you done for these people?'

'About three for *Styled* and half a dozen for other people, including the first fashion show in Manchester . . . they want me to go abroad for a Christmas shoot, but I wasn't sure if I could fly . . .'

'If you're over twelve, you can fly provided you're accompanied by an adult of sixteen or over who is willing to sign for you, under that and you would need my permission as well as an escort . . . but that isn't the point.' As always he answered with honesty and simplicity. 'You've been lying to us, Francie . . .'

'Only a little white lie,' she said, seeing disappointment in his eyes. 'I only wanted a bit of fun and it spiralled out of control . . . the contracts keep mounting up . . .'

'No wonder you've got behind with your art.' Sebastian's eyes flashed angrily. 'You know what a fool you've been, letting these people exploit you, so I shan't lecture you, Francie, but you can't do any more. My lawyers will sort this mess out and I'll do my best to fix things with the college – but you must give me your word to knuckle down to your art and forget this nonsense.'

Francie wanted to tell him how lovely it had been working for the nicer magazines. She hadn't wanted to do those pictures of her lying half-naked and staring up into the handsome face of a male model clad in very little as far as the photos showed, except that he'd kept swimming trunks

136

on all the time – but from the way a towel was draped across his backside, it would appear that he had nothing on and she had little but some artfully draped silk to cover her body. She had actually worn a flesh-coloured body former underneath but it looked as if she were naked after they'd touched out any lines. If her father ever saw those pictures he would kill her!

'I promise,' she said. 'I don't want to lose the scholarship to study in Paris, Dad . . .'

'Well, I'll do my best for you,' her father said, 'but I can't promise you, Francie. I shall have to speak to your headmistress and hear what she has to say . . . and I'll keep that wretched contract.'

'I'm sorry I let you down . . .'

'It wasn't your fault. You were foolish, but too young to understand what you were getting into. I know who to blame and believe me they'll be sorry by the time my solicitor gets through with them . . .' He made a note on a pad on the desk, and then handed the magazine back to her. 'Go and see if your mother needs anything, and I'll make that call to Miss Honiton now . . .'

'It's a pity you didn't telephone me the instant you suspected something odd was going on,' Sebastian said coldly into the telephone.

'I thought it was just a piece of innocent fun at first,' Miss Honiton replied. 'It is a case of not wanting to tell tales, Mr Winters. When I realised it wasn't just a one-off thing I warned Francie that she was in danger of losing her scholarship.'

'Has her work deteriorated so much?'

'It has suffered. As I told her, she has to live for her art if she wants it to live for others . . . it is in all honesty nothing that a little more time spent at her easel wouldn't cure, but I wanted to shock her.'

'She will work here and I'll see this other business is sorted out. The contract they made her sign is ridiculous, if not to say dubious and down-right illegal. I'm handing it over to my lawyers. Francie was duped into signing it – and she was under age. At fourteen, she needed my consent to enter the contest and they know it. I haven't spoken to this Kathy person yet, but when I do she will wish she'd thought twice about using an innocent girl . . .'

'I'm so glad Francie made a clean breast of it,' Miss Honiton said. 'She does need to work for her exams, but I know you have everything she needs there with you – and I'll send a copy of her coursework through the post. She will miss the lectures, but I can send tapes so she can listen and that may help her. It would be a shame if Francie didn't pass the art exams she has coming up this term – and I should then be obliged to give the scholarship to another pupil. In fact, my advice would be to remove her from the school and allow her time to make up her mind as to what she truly wishes to do.'

'Are you telling me you no longer wish her to be one of your pupils?'

'No, I have great faith in her ability, but I do not believe that art should be forced on anyone. Unless Francie truly wishes to continue she will not achieve her full potential. She needs to commit one way or the other . . .'

'Yes, she will, I promise you . . .' Sebastian said. 'Thank you for listening, but for the moment Francie is needed here with her mother . . .'

'Of course. Thank you for letting me know so quickly . . .'

Sebastian replaced the telephone. He glanced down at the magazine pictures of his youngest daughter and felt a shock as he saw quite clearly that Francie wasn't a child . . . or perhaps it was because he was her father that he thought she looked like an innocent waif, which could make her vulnerable to predators. It was her very innocence that would appeal to men of all ages. She'd smiled at him like that on the beach, but she was his daughter and he loved her as a father should; appreciating and loving her immaturity, but even he could see that she was that elusive thing, a child-woman. A part of him felt proud of her beauty and the sweet innocence he saw in her face, but he also felt that this new world she'd entered held too many dangers for a girl of her age and he was angry that she'd been tricked into it.

God! He would like to tear that Kathy woman

limb from limb! It was just as well he had more important things to do first, because it would give him time to clear his head, but he would certainly deal with the woman when he returned.

CHAPTER 9

They'd been working non-stop all morning when Marie told Betty to take her break and enjoy the unusually warm sunshine. It was October but it might have been high summer, because the heat had been intense and sweat was trickling down Betty's back beneath her thin blouse.

'Go for a walk, ma enfant,' Marie told her with a smile. 'The customers will sit for hours over their wine now we have finished the midday rush. It is only Michele, Jean and Renoir . . . and they have no money to spend . . .'

Her eyes sparkled with mischief, because the artist she teasingly named Renoir was really a young Englishman who was trying very hard to follow in the footsteps of the famous Impressionist but was not truly very good.

'You are wicked,' Betty told her and went off with a smile on her face. Not far away there was a beautiful park where she loved to walk when she had the chance. She found a bench under a shady tree and sat down to rest. Her hair had grown longer and she wore it twisted into a pleat

141

at the back of her head and held with pins while she worked, but now she removed the pins and shook it loose. Since she'd had a little more money to spend, Betty had been to the hairdresser and had the all-over lightening that she'd always wanted and she knew her hair, which previously she'd had cut much shorter and bleached, was now a proper strawberry blonde and she loved it. She just wished she had someone to take her out . . . someone to wear the new dress she'd designed and made for herself, after finishing Marie's.

Her friend had loved the dress and was planning to wear it when she closed the café for two weeks in November and went to stay with her cousin at her villa in the South of France.

'Hortense will adore it,' she'd told Betty. 'You are very talented, my little one, and do not let anyone tell you different.'

Marie was so kind to her, but Betty knew she was biased. Lost in her thoughts, Betty was not at first aware that she was being watched. Glancing up as she felt a prickling sensation at her nape, she saw that two men were staring at her and seemed more than a little interested. When she realised that one of them was Pierre she felt a jolt of something rather like pain shot through with regret, because it was the first time she'd seen him since he'd thrown her out.

Betty's heart raced as the men walked over to where she sat. Part of her wanted to get up and run but pride held her where she was, refusing even to acknowledge him until he spoke to her.

'Betty, you look . . . gorgeous,' he said in that voice that could melt her insides. 'What 'ave you done to yourself?'

'Hello, Pierre,' she said, ignoring his question. 'I've been working . . . and I have to get back to work now . . .'

'Why you must rush?' Pierre asked, his smile making the blood pound in her veins and her heart race. 'Stay and talk to us . . . my friend Marcus wants to meet you . . . Marcus this is Betty, the young English girl I told you of . . .'

Something about his companion's heavy-lidded eyes as they moved over her sent shivers down Betty's spine. She thought he might be French-Algerian or perhaps Turkish, and something in his manner was menacing. She saw an expression that might have been anger or excitement in his eyes, but his smile did not waver as he told her she was very lovely and he was happy to make her acquaintance.

'Betty, 'ave you nothing to say to my friend?'

'Monsieur is very kind,' she replied coldly. 'Now, if you will excuse me – I must return to work or I shall be late.'

'Betty,' Pierre chided playfully. 'You know 'ow much I love you, ma cherie. I am sorry that we parted so badly, but I was – 'ow you say, under great anxiety. Now everything 'as changed . . . and I want you to forgive me . . .' He looked at Marcus, who inclined his head. 'You let me take you out this evening . . . we go to the cafés and see our friends and perhaps watch the cabaret . . .'

For a moment Betty was tempted, because she would've liked to see her friends, and she'd thought she loved Pierre, but then she shook her head. She'd been a fool once and she had no intention of falling into the same trap twice, even if her heart had leaped at the sight of him.

'I'm sorry, I don't have time,' she said coolly. 'It was nice seeing you again, Pierre . . . Monsieur . . .'

She walked away, her head in the air, aware that the men were watching her. She might have forgiven Pierre, because a part of her was still attracted to him despite the way he'd treated her, but something about Pierre's friend had made her uneasy. There was a look in his eyes that made her feel cold all over and instinct told her to stay well away from men like that. All he could want from a girl like her was to use her. Betty knew that if Pierre had been alone she might well have welcomed the chance to visit the cafés and have an evening with the friends she'd made when she first arrived in Paris . . . but she hadn't liked the calculating look in the other man's eyes, as if he were stripping her naked.

She walked quickly, not looking back over her shoulder and so failed to notice that she was being followed. For a moment Betty thought of her mother and was caught by a wave of longing for her home. She wished she could see her mother and Francie

. . . but not Sebastian. Oh no, she hadn't forgiven him . . . and yet something inside was hurting so bad and she wanted to see his smile and feel his arms about her.

Knuckling away her tears, Betty entered the café and went through to the back kitchen. She stood in front of the spotty old mirror and twisted her hair up into its neat little pleat and then picked up her tray and went back into the café. There were cups and glasses to clear and tables to clean . . .

'Have you heard anything since Sebastian left for France?' Beth asked when she visited that morning. 'Frank came to see us last night and he's very worried – he wondered if there was any news of Betty . . .'

'Frank? I don't think I've met him?'

'You wouldn't; he met Betty at our house,' Beth said. 'I believe he, Jenny, and Matt all went to a skiffle concert once: Lonnie Donegan, I think it was – and they may have gone to the flicks or a jazz club a couple of times. He's a year or so older than Matt, though they were at college together, but he's not a Londoner. He lives in Cambridge; he designs stuff for airports . . . Matt says he's clever and he travels all over the place, because people want his advice about the problems of modern travel. Frank is trying to make travelling by air more comfortable for passengers, because he thinks holidays in Spain and France are going to be the norm one day in the near future . . .

affordable for the many and not just the privileged few . . .'

'That sounds wonderful,' Lizzie said and sighed. 'Why couldn't Betty have fallen for him instead of this Frenchman?'

'Who knows what goes on in the mind of young girls these days?' Beth said. 'All they seem to think about is clothes and make-up, music – and film stars . . .'

'Have you seen those pictures of Francie?' Lizzie asked, her gaze narrowing. 'Sebastian wasn't very pleased about them – but they didn't look too terrible to me, though they do make her seem at least eighteen instead of nearly fifteen . . .'

'Francie showed me,' Beth said. 'She was a silly girl to get pushed into it in the first place, though of course I see the attraction, and I think those people took advantage of her innocence, made her feel she was legally bound to them because she entered the competition.'

'I think she was excited and flattered too . . .' Lizzie said. 'I don't really mind her doing it myself, though I know Sebastian is upset – he thinks she's out of her depth amongst people like that . . .'

'He may be right, Lizzie. It makes me glad Jenny got married so young, even though I was dubious about it at the time . . . but I suppose we weren't much more sensible, were we?'

'Not much . . .' Lizzie laughed and some of the tension left her. 'You fell for Mark and got caught out – and I married Harry and that all went wrong,

146

but we both came through it all right. I tried to tell Sebastian not to be too hard on Francie, and I know he won't make the mistake he made with Betty. He hasn't stopped blaming himself for her running off . . . I just hope she's safe with this Pierre and not in any trouble . . .'

'He'll find her,' Betty said. 'Sebastian won't give up, Lizzie . . .' She hesitated then, 'You two are still all right together, aren't you?'

'Yes. Why do you ask?' Lizzie frowned, because Beth couldn't look her in the eyes and she knew that expression of old. 'Come on, Beth. I know you're holding something back – please tell me . . .'

'I don't want to upset you, love . . . I'm sure it was nothing important . . .'

'Did you see Sebastian with a woman?'

Lizzie's direct question made Beth stare at her. 'So you know . . . I was sure it didn't mean anything . . .'

'Aunt Miriam saw him with a woman in a dress shop in Knightsbridge. She thought he'd been buying her clothes – and I'm sure she's convinced that he's having an affair . . .'

'If he is he must be mad,' Beth said. 'I saw them coming out of a block of flats in Southwark. A row of lovely old houses that have been turned into flats now, much nicer than the high-rise flats the council are sticking up all over the place, and probably expensive . . .'

'What were you doing out there?' Lizzie raised her brows.

147

'Jenny's husband is after a vacant flat. She wanted to stay with us until the baby is born but her husband is buying a flat for them – it's a ground-floor apartment with two bedrooms and the use of the garden. He thinks it will be a good investment for the future – they can let it if they're posted abroad again and he thinks it will rise in value. I went to have a look with Jenny . . .'

'What is this woman like? Is she very pretty?'

'She's older than you – and she's not at all pretty. She might have been once but she appears washed out and . . . I thought she might have been very ill . . .'

'You had a good look at her then?'

'Yes. She was well dressed, but plainly – nothing special about her . . .'

'I see . . .' Lizzie nodded. 'It would be easy to jump to conclusions, Beth, but Sebastian loves me. He's worried to death because I'm having this baby – and he insisted that Francie stays home and does her college work here, because he didn't want me to be alone.'

'You're hardly alone with that nurse and Aunt Miriam fussing over you . . .' Beth shook her head. 'I'm sure there is nothing in it, Lizzie – and I'm sorry if I've upset you.'

'You haven't,' Lizzie assured her. 'I'm determined not to be silly about this or judge Sebastian until I know the truth . . .' Determined not to show any distress, Lizzie fished under the eiderdown for her sketchbook. 'I've been forbidden to work, but I had some ideas and I can't bear just lying here day after day. Could you take these into Romany for me? It's just some variations on our spring line for next year . . . ask her if she has time to pop in for a visit. I want to talk about some new ideas for the summer . . .'

'Surely you don't have to worry about that so soon? We haven't had Christmas yet . . .'

'Hats are much harder to sell these days,' Lizzie told her. 'The younger generation don't wear them as much as we used to, unless it's for church or a wedding – except for the Ascot race days, of course. I don't think that will ever change . . . not as long as the Queen mother and Queen Elizabeth love them . . .'

'I still love my hats, Lizzie.' Beth sighed and smiled. 'I wear them whenever I get the chance . . .'

'Well, why not?' Lizzie looked at her questioningly, because she knew her friend so well and something was wrong. 'Are you worried about anything, love?'

Beth shook her head, but Lizzie could see she was holding back and she gave her a straight look. Beth saw it and burst out laughing.

'That's the trouble with us – we know read each other's minds . . .' she admitted. 'Tony and I are all right – but I worry about the kids. Jenny isn't carrying the baby as well as she might. Tony says I worry too much, but you know what it's like, Lizzie . . . and Matt doesn't want to take over the

149

shops from his father. I think he has some idea of being a sports journalist . . . or writing books.'

'There's nothing wrong in working as a journalist or in writing books . . .'

'You try telling that to Tony. He says it's pie in the sky stuff and that Matt should go into the shops and use his education to improve them . . . he wants more shops, a whole fleet of them . . .'

'Men and ambition,' Lizzie teased. 'I shouldn't worry, love. Matt can write in his spare time and Jenny will probably get on much better than you think . . . look at me. I've been condemned to bed under dire warnings . . .'

'Compared to your troubles mine are nothing,' Beth said and leaned forward to kiss her. 'Make sure you rest, love. We could none of us manage without you. Now I'll take the sketches and go before your dragon lady comes after me . . .'

CHAPTER 10

Francie stood at the easel her father had bought her when she was thirteen and he'd realised that she was serious about her art. She'd stretched her canvas and prepared it with a light colour-wash and now she was ready to start, but her head was empty of ideas. At college it was better, because the lectures gave the students an idea of what they were supposed to be working on and everyone worked in little groups, which meant it was easy to get into the mood – and of course there was wonderful scenery to inspire you. She looked out at the garden, which she loved in spring and summer when it was filled with blossom and pretty flowers. A few roses were clinging to their stems despite the drop in temperature of late but they looked forlorn and straggly, and moisture was dripping from the bushes, making the whole scenario dank and dismal. For a moment she felt so miserable and worried about her sister . . . where was she and was she all right?

Suddenly, she was filled with inspiration and she turned the easel so that she could look into the garden. Now she saw the dark mystery of a winter garden and she mentally placed the girl in the photograph in that scene . . . there would be something piquant and appealing in setting that pose in a drenched garden. The girl would wear a thin almost transparent dress that clung to her legs, concealing as much as it revealed, because just a glimpse was better than naked flesh. Of course the face would not be hers but a face dragged from somewhere in the deep recesses of her mind . . . a sad, mysterious face that cried out for love and understanding. Something rather like the *Lady of Shallot* perhaps in a Renaissance painting, with red long hair . . . but the face would be in shadow so that you could only really guess at her identity, although Francie knew that she was aware of the identity of the beauty she wanted to paint.

She mustn't make it too obviously Betty, of course, because her parents wouldn't approve . . . but she would catch the sadness she'd sometimes seen and wondered at in her sister's face . . . as if she was looking for love.

Francie frowned. How could the sister she'd always looked up to and admired not know how much she was loved? Francie would make the picture her tribute to Betty . . . and perhaps one day, when she came home, because she must come back to them, mustn't she? – Betty would understand how much they all cared for her.

Betty stood looking out over the River Seine. It looked dark and mysterious as evening descended and the bobbing lights came from the boats that still plied their trade up and down, past the cafés with their insides blazing with light and the sound of music and delicious smells tantalising as you drifted by.

She sighed, knowing that she felt lonely and confused. It was the reason she was standing here wearing her new dress and looking longingly at the lights of the cafés, wanting to be a part of it all again. Marie was kind and generous, but she wasn't young, and Betty wanted to have fun, as she had when she first came to Paris.

Perhaps it was just that she was missing home and her sister in particular. It was Francie's birthday and Betty had a gift for her, but she hadn't sent it, though she'd popped a card in the post to her sister's college. She was torn between a longing to go home and make it up with her family and her desire to make something of herself first. If she'd found a good job in a fashion house she could have popped home and told them all how well she was doing . . .

Oh, what was the matter with her? Of course she couldn't just breeze in and expect everything to be fine. Her father was never going to forgive her – and yet she did miss being with Francie and her friends. A wave of loneliness swept her and she felt the tears on her cheeks.

It was because she'd seen Pierre again, of course. That meeting had unsettled her and made her wish she'd agreed to let him take her out – if he'd been alone she was sure her decision would've been different. Did she dare go to their favourite café alone? She was almost certain to meet friends, people she knew and missed. Perhaps Helene or Veronique or Jacques would be there and she could join them for a drink and listen to gossip and music coming from a wireless. Or one of the musicians who sometimes came to play if it was a cabaret night . . .

Crossing the road, she hesitated, turned back and began to walk off as her courage left her, then she stopped and made herself go back and enter the busy café. It was packed with chattering customers enjoying themselves; every table was occupied and she could hear someone singing, a rich deep female voice that sent shivers up her spine. Betty let her gaze travel round the room and saw that Veronique and Helene were both there together with Jacques. There was no sign of Pierre and Betty wasn't sure if she was sorry or pleased. She'd loved him at the start, but he hadn't treated her well . . .

'May I join you for a drink?' she asked hesitantly, and Veronique looked up and gave a genuine cry of pleasure.

'Betty,' she cried. 'We wondered where you were. Pierre thought you'd gone back to England . . .'

'No, I've been working hard to earn a living since . . .' Betty's last words were lost as all three of her friends jumped up and embraced her, kissing her cheeks and exclaiming at how lovely she looked.

'I thought you beautiful before, but now – you are manifique!' Jacques told her and rolled his eyes. 'You have the new lover – he has done this for you? Tell me at once. I am jealous . . .'

Betty laughed as they drew out a chair for her and filled a glass with some of the red wine from their jug. It was a cheap house wine, but tasted of ripe fruit warm from the sun and she drank it carefully, knowing how easily such wine could go to her head.

'There's no man,' she said and smiled at him. 'I thought I was in love with Pierre – and now I am alone . . .'

'Pouff!' Helene made a rude noise and an even ruder gesture. 'Pierre is the fool. He 'ad a treasure in you but 'e could not see it . . .' Her gaze went hungrily over Betty. 'Your 'air is enchanting – and where you buy such a dress? I love it and must 'ave one . . . they make in red?'

Betty laughed, already drunk with the excitement of being with people who seemed to genuinely like her and welcome her company. It was their warmth and witty conversation that she'd missed since the breakup with Pierre. 'It is available in any colour you want – if you buy the material and let me measure you, I can make it just as you wish . . .'

'So now you work for a great fashion house . . . it must be Dior,' Veronique said and clapped her hands. 'Who designed this, Betty?'

'I did . . .' Betty laughed as they made her get up and do a little twirl. 'I work in a café serving drinks and coffee . . . I designed the dress and made it myself on Marie's sewing machine. I made a dress for her too – but not this one . . .'

'You will make one for me,' Veronique demanded. 'I love this . . . but can you design something just for me?'

'Yes, if you don't mind waiting for a while. I'll have to think about what would be best for you . . . what is your favourite colour?'

Veronique was about to reply when they were interrupted. For a moment everyone went quiet and the back of Betty's neck prickled. She glanced up and saw Pierre standing very close, smiling at her in the way that had always made her melt inside, and she knew that a part of her had been subconsciously waiting for him to arrive.

'Betty, you came back to us,' he said and the warm chocolate tones of his voice made her melt inside. 'I am so 'appy . . . you don't know how much I miss you, darling. I make a mistake terrible and I am so sorry . . .' he rolled his r's, his accent very soft and French, making her tingle with remembered pleasure.

Betty didn't answer: she couldn't because her emotions were all over the place. This was what she'd longed for on so many lonely nights – to be with her friends and Pierre and to see that look in his eyes. A part of her was still angry with him, and yet she could feel herself dissolving in the warmth of his smile.

'Do not listen to him, Betty,' Veronique warned in a whisper and captured her attention.

While they spoke, she was aware of Pierre sitting down and ordering her favourite white wine, less dry and rough than the red; she'd often drunk too much of it when Pierre was in the mood for splashing out – but it didn't do to mix the two and so when he offered her a glass she shook her head.

'I'll stick to the red,' she said and Pierre shrugged, but as soon as her attention was drawn back by the two girls he filled her glass with more of the house wine. Betty ignored it until Pierre lifted his to toast her return and then the friends followed suit with toasts to her hair and her dress and then to anything that came into their heads. Betty merely sipped, though her friends were drinking heavily.

Pierre topped up her glass, but when he left the table to speak to someone, Betty swapped her full one for Jacques' empty glass. He grinned and sipped it and then winked, kissing his fingers to her.

'As wise as she is clever,' he murmured softly.

After that, Jacques obliged her by drinking most of the wine Pierre placed in front of her, leaving Betty to sip occasionally, while he got steadily drunker.

'I shall see you 'ome, Betty,' Pierre said as she got up and swayed slightly. Betty wasn't drunk, but she knew Pierre had intended her to be. 'You not safe to walk 'ome alone . . .'

Veronique leaned towards her, whispering, 'Be careful, my friend. He is not to be trusted . . .'

'I know, but I'm curious how far he will go . . .'

'What are you two whispering about?' Pierre demanded.

'I want Betty to make me a dress. She is so talented and clever,' Veronique said quickly. 'You do not deserve her, Pierre.'

'Betty knows I adore her,' he replied smoothly. 'You've drunk enough, Betty. Come, we go . . .'

She went with him docilely, not sure why she didn't just walk off. Yet a part of her wanted him to love her; she craved real affection and she'd believed Pierre when he'd told he loved her. But then he'd thrown her out because it no longer suited him to have her around. Now, he seemed to want her back – why?

Betty was sober but she needed to know for sure whether Pierre loved her – or whether he had always been using her.

Veronique's warning had rung bells in her mind and Betty knew that she must let Pierre believe she was as drunk as she would've been had she drunk all the wine he'd poured for her – but Jacques had gone along with her masquerade. It seemed that he and the girls were her friends . . . and that thought made her stronger inside.

She swayed against Pierre slightly as they strolled through the quiet lanes, and he put his arm about her, kissing her neck. 'You don't want to go 'ome, do you, my darling?' he murmured against her ear. 'You'd prefer come 'ome with me, no?'

'Go to my home . . .' Betty said in a slurred voice, but his grip just tightened on her.

'No, I'm not letting you go in this state,' he said. 'I take care of you, Betty. We 'ave fun like always – but this time it will be even better . . .'

'No, I don't want to,' she said, introducing a slightly truculent note into her voice, as she had sometimes in the past. She knew they were almost there, the lanes here were ill lit and deserted apart from two men singing loudly as they lurched their way back to their lodgings. He was taking her to his apartment; she knew it but allowed it recklessly because she wanted to be sure how he truly felt about her. If Pierre loved her, he would tell her how sorry he was for what he'd done and beg her to forgive him. She would allow him to think she was drunk just until she knew what he intended.

'Look, we're 'ere,' Pierre said and Betty knew it was what he'd intended all along. 'I give you good wine, better than you 'ad this evening . . . and then we have fun. You see 'ow sweet it taste . . .'

Betty stumbled at the first stair and Pierre swung her up in his arms, carrying her up the wooden steps. Once inside, he carried her straight to the bed and dumped her down on the crumpled sheets. Betty gave a little moan and held out her arms to him, willing him to come to her and confess how much he loved her and wanted her.

'Do you love me?' she asked. 'Do you want it to be as it used to be?'

'Foolish little one,' he murmured, and she could

smell the wine and cigarettes on his breath. 'I want you amenable . . . you no refuse me tonight, Betty. This is important . . . a matter of life and death . . . I 'ave to keep him sweet and he wants you . . . it's the only way I can pay . . . besides, you owe me for what your friend did . . .'

Betty had no idea what he meant. All that registered was that he hadn't brought her here because he loved her! He was going to use her – to give her to that man she'd met in the park. She'd been a stupid fool to think that he'd wanted to make amends.

Betty's nerve ends prickled and it was all she could do to lie still and not jump up and run, but she knew it was too late for that now. Veronique had known what she was talking about when she'd told her not to trust him. She'd been a fool to come with him, but a part of her had hoped that he truly missed and loved her. Betty lay back against the pillows with her eyes shut as he moved away from her, hoping he would just go and leave her alone if he thought she'd fallen asleep, but then she opened them cautiously, watching him, sensing that he had something planned. Pierre was pouring wine into two glasses, but he slipped a powdery substance into one of them and stirred it with his finger, and Betty's instinct told her that was the glass meant for her. Pierre wanted to make sure that Betty couldn't resist what he was planning to do to her . . .

She lay tense, fearful, yet alert and tingling with

suspense as he brought the glasses back and placed them on the little table, pushing hers close to her, and then he put his arm about her and sat her up against the pillows.

'Open your eyes, Betty. I 'ave something special for you – once you taste it you beg me for more. I knew you were valuable when I found you, but you needed breaking in and Marcus, 'e told me 'ow to do it. He knows all about such things, special things that bring erotic pleasure . . . and you 'ave a wonderful time.' He laughed nastily, sending chills down her spine.

Betty shuddered inwardly as she guessed what kind of a life was being planned for her. Pierre thought her an innocent fool and she had been stupid to believe in him and trust him, but now she was well aware of the danger she was in.

He put the glass in her hand and then his phone rang in the studio. Pierre swore and allowed her to relax back against the pillows.

'Drink it all, Betty and then I'll be back – and I promise you never see things the same again . . . my little prude . . .'

Betty lay as if frozen until he left to answer the phone; the realisation of what he intended for her flooded through her and then, jerked into action, she swapped glasses, placing her glass where his stood on the little bedside chest and taking his. She sipped it so that the taste and smell would be on her lips, then leaned over the bed and emptied the contents onto the floor beneath and then lay

161

back, letting the last remnants of the drugged wine spill on to the bed. Now she was alert, fearful of his next move and trying to work out how she could escape the fate he intended for her, and praying he didn't notice the spilled wine. If he drank the wine he'd intended for her it might render him incapable and was her best chance of escape. He was evil, merciless, and she knew him now for the devil he was and she could only pray her ruse would work as she lay with closed eyes and waited for his return . . .

'He's coming . . .' the hateful voice, a voice she'd thought she loved, said close to her ear, 'and then 'e give me what I want, my precious fool. He like the ménage à trois so we share you and then each other . . . is time you learned what it's all about, my little English prude, and the drug I've given you will make sure you can't resist. Marcus gave it to me; 'e told me it's specially designed for girls like you, to bring you under control. You cannot resist but you know what's happening . . .'

Even though the revulsion and fear trailed through her, she made no protest as he partially undressed her, touching her breasts intimately, and laughing as she gave a faint moan, and then he left her abruptly. She heard him pick up his wine glass and knew with a sense of expectation and glee that he was drinking the wine he'd meant for her. He had no suspicion that she'd managed to switch the glasses when he answered his phone and he must have drunk it all just as he thought she had, because she heard him swear and then felt his weight as he suddenly slumped on the bed next to her. Pushing his weight away from her, she scrambled over his body and out of the bed. He made an attempt to grab her ankle, cursing in a blurred voice as he couldn't hold her; it told her clearly what effect that foul drug would've had on her if she'd drunk from the glass he'd intended for her.

'Damn you,' Pierre muttered thickly. 'Marcus kill me if he no get you . . . Betty . . . 'elp me . . . payment for the debt . . .'

'I hope he does . . .' Betty muttered. 'I loved you, but you're evil . . .'

Evading his grasp as he fell back useless against the pillows, she'd grabbed the clothes he'd taken from her, and fled, down the wooden staircase to the alley below, knowing that she must be gone before Marcus arrived. She'd tricked Pierre, but his friend would grab her and make her a prisoner if he caught her. She hid in the shadows and hurriedly pulled on her dress as she saw the man who had paid for her walking eagerly towards the wooden steps that zig-zagged up the outside of the wall to the small garret studio. A sense of revulsion swept over her as she realised how close she'd come to a life of shame and despair. How could she have become involved with men like these? But she must get away – far away before someone came looking for her . . .

As soon as he opened the door and went in,

she ran and ran . . . the fear of being caught, imprisoned and forced to serve whatever man was brought to her, making her unaware that her feet were bare on the sharp cobbles until she paused for breath, believing that she was safe for now, though for the moment lost in the maze of dark alleys. Not far away were the seedy nightclubs of Montmartre and the café where she'd spent happy evenings with her friends. She'd walked these streets so often in daylight, and she could find her way now if she took a deep breath and started to think calmly.

Pierre had sounded frightened of the man he called Marcus – his friend and a businessman who had promised to help him with his career as an architect, and yet it seemed this man had perverted sexual tastes. He liked three in a bed and he wanted young girls, but he wanted them drugged with opiates, abandoned and incapable of refusing any deviant act he demanded.

Why would Pierre trick her into something like that? She'd hardly heard what he said as she escaped from him, her terror at being caught by this evil man blurring her mind as she fled. Yet now she recalled Pierre's words . . . Marcus would kill him if he didn't get her . . . and payment of a debt.

Did he owe this man a lot of money he couldn't pay? And why did he want her in particular – or was she just the easiest prey for Pierre and the man he feared?

164

Gradually, she recovered her breath and became calm enough to recognise her surroundings. Her feet were cut and sore, but unconsciously, she'd been running in the right direction to find a safe harbour, though it would only be safe until Pierre came looking for her again. Once she'd thought she loved him, but now the very thought of his touch made her sick with shame and she wished a thousand times that she'd never met him. In that moment she knew she must get away from this place. She'd believed she'd found a way to live and find happiness, but what he'd done tonight had convinced her that he would never let her go free while she was of use to him.

She must go back to England, though she could never go home. Yet in her own country she could find a place to hide and perhaps in time she would find a new life. It was no longer a matter of choice, but the only avenue left open to her . . .

CHAPTER 11

'I sad to see you go,' Marie said when Betty told her she had to leave. 'Why you run from this man, my enfant? You let him come 'ere and Marie will tell him what 'appen if he try to touch you again . . . I cut 'is manhood off with my chopper!' She brought the heavy cleaver she used to cut meat down on the wooden chopping block with relish and Betty laughed. 'See, Marie protect you . . . you never go near 'im again. He never touch you no more . . .'

'I would never give him the chance,' Betty shuddered, because she had only told her a part of the story. It was too awful and her friend would insist on going to the police if she knew it all. 'I was so naïve, Marie. I still thought he might love me, even though my friends warned me he was not to be trusted . . .'

'You stay for a few days, yes?'

'Yes, of course. I don't know if Pierre knows where I work . . .'

'Perhaps I kill this pig and then you stay with me . . .'

Betty laughed at her fierce expression. She

wished that she could go on living with Marie and working here, because the warm sunshine suited her and she didn't relish the thought of thick fogs and dank mornings that characterised the British winter.

'I'll come back and visit one day,' Betty promised, 'when Pierre has forgotten me . . . but he's dangerous, Marie – dangerous and evil and so are his friends . . .'

'I never forget you,' Marie told her and there were tears in her eyes as she embraced her. 'I 'ate this man, who treat you so bad . . .'

Betty smiled but said nothing. She knew she should feel hatred for him too but all she could feel was anger and contempt that he should imagine her to be such a fool. It made her sad that he'd been willing to use her like that – and if she'd drunk half the wine that Pierre had poured for her that night, she would have been easy to control.

A shudder ran through her as she thought of her likely fate. Once hooked on that foul drug, some kind of opiate she guessed, she would have sunk into a life of dependency and degradation. Her fear of Pierre had faded once she was safe with Marie, because he was unlikely to try abducting her off the streets. She'd decided that it was best if she went back to England soon but before she went, she would make a dress for Veronique and she would visit her in her lunch break, because she couldn't go out to the café alone at night . . .

*　　*　　*

When Veronique heard what Pierre had done, she went wild and shouted a lot, gesticulating with her hands and telling Betty she should go to the police.

'Pierre is vindictive and he will not forgive that you made a fool of him,' she warned. 'I knew that he liked to visit houses where they gratify 'is perversions . . . but I no think he do such a thing to you, ma cherie . . .'

'It was partly my fault. I let him believe I was drunk, but I wanted to discover if he loved me – and now I know . . .'

'He 'urt you, Betty,' Veronique said and twisted her mouth in disgust. 'He no longer one of us – when I tell Jacques 'e make clear that we not want to know him . . .'

'I'm going back to England soon . . .'

'But you stay for a while, and you come to the café – and we protect you. We walk 'ome with you and if he try to touch you, Jacques will stop him . . .'

Betty laughed and agreed, because Pierre was too much of a coward to do anything on a busy street in daylight and if her friends protected her in the evenings she would be safe; he would only move against her in the seclusion of a deserted alley late at night.

'All right,' she promised. 'Just while I make your dress and save a little more money – and then I must go home to England . . .'

Marie was waiting downstairs when Betty's friends walked her home a few nights later. She'd drunk only one glass of wine, but there had been no sign of Pierre and Jacques told her that he wasn't at home, because he'd been round there to have it out with him.

'What he did was despicable,' Jacques had looked angry. 'You must never go anywhere with him again, Betty . . .'

'I shan't,' she'd promised with a smile. 'It was foolish but I'd hoped he still cared. Now I know he never loved me. Thank you for drinking my wine that night – he believed I was drunk and so I was able to escape him, and to make him suffer a little for what he did.'

'If he is ill it is good,' Jacques had said, looking grim. 'If he show his face 'ere again, I make him sorry . . .'

'He isn't worth it,' Betty had said and smiled at her friends, because their friendship had given her back her pride and her confidence, and she was feeling happy when she walked in that evening. However, the look on Marie's face made her go cold all over.

'What has happened?' she asked.

'A man came to the café looking for you, ma enfant,' Marie told her. 'He say it important that he speak to you . . . I say you not work 'ere. I say I not know you . . .'

'Pierre?' Betty shuddered. Had he found her?

'He not French,' Marie said. 'I think English, but I no think you want to see him . . . he look stern . . .'

'Did he leave his name?' Betty wondered who else would be looking for her and then she thought she knew, nodding her head as Marie went on,

'He no say but . . . he is your father, yes?'

'I think perhaps it might be him,' Betty agreed and felt a pang of regret. If Sebastian had come after her perhaps he did care after all? The child in her wanted to run to him and tell him everything so that he would take charge and make it better, but she knew she couldn't inflict such pain on him. It would either make him disgusted with her or he would blame himself. Marie was looking at her oddly, waiting for an explanation. 'Not my father – my stepfather . . .'

'Ah, I understand. It is he you run away from? Did he beat you?' Marie arched her brows.

'No, nothing like that,' Betty said and smiled oddly, because her experiences with Pierre had taught her that Sebastian had done nothing other than try to help her. 'He refused to let me work in my mother's workshops – and said I had no talent . . .'

'Pouff! Then he is fool,' Marie said and nodded. 'Yet, not so much stupid . . . he no believe me when I say I not know you. He tell me he will be back and I was to tell you it was important . . .'

Betty nodded uncertainly. She had no idea how Sebastian had found her place of work, but she knew how persistent he could be. If he was convinced Marie was lying for her, he would keep returning until he found her . . .

'He say to give you this . . .' Marie held out a sealed envelope, looking doubtful. 'I not know if to give . . .'

'Yes, thank you,' Betty said and kissed her. 'Dad would never hurt me. He might get angry but he would never harm me . . .'

She took the letter and went upstairs to her room. Her heart was racing and she was half-afraid to open it, and yet she couldn't wait to see what he'd written. She tore it open and scanned the few lines inside.

Forgive me; your mother needs you. We all want you back. Please come to the Hotel Meurice in the 1st arrondissement, opposite the Tuileries Garden, tomorrow at three. I shall wait for you there – but if you do not come I will come back to the café until I find you. I was wrong, Betty. Please give me a chance to show you that I do care . . . Sebastian.

Betty felt the sting of tears, because the note was so typical of Sebastian, brief and to the point. No flowery apologies or promises, just the truth. She brushed her eyes and swallowed hard, as a wave of longing swept over her and she knew she would meet him as he asked . . . because she loved all her family and she'd missed them so terribly. And yet she was so ashamed. Sebastian would want to know what she'd been doing . . . if she knew him, he would already have all the facts but he would expect an explanation.

Sebastian frowned as he drank his rich dark coffee. That woman had so obviously been lying, trying to protect Betty – and he could guess why. His informants had told him the unvarnished truth: Betty had got into deep waters with a man who needed a good thrashing.

Sebastian had gone after Saint-Jacquez intending to do just that, but when he got to the cheap apartment where the fellow lived, he'd discovered it shut up and deserted. A man had come from the shop beneath after Sebastian had banged on the door for several minutes.

'Gone away,' he'd shouted. 'What you want with that devil, Monsieur? He scum – better you do not find him . . .'

'He's lucky I didn't,' Sebastian muttered, still seething with rage. 'I might have been tempted to kill him . . .'

'Someone should do it,' the man agreed. 'He owes me one hundred francs in rent and he goes with no word. Pouff! He will find his things no more if he returns. I sell them for my money . . .'

'Good luck to you,' Sebastian said and meant it.

He walked away knowing that it was better he hadn't found Pierre at home. Murder was a hanging offence and Sebastian could cheerfully have killed the man who had taken his innocent daughter away from her home and the people who loved her.

He'd discovered all he needed to know about Pierre by asking at the various cafés and bars. Most people were willing to talk, especially if he offered money. Pierre Saint-Jacquez owed money almost everywhere and was not liked. Several of those Sebastian had talked to claimed he owed them hundreds of francs – and that was very probably the reason he'd fled his usual haunts. It was unlikely that he was still in Paris. All Sebastian had had to do then was to find Betty.

It had taken him the best part of a week, because she was not well known. He'd tried some of the fashion houses and no one remembered seeing her, even though he'd thought a vendeuse in the House of Vennier was lying when she'd denied all knowledge of Betty. After the fashion houses he tried the cafés and bars, because Betty had very little money so she had to work somewhere, and at last he'd found someone who suggested he should visit Madame Marie's café in the Boulevard de Rochouart.

Sebastian had gone immediately to Madame Marie's establishment, but she denied all knowledge of Betty. However, her manner was so guilty that he knew she was merely lying to protect the girl and in the end he'd asked for paper and an envelope. He'd scribbled a few words to Betty, telling Madame that he would return until Betty was ready to talk to him . . .

'Monsieur Winters?' The receptionist came up to him as he finished his coffee. 'A telephone call for you, Monsieur . . .'

'Yes, of course, thank you.' Sebastian followed her into reception and picked up the receiver. 'Sebastian Winters . . .'

'Seb, I've got that information you've been waiting for – but you'll have to leave immediately. You have an appointment: Monday, at half-past ten in the morning at the Magdalena Bar in East Berlin. You'll find all the papers, including tickets for your flight to East Germany and three return tickets, and your luggage in your hire car outside the hotel . . . your plane leaves in two hours so you'll need to move fast . . .'

'I have things to do first,' Sebastian protested. 'I have to see my daughter . . .'

'Betty is safe. Gretchen's life is in danger, as is that of the man who has risked a lot to get her out of where she was being held . . . if you're not there on time it will be too late to save either of them. This is important, Seb.'

'It's important that I see my daughter . . .'

'I'll get a message to her,' Jack promised. 'Tell me where she's working . . . I'll get one of my chaps to take a message round.'

'That isn't good enough. I'll call there on the way to the airport.'

'Just don't miss the flight. Look, Seb, you wanted to get the girl out and I arranged for her to be brought as far as Berlin; miss this chance and you can give up all idea of finding her alive. Betty is OK. I give you my word nothing will happen to her. If you're worried about Saint-Jacquez you can forget him. We have our eye on him and he isn't in Paris . . .'

'How did you manage to fathom all that out?'

'All things are possible when needs must,' Jack answered. 'Your bill is paid at the hotel – and you will be bringing two passengers back with you; the hire car is waiting for you outside. A man will drive you to the airport and then return the car; there will be another waiting near the airport the other end and you'll be met and given all you need . . . your cover story is in place. Follow your instructions to the letter . . . you have to go right now . . . Do this for me, Seb, and for the sake of two lives . . .'

The phone went down abruptly and Sebastian stared at it in annoyance. He didn't want to leave Paris when he'd just found Betty and arranged a meeting, but he knew that Jack wouldn't have told him it was crucial to move now if there was room to manoeuvre. If he wanted to get Gretchen out, he had to follow Jack's instructions in every detail. All he could do was to leave a letter for Betty and postpone their meeting.

He asked for pen and paper and wrote a swift note, reviewing it with a frown. It was hardly adequate, but Betty would understand that something important had come up. He placed some money inside, in case she didn't have enough for what he'd asked and sealed it, giving it to the receptionist with instructions to give it to Miss Betty Oliver when she asked for him. He hoped that Betty would take the money and go home, because he wasn't sure how long he would be away – and it was possible that things could go wrong. Besides, he wasn't sure that she would respond to his invitation. He would probably have to return to the café and fetch her in the end . . . and in the meantime he could not afford to lose his chance to get Gretchen out of East Germany . . .

Ten minutes later he asked the driver of the hire car to wait while he paid a quick visit to Madame Marie's café, but even as he walked quickly towards it, he saw that it was closed and there was no sign of anyone. He rang the bell and banged on the door but no one answered. A blast of the car's horn made him look over his shoulder; they were holding up the traffic and needed to get going if he was to catch that plane.

Cursing, Sebastian went back to the car, unaware that someone had looked out of the window above the café. He had no time to look back, no time to try again, because if he missed that flight Marianne's daughter might be lost forever . . .

CHAPTER 12

Betty dressed carefully for her meeting with Sebastian. She didn't want him to think her life had been all drudgery since she'd left home. Yes, she'd made a terrible mistake trusting Pierre, but it had taught her something important, and she'd grown up. She'd been an innocent child when she ran away, but now she understood so many things that she hadn't before – and she was beginning to make a good life here in Paris. If she could be sure that Pierre would leave her alone, she might have been tempted to stay.

Veronique's dress was finished and she'd gone into raptures over it, declaring that it was as good as anything she'd worn for the fashion house she worked at.

'You should be in our workshops, ma cherie,' she'd told Betty when it fitted her like a second skin, clinging softly over her hips and breasts, showing off her narrow waist to perfection. 'I adore it, Betty. One day you set up your own house and I work for you, yes?'

'You would be welcome,' Betty said and embraced her, loving her friend for being so enthusiastic.

Veronique's genuine delight in the gown made up for the slights that others had offered her – even though she'd been able to ignore Madame Vennier's insults when she discovered a dress almost exactly like one of her stolen designs in a shop window. Betty was ready to forgive the quarrel with her father too as she walked through the lovely gardens on her way to the hotel Sebastian had chosen.

She would miss the warmth and the scents of Paris, the sweet fragrance of flowers and the equally enticing one of garlic and delicious cooking well laced with wine. She'd begun to feel very much at home here. She'd come to Paris in late August and it was now the end of October; just two months though it seemed like a lifetime, and she felt as if she belonged here. She loved the beautiful old city, its magnificent ancient buildings and its wonderful shops – but there was another city tugging at her heart, and the people of London who had been such a large part of her childhood. To work there as part of a fashion team would be her dream come true. She'd thought first of her mother's workshops, of making beautiful hats – but now Betty knew where her talents lay and what she intended to do with her life. She would try to find work in a London fashion house, beginning in their busy workshops and then, gradually, perfecting her own designs. It was a glittering dream that danced before her eyes like a butterfly of silver, always out of reach but on the horizon so that she could see it and, if she tried very hard, reach out and touch it.

The Hotel Meurice was in front of her. She stood outside its imposing entrance and smiled at the old-fashioned elegance of it. The hotel had been entertaining the rich and important for years and its elegance had undergone many changes over the course of its history, but it looked expensive, exclusive and exactly what Sebastian would choose.

Betty went inside, pausing for a moment and taking in the richness of marble, glittering mirrors and soft carpets, breathing in the smells of leather, exotic perfume and money. Walking up to the desk, Betty was glad that she'd bothered with her appearance, because the receptionist looked at her as if she were something the cat had brought in, and had she come in a pair of her worn-out jeans and a loose blouse she had a feeling she would have been immediately shown out by the uniformed porters.

'Yes?'

'I've come to meet my father, Mr Sebastian Winters . . .' Betty lifted her head proudly.

'Just one moment . . .' The girl referred to her register. 'I am sorry, Mr Winters left yesterday in something of a hurry . . .'

'He left yesterday?' Betty was stunned. 'Are you certain? I'm Miss Oliver . . . did he leave a message for me . . .?'

The girl looked as if she doubted it, but checked the pigeonholes and then took out an envelope with the hotel's logo on it. 'Miss Betty Oliver?' she asked, screwing up her nose as if there was a bad smell. 'Do you have any identification?'

'Yes, I have my passport,' Betty said and offered it. The girl looked at it for a moment and then returned it together with the envelope.

Betty walked from the hotel, feeling numb, shocked and hurt. She'd come here in a mood of optimism, but once again she'd been left feeling as if she were of little importance. She couldn't believe that Sebastian had asked her to call and then left without contacting her to let her know. He must have been in a great hurry . . .

She tore the envelope open and saw the money. Frowning, she thrust it back in the envelope and extracted the thin sheet of writing paper.

Forgive me, Betty. Something extremely important has come up and I have to leave at once. I'm sorry to leave you in the lurch and there are reasons why I cannot explain more at this time. It may be a while before I can get back, so don't wait for me. Take the money and go home. Your mother needs you. Francie is with her but you should be too. We'll talk when I get back – until then be patient and I'll make it up to you. I promise things will be better. The future isn't as black as you may imagine and I love you and I've missed you terribly . . . Sebastian. X

Betty stared at the note, her feelings all over the place as she struggled against anger, bewilderment – and then anxiety. Twice now Sebastian had told her that her mother needed her. Was she ill? Surely he would've said if that were the case? She was hurting inside because once again he'd put something or someone else before her. It seemed to her that he'd done it so many times in the past, but she'd thought this time it was different. She'd thought he really had come to Paris to look for her, but she was just one item on his agenda. He said he loved her but then he wasn't there when she needed him. He said he was her father but fathers didn't let their daughters down. Nothing could be more important to a father than the daughter he loved. Wasn't the truth that he'd wanted her mother and just taken Betty as part of the deal – and why had he just gone rushing off like that without letting her know? Didn't he realise how that would make her feel?

Betty sat in the gardens for ages, watching the people come and go, and the hurt festered inside her. Everyone seemed busy, happy and smiling with somewhere to go and someone waiting for them. People chattering, laughing, children playing and babies crying, all of it combining to make her feel so alone. She'd bolstered her courage to come here today and face the man she'd once thought of as her father, ready to confess her mistakes and her regret . . . and now all she could feel was anger. How could she go home or tell him the

181

things she needed to confess if she was just extra baggage that had come when he married Mum? Tears stung her eyes, because God knew that Betty wanted him to love her; she desperately needed him to be her father, but he was just Sebastian, her mother's husband . . .

The temptation to go off somewhere he couldn't find her was almost overwhelming, but Betty knew her best chances of finding the kind of work she wanted were at home in London. Besides, she was worried about her mother. Sebastian had told her she needed her – why? Betty felt a wave of anxiety wash over her as she wondered what could be wrong. Her mother had always seemed strong, full of life and happy. Was Sebastian lying to make her feel guilty . . . or did her mother really need her?

Sebastian's letter had stirred up her feelings for her home and those she loved there. She missed her mother and Francie, and in her heart she missed her dad too. If only she could truly count on him as a father. It hurt her so much to think that he'd thought something else more important than keeping his appointment with her though.

Perhaps it really had been very important that he leave Paris quickly. She would return to England and visit her Aunt Miriam. She would visit her mother too and phone Francie at college, something she ought to have done before this, but she wouldn't stay under Sebastian's roof for long. Betty was no longer a child and she was determined to make a success of her life.

Betty would use Sebastian's money to get home, as he bid her, because she needed her own to get started in London – but he wasn't her father and he couldn't tell her what to do, even if he was her legal guardian. A real father wouldn't have let anything take him away from an important meeting with her . . .

'Lizzie darling . . . how are you?' Sebastian's voice was very faint, as if the line was poor from wherever he was. 'I'm sorry; I'm going to be away a bit longer than I'd planned . . . I can't tell you now but I promise I'll explain everything when I get back.'

'I'm fine, Sebastian, just missing you – and worried about Betty. Is there any news?'

'Betty is all right, Lizzie. She's in Paris, working at a café. I've contacted her and she should be home soon. I had to leave before I spoke to her, but I've left her some money and told her to come home . . . I just wanted you to know how much I love you all. My flight is being called. I have to go . . . I'm sorry, my love. I'll be home when I can . . . just remember I love you . . . I'm sorry . . .'

The line clicked off and Lizzie stared at it in bewilderment. Sebastian had sounded so strange, unlike himself and worried . . . almost as if he thought he might not come back . . .'

Coldness spread down her spine and she trembled as the fear gripped her. She was taken back to the war years, when Sebastian had left her for unknown destinations and she'd known he might never come back. Was he still caught up in dangerous work for those people? She remembered the mysterious Jack and wondered what Sebastian had got caught up in this time. Before he left for Paris he'd mentioned there was something he wanted to tell her one day, and she'd felt it was important – but what did he mean Betty was safe and should be home soon? Why hadn't he brought their daughter back himself? Surely nothing could be more important to him than bringing his girl home? He spoke of loving them all, but he must know that Lizzie was desperate to see her eldest daughter, to hold her in her arms and know she was safe. Why hadn't he brought her home himself?

'Was that Dad?' Francie asked from the kitchen doorway. She was dressed in a long skirt, one of Betty's, Lizzie thought, and that top was definitely her sister's. She had paint smeared over her face and hands and on the long white shirt – probably one of Sebastian's old ones – she wore over the skimpy top.

'Yes, he was in a hurry.' Lizzie painted a cheerful smile on for her daughter's sake. She didn't want Francie to know how desperately anxious she was for her sister. 'Your father says Betty is all right and may be home soon – so that's good news, isn't it?'

'Yes . . .' Lizzie nodded and followed her into the kitchen. 'Yes, but I wish she would get here,

Mum. I don't know why she hasn't telephoned us – it isn't like her to just go off like this . . . and she could've at least phoned me. I wouldn't have nagged her . . .'

'No, it isn't like her, but I'm sure she has her reasons for not getting in touch . . .'

'She probably thinks Dad would bite her head off,' Francie said and looked serious. 'Betty has always been a bit insecure, Mum. I don't know why – maybe because her own dad died before she was born, but we all love her – why doesn't she know that?'

'I think it may be my fault. I was always working, always busy, when she was a baby, and I left her with other people while I took care of the business. I didn't have much choice, Francie. I couldn't just stay home and take care of her . . . and perhaps that made her feel that she wasn't important . . .'

'But surely she knows. I hate her not being here to share secrets . . .' Francie smiled, 'but she'll know we love her when she comes home, won't she?'

'I'll do my best to make her understand . . .' Lizzie smiled lovingly at the girl who seemed so much older than her years and wiser . . . far wiser than she'd been at her age. 'I love you both – you do know that, don't you?'

'Of course I do.' Francie grinned at her. 'I'm thirsty and hungry. Is there any food in the fridge?'

'I'm sure there are lots of things,' Lizzie said and

smiled, because Francie's ability to take things in her stride kept her sane; she was so like Sebastian in that way and Lizzie had to be the same, she had to trust that he would come through as always. 'Would you like a cup of tea – or some Vimto?'

'That's Betty's favourite,' Francie said. 'Keep it for her, Mum. I'll have fizzy orange juice – and you sit down while I make the lunch. Just because the nurse said you could get up, doesn't mean you can start working . . .'

'Thank you, my darling,' Lizzie said and smiled as she sat down to watch her daughter prepare their meal. 'How is your latest painting coming on, Francie? Can I see it yet?'

'Not until it's finished – and not until Betty is here,' Francie said. 'It's for her, Mum. I did it to show her how much she means to us – because I don't think she knows . . .'

Lizzie's throat caught with tears as she heard the love and sincerity in her daughter's voice. 'Surely, she can't doubt it? I love both of you, Francie; I always have. I was lucky with you, because I was able to spend more time with you. Betty was a baby in the war and things were so difficult then . . .'

Francie moved towards her, putting her arm around her waist. 'Tell me about Betty's father, Mum. Something happened to him, didn't it?'

'He was killed in a car accident . . . but we'd quarrelled and his uncle blamed me for it.'

'Did you meet Dad after Betty's father was killed?'

'No, I first met him at Bert Oliver's workshops. He was very good-looking and I thought he was just flirting with me. I was married to Harry and for a while very unhappy . . . and then Harry died and in time Sebastian came to me and . . .' Lizzie shrugged. 'I've been very happy ever since . . .'

'Even though Dad goes away such a lot?' Francie looked at her anxiously. 'Sometimes, I feel really cross with him. You need him here, Mum – we all do. Betty . . . well, she'll need love and help to settle again. We don't know what's happened to her in France . . .'

'You're very wise, my darling,' Lizzie said and gave into the temptation to kiss her. Francie gave her a fierce hug and went back to preparing the omelettes, meltingly soft and moist in the middle and just slightly brown outside, the way they liked them.

Francie then prepared the salad, using a little of all the ingredients in the fridge: Cos lettuce, tomatoes, grated carrot, beetroot, apple, as well as some olives, walnuts and gherkins in the cupboard, and whisking olive oil and white wine vinegar with a little mustard.

'Shall I pour this over – or will it upset you?' she asked as Lizzie ladled the omelettes on to two plates.

'I love your dressings,' Lizzie said. 'How did you know I had a craving for olives?'

Francie giggled. 'I remembered you telling me

187

that Dad had to search all over London when you were having me. Not many shops stocked them then, but a few more do these days.'

'We get these from a small Italian grocer in the East End,' Lizzie told her. 'I prefer them to the Greek olives and Beth buys some for me whenever she thinks about it. Ed brought me these when he visited yesterday . . .'

'Ed's lovely; we don't see him enough . . .'

'He's busy and he has his own life.'

'Yes, you were lucky to find him and Beth when you were young, because not everyone makes friends for life,' Francie said and smiled as she popped a few more olives into the salad bowl and sprinkled the dressing over. 'I was lucky to have Betty as my big sister – but you didn't have anyone at all when you were growing up.'

'No, but then I had Beth, Ed, Miriam, and my other friends – and then my daughters,' Lizzie said. 'I've been so lucky . . .'

'Betty will come home, won't she, Mum?' Francie asked, suddenly anxious.

'Yes, of course she will, darling,' Lizzie said but she turned away to pour them both a drink of orange squash.

She could only pray that Betty would be here soon, because after that phone call from Sebastian she was very much afraid that he might not return this time. Lizzie knew her daughter and she understood the way Betty thought. She would wonder why Sebastian hadn't brought her home himself, and probably feel let down and annoyed. Lizzie felt the same, because what could be more important than seeing Betty safe home with her family . . .? What had made him go off so suddenly?

CHAPTER 13

'**M**um isn't really ill, is she?' Betty asked Aunt Miriam as she followed her into the large, old-fashioned kitchen. In late October the low wintry sun slanted across the floor, making the worn tiles look red and rich from years of polishing. It looked exactly as it always had, with its rush mats scattered about the floor, the pine cabinets and the deep stone sink. At least nothing ever changed here and its familiarity was reassuring. Even her aunt had been the same as always, as if Betty had never been away. She'd just told her to come in and given her a kiss on the cheek, saying she was glad she was home even if she was a naughty girl. 'Sebastian's note said she needed me . . .'

'She's having a baby and you may recall that she was warned against it years ago. She's not young anymore, Betty, and having a child is always a risk for older women, but she's always wanted a boy and she's over the moon that she's pregnant again. Your father is concerned about her health, but you know your mother – she's as stubborn as you are, my girl and she wouldn't consider the idea of a termination . . . and of course I'm happy for her, though worried too.' Aunt Miriam gave her a stern look. 'Now, what did you mean by upsetting us all like this, Betty?'

'I'm sorry if I worried you,' Betty apologised, feeling ashamed, the more so because of her aunt's warm welcome as she'd walked in the door. 'I did send you a postcard – did you get it?'

'Yes, I did and I showed it to your mother. Your father was very upset, Betty. I know he shouldn't have lost his temper with you . . . but your mother didn't deserve to be hurt like that and you were rude to them both . . .'

'I know but I was upset . . . what they were saying about me, discussing me as if I were a stranger . . . saying I couldn't design hats as well as Mum . . .' Betty shrugged her shoulders. 'Ed said I was just as quick to pick up the work as Mum . . . so why doesn't Dad think I'm any good?'

'It was a private conversation you were not meant to hear – and no excuse for what you did . . . hurting you mother like that!'

'I was hurt too,' Betty said defensively. 'Dad said I had no talent for designing hats and . . . I've never been able to make him proud the way Francie can . . .'

'Betty, that just isn't true,' Aunt Miriam told her and shook her head. 'He's always been like a father to you and he's always been proud of you.'

'He wanted Mum and he had to take me too . . .'

'Nonsense! Do you really think Lizzie would

have gone along with that? She would never have married him in the first place if he hadn't shown that he cared for both of you. Your mother was such a brave woman. She was left with you to care for after your father died – and Bert threw her out. I was so angry with him, but he thought she'd let Harry down and it was quite the other way round . . .'

Betty was silent, absorbing her words. 'What did my father do that hurt Mum?'

'Don't expect me to tell you that, Betty. Your mother only told Bert because he was so awful to her – and he wanted to know the truth, but I was ashamed of Bert. He tried to ruin her at one time . . .'

Betty was shocked. 'I thought he cared for her – he left her his business . . .'

'That was after he came to his senses and realised I couldn't manage without her. Fortunately, she had Sebastian behind her and he would never have let her down so she didn't go under . . .' Aunt Miriam sighed and put the kettle on the stove. 'Well, you're back now, so have you made it up with your parents?'

'I haven't seen anyone yet. I came here first . . .' Betty hesitated, then, a little defiantly, 'I'm not going back to school or college. I'm going to work in a fashion house so that I can learn the business – and then I want to design clothes. Don't say I haven't the talent, because I have!'

'I wouldn't dream of saying anything of the sort.

You know this house, my money and shares in the workshop will come to you – if you wanted help to set up your own place I'd sell my shares and give you the money . . .'

'I'm not ready yet,' Betty said. 'I want to work for someone else first and learn my trade from the bottom and then . . . if I work hard and learn the trade I could be successful.'

'I think that's a sensible plan, my love. I know you'll do it, Betty. Your uncle was a brilliant cutter in his time and your mother is clever at her hat making. If you want to design dresses then go ahead . . .'

'Will you let me make you something – and then wear it without telling my parents where it came from . . . to see what they think of it?'

'If you have belief in yourself, no one else's opinion matters,' Aunt Miriam said, 'but I'll back you up all the way.'

'Thanks,' Betty hugged her. 'I'm going home for a few days to see Mum and give Francie her birthday gift, but I don't want to stay there – can I live with you for a while?'

'For as long as you wish,' Aunt Miriam said. 'If your father allows it . . .'

'I'll talk to him,' Betty said, 'but if he says no I'll find myself a room somewhere. Don't worry, I shan't disappear, but I don't want to live at home . . .' She shook her head. Sebastian's careless desertion of her in Paris was still too raw and painful. Aunt Miriam had got through to her a little, but she still wasn't ready to forgive him or accept that he really was her dad. 'I wanted to talk to you first – but I'd better go home . . .'

'Frank, I thought you would want to know,' Matt said as he ordered coffee for two in the popular cafe. Someone had put a coin in the jukebox and Tab Hunter was crooning about young love. 'Betty got home and it seems she's OK – but I thought one of us ought to pop round to her aunt's and see if she wants to talk. If she's in any kind of trouble she may need our help . . .'

'I'll go round one evening and ask her out for a coffee or something . . . you know you can rely on me if anything is wrong . . .'

'Supposing she's having that devil's baby?' Matt said, watching his reaction carefully. 'I know it's illegal – but we could probably find someone to get rid of it for her . . .'

'No! She's not going through that,' Frank said firmly. 'If she's in that kind of trouble I'll marry her.'

'Are you sure, Frank? I know you care for her but that's a big commitment . . .' Matt looked him in the eyes, because he needed to know what Frank felt.

'I love her, Matt. I don't blame her for what happened. I could kill that bastard – but she was just a kid and she doesn't deserve to be made to suffer for it any more than she has. She might not tell me, but she talks to you – ask her if she needs help and if she does . . .'

'Right, I'll have a word with her – and if you're interested I think you're a great bloke, Frank.'

'I'm not making a sacrifice. I love her . . . one day you'll know what that means . . .'

'Fine,' Matt grinned at him and fished for a coin in his pocket. 'I'm going to see if there's any decent Jazz on that thing instead of all this daft love stuff . . .'

He placed his coin in the jukebox, a frown marring his forehead. Frank wasn't the only one that wanted to kill Saint-Jacques for what he'd done to Betty. He had no intention of telling his friend, but if he ever got the chance he might do just that . . .

Lizzie was sitting in a comfortable chair in the large sitting room overlooking the garden. It was a pleasant day, the wintry sun having broken through misty clouds after lunch and she had her sketch pad on her lap, a box of her favourite pencils and pastels next to her on the arm of her chair, but for some reason she hadn't drawn a thing so far. Sebastian's call had unsettled her and she couldn't help wondering where he was and what he was doing.

She heard a door knocker and Lizzie's cleaning lady had gone to open it . . . Beth was in the kitchen making tea for them. Romany had said she might come over to discuss the Christmas promotions, so Lizzie wasn't expecting anything when the door opened and someone entered. It took a moment for her to realise that it was Betty, looking nervous and clutching a little posy of flowers. For that second Lizzie stared in disbelief and then jumped up, overturning the box of pencils and sending the sketchbook flying.

'Betty, my darling, you're home!' she cried and opened her arms wide.

Betty came flying across the room and into her arms and then they were hugging and kissing, both of them crying.

'Oh, Betty, I've been so worried – and Sebastian has been wretched, terrified something had happened to you and blaming himself . . .'

'Mum, I'm sorry you were worried,' Betty said and wiped the tears from her mother's cheeks with her fingertips.

Lizzie touched her hair, feeling the joy at having her daughter home flood through her. 'How lovely you look – and so grown-up. What have you been doing in Paris?'

'I've been a fool, Mum. Going off like that and upsetting everyone. I'm really sorry for what I did. I didn't realise what I was getting into . . .' Betty gave a little sob. 'I'm really glad to be back . . . if you can forgive me'

'Of course we will! You're our daughter and we love you. Sebastian loves you. He's so sorry for what happened . . . there is no excuse for him raising his hand to you, but he had a lot on his mind, worries over the business and other things, I imagine. He shouldn't have done it and he has told me he will never do such a thing again, but you were wrong too, Betty. You shouldn't have said those things . . . and you should never have run off with a man like that. It was dangerous and foolish and we might have lost you for good . . .'

'Mum, I'm so sorry. I made a mistake. Forgive me, please? I was so mixed up and unhappy. You won't hate me, will you?'

'Of course I shan't and I have forgiven you, though I do want to know what happened out there. . . .' Lizzie looked at her anxiously. 'We were so worried . . . were you with friends? You should've let us know where you were . . . just a phone call would have been enough.'

'I know. I'm so sorry . . .' Betty bit her lip. 'I can't tell you yet, Mum. I want to but not yet . . .'

'I shan't force you, but I think we should talk . . . as women and friends . . . don't you?'

Betty nodded, tears slipping down her cheeks. 'I feel terrible, Mum. I just can't tell you some of it . . . please don't make me . . .'

'You don't have to tell me it all . . . but tell me as much as you can about what happened, Betty, please? You can't simply disappear and not give us an explanation . . .'

'I was with a man but . . . it didn't work and I was on my own for a while. I've made a lot of friends in Paris; I've worked hard in a café but I've also worked on my designs and I know what I'm going to do with my life now,' Betty said. 'I'm going to work as a seamstress in a fashion house, learn the business from the bottom up – and then I'm going to design clothes. Not hats like you, Mum. Your designs were so good I couldn't better them, but I've always loved making dresses . . .'

'And you do it well,' Lizzie agreed. 'Romany might be able to help you find a job. She has a lot of contacts in the rag trade and she thinks the world of you, Betty. I'm sure she'll help you get started . . .'

Betty stood back and stared at her. 'You wouldn't mind? You don't think I should go back to college as Dad said?'

'No, not now, Betty,' Lizzie said. 'You've had a taste of working for a living and you've proved you can survive on your own.' She smiled at her daughter. 'Sebastian only wanted what he thought best for you, darling – but this time he will listen, I promise.'

Betty drew away. 'He asked me to meet him at a hotel, Mum, but when I got there he'd checked out in a hurry. He left me a note and the money to get home . . . but why did he just go off like that? I'm sure the girl in reception thought I was a floozy; it was so humiliating . . .'

'I don't know, but be sure I'll ask him about it.' Lizzie drew her down to sit on the squashy seat beside her, wanting to hold her close so that she wouldn't ever leave again. 'Your father is mixed up in something,' she said. 'I think it's some kind of secret work, something to do with the last war . . .'

'That's been over for years,' Betty dismissed it with a shake of her head. 'How can it have anything to do with that?'

'No, my darling, it isn't over, not for everyone. There are still people without homes or have family that they can't trace . . . so many people were lost and misplaced during that awful time . . . I don't really know exactly, but I just feel it's all mixed up with what he was doing in the war . . .'

Betty sat up straight and stared at her. 'Do you think he could be a spy . . . but that would be dangerous?'

'I'm not sure he's a spy but . . .' Lizzie broke off as they heard Francie's voice outside the door. 'Don't say anything to Francie. We don't have to worry her yet . . .'

Betty nodded and stood up as the door was flung open and her younger sister came bursting in wearing Betty's clothes, which she'd managed to get paint all over, a paintbrush tucked behind one ear.

'Beth just told me! She said not to come in yet because you'd want to talk to Mum, but I couldn't wait. Betty, you're home . . .' Francie cried and hurtled towards her. 'I'm so glad! So glad! Where the hell have you been?'

'Working in cafés,' Betty said and laughed as Francie pulled a wry face. 'It was fun, but I'll tell you all about it later. Why aren't you at college – and who told you, you could wear my things?'

Betty teased and Francie laughed in delight. 'I'm sorry I wasn't here for your birthday, love, but I've got a present for you – and I did send a card to the college . . .'

'Oh, thanks,' Francie hugged her. 'You don't mind about the skirt, do you? I always liked your clothes, and you left this behind . . .'

'I don't care if you wear my things, Francie. I'm going to be making lots now . . . and you can tell me what you like and what you hate . . . and be my model . . .'

Francie went white and looked at Lizzie. 'No, I didn't tell her,' Lizzie joined in the teasing. 'Betty, your sister is in disgrace with Sebastian for becoming a famous photographic model . . .'

'What have you been doing, Francie?' Betty put her arm about her. 'It sounds exciting?'

'Yes, it was . . .' Francie told her about the competition and how she'd been given a contract and had her pictures in several magazines.

'And your father isn't too pleased, because he's afraid she'll be too famous to know us . . .'

'Mum!' Francie giggled. 'I'm not famous – but I might be if Dad wasn't so cross about it. Miss Honiton threatened to kick me out of college if I let my work slide and to rescind the scholarship in Paris . . .'

'The mean old devil.' Betty hugged her sister. 'You'll love it there, Francie – I thought your art meant everything to you?'

'It did – it does,' Francie said, 'but it was fun

doing the photo shoots. I've just got the latest magazine. I daren't show it to Dad – but I think it's good . . .'

'You haven't shown it to me either,' Lizzie said and frowned. 'Is it very awful, Francie?'

'Dad is going to think so,' Francie said and produced the magazine from under a cushion on the sofa. It came through the post this morning and I hid it because I was afraid of what you might say . . .'

Betty took the magazine and flicked through until she found the pictures. She frowned over them for a few minutes and then nodded. 'Dad will hate them, Francie, because they make you look older – and so sexy, but they're really good. You're gorgeous, and this photographer has done a fantastic job . . .' She used the word Dad talking to her sister without realising it and then frowned, because she would be a fool to slip back into the old ways. He'd shown how little he cared when he left her in Paris. She handed the magazine to Lizzie. 'Look at it sensibly, Mum, and not as a mother . . .'

Lizzie looked at the spread of several rather lovely photographs of her daughter. Francie was delectable, beautiful, leggy and very enticing – but much too knowing and grown-up for a very recent fifteen-year-old. She was wearing filmy clothing that seemed to reveal her flesh through it, but there was nothing that Lizzie wouldn't have accepted in any other model.

'I was wearing a bodysuit underneath, Mum . . . it isn't as bad as it appears.'

'She isn't naked,' Betty said, 'and I think she looks beautiful . . .'

'Yes, I do see, Betty,' Lizzie agreed, 'but your father is going to hit the roof, Francie! I think he will sue the pants off the person who made you have these taken . . .'

'Then don't show him, Mum,' Betty said. 'What the eye doesn't see the heart doesn't grieve for . . .'

'That is quite enough, Betty! We'll have no more lies in this family. Your father will be angry, Francie, but I'll do what I can to calm him down.'

'I *was* wearing a flesh-coloured leotard under that filmy thing, Mum, honestly,' Francie pleaded with her eyes. 'I said no at first, but Kathy said I had to . . .'

'Sebastian will murder her when he gets back . . .' Lizzie said.

'He can't know,' Betty said. 'By the time he gets home these magazines will be off the stands. Are there any more to come, Francie?'

'Not like these,' Francie said and grinned at her. 'It was fun though – and I wouldn't mind working for a magazine again . . . but not quite like these . . . more fashion photography.'

'You'd do well in Paris. Veronique would have you working with her like a shot . . .'

'Who is Veronique?' Francie wanted to know, listening in fascination as Betty told her about her Parisian friends.

Lizzie watched her girls talking, half-listening to their chatter but just happy to have them both here and safe.

Lizzie was torn between her love for her husband and anger that he could risk all they had for this secret work. Surely he'd given enough in the war? It was time he gave it up, whatever it was, and spent time with her and his children.

Oh, God! Please let him come home . . . she didn't know how she'd bear it if she never saw him again . . .

CHAPTER 14

Sebastian saw them sitting together at a table in the corner of the shabby bar: two men and a woman, one of the men obviously a German official from the look of his uniform. They were the only customers, which wasn't surprising to Sebastian; the place smelled of spilled beer and something more unpleasant coming from the rear of the bar. He conquered his distaste for the whole affair, which seemed somehow sordid and far from what he'd imagined, because all the false papers and Jack's strict instructions about their identities made it seem unreal. Was this truly the girl Sebastian had been searching for or had he been tricked?

As he approached the table, the girl looked up and his heart jolted because Karl's eyes were looking straight at him, and he knew in that moment that this thin, pale-faced girl was his friend's daughter. The man next to her was in his thirties, also thin and gaunt-looking, he had long hair that straggled into his neck and looked as if it needed a damned good wash. According to the papers Sebastian had been given for him, he was a small-time crook who was wanted by the British government for theft committed in London and on British ships, a man who worked on liners as a steward and stole from the passengers and crew. Sebastian had been told that he was actually travelling with them, because he was Gretchen's lover – according to what he'd been told.

'Herr Schmidt?' Sebastian asked of the officer and took the papers he'd been given from his pocket. He saw the man stiffen and then relax as the papers were offered; as if he'd half thought Sebastian would pull a gun. 'You're here to hand my prisoner over to me I think?'

'That is correct, sir,' the officer replied, his English perfect but with a heavy German accent, 'please sign here . . .'

Sebastian signed with a flourish the name he'd been given, but in such a way he hoped it was unreadable, because he didn't want to end up in a German prison accused of using a false identity, and all this could yet turn out to be a trap.

'Thank you.' The officer handed over some documents, inclined his head and then said, 'If I were you, I should leave for the border immediately, sir. It isn't safe here these days . . . and I can't guarantee your life once you leave this café . . .'

He walked quickly from the room, leaving Sebastian stunned and disbelieving. What the hell did Jack think he was playing at! This was supposed to be a straightforward hand over. He hadn't reckoned with any cloak and dagger stuff, though there was always danger on these missions, because people double crossed you for personal gain. Sebastian had fumed as he read the letter from Jack detailing the plan, which seemed pretty straightforward in essence. He was supposed to be a plain-clothes police officer here to arrest and deport Eric Schiller and, at the same time take home the girl who was supposed to be Sebastian's daughter according to the papers he had been given for her, and who had fallen ill on a visit to her mother who lived in East Germany. He had papers signed by some official in East Berlin to take Gretchen and Schiller, her supposed lover, through the border controls into West Germany and then into France, and his instructions were to pick them up from the bar and drive straight to the nearest border, present the papers and get the hell out again.

Everything has been taken care of, bribes paid to guards and it should be straightforward – but we need Eric Schiller so make sure you get him through. I know you can do it. Destroy this. Good luck, J.

Jack's careless note seemed less than reassuring now. Sebastian had been watching the couple's manner as he dealt with the German police officer and doubted very much he'd been told the truth about them being lovers. Eric Schiller might be a small-time crook wanted for theft, but he was more likely someone the British government wanted for their own reasons. By the look of him he'd been held prisoner for a while and not well treated.

'Gretchen, my dear,' Sebastian said when the girl stood up nervously to greet him, 'I trust you are feeling better – and your mother?'

'She is very good,' the girl replied in a thick guttural voice, her English obviously poor, but her answer correct. 'You are well, Father?'

'Better for seeing you,' he replied and meant it. He would be glad to get her home to her mother Marianne, and see an end to this business – and this was definitely the last time he would be drawn into one of these missions. 'We should leave quickly. I have to be back in London and it's not safe here for any of us . . .' He turned his gaze on Eric Schiller, keeping up the pretence. 'Herr Schiller, I have a warrant for your arrest. Do you come willingly or must I handcuff you, sir?'

'I think you should handcuff me, Inspector,' Eric Schiller replied in a far smoother and more educated voice than Gretchen's, although still heavily German. 'But give me the key when we get in the car – just in case . . .'

Sebastian inclined his head, slipping the handcuffs on and locking them with a snap. As they were about to leave, he caught sight of the bartender reaching for the telephone and felt coldness at his nape. It was all going too smoothly for Sebastian's liking and there was something wrong – something had always been wrong with this, but he couldn't put his finger on it. He just had a sense that he was being lied to by everyone.

He led the way outside to the car, which he'd left down a side alley. Sebastian and Gretchen got into the front, and Eric took a back seat. Sebastian leant over and gave his back seat passenger the key to the handcuffs.

'I'm not sure what is going on here,' he said. 'I came for Gretchen but was told to bring you out as well – but I shan't hesitate to sacrifice you if it means our safety. Do you understand?'

Eric Schiller grinned and looked vastly more human and attractive. 'I understand perfectly, old boy,' he said in a cut-glass English accent. 'I wouldn't dream of asking you to do anything else.'

'Eric . . .' Gretchen looked at him, a strange expression in her eyes. 'Please don't do anything foolish . . .'

Suddenly, as the other man's eyes softened, Sebastian wondered if he'd been wrong about these two. Perhaps they were lovers, though their demeanour hadn't suggested it in the bar.

'The bartender was watching us,' he said. 'As we left he made a telephone call. I think they will be waiting for us if we try to cross over the border here as I was instructed. We'll just wait for a moment and see what happens.'

'It might be better to take the scenic route home rather than to try crossing over into the West section at any point they might look for us,' Eric said in his upper-class English voice. 'Do you happen to know your way to Austria and then to Switzerland – or would you prefer me to drive?'

'I know the way,' Sebastian said grimly. It would mean a detour through quiet country roads, avoiding all the usual crossings and checkpoints, to slip across borders illegally, and a long delay on his return to France. He could only hope that Betty had taken the money he'd left for her and gone home. 'If I need directions at any time I'll let you know – in the meantime, pray to whatever god you choose, because I think you were never meant to leave here alive, Mr Schiller.'

'Just call me Eric,' he said and sat back with a little smile on his face. 'I'm certain you're right, Mr Winters – and I do thank God they sent you, instead of some official policeman who always follows his orders.'

'You'll find a gun in the shoe box on the seat next to you,' Sebastian said. 'Please don't use it unless you absolutely have to . . .'

'What a resourceful man you are,' Eric said as they saw a large black car draw up outside the inn and then two men, in dark coats and trilby hats that were pulled down over their brows, jumped out and rushed inside. They were clearly looking for Eric and probably members of the Russian secret police. Had they found him, he could well have disappeared forever.

Sebastian waited in the shadows until the men came out a few seconds later, got into their car and raced off with a squeal of brakes in the direction he had been intended to take. He reversed gently and drove two blocks down the road, parked the car, got out and led the way to a small and rather dirty-looking van.

Unlocking the door, he got in and allowed Gretchen to sit beside him. Eric was obliged to climb in the back amongst the boxes stacked there. He investigated and discovered pair after pair of beautiful shoes.

'How did you set this up?' he asked.

'Before I left England, I asked a close friend of mine, who sells shoes for me all over Europe, to drive his van here and leave it for me. He returned to France by train and gave me the keys, and is now safely back in England with his family.'

'So you were suspicious even before you came. How resourceful of you, Mr Winters. What is your alibi now?'

'I am myself, Gretchen is still my daughter – and your name is Jack Havers, a member of my staff. You work as a travelling salesman for me selling hand-stitched English shoes. We have outlets in West Germany, Austria, France and Switzerland and we're trying for markets in the Eastern zone of Germany and Poland . . .'

'How quickly one goes up in the world,' Eric said and smiled oddly. 'Next time I find myself in a sticky situation, I shall certainly ask them to send you.'

'Don't bother, I shan't come – and we're not

out of this one yet,' Sebastian said but smiled to himself.

Something was definitely not as it seemed here, but he'd been sent in to do a job and he would do it – even if the result wasn't quite what their masters had planned . . .

CHAPTER 15

'I've got something to show you,' Francie said, looking at her sister shyly when they'd left their mother, Beth and Romany to talk shop and had gone up to Betty's old bedroom. 'I did it for you, Betty – because I wanted you to know I understand . . .'

'In your studio?' Betty smiled and followed her sister back down the stairs. They'd left Romany and Beth talking to their mother about various aspects of the millinery business after they'd all had tea together.

Earlier, Romany had promised to help Betty find work with a friend of hers. 'He was asking if I knew any promising girls,' she'd said. 'Have you got anything you've made I could wear to his party?'

'I could make you an evening dress if you like,' Betty said, her gaze moving over the tall well-built woman who had been such a friend to them all since she joined the workshop team. 'I do have an idea I think would please you . . .'

'Can you do it in a week?'

'Yes, if I can use Mum's machine?' She hesitated.

'Will you be using it to make clothes for the baby? Perhaps I could help with that too?'

'Of course you can, my love. I've bought some linen and a few bits of lace and voile for the cot, but I think we need mostly knitted things for a start – and we've got the christening robe I had for Francie. Unfortunately, you had a second-hand one, because it was in the war, but Francie's is like new . . .' Lizzie said. 'Where will you buy the material for your dress, Romany?'

'Oh, I've got some material I love but I've never done anything with. I'll drop it over early in the morning – if that's all right?' Romany asked.

'Yes, please.' Betty was thrilled with the idea. 'I'll take your measurements then, though I think I know them from that suit you had made for Jenny's wedding. I went with you to buy the material . . .'

'I hadn't forgotten.' Romany smiled at her. 'It's good to have you back, Betty.'

Betty's bedroom was just as she'd left it, except that the things she'd smashed before she ran away had been removed and everything was immaculate. Francie hovered over Betty as she unpacked the few things she'd brought home with her. She'd left one suitcase at Aunt Miriam's because in her own mind she was still set on going to live there – but of course she would need to break it gently to her mother.

'This is lovely,' Francie said, fingering some delicate underwear edged with lace. 'Did you buy it in France?'

'No, I made it, but I copied some things I saw in a wonderful shop there . . . they were so expensive, Francie, and I made these for a fraction of the price.' Betty smiled and took a small package wrapped in tissue from her case. 'These are for your birthday, Francie. I would've sent them but then I decided to come home . . .'

'Thank you,' Francie hugged her and then tore the tissue off to reveal a delicate cream silk vest and two pairs of exquisite French knickers edged with coffee-coloured lace. 'Oh, I love them. Your birthday presents are over there on the chest of drawers, Betty. We all bought you a gift, even though you weren't here . . .'

'I'll open them later,' Betty said and hugged her. 'I do love you, Francie – and I missed you . . .'

'I missed you, too.' Francie held the underwear up against herself in front of the dressing mirror. 'I wish I had your talents, Betty. These are lovely and so are the clothes you're wearing . . . they're simple and just you, but I love them.' She hesitated, then, 'I've bought some knitted things for the baby, but I haven't told Mum yet. She's a bit nervous of getting things too soon . . . just in case . . .'

'I know, but I shall make a few things in secret and keep them until he or she is born. I hope mum gets a boy this time, don't you?'

'I don't mind as long as they're both all right . . .' she looked wistfully at Betty's clothes. 'I wish I could make things like this . . .'

'You can buy nice things from the shop, Francie – but your talent is so much more. I wish I could paint the way you do . . .'

'Tell me about France,' her sister said. 'Did you have a lover – was he wonderful?'

'No, I didn't have a wonderful lover,' Betty said, because Pierre had been evil and she could never tell her innocent sister about him or what he'd done to her. 'I had friends and we went to the cafés and drank cheap wine and listened to the music, but I had to work hard to earn a living. I tried to sell some of my designs but they weren't interested – though I know one of them stole three of my ideas for evening dresses . . .'

'How wicked! Why didn't you go to the police?'

'I had no proof – why would anyone believe me over her?'

'I would,' Francie said and hugged her.

'You're my sister.' Betty smiled and put an arm about her waist. 'When am I going to see this picture of yours?'

'Now, if you want,' Francie was nervous as she led the way to her studio, which was an annexe built on specially for her with lots of windows and skylights so that she always had good light for her work. 'I'd like to know what you think . . .'

She took the cover from the easel, revealing the painting of a girl standing in their garden on a misty morning. She was wearing a long skirt rather like one Francie was always borrowing from Betty and a loose flimsy top that showed a hint of her breasts; her red straight hair flowed onto her shoulders and her face was in shadow. There was an air of mystery about the girl in the picture but also of sadness . . . an inner loneliness that Francie had sensed in her sister so many times.

Betty stood staring at it for ages and Francie's nerves were stretched as she waited for a response. Would Betty hate it or would she realise it was her and yet not her – would she see that it had been done out of love, because Francie wanted her to understand that she knew?

At last Betty turned to her and there were tears on her cheeks. 'It's me, isn't it?' she said and it wasn't truly a question. 'You know – you've always known . . .'

'I don't understand why,' Francie said moving towards her. 'We all love you – I would hate it if you were hurting inside and didn't know how much we care . . . I care . . .'

'I know you do.' Betty put her arms about her, holding her tightly as their tears mingled. 'I know Mum loves me, and Sebastian has been a good father to me. He spoils me but he isn't my father, Francie, and no amount of wishing can change that . . . Perhaps it's just something in me . . . something I can't help. Insecurity or restlessness, a need to be loved . . . I think my real father may have been like that . . .'

'Dad does love you,' Francie said. 'I've seen him look at you and smile and I know he really thinks of you as his daughter. You're one of us and we all want and love you – and I wish you could believe that, Betty.'

'I suppose I do in a way. I was always a little jealous when we were younger, but I've grown up now and I realise how much I had . . .' Betty said as she hugged her sister. 'I missed you so much when I was in Paris, but I couldn't write and tell you, because I didn't want anyone to know where I was. Something happened and . . . it wasn't glamorous or exciting, Francie. I've regretted it so much and I have felt alone sometimes, just as I look in your painting, but I'm never really alone because I've got you, Francie, and I don't ever intend to lose you again – and I think that painting is wonderful.'

'I think it's the best thing I've ever done,' Francie said and smiled at her. 'I need it for my exams, but afterwards it's yours. I did it for you because I love you. I kept wondering why you didn't write or phone, but I thought you were just busy and I was too . . .'

'I know and that painting is brilliant,' Betty said. 'Being in Paris has changed me, Francie. I need to be more independent and once Mum is feeling better and I have a decent job I'm going to get my own place – but I'll always want you to come and stay. Promise you will?'

'You're my sister,' Francie said and covered the painting. 'Don't leave Mum too soon, though I'm not going back to college until Dad gets home. Mum won't say where he's gone, but I know she's worried about him, just like she was over you.'

'Yes, I think she's right,' Betty agreed. 'What do you think he does when he goes away? He always says it's business but . . . you don't think he has someone else?'

'He wouldn't!' Francie cried. 'Oh, Betty, you can't think he would do that to Mum? He was so worried when he knew she was having the baby . . .'

'I always believed he loved her . . .' Betty nodded. 'Well, it's a bit of a mystery, isn't it? He asked me to meet him at his hotel, but when I got there he'd checked out in a hurry – why would he do that? It can't just be business, Francie . . .'

'I know he's upset about something else,' Francie said. 'I saw him looking through some accounts . . . and I heard him talking to someone on the phone and he sounded annoyed. I think the business may be in trouble – his business, not Mum's. She's still doing well . . . even though lots of women only wear hats for church, or weddings and funerals nowadays . . .'

'I love those little bits of fluff and feathers Mum designs to wear on the side of your head,' Betty said.

'Oh those, but they're different, hardly hats at all,' Francie said and then laughed. 'They cost an awful lot of money in the shops though . . .'

'We ought to go window shopping together as soon as Dad gets back,' Betty said, slipping into the old familiar way of calling Sebastian her father, because it was impossible not to when she was with Francie. 'Go in and try lots of things on like we did when you were on holiday last year – but first of all I've got to make Romany's dress and you can help me when you're not working . . .'

'Yes please! Show me some of your designs,' Francie begged and they went back to the bedroom together, arms about each other's waist and the best of friends . . .

CHAPTER 16

'Stop the van here,' Eric said suddenly as they approached the border with Switzerland. 'If we're right, my enemies have probably worked out where we're heading by now. You should take Gretchen through yourself – and I'll make my own way through the woods.'

Sebastian stopped the van and turned to look at him in the back. 'I've been thinking much the same thing,' he said. 'Do you want to meet up the other side of the border and travel back to England with us?'

'No, I think I'll carry on alone; I can't be sure what sort of a reception is planned for me and I prefer to work as a loner,' Eric said and leaned forward, offering his hand. 'Thank you for saving my life – I shan't forget it . . .'

'I did my duty as a decent fellow human being,' Sebastian said. 'Take the gun – have you got money and the papers I gave you?'

'Yes, thank you,' Eric said. 'I'll be in touch when you are settled in England, Gretchen . . .'

Tears ran down her cheeks. 'Please don't leave me. I can't face it without you . . .'

Eric leaned forward and kissed her gently on the lips. 'It will be better where you're going, Gretchen, and you can trust Sebastian. He'll see you safe . . .'

'I don't want you to leave us . . . you might be killed . . .'

'It's best for all of us,' Eric insisted and put her firmly from him. 'You have to forget what they did to you, Gretchen. You have a new life ahead now. You don't need me or the past . . .'

She gave a little sob as Eric got out of the van taking his haversack, which was all he'd brought with him and the gun in his pocket. The handcuffs had been removed long ago as they travelled, buying food on the way.

'He'll get through,' Sebastian tried to reassure the sobbing girl, but she threw him a look of dislike and ignored him.

As they approached the barriers between the two countries, Sebastian sensed the tension in her. She shot a scared glance at him as the guard came forward and looked into the window.

'Is there anyone else with you, sir?'

'No, it's just me and my daughter,' Sebastian said to him in his own language. 'She came to Germany to visit her mother who was ill, and is now returning to her home in England with me.'

'Why do you wish to visit Switzerland?'

'I wanted to share the beauty of the mountains with my daughter. It's November and we may go skiing for a couple of days if the slopes are ready . . .'

'It's a bit early in the season yet, but they tell me you may find enough snow higher up.' The man nodded. 'May I look in the back of the van please?' he asked and shifted the rifle over his shoulder.'

'Of course.' Sebastian got out and went to open the back, revealing all the boxes of shoes.

'What is in these please?'

Sebastian looked at the man's feet. He was a good judge and thought him a size ten English. Picking up a box containing one of the finest pairs of shoes they'd ever sold in size ten, he handed them to the guard. 'Just your size . . .'

The guard opened the box and for a moment his eyes gleamed. 'They are very fine – and very expensive. I have always liked English craftsman-ship . . .' this time he spoke in perfect English.

Sebastian replied in the same, 'Take them as a goodwill gift – to show that there are no hard feelings between us as nations now . . .'

The man hesitated and then he shook his head, handing them back. 'I don't take bribes, sir.'

'It's not a bribe,' Sebastian said. 'I'm looking for people to act as agents for my shoes in Germany and Austria. Take them with you – and if you think we can do business contact me at the address inside the box. It might be good for us all . . . business isn't against the law in Germany, is it?'

The guard seemed to hesitate, then nodded and took the box. 'You can go,' he said. 'Your papers are in order.' He took the box into his hut and operated the barrier to let them through to the Swiss side.

Sebastian was aware that Gretchen was shaking beside him as they drove on past the friendly Swiss officer on the other side of the border, who welcomed them to his country and directed them forward after a brief glimpse of their papers.

'It's all right,' Sebastian said when they were clear of the border posts. 'Your papers were always in order – it was Eric they were after . . . whoever they are . . .'

'He knows things . . . I'm not the only one he's helped get away, but they suspected him and he was imprisoned and beaten, but he escaped and hid in cellars for some months, and that's when I met him; he was kind to me and I love him . . .' Gretchen said, her voice harsh with emotion. 'He has a lot of information in his head. He told me that nothing is written down but there are photos, tapes, which he had smuggled out to Switzerland by friends. That's why the British want him and his enemies want him dead. He helps people like me . . .'

'Where were you?' Sebastian asked, but she only shook her head. He saw pain and fear in her face and decided not to push her. If she found the courage to trust him she would tell him in her own good time. Now he had to get her to England and safe in her mother's care. Only then would he be free to finish his own business . . .

★ ★ ★

'We need to get you some more clothes,' Sebastian said to Gretchen when they boarded the plane for England. She was already wearing a tweed suit he'd purchased in Switzerland for her, but she needed far more than just a couple of nightgowns and the suit, which was all she'd bought so far with the money he gave her. 'Your mother wants you to be happy, Gretchen – and so do I. Karl was my good friend . . .'

'They told me he worked for the Nazis and was a war criminal . . .'

'Trumped up charges they used as an excuse to execute him,' Sebastian told her. 'Yes, he did work for the Nazis, and perhaps some of that work was used against Jews, but Karl never intended it to be so – whatever they forced him to do, he did for your sake and your mother's . . . to protect you and keep you out of the camps.'

'It might have been better to have died in the camps. At least I'd have been with her and not in that place . . .'

'What kind of a place, Gretchen?' Sebastian asked softly, but she simply shook her head.

'You can't change what happened,' she said and her eyes were bleak. 'You can't give me back the childhood I lost – or take away the nightmares. If my mother had taken me with her I could've been with her.'

'She was having a child and your father wanted her safe. He intended to bring you out himself, and he would've given half a chance – but they arrested him, tried him and shot him, and they sent you to an orphanage.'

'Orphanages are supposed to be where they send children to be cared for . . . I wasn't . . .'

'I'm sorry that bad things happened to you there, Gretchen,' Sebastian said. 'As you said, I cannot change the past or undo what was done to you – but I can help you to have a better future.'

'Why did Eric leave us?' she asked, looking at him accusingly. 'He thought you would betray him . . .'

'Not me; he is too clever for that, but someone did. I had the feeling something was wrong from the start. I would've tried to get him through – but he thought he could make it through the woods himself and avoid trouble for us. He's a wanted man. They were looking for him, Gretchen, and he made it much safer for us by doing what he did . . .'

'He has enemies because he knows too much . . . secrets the Russians don't want the West to know – and he helped me get away. You could not have found me if Eric hadn't found me first . . .'

'Yes, I see,' Sebastian said. 'You are grateful to him . . .'

'I love him,' Gretchen said fiercely. 'I know he would never marry me – no man would after what I've done, but he was kind and he was my friend, and I loved him . . .'

'Then you should be glad he got away safe,' Sebastian said. 'I am sure he knew his way through those woods, Gretchen. I think he's done it before

– in fact I'm not sure he needed my help to get him out . . .'

'If you had not seen that man reach for the telephone he would have gone to the border and trusted those papers.' She looked at him and for a moment he saw a glimmer of respect in her eyes. 'When we get to London you will show me where to buy a new dress please?'

'Yes, of course, and I'll help you to find a job – what would you like to do?'

'When I look at magazines from the West I see much lovely food,' Gretchen said. 'They never fed us and I was always hungry. Can you help me find such a job?'

Sebastian laughed. 'Oh yes, I think I can help with that, Gretchen. Your mother wants a café of her own and I think you could set one up together with a little help from me . . .'

And a few others, Sebastian thought. He'd been set up for this job and it could have ended in one or all of them being killed – and someone was going to pay for that. Gretchen and her mother would get what they deserved if he had to strangle Jack to get it . . .

'These things are so beautiful so expensive . . .' Gretchen exclaimed over the dresses, skirts and soft knitwear the showroom assistant had brought for her to try. 'I do not know what to choose.'

'Try them all and see what fits best and which of them suit you . . .'

Gretchen gave him a shy look, clearly overwhelmed by the kindness she'd seldom experienced in the past. She tried on eight dresses and Sebastian chose six of them, two skirts and two twinsets, and a winter coat, which she would soon need. He asked if she wanted a hat but she said no, she did not think she would wear them, and if she did it would be a sensible felt hat, not one of the frivolous bits of fancy the shop sold. Sebastian smiled at that and decided not to mention it to Lizzie.

They left the shop with several smart paper bags. Sebastian told her to get in the car. She would need some shoes, he suggested, but she refused to let him spend any more money.

'I bought two pairs in Switzerland,' she said. 'Now please take me to my mother – you must have much to do . . .'

'Yes, of course and then I need to get straight back to Paris. There are a few things I have to do,' Sebastian said and turned his head to smile at her. 'I shall help your mother fund her café, Gretchen. I promise – but for the moment there is an important matter I have to attend to in France . . .'

'You are so good and I was unfair,' Gretchen said. She leaned towards him and kissed him. 'I want to thank you for saving my life – and to ask if you will let me know if you hear from Eric . . .'

'I only did what any decent man would do, and if I hear anything, of course I'll let you know . . .'

Gretchen gave a sob and put her arms around him, hugging him as the emotion took hold of her.

Sebastian did not push her away. Gretchen had been abused, insulted and made to feel worthless too often. Instead, he put up his hand to touch her face and smile at her.

'You are a pretty girl, Gretchen. Perhaps you can't see it now, but when you're well again and the memories begin to fade you will be lovely – and here in England, you will find happiness. I promise it will come, my dear.'

'You are kind but you cannot change the past,' she said and the look in her eyes smote at him, because he knew it was true. Had he been able to rescue her years ago, all the bad things might not have happened to her, but at that time he'd still been busy here at home, and had no idea of what was happening to Karl and his family.

He looked at her sadly, feeling her pain. 'No, I cannot do that, but I can help you to find a place where you may discover at least peace,' he said and then turned to drive off.

He had no idea that he'd been watched by two young women ever since he left the shop, his mind was already on Paris and what he would find there . . . but first he had to send some flowers to his wife and tell her he was thinking of her. He considered ringing her but she would ask too many questions he couldn't answer on the phone.

If Betty was already back with her mother so much the better, but Sebastian had unfinished business in Paris and he wanted it over so that when he was home he could stay there. Jack had told him that Saint-Jacquez was no longer in Paris, but Sebastian needed to talk to his friends and find out all he could. That man had mistreated his daughter and if Jack was right, he was dangerous. Even back in London, Betty might not be safe. If she was still in Paris he would bring her home, and he would make sure the French authorities knew what had been going on so that if the man ever returned he would be arrested.

CHAPTER 17

'That was Dad wasn't it . . . with that girl?' Francie's face was white with shock as she looked at Betty, her lovely eyes begging her to say no, to tell her that she was mistaken.

'Yes, it was Sebastian,' Betty said oddly and Francie saw that she was furious, her voice bitter and hurt.

'I can't believe he would do something like that,' Francie said in a voice so low it was almost inaudible. 'There has to be an explanation. She wasn't much older than you . . .'

'No, but obviously he thinks a lot of her,' Betty said coldly. 'Mum thought he might be doing secret work to help refugees, people who were lost after the war . . . but you saw the way he looked at her . . .'

'And all those bags of clothes . . .' Francie stared at her in horror. 'Mum can't ever know, Betty. She thinks Dad loves her . . . and he's having an affair behind her back.'

'We shan't tell her,' Betty said firmly. 'You must promise me, Francie. You won't let Mum know what we saw today. If she thought he was having an affair with a woman half her age . . . and she's having his child even though she could die . . . I hate him so much!'

'No!' Francie cried, tears in her eyes. 'You mustn't hate Dad, Betty. Please, don't turn against him. I know he cares for you . . .'

'I'm sorry, love. But I can't stay under his roof, Francie.' Betty said. 'I'll tell Mum tonight that I need to live with Aunt Miriam . . .'

'Oh, Betty, do you have to go?' Francie looked at her miserably. 'I was enjoying being with you so much – talking about Paris and having fun. I wish we hadn't seen them. Why is he even driving a hire car? It's as if he wants to hide from us . . . We were having such a lovely time . . .'

'We're still having fun, and we're going to buy a present for the new baby,' Betty said, lifting her head in defiance of what she'd witnessed. 'I refuse to let him ruin our day. We're going to enjoy ourselves, Francie – and I'll always be there for you, and I'll visit when I know he's not around, but I couldn't be in the same room as him now.'

Francie looked at her sister sadly. Betty seemed so bitter against their father and that hurt her, but she could see that nothing she said would alter her mind. 'All right, we'll still go shopping and try lots of stuff on . . . but not in there . . .'

'Why don't you want to stay here with us?' Betty's mother asked her that evening. 'I thought you were enjoying yourselves, being together again? I was

231

hoping we might all go to the theatre one night to see Julie Andrews in My Fair Lady . . .'

'I have enjoyed being with you and Francie, and I'd love to see that show with you, Mum,' Betty said, 'but I want to stand on my own two feet, Mum, and I can't do that here. Aunt Miriam treats me as an adult. When Sebastian gets back he'll either try to stop me – or give me lots of money, and I don't want money from him . . .'

'Why have you turned against your father?' Mum asked sadly. 'He does love you, darling. In your heart you must know it . . .'

Betty stared at her in silence and the truth burned on her tongue but she held it back, though every little inch of her was longing to let out the stream of vitriol she felt against Sebastian. For a while after she came home and talked with her sister Betty had been inclined to forgive him, because he was Francie's dad too, but after what she'd seen she was furious with him again.

'Why did he just go off and leave me stranded in Paris if he cared for me – what was so important that he couldn't take the time to tell me he had to leave?' she channelled her anger into a safer stream.

'I don't know for sure,' her mother said and frowned. 'Perhaps he's been doing some special work for the government again.'

Betty shook her head, denying it. Sebastian was having a passionate affair with a girl half his age! She would never forgive him for caring more for that girl than he did for her mother.

'I won't live in his house, Mum.'

'You won't just disappear again, will you?'

'No, I promise I shan't do that,' Betty said, softening as she saw the sadness in her mother's eyes.

'Come and kiss me, darling. You can at least stay another night, Sebastian told me not to expect him for another night at least – he's got some business to finish.'

'You've spoken to him?'

'No,' she frowned. 'It was odd really – he sent me a big bouquet of beautiful roses and a little note to say he hoped to be with me very soon and he loved me . . .'

Guilty conscience! Betty's hands clenched. She was so furious with him for the way he was treating her mother. Oh, she could kill him! Mum was so trusting, so loving and sure of her husband's devotion. She ought to know the truth and Betty would've warned her, but it would hurt her – and Betty's desire to protect her and Francie was fierce.

'Well, I shan't try to hold you, but ring me and visit when you can,' her mother's words cut into her thoughts.

'We can meet for coffee or lunch, Mum, and I'll visit, keep an eye on Francie for you and take her places – I love you and I shan't desert you, but please understand that I can't live here . . .'

'Yes, we'll meet – and I hope one day you will understand your father and forgive him, darling. Because I know he loves us all very much . . .'

★   ★   ★

Lizzie wondered what had happened to make Betty so angry with Sebastian. She'd thought she was reaching her, helping her to forget the things that had hurt her in Paris, because she knew there were things that her daughter wasn't telling her.

Lizzie loved Sebastian and she knew he loved her – but why had he sent her flowers and a note rather than telephoning and letting her know what he was doing? It was a tiny little prick of doubt, a little thorn in her flesh that once planted would not go completely.

Lizzie's hands rested on the gentle swell of her belly. She believed her son had settled into the warm nest of her womb and was safe now, because she felt so much better . . . stronger. She wasn't an invalid and she didn't intend to behave as though she were, staying in the house all the time and neglecting her business.

Lizzie Larch had survived a war alone except for her friends; she'd survived hatred and vindictiveness and she could survive a baby, even if it was rather late in life to be having another. She smiled and decided what she was going to do. It was time Francie made plans for returning to Art College and she was going into the showroom to talk to Romany and work on a few special hats for the window. There was absolutely no reason why she shouldn't . . . and she was going to put all her silly thoughts away to a small corner of her mind where they couldn't hurt her . . .

*　*　*

'I can tell you no more, Monsieur . . .' Marie threw up her hands in dismay. 'You demand of me where your daughter is and I tell you she go to meet you at the hotel and when she return she angry . . . so angry! She pack her things and say she go home and I see her no more . . . as for her friends I know only Veronique as I tell you . . .'

'If you're hiding Betty I shall find out and come back . . .' Sebastian warned.

'Pouff! These English! Why they no listen?' She threw up her hands in disgust, her plump face outraged. 'I tell you, she go back to England – perhaps to her home.'

He smiled oddly. 'Thank you, Madame Marie. I shall pray she is there when I get back to England . . .'

Sebastian walked swiftly back towards his hotel. He hoped that the Frenchwoman was telling him the truth and his daughter would be there when he got home. He'd returned to France partly for his daughter's sake, but also because he had to know what had been going on here. He would talk to Veronique and anyone else Betty had been friendly with and discover what they knew of Pierre Saint-Jacquez. Jack had told him that the man was suspected of being involved in smuggling young girls out of the country and that these girls were never seen again. Sebastian needed to talk to the French police and discover what they knew of the man, but first he would talk to Betty's friends. At the very least they might know something that could help him discover where the man had disappeared to, because Sebastian was determined that he would be traced and punished for what he'd done to his daughter.

He would have normally been content to leave it to Jack, but he wasn't sure if he could still trust a man he'd thought of as a friend. Jack had betrayed him in some way. What happened in Germany showed there was a traitor somewhere, and Sebastian wasn't sure if it was Jack or someone else in the department. He needed to talk to the man who had driven his hire car to the airport and given him the false papers. Jack had risked all their lives . . . and he had some explaining to do.

His mouth was set grimly as he joined the queue for the flight back to London the next day. He'd tried to phone Lizzie twice but there was no reply and his imagination was running riot. Supposing she'd had a fall and the baby had come early or . . . But that way lay madness. In a few hours he would be home and he knew there would be some explaining to do. Lizzie was going to be angry because he'd left Betty to get home herself. He just hoped she was home, because otherwise it would be back to square one and he just didn't have the energy to cope with that all over again. He'd rescued Gretchen, but if Betty had disappeared again he would never forgive himself . . .

God, he was tired. He had a nagging pain in his

chest and realised it must be indigestion . . . it was all the worry and rushing about, grabbing a sandwich on the run. He would go to the doctor when he got home and get something to ease it . . .

CHAPTER 18

'Where is your mother?' Sebastian asked of his daughter as he put down his battered leather suitcase in the hall. 'And is Betty here? I was told she'd come home . . .'

'Betty was here but she took her things and moved in with Aunt Miriam,' Francie said. 'She doesn't want to live here – she says you don't really care about her. I don't know what you've done to her, Dad . . .'

'What I've done?' Sebastian asked curtly. He was too damned tired for this and he'd just spent the last hour threatening an old friend with hellfire for no good reason. Apparently, Jack was furious because he hadn't got Eric back for them.

'He's damned important to us, Seb. I thought you understood it was vital he talked to us. What the hell did you let him slip away for? We don't even know if he got through alive.'

'I didn't hear any shots – and he wanted it that way,' Seb said. 'Obviously, I don't have clearance to know everything – but I've been used and I want compensation . . .'

'You want money? You never have before . . .'
Jack looked disbelieving.

'I'm in financial trouble, but it isn't for me – I want help for Gretchen and her mother. You've no idea what that girl has been through . . .'

'I think I might guess,' Jack said. 'Look, I'll do what I can, Seb, but our masters aren't known for their generosity. Think yourself lucky you got papers to get them both over here . . .'

Sebastian admitted that he'd been fortunate, because not all refugees were granted asylum, especially with Karl being labelled a war criminal, and yet he felt aggrieved that he'd been asked to bring Eric out when those who planned it must have been aware it could ruin Gretchen's chances of escape.

'Well, do what you can for me,' Sebastian said. 'I'm glad you didn't deliberately set out to get us all killed – but someone did. You must have a traitor in the camp . . .'

'I'm on to it, Seb, believe me. Look, I'll try for at least some of the money – but I want something in return . . .'

Sebastian's gaze narrowed dangerously. 'I think I've given enough. It's time for me to retire and look after my family . . .'

'If Eric gets in touch, promise me you'll let me know when and where the meeting is set up – no one else, whoever asks. Even if it's the damned Prime Minister or the archbishop of wherever . . . will you give me your word?'

Sebastian studied him for a moment. 'I'll trust you, Jack. Obviously, you need to be careful, because someone wanted to ruin your plans – and that means you can't trust anyone.'

'Except for you.' Jack offered his hand. 'I trust you, Seb – and that's why I know that if Eric contacts anyone it will be you . . .'

'Daddy, you haven't answered me,' Francie's voice broke through the haze of thoughts and pain in Sebastian's mind. 'Betty hates you now and there has to be a reason other than what we saw . . . because I don't hate you even though I think it's despicable to deceive Mum . . .'

Sebastian blinked at his daughter. Everything looked vaguely red and he could hardly breathe for the pain in his chest, which was so much worse now.

'What are you talking about . . .' he started to say but then his tongue seemed to stick to the roof of his mouth; his eyes rolled, he gave a sigh and lurched forward, falling to the ground at his daughter's feet.

'Dad!' Francie screamed and knelt by his side. 'Oh, Daddy, please don't die. I didn't mean to upset you . . . please, don't be dead . . .'

The door opened behind her and Beth walked in. She took one look at Francie's frantic face, then bent over Sebastian, working her finger into his mouth, making sure that he didn't swallow his own tongue and choke and then turning him on one side so that his airways were not restricted.

He was still breathing but seemed to be unconscious so she left him and quickly snatched up the telephone receiver, dialling a number she'd used on Lizzie's behalf recently and knew by heart.

'Doctor Staples' surgery – how may I help?'

'We have an emergency here,' Beth said, sounding calmer than she felt. 'Mr Sebastian Winters has collapsed and I think it must be a heart attack. He is unconscious but breathing and his airways are not constricted. Can you please send a doctor – or the ambulance . . .?'

'I think you need an ambulance,' the receptionist said. 'Are you the patient's wife?'

'No, I'm a family friend, but his daughter is here and we shall both be going with him in the ambulance . . .'

'The ambulance will be with you in about ten minutes, madam. Can someone let Mrs Winters know please?'

'Yes, we'll do that now,' Beth said, and looked at Francie as she replaced the receiver. 'I'm going to ring your mother. Fetch a blanket and a cushion; keep your father warm and comfortable. We'll just have to pray the ambulance gets here fast . . .'

Lizzie sat in a taxi heading for the hospital to which Sebastian had been taken. Beth had told her to remember her unborn child and not to panic, but Lizzie's fear was threatening to choke her. She couldn't lose Sebastian now. He was older than her but still looked and acted like a young man – and perhaps that was half the trouble. He'd been working too hard for years and it was time he slowed down and took things easier . . .

She'd been talking to Romany about the new spring and summer lines for next year, because you always had to plan several months ahead, and think about what was likely to be in fashion. Privately, when Betty was in the showroom serving a customer, Romany had told her that she had been talking about the girl to one of her contacts.

'Walter is interested and he certainly liked Betty's work,' she'd told Lizzie, 'but don't say anything to her yet. He can be very fickle and he may change his mind. Wait until he says he wants to see her – at the moment he's just asked to see more of her designs . . .'

'I'm not sure Betty will let her sketch pad go,' Lizzie warned. 'She did that in Paris and three of her designs were stolen.'

'That won't happen this time, I give you my word. Walter . . .'

Lizzie never did get to hear the rest of what she was going to say, because the telephone rang and Beth's news had Lizzie rushing to order a taxi. Betty had entered the workroom just as Lizzie was about to leave but she hadn't asked her to go with her to the hospital, because she knew Betty was still angry with her father.

'I'll telephone you as soon as I hear anything,' she said and kissed Betty's cold cheek. 'Don't worry, love. He's on his way to hospital and I'm sure he'll be all right . . .'

'I didn't want this, Mum . . .' Betty was white-faced. 'Please let me know soon . . .'

'Yes, of course, love,' Lizzie promised, but then the taxi arrived and there was no time. Perhaps some good would come from this, she thought, and prayed that Sebastian would recover. It was ironic that just as she felt her son was safe inside her womb her husband should be taken ill . . .

Lizzie arrived at the hospital to find Beth and Francie sitting together in the waiting area of the emergency department. Beth got up and came to embrace her.

'He's stable,' she told Lizzie. 'The ambulance men gave him some treatment and I think he came round just as they got him here. He's in that cubicle over there, love. The doctors are with him now and we were asked to wait here . . .'

'I can't see him yet then,' Lizzie said and embraced Francie as she came to put her arms about her. 'Don't cry, love. Your dad is a fighter and I'm sure the doctors can help him . . . but I wish I'd known he was ill . . .'

'He probably didn't know,' Beth said. 'I don't claim to have much knowledge, Lizzie, but I do remember from nursing training that we were told patients often had little or no warning of a first heart attack . . .'

'He's always been so strong,' Lizzie said close to tears. 'Oh, Beth, I can't . . .' she held the next words back, because Francie's white face and big dark eyes told their own tale.

'Sebastian is as tough as old boots,' Beth said staunchly, looking at Francie and then at Lizzie. 'It was probably just a warning, love, but I thought it was best to get an ambulance quickly . . .'

'Beth was wonderful,' Francie said. 'If she hadn't been there I shouldn't have known what to do . . .'

'I did very little,' Beth said with a wry look. 'I might have managed some chest massage and mouth to mouth resuscitation if it had been needed, but it wasn't – which is why I think this is probably just a warning . . .'

As if to endorse her words, the curtains of the cubicle were swished back and Lizzie saw Sebastian sitting up against the pillows and talking to the doctor. She jumped to her feet and walked swiftly to his bedside.

'Sebastian, darling . . .' she cried and bent to kiss his cheek. 'Thank God! I was so frightened when they told me you'd collapsed . . .'

'I'm sorry to worry you all,' Sebastian said. 'It was just a bit of nonsense. Nothing to worry about . . .'

'I didn't tell you that, Mr Winters,' the doctor said with a straight look at Lizzie. 'It was a sharp warning to slow down. So no rushing about for a while. I'm going to send you up to a ward and we'll be doing tests tomorrow to discover just what sort of condition your heart is in. Something is wrong or you wouldn't have had this attack. At the very least you're going to have to take things easier . . .'

'He needs a holiday at home,' Lizzie said. 'He's been away far too often of late, and I'm going to make sure he spends more time with his family.'

'There speaks a sensible woman,' the doctor said and smiled at her. 'It will be about half an hour before they take you up to the ward, Mr Winters. After that I suggest you go home, Mrs Winters. Your husband needs some bedrest and we're going to see he has a good long sleep before we do the tests.'

'I don't want to stay here longer than necessary . . .' Sebastian protested.

'You told me to stay in bed when it was necessary,' Lizzie said, giving him a straight look. 'You'll stay here until the doctor says you can come home – otherwise you'll be hearing from me.'

Sebastian smiled and relaxed against the pillows. 'You win, Lizzie Larch. To be honest with you, I could do with a rest . . .'

Betty finished for the evening and said goodnight to Romany and the other girls, leaving Romany to lock up as usual. She'd waited nervously all afternoon for a phone call to say how Sebastian was, but none had come. It was stupid but it hurt because her mother hadn't rung her as soon as she knew the situation – and the way Mum had gone rushing off without even asking if she wanted to go with her made her feel like an outsider.

Betty understood her mother's thinking. She'd been so angry with Sebastian, but she would never do anything to make his condition worse. Of course she wouldn't! She didn't want him dead, even though she'd said she hated him . . . Tears stung her eyes and she almost bumped into the man coming from the busy café ahead of her. She swayed and his hands shot out, steadying her. Blinking hard, Betty looked at his face and gave an exclamation of surprise.

'Frank! Frank Hadley,' she said. 'What are you doing here?'

'Killing time in the hope of catching you when you left,' Frank said. 'Matt told me you were helping out here . . . so I thought I'd hang around for a while . . .'

'Oh, Frank, why didn't you come in and ask for me?'

'Wasn't sure you would want to see me . . .'

'Of course I do – you're a friend . . .'

Frank studied her intently and then he put out a finger to wipe away her tears. 'Then why are you crying, Betty?'

She caught back a sob and brushed at her eyes. 'It's daft,' she said in a choked voice. 'Sebastian has had a heart attack and Mum was going to telephone but she hasn't and I'm afraid something has happened . . .'

'Why don't we go to the hospital and find out?' Frank said. 'I've got my car here . . .'

'I can't go to the hospital,' Betty said. 'You don't

understand, Frank. We fell out . . . and they might not want me there . . .'

Frank took her arm. 'Where are you living, Betty?'

'With Aunt Miriam . . .' she hesitated then. 'I know it's a lot to ask, but would you phone for me?'

'Of course. Don't you know I'd do anything for you?' He smiled at her in a way that made Betty blush and look down. 'Come on, there's a phone box just a few yards up the street . . .'

Betty nodded and followed him into the cramped interior. They had to squash in together, but she didn't mind because Frank was Frank and she was always comfortable with him. Thankfully the phone was working and he had a pocketful of change, which he inserted at the operator's command.

'Ah yes,' he said, nodding at Betty when at last he was put through to the Nursing Sister that could help him. 'It's about Mr Sebastian Winters. We wanted to inquire how he is please . . . Yes, I am a relation. I'm his son-in-law . . .'

Betty gasped at the barefaced lie, but Frank just grinned at her.

'So he's resting for now – tests in the morning but you think he'll come home in a couple of days. Thank you, Sister Morrison. My wife was extremely worried . . .'

'Frank, how dare you?' Betty said, looking shocked as he replaced the receiver. 'Telling her lies . . .'

'Only a little one,' Frank winked. 'She wouldn't have told us anything otherwise – and you were very worried, so where's the harm in bending the truth a little?'

'You're not my husband. We're not even courting . . .' Betty's cheeks were on fire because Frank was making no effort to move and let her out of the cramped phone box.

'That's something that could easily be arranged,' Frank said with a cheeky grin. 'I shall be working here in London for at least the next few months, Betty. I did a report on the new facilities at Gatwick and now I've been asked to do one for another airport. They've offered me a chance to work on various designs for the new terminal and the facilities and that means I'll be around for ages – and you know you're special to me . . .'

'No!' Betty gave a cry of anguish. 'Please don't say that, Frank. You don't know me. You don't know what I've done . . .'

She squeezed past him out of the box and started to run up the street. Frank came after her and grabbed her arm, swinging her round to face him, holding her gently but firmly as he gazed down at her. Betty couldn't look at him; she was afraid to gaze into those honest eyes.

'I know you, Betty,' Frank said. 'I know that whatever happened in Paris wasn't your fault – Pierre Saint-Jacquez is a devil. It's all my fault. I wish I'd told you everything back then, when I knew you were falling for him. I'm not much of a catch for you and you could do much better – but I'll be around if you need me . . .'

Tears trickled down Betty's cheeks. She shook her head, too ashamed to look at him. 'Please don't, Frank,' she whispered. 'It wouldn't be fair . . . I'm not fit . . .'

He gave her a little shake. 'That's enough of that,' he said harshly. 'I don't care what you did – what he made you do – you're lovely to me and always will be.'

Betty swiped her hand across her eyes. 'Thank you for phoning the hospital for me, Frank – but my plans don't include romance.'

Reluctantly, he let her go and stood back. 'If you need help or you want to see me, Matt knows where to find me,' he said and then turned and strode away.

Betty watched him go. She wanted to call him back, to feel his comforting embrace and know that someone cared for her – but that wouldn't be fair. Frank was kind and generous and she couldn't take advantage of him – besides, she was afraid that even if he admired her now he would come to despise her when he realised just what had happened in Paris.

'You ought to go, Beth,' Lizzie said and glanced at the gilt and enamel mantel clock. 'Tony and Tom will be waiting for their meal . . .'

'I rang Tony and explained. He said they would have fish and chips – and he's taking Tom out for a treat.' Beth looked at her in concern. 'I didn't want to leave you alone, and Francie is too weepy at the moment. She hasn't come up against serious illness before . . .'

'No, our children are lucky,' Lizzie said and smiled at her best friend. 'They haven't had to cope with the hardships we had, Beth – and thank goodness for that. Sebastian has always tried to protect them from harsh reality – and perhaps that's wrong. I don't know what she would do if . . .'

'It isn't going to happen,' Beth reassured her. 'You mustn't get into a state, Lizzie. The doctor said that Sebastian had been lucky. It was just a warning to slow up.'

'Yes – and the worry over Betty . . .' Lizzie gave a little cry of distress. 'I meant to ring the workshops earlier and let her know. I'll have to telephone Miriam . . .'

'Are you sure you feel all right?' Beth said. 'You looked very white when we came home in that taxi. I was worried that you might faint or something . . .'

'I'm fine,' Lizzie said. 'Physically well – but I must admit I feel tired and weepy. I was afraid I might get to the hospital and be told he'd died.'

'Yes, I know . . .' Betty sighed. 'Are you sure you will be all right?'

'Yes, of course. I'm going to ring Miriam and speak to Betty now – and then I'll see what Francie is up to . . .'

'She told me she would be in her studio,' Beth said and smiled. 'She's such a talented girl, Lizzie.

I'm glad that modelling thing was just a flash in the pan. She should keep on with her art – that picture of a girl in a garden was wonderful. I think it's beautiful . . . quite arresting . . .'

'Yes, she's captured the sadness in Betty's face so well . . .' Lizzie smiled. 'Francie doesn't say it is her sister, but I can see it. I wonder what Sebastian will think when he sees it.'

'Well, I'm sure he will be home soon,' Beth bent to kiss her cheek. 'I shall go then – but don't overdo things, Lizzie. Think of yourself and the child . . .'

CHAPTER 19

Francie painted with frantic haste. The light was dying and she wanted to make a start. She had to get his face on canvas before it faded from her mind – the haunted, anxious look she'd seen in his eyes when he'd asked about Betty. Perhaps if she could convey that feeling to her sister she could ease the festering hurt inside Betty.

Brushing a hand over her cheeks to dash away the stupid tears, Francie poured all her love and passion into the picture she was painting of her father. Like Betty, she'd been furious with him when she'd seen that tender scene in his car. How could he look at another woman in that way? Francie had wanted to fly at him with her accusations and beat his chest with her fists, but she hadn't because she didn't want to upset her mother. Except that she'd been on the point of accusing him of betraying her when he'd suddenly collapsed at her feet. Francie had never been so scared in her life. She'd been terrified he would die, unable to move, too ignorant to help him.

Thank goodness for Beth. Mum's best friend. Beth had acted calmly and competently, even though she'd admitted that she'd forgotten most of her nursing training. Yet still she'd known enough to do what was needed. Francie was determined that she would learn first aid – just enough to help if anyone she loved was in that kind of trouble again, but she could never be a nurse as Beth had been. She was an artist and she needed the outlet it gave her when she painted as she was now, fast and furious, the paint going on in bold sweeps and with a sure touch that lit her from inside.

Oh, she'd had fun with the modelling, and if her father hadn't objected she would have liked to go on with it for a while, but perhaps both he and Miss Honiton were right. Art wasn't a job, it was a vocation, as nursing was for some people. You had to live it as she was living it now . . . moved by fear and love into an outpouring of emotion on the canvas.

'Where have you been, Betty?' Aunt Miriam demanded when Betty entered the sitting room later that evening. 'Your mother phoned and was worried when I told her you weren't home. She has rung you twice and wants you to get back to her right away . . .'

'I'm sorry if you were both worried,' Beth said. 'I'll ring her now if that's all right?'

'Of course. This is your home, my love. I was just worried – but your father is all right. Not well but still alive and in the best place . . .'

'I know. Someone phoned the hospital for me,' Betty said. 'I was restless – and I've had a bun and some coffee in a café, so don't worry about my not having supper.'

Francie answered the phone. 'Mum's having a bath,' she said. 'Where did you go, Betty? Mum was worried. We were up the hospital for ages, waiting for Dad to be moved into a ward.'

'The hospital say he has to have some tests . . . do you know what they are?'

'No, they didn't tell us anything – except that Dad has to rest more. Mum says he's banned from going on trips overseas – so don't go off to Paris again, will you?'

'No chance of that,' Betty smiled oddly. 'You will be the one to visit Paris next, Francie – when you take up that scholarship . . .'

'I might not get it,' Francie said. 'I can't settle to this year's coursework. It's not the kind of art I want to do, but they insist that we can express ourselves in various ways. I can only paint one way . . .'

'You should go back to college. You would have tuition there . . .'

'No, not while Dad is ill,' Francie said quickly. 'Mum was exhausted sitting at the hospital. You should come and see her tomorrow, Betty.'

'Yes, all right,' Betty said. 'You're a lovely sister, Francie.'

'Betty, the first thing Dad did when he got in was ask about you . . .'

'Really?' Betty sighed. 'I care about him, of course I do. I pray he'll get better but . . . why was he with that girl?'

'I know what we saw, but it doesn't make sense that he would have another woman . . .'

'We both saw him with her,' Betty said coldly. 'She was half his age and he'd bought her lots of clothes; he's having an affair . . .'

'No, he can't be,' Francie said. 'I know he was with her and they'd just come from that shop . . . but don't you think there could be another reason?'

'None that I can think of,' Betty said. 'He's our dad and I know you love him – but if he hurts Mum in her condition . . .'

'He won't,' Francie said. 'He worries about her. He kept telling her to go home and rest at the hospital. I'm sure it wasn't what we thought . . .'

'You've got more faith in him than I have,' Betty said. 'All right, love – tell Mum I'll come for lunch tomorrow, but don't go to a lot of trouble.'

Francie stared as her sister put the receiver down and then she heard another click and frowned. It sounded as if someone else had been listening into their phone conversation . . . had Mum picked up in her bedroom? Oh, she did hope not. It would hurt her so much if she learned of her husband's betrayal in that way.

Racing upstairs, Francie went into the bathroom and saw her mother towelling down. She felt a surge of relief as she smiled.

'Are you all right, Mum?'

'Of course I am, darling. Who was that on the phone?'

'Betty rang to apologise because she wasn't home – but she's coming for lunch tomorrow . . .'

'Oh good,' Mum smiled again. 'We'll have the chicken. We all like that, don't we? You can make us a nice salad starter – and we'll have some tinned peaches and cream for afters. Just a nice simple dinner . . .'

'Mum, you don't need to cook for us . . .'

'Francie, I'm much better now, my darling. Believe me. I was upset earlier, because your father has always been so strong – I always knew everything would be fine when he was here . . .'

'You must try not to worry. The doctor said you should rest, Mum.'

'Your father has to rest too – so we'll both sit about and be lazy together when he's home. It's a pity the weather isn't better so that we could sit in the garden, but it is winter now.'

'It will be Christmas before we know it,' Francie said and handed her mother a lovely white robe to slip on.

'And you have exams before then,' her mother said. 'You should return to college next week, love.'

'I'd rather stay here with you,' Francie said.

'You don't want to lose your scholarship, Francie. Your father and I will be fine, I promise you.'

'Honestly, Mum, I'm perfectly all right here,' Francie said. 'I'm doing some of the best work

'I've ever done and I would hate to lose the feeling I have for it – I can work better in my studio.'

'Well, we'll see what your father says,' her mother promised. 'Pop down and put the kettle on, love. I could do with a cup of tea . . .'

Lizzie sat on the edge of the bed staring into space. She'd rushed to the phone in her bedroom as soon as it rang, fearing that it might be the hospital to say that Sebastian had had a relapse. Hearing Betty's voice she'd been going to cut in but something made her wait – and she'd waited too long.

Lizzie had been so stunned when she heard Betty say Sebastian was having an affair that she hardly took in the rest of it. No, it couldn't be true . . . it just couldn't, because she knew he wouldn't do that behind her back. If it was over – if he wanted another woman – he would tell her, wouldn't he?

He'd had something on his mind for a while now. She'd known there was a problem he wasn't sharing with her – he'd even said he had something to tell her when he got back from looking for Betty.

Could it be that the dream had come to an end? All those years of loving Sebastian, of being so happy, successful in her chosen business and with two wonderful daughters – had they finally ended? Perhaps he'd found a new love . . . a much younger woman?

It would break Lizzie's heart if that was the case, but a part of her still refused to believe it even though her daughters had seen their father kissing a girl half his age.

Why would Sebastian do such a thing, unless he'd fallen in love? She wanted to ask him for the truth, to have this out in the open, but knew that she couldn't. Sebastian needed rest and the doctors had told her that too much stress might bring on another attack.

Lizzie was just going to have to be patient and hope that it wouldn't be as bad as she feared . . .

CHAPTER 20

Francie read the letter three times before she could take it in. It was an apology from *Styled* magazine, telling her that they hadn't known that Kathy had tricked Francie into making her Francie's agent. They wanted to assure her that she was in no way legally bound to them, but they would like to feature her in their magazine again and they set out their terms, which. were far more generous than in the past and Francie was sorely tempted.

She loved her art, of course she did. Sometimes she lost herself in it for hours and hours, but she was young and she also wanted some fun. It would be exciting to do the shoot for a spring campaign in Austria. She would be chaperoned by their new fashion editor and they could assure her that she would not be asked to do anything she disliked.

Francie read the letter through once more and decided to go along to the magazine's head office and discuss the project, because it sounded so exciting – and surely she was entitled to some fun before she settled down to her serious work?

She folded the letter carefully and placed it in

her bedside drawer. Since the shoot was taking place abroad, she ought to get her parents' permission. Francie knew that her father would never agree to her going to Austria with strangers . . . not after Betty's escapade. If she was back at college, as she could be, perhaps they wouldn't have to know until afterwards – and if the pictures were just of beautiful clothes and not too sexy perhaps they might even agree that she could take a couple of years off from her art, because painting was in her blood so she would be able to return to it easily.

Betty kissed her mother's cheek, relieved to see that she looked perfectly well and had got the colour back in her face. She glanced at the table, which had been set out as if for a special occasion, and felt a pang of regret. If her mother considered she needed to make an effort when Betty came to lunch it was relegating her to the position of a guest.

'How is Dad' she asked and went to the fridge to get herself a drink of her favourite fizz. 'Have you rung the hospital this morning?'

'Yes, they say he's doing very well, but is a little tired and they've requested that he has only one visitor this afternoon . . .'

Betty nodded and looked sympathetically at Francie. 'Well, I suppose they know what's best for him. Perhaps he'll be home soon . . .'

'Yes, I'm sure he will,' her mother replied and

nodded. 'Let's sit down and eat our salad; the chicken is almost ready . . .'

'It smells good,' Betty said. 'You needn't have gone to all this trouble, Mum.'

'I was going to cook it anyway,' Mum replied, giving her an odd look. 'How are you getting on at your aunt's house?'

'Oh, it's all right,' Betty said. 'She can't cook like you, Mum – but I don't want that much anyway. I have a sandwich for lunch and some soup or toast would do when I get home, but she won't hear of it . . .'

'Miriam is looking after you. I'm glad, because you would obviously neglect yourself. You have a lovely figure; you don't need to slim . . .'

'I'm not trying to,' Betty assured her. 'Anyway, look at Francie. It's no wonder the magazines wanted her to model for them . . . she's like a twig.'

'I am not,' Francie flicked a piece of lettuce at her. Betty laughed and wagged a finger back at her. At least her sister was the same as always. 'It's lovely being all together, us three . . .' she said and looked wistful.

'Yes, lovely,' Mum said and reached out to touch their hands in turn. 'Are you going to show Betty what you've been working on, Francie?'

'It isn't finished so I don't want anyone to see yet . . .'

'I'll see it another day,' Betty agreed. 'Oh, I've got a bit of news – Romany has arranged for me to meet someone this evening, the director of a fashion house. I know their clothes and I like them, even though they're not in the top rank yet, but it would be fun to work for them . . . get some experience . . .'

'Lucky you!' Francie said. 'I enjoyed doing fashion shoots – all the glorious clothes and the things I got to keep . . .'

'Well, I've been working on something too,' Betty told her. 'It's for you, Francie, but I'm going to show it to Mr Walter first – because he wants to see examples of my work made up . . .'

'Oooh! What is it?' Francie said excitedly. 'A dress or a skirt?'

'I'm not telling,' Betty teased. 'I think you will like it – and that's all I'm saying . . .'

'Beast!' Francie pulled a face at her and they both giggled. Mum was watching indulgently and looking happy. Suddenly, Betty wished she could go back . . . before the quarrel that had sent her rushing to Paris. 'I love you,' she said to her sister emotionally. 'And you, Mum. Always remember that . . .'

'Well, Miss Winters, I think you have some talent,' her prospective employer said, looking at her thoughtfully. 'Your work is naïve as yet and you need some professional training – but on the whole, I believe we should be willing to give it to you . . .'

Betty stared at him, her heart pounding. They'd

met in his office at the back of his extensive work-rooms and she'd been on fire with curiosity as she passed shrouded dummies with garments hidden from her view. Piles of beautiful materials were on the shelves, because everything had been put away before the girls left for the evening, but she could smell the new cloth and the faint perfume in the air and felt tingling at her nape at the thought of working here.

'You mean you will give me a chance to work for you?' Betty could hardly contain her excitement as she looked at the tall thin man with his long straight hair and heavy glasses, behind which his intelligent eyes seemed to be larger than natural.

'Providing that you understand you must start from the bottom and earn your place here,' Mr Walter said. Walter Bonham's fashion house was a rising star in the rag trade, not yet a designer of the first rank, but an exclusive range that wealthy women in their middle years loved to acquire and wear. 'You will not be a designer for some time, perhaps never in this establishment. If you choose to work for me, I shall teach you how I like things done and expect you to forget your old habits . . . do you wish to accept that my word is law here?'

Betty didn't hesitate. She knew only too well that she had much to learn. It was what she wanted, and she would have worked for him for nothing, but the wage he offered was the same as she was getting working with Romany – three pounds and fifteen shillings a week.

'It would be a privilege to learn from you, sir.'

'Mr Walter if you please – and you will be Miss Winters until we know you better. Our customers often come to us for bespoke clothes – based on our new lines but made to measure and with small changes. Always remember the rules of correct address if you are called into the changing rooms to assist with fitting . . .'

'Yes, Mr Walter.'

'Good,' he smiled at her and then at Romany. 'I have to thank you for bringing me a girl with talent. I am surprised you did not wish to keep her with you?'

'Betty's flair is for clothes not hats, though she is an excellent seamstress and we thought something more suited to her talents . . .'

'Your loss is my gain,' he said, beaming at them. 'Miss Winters, I need you here at eight in the mornings and your immediate supervisor is Miss Elaine Robson – you will meet her next Monday. And now I have another appointment . . .'

Finding themselves dismissed, Betty grinned at Romany as they left the workshops. 'He knows his own mind, doesn't he?'

'I believe he's a bit of a tartar to work for, and don't make the mistake of calling Miss Robson, Miss Elaine,' Romany warned. 'That's his privilege not yours – but it's probably the best place you could choose to learn your craft, love.'

'I'm so thrilled he's given me a chance,' Betty said and hugged her arm. 'Thank you for recommending me – and I shan't let you down, I promise.'

'There's someone on the phone for you, Betty,' Aunt Miriam said as she came into the sitting room later that evening. 'He didn't tell me his name . . .'

'Oh . . . all right . . .' Betty frowned as she went into the hall to answer the call and wondered who would be ringing at this hour. She wasn't sure whether Mr Walter had this number or not and couldn't think who else it might be.

'Betty?' a voice she knew sent shivers down her spine. 'How are you, my little deceiver?'

'What do you want? How did you get this number?' Betty asked. 'After what you did, I can't believe you have the cheek to call me . . .'

'Oh, I'm going to do more than that,' Pierre said in a tone that made her tremble. 'You cheated me, Betty, and you owe me. One of these days I'm going to collect . . .'

The phone went dead, leaving Betty feeling chilled and apprehensive. Pierre couldn't really be threatening her? Yes, she'd switched glasses, causing him to suffer the effects of the foul drug he'd prepared for her, but surely he couldn't be so vindictive that he would pursue her to London to get his revenge? Of course he'd known that she often visited Aunt Miriam when he was here in the summer, and it hadn't taken him long to find her. He was evil and she mustn't forget what he'd planned for her that night in Paris. She felt a trickle of fear because she had no idea what to do. If her father had been well . . . but he wasn't and she couldn't tell her mother or her sister or even her aunt, because it would mean confessing the whole story and there was no one she dare tell . . . unless maybe she could talk to Matt . . .

They'd been brought up almost as brother and sister and he might just understand . . . and yet if he looked at her with disappointment or disgust it would be more than she could bear. No, she must keep it to herself and pray that Pierre was just trying to frighten her.

'Who was it, love?' Aunt Miriam asked when Betty returned to the sitting room.

'I'm not sure,' Betty lied. 'The line was a bit crackly. I couldn't hear properly. It might have been one of my friends from Paris . . .'

'Oh . . . I could hear perfectly,' her aunt said, looking puzzled. 'Never mind, if he wants to talk he will ring again . . .'

'Yes, I expect so,' Betty picked up her sketch-book, looking at her latest drawings of an evening gown.

She groaned as the front door knocker sounded, a feeling of fear shooting through her. It couldn't be Pierre, could it? He wouldn't dare to come here . . .

'I'll go,' Aunt Miriam said. 'I'm about to make a cup of chocolate . . .'

Betty was apprehensive as she heard the male

voice and then her aunt opened the door and admitted someone into the room, before leaving them to go off and make their drink. She gave a sigh of relief as she saw it was Frank.

'Frank,' she said, standing up to greet him. 'What made you come round this evening?'

'I wanted to make sure you're all right, ask after your family . . .' Frank said and the look in his face was concerned and caring. Betty's heart caught with pain, because she liked him so much and she didn't want to hurt him. 'You seemed so upset the other night – and if that was my fault, I want to apologise.'

'Of course it wasn't, Frank,' Betty said. 'You know I like you – but . . .' she stopped and shook her head. If only she could confide in Frank, but no – she couldn't tell him yet.

'I know you don't love me the way I love you,' Frank said, his eyes never leaving her face, 'but that doesn't mean we can't go out together, does it? I've got tickets for a dinner and dance for my firm. I'd love you to come with me, Betty.'

Betty hesitated, but then realised that unless she was going to lock herself away it was the best thing she could do. She wasn't in love with Frank, but knew she might never love anyone. Pierre had destroyed her trust – and yet she trusted Frank.

'Yes, all right,' she said and smiled shyly. 'When is it for?'

'A week on Saturday,' Frank said. 'I'll pick you

up and bring you home, Betty. It's just as friends . . .'

Betty laughed, because at that moment he was looking at her with the eyes of a little puppy dog. She felt some of the fear and sadness caused by Pierre's phone call fall away.

'Friends? Yes, I can do that, Frank,' she agreed just as her aunt returned carrying a tray of milky chocolate drink with a jug and three mugs.

'I brought enough for you too, Frank,' her aunt said and set it down. 'Was it you trying to get through on the phone earlier? Betty had a call but she couldn't hear what he said . . .'

'No, not me . . .' Frank looked at Betty, who gave a little shake of her head. If Frank knew that Pierre had threatened her he would try to do something about it, and she didn't want him to get hurt.

For a moment Betty longed for her father to be well and strong and on her side. She was certain that Sebastian would've sorted this out, but of course she couldn't tell him either, because he was ill and the doctors were saying he mustn't have any stress . . . she might just have been able to tell Matt, but he hadn't been round to see her. Betty wondered why. Was he disgusted with her for going off to Paris with Pierre? The thought made her eyes sting with tears and once again she wished she'd never met the charming Frenchman.

'Thank you, Miriam,' Frank said and took his drink. 'How kind of you – it's just what I need on a chilly evening . . .'

'Well, it's only six weeks to Christmas now,' Aunt Miriam said, 'and the nights are very cold. It was good of you to come round to see us – how is your mother?'

'Very well,' Frank replied. 'I haven't seen her for a few weeks, but I phone most nights just to say hello . . .'

'What a good son you are,' she beamed at him. 'That's the sort you want, Betty, a good reliable man who always thinks of others . . .'

Frank raised his brows at Betty as Aunt Miriam turned away to pour the cocoa and it was all she could do to stop bursting into laughter. The last thing Frank wanted to be described as was a good reliable man . . . it was good to be with him and to forget for a while all the things that had hurt and frightened her . . .

CHAPTER 21

Francie had dressed simply in a pair of American-style jeans and a tight jumper that accentuated her firm breasts, choosing to wear a pair of high heels with the outfit. Her hair was swept back in a ponytail and she wore only a smear of pale pink lipstick, her face still a little tanned from the summer.

Some builders working near the magazine's offices whistled and called out as she passed, but Francie didn't turn her head. She wasn't interested in men – or at least not in any of the men she'd met thus far. She'd liked the grip who worked for *Styled* but she was too young to get serious about any man. Francie enjoyed going out with a group of friends to the café or youth club nights, and she missed going about with Betty, but her elder sister was often too busy.

The receptionist inside the impressive building put through a phone call and asked Francie to wait, which she did, sitting on a plastic-covered single chair that made her feel as if she would slip off if she breathed too deeply. The whole place was shiny and slippery with a lot of stainless steel and plastic everywhere.

After a few minutes a woman in a smart black dress, with a huge white collar that stood up at the back and framed her neck, and red high-heeled shoes, came towards her and introduced herself. 'I'm the editor's secretary,' she said, smiling in a way that made Francie think of a crocodile. 'Will you come up please, Miss Winters? Miss Arlene will see you in a short time . . .'

Francie glanced at her watch. She was on time, but it seemed as if the editor intended to keep her waiting. Perhaps she'd heard something about the way Francie's father had threatened the magazine with the law if they forced her to do anything she didn't like again.

Shown into an outer office with yet more plastic and steel, Francie perched on the edge of the uncomfortable settee and waited. Half an hour passed and no one came for her. She looked at her watch and then expectantly at a girl who came out, followed by another two girls. They looked at each other and giggled. Francie glanced at her watch again and then stood up. She was on the point of leaving when the door of the office opened and a woman came out. She was wearing a silver grey wrap-over dress that looked like haute couture and clung to her hips like a silken sheath, and she smiled at Francie.

'I'm so sorry to have kept you waiting, Miss

Winters,' she apologised. 'I was caught up in something – a load of pictures came through of another model and they are impossible to use. We've had to reschedule the whole magazine – and, as a matter of fact, we want to use some of your material again. We'd like to take a couple more shots today, at a studio nearby – and reuse some of the old stuff . . .'

'I'm not sure . . .' Francie was doubtful. 'Some of that stuff was very upsetting for my father . . .'

'Oh no,' the woman said and held out her hand. 'I'm Arlene. May I call you Francie please? I assure you we have no intention of using those particular photos. It was quite wrong of Kathy to force you into agreeing to that work when it was so obviously not appropriate for you . . .'

'My father was so angry,' Francie nodded agreement and followed her into an office where she was relieved to see there were more comfortable chairs and a small table with a coffee tray, as well as a large desk covered with lots of pictures. 'He didn't want me to do anything like that again . . .'

'Well, these are quite tasteful,' Arlene said. 'Just have a look at them. You have my word that we shan't use anything your father could object to . . .'

Francie looked and smiled. They were some of her favourite shots, taken of her wearing outer clothes for a trip to the zoo, and pictured her with various animals in the background, including one of her holding a koala bear.

'Oh, yes, I loved those,' she said. 'Even Dad couldn't object to them . . .'

'Then that will fill a big hole for us – and if you could pop round to the studio and have a couple taken there in a day dress and some designer jeans rather like your own . . . and if they turn out well we might just feature you on the cover . . .'

'Yes, all right,' Francie said, sucking in her breath, because she still wasn't sure her father would be very pleased about it, but she couldn't see anything wrong with just doing the odd shoot now and then, especially when it was harmless like the zoo pictures. 'Thank you – I'd love to . . .'

'Have you had a nice day with your friends?' Lizzie asked when Francie got in that evening. She noticed the colour in her daughter's cheeks from the fresh air. It was a cold November day but the sun was bright and the air crisp with frost, but that didn't explain the excitement in Francie's eyes. 'What did you do?'

'Oh, hung out with a few old friends, drank coffee and tried on some divine clothes,' Francie said. 'What about you, Mum?'

'I've been to see Romany and Ed,' Lizzie said. 'Everything is going well and I've got lots of ideas for next year's spring and summer lines . . . and visited your dad, of course'

'How is he?'

'A little better I thought . . . we just have to see the results of those tests . . .'

'Fingers crossed.' Francie gave her mother a hug and then started to set the table for two. 'I'm not very hungry this evening, can we just have salad?'

'Yes, of course, if you like . . .' Lizzie looked at her. 'It's no wonder you're so thin, darling. You never eat enough to keep a sparrow alive . . .'

'Cheep, cheep,' Francie said and flapped her arms. 'I'm thin because I was meant to be. If you want to know, I've had loads of coffee, two iced buns and a cream doughnut . . .'

'All that and you never put on an ounce . . .' Lizzie laughed and looked at her daughter a little enviously. 'If I sniffed a cream doughnut I'd balloon to size sixteen in an instant . . .'

'I bet you've hardly put on a pound since you had me . . . you're only a small twelve now . . .'

'I was . . .' Lizzie smiled and placed her hands lovingly over her tummy, 'but look again, darling, I'm already blooming, which means your brother is growing fast. Shall we just have a lovely fruit salad and not bother with much else . . .'

'Lovely,' Francie said. 'I'll do some work this evening, Mum . . .'

'Me too,' Lizzie agreed and looked anxious. 'You're not neglecting your coursework, are you?'

'No, of course not,' Francie said but didn't quite meet her eyes.

'Oh Francie . . .' Lizzie sighed. 'I know you enjoy meeting friends and having fun, and I'd never try to stop you, darling – but you must try to pass those exams. Your future might depend on it . . .'

Francie lay on the bed and looked through the back issues of *Styled* that Arlene had given her. She liked the magazine, and she'd liked Arlene, even if she had kept her waiting – but most of all she'd liked having her photographs taken by Michael.

He was so good-looking in his tight leather trousers and black silk polo . . . rather like James Dean, but less moody. He'd been so easy to work with and so complimentary.

'You were made for the camera; it adores you,' he'd said. 'You're a beautiful girl, Francie – and I do hope I get the chance to work with you again.'

He'd smiled at her when they'd finished. 'Good work, Francie,' he'd said. 'I hope we'll work together in the future . . .'

Finding some photos in the magazine, which had his name printed underneath, Francie looked at them and smiled. There was something special about his work and she felt pleased that he'd taken her pictures.

Sighing, she put the magazines back in her bag and went down to her studio. Perhaps she'd better have a go at some of the coursework Miss Honiton had sent her, though it didn't inspire her at all. Francie thought it stupid that she was required to do stuff she would never paint from choice. Her style was individual and surely it was better to

275

work at what she liked rather than force something that did not come naturally?

Oh well, she could splosh a few bits of paint about and have fun. If she returned to college soon she might be able to get away for a few days for that photo shoot in Cornwall, but after that she would have to think things through and decide what she really wanted to do, because if it was modelling, she need to talk to her father . . . and she couldn't do that until he was properly well again . . .

CHAPTER 22

'Why don't you ask Sebastian?' Gretchen inquired as her mother looked longing at the details from the estate agent that Saturday morning. 'You have the rent money for six months – we just need a loan to start . . .'

'He has done so much for us already,' Marianne said and frowned. 'We should need at least five hundred pounds to buy all the equipment and stock up with food and drink for the opening day and to keep us going for a while . . .'

'He promised to help us,' Gretchen insisted. 'You should remind him . . .'

'Yes, but that was two weeks ago,' Marianne reminded. 'He would contact us if . . . no, I cannot ask, Gretchen. Sebastian risked everything for our sakes. It would be wrong to demand more.'

Gretchen's face hardened. 'You are too soft, Mutti,' she said. 'Men lie too easily. He promised . . . you should tell him the perfect premises are available. My father saved his life – what is five hundred pounds for a life?'

'No, Gretchen,' Marianne replied sharply. 'You are too hard. I know you've suffered dearest, but we already owe Sebastian so much – we must wait and see whether he comes back to us . . .'

Gretchen shrugged and reached for her jacket. 'I shall be late for work . . .' she kissed her mother's cheek and went out, a little annoyed with her.

Sebastian had promised he would come to see them and make sure they were settled. He had not even telephoned since the day he brought her home – and he'd promised to let her know if Eric was safe. It seemed he'd just forgotten them. And to a girl who had been let down so many times by men that meant he didn't care about her or her mother. He'd just said things he didn't mean to please them.

Gretchen had found work at the café her mother cooked for but only washing up and she hated it. Her life was better in some ways than it had been, but she'd expected much more once she'd escaped to the West. The bitterness of years of misery surged inside her.

Why shouldn't they have a chance of a better life? Gretchen's thoughts hardened as she walked to work. If Sebastian kept his word she knew that they could make a go of the café they'd viewed on her half day from work. Gretchen would cook and help in the kitchens and they could have a girl to serve the customers – but they would be working for themselves, and she was tired of taking orders. Besides, she didn't like the way her boss had been looking at her recently. He hadn't laid a finger on her, but she sensed he was only waiting his chance and Gretchen wasn't prepared to be mauled or used; she'd had enough of that in the past.

She would ring Sebastian at home. His number was in her mother's book and she'd copied it down on to a scrap of paper. Going into the nearest phone box, she asked for the number and then inserted her money in the box. The phone rang three times before it was picked up.

'Hello,' a woman's voice said. 'May I help you?'

'Is Sebastian there?' Gretchen asked. 'It's important. I need speak with him urgently . . .'

'I'm afraid he's resting,' the woman said. 'Who is this please? Can I take a message?'

Gretchen hesitated, then, 'Please ask . . . no, don't bother . . .'

She replaced the receiver, pushed the button to get back the money she hadn't used and left the kiosk. It had been an impulse. Gretchen wouldn't have hesitated to ask for money if Sebastian had answered, but somehow she couldn't ask the woman if he would ring her . . . Marianne had told her he was married and it wouldn't be fair if that was his wife on the phone, because she might have thought Gretchen was his lover . . .

Besides, a part of her problem was that she was feeling worried over Eric. He'd risked a lot to get her away from the men who were holding her prisoner in that wretched place and, unused to kindness from men, Gretchen had thought he might care for her. She'd felt close to him and safe for the first time since she'd been taken from her family, and she couldn't quite get him out of her head. But she was foolish because the truth was that all he'd felt for her was pity.

She had her mother now and they had to stand on their own two feet and make a life together. Her mother was right, they couldn't ask Sebastian for more . . .

Lizzie stared at the phone receiver before replacing it. She wondered who that woman could have been. The voice was definitely not English . . . one of Sebastian's business contacts perhaps? Yet if that were the case, why hadn't she told Lizzie what was so important that she'd rung him at home?

Lizzie had contacted his manager at the fashion shop and the factory concerning his illness, and was pretty sure they would not have rung unless it was an emergency – but if that were the case the woman would have told her, surely?

Could she be the mystery woman in Sebastian's life?

Lizzie's throat tightened with anguish. If she was Sebastian's mistress she must be wondering why he hadn't contacted her – perhaps worried and in distress . . .

Lizzie tried to dismiss the call, but it wouldn't go away as she prepared a light lunch for herself and Sebastian. On his release from hospital, he'd been told to rest as much as possible and not to do any form of work for at least a month.

'His condition has been brought on by overwork and stress,' the doctor had told Lizzie in private. 'Although, I think this was just a warning and the tests show no lasting damage has been done, he must take it easy. He is fretting in hospital and so I am allowing him home, on condition that he sticks to a strict regime: rest, a sensible diet – and no stress. Keep him away from his work at all costs, Mrs Winters.'

Lizzie had agreed and so far Sebastian had been following the rules. She knew it wouldn't be long before he refused to stay in bed. She didn't intend to have Sebastian worried about anything – and even though the mysterious phone call played on her mind, she had no intention of asking him anything about it . . .

She was laying the table when he came down-stairs wearing a silk dressing gown over black and gold striped pyjamas. He was still such an attractive man. It wouldn't be surprising if a much younger woman had fallen in love with him. Lizzie's heart turned over as he smiled at her and sniffed the air in anticipation.

'Fresh salmon cooked in wine?' he asked, brows rising. It was a favourite of his, and Lizzie cooked it with green beans, creamed potatoes and a sauce, with a green salad as a side dish.

'Yes – are you hungry?'

'I am now,' he said, but she thought he was just

trying to please her. He ate very little these days and she sensed that his smile hid more anxiety than was good for him. 'Can we have wine?'

'The doctor said a small glass once a day,' Lizzie said. She watched him as he went to the refrigerator and took out a bottle of white wine, pouring it in to two small glasses. 'Lunch is ready now . . .'

Sebastian's gaze followed her as she dished up their meal. She was aware of him, sensing that he wanted her to say something but she couldn't because if she did she might demand to know who the mystery woman was – the woman her daughters had seen him kissing.

'Who rang just now?' Sebastian asked, giving her an odd look.

'Oh . . . just Romany,' Lizzie lied and avoided his gaze.

'Ah . . .' Sebastian nodded. 'Where is Francie?' he asked as he noticed that just two plates had been set. 'Isn't she joining us for lunch?'

'She had a letter this morning and said she wanted to meet someone in town. I think it may be a friend from college and they're going to have coffee and a sandwich somewhere . . .'

'Oh . . .' Sebastian tasted his salmon. 'Lovely. You're such a good cook these days, Lizzie. But you should have more help in the house – especially at the moment . . .'

'I feel wonderful,' she said and looked at him lovingly, wondering how she could even doubt his love for her. 'I was thinking we might have a little holiday somewhere warm once the baby is born, Sebastian – all three of us. Betty too if she would come, but I don't think she will. She's very angry with you for some reason . . .'

'Because I didn't meet her at the hotel as I promised,' he said. 'I'll have a talk with her and explain . . .' Sebastian hesitated, then, 'First there's something I have to tell you, Lizzie . . .'

'Do you think it's a good idea?' Lizzie said and started eating, then sipped her wine. 'It can wait until you're feeling better . . .' She ate a piece of the salmon. 'This is really nice. I bought it from the new Mac Fisheries . . .'

'Unfortunately, I can't put it off much longer,' he said and looked upset. 'You have the right to know, Lizzie . . .' He ate another piece of salmon and nodded. 'This is lovely, darling . . .'

Lizzie enjoyed her meal, watching as he ate slowly, clearly not very hungry despite his comments about her cooking. A chill went through her and she closed her eyes for a moment. Perhaps Sebastian was about to tell her that it was over and he wanted to be free – free to marry another woman.

'At least eat your lunch first . . .' she said, trying to put it off to the last moment. He ate a little more and then pushed his plate away, most of the food uneaten. 'Eat a little more, Sebastian, please . . .

'It was delicious, but it will take time to get my appetite back. Why don't we take our drinks into the sitting room? I want to be sure I have your attention.'

Lizzie's throat was tight with emotion. It had come at last and she did not know how she could bear it, but there was no putting Sebastian off when he got that determined look in his eyes.

She picked up her drink and followed him into the hall just as the telephone rang. Lizzie frowned as she answered it. If it was that woman again she would just put the phone down on her . . .

'Lizzie?' Aunt Miriam's frantic voice came over the phone. 'Is Betty with you?'

'No, isn't she with you?' Lizzie felt the fear tingling at the nape of her neck.

'She went to work yesterday morning as usual but she didn't come home last night. I didn't worry because I thought she might have gone out with Frank – that nice young man who came round and had hot chocolate with us . . . but I telephoned his number and there was no answer. They're supposed to be going to a dance this evening . . . you don't think they've run off together?'

'Has she taken any of her things?'

'Just the bag she always takes to work with her. I telephoned Romany and she said she was happy at work on Friday, talking about starting her new job with the fashion house next week . . . but a neighbour brought Betty's bag round this morning. She said she found it outside her house . . .'

'Oh no . . .' Lizzie's hand shook and she looked fearfully at Sebastian.

'What's wrong, Lizzie?' Sebastian took the receiver from her hand and barked into the receiver. 'What happened, Miriam – tell me from the beginning . . . I need to know anything unusual . . . anything that happened you didn't quite understand . . .'

'Betty didn't come home last night and her work bag was found outside my neighbour's house.' Miriam was silent for a moment, then, 'There was the odd phone call the night Frank came round to ask her to the dance,' she said slowly. 'A man with a French accent asked if Betty was here, but when she went to answer it she said the line had gone funny . . . at least that's what she told me . . .'

'Could she have run off with someone?' Sebastian demanded and Lizzie saw the cold anger in his face. 'Think Miriam! This is important . . .'

'No, I'm sure she hasn't. I know she was looking forward to the dance – and she was over the moon because she'd been offered a new job at that fashion house . . . she rang Lizzie about that . . .'

'What made you think the call was from a Frenchman?'

'Just the way he spoke – his English was good, but his accent sounded foreign to me . . .'

'I'm coming round there shortly,' Sebastian said. 'I want to look through her things – see if there are any clues . . .'

'Supposing Betty is staying over with a friend? She will be angry that I let you go through her stuff . . .'

'Then she should have let someone know where she is,' Sebastian said and put the phone down hard.

'Sebastian,' Lizzie said, looking at him anxiously. 'Don't get yourself into a state and please don't be angry with Betty. I don't believe that she has just run off. I am sure she wouldn't do this to us again . . .'

'Are you? Then why isn't she at home with us? Where is she?'

Lizzie bit her lip. 'I think something may have happened to her, Sebastian.' Before he could say anything, she said, 'Come and look at the picture Francie painted of her sister. I think it says more than I could in a thousand words . . .'

'What has a portrait got to do with Betty going off?'

Sebastian looked uncertain but followed her into Francie's studio. The weak wintry sun was slanting through the skylights drawing his eye to the easel but the picture there was covered, and Francie's tribute to her sister stood on a chair away from most of her other work.

'My God!' Sebastian stood as if turned to stone. Lizzie saw his face working with emotion. 'Is that really how Betty looks?'

'Not always. Sometimes she is happy and laughing, just the way she used to be – but Francie notices things most of us miss and once I'd seen this I could see it for myself. Betty is desperately unhappy about something . . .' Lizzie was trembling. 'I think something may have happened to her . . . Do you think that man could have come looking for her – the one she went off with before?'

Sebastian frowned. His first anger had evaporated and as he gazed at Francie's portrait of her sister, he remembered what he knew of Pierre Saint-Jacquez. Now his anger was directed another way . . . if that man had harmed his daughter he would kill him!

'Take a taxi and go round to Miriam's house,' Sebastian said. 'Have a look through Betty's things – if she comes back she would resent that less than if I did it. I've got some phone calls to make. I'll telephone the hospitals first and then some friends of mine . . .'

'Supposing she's lying somewhere . . . hurt . . .' Lizzie's face was wet with the tears she couldn't stop. 'Oh, Sebastian, I can't bear to lose her again . . .'

'You mustn't upset yourself, darling,' he said and put his arms about her, kissing her hair to comfort her, but she could feel the tension in him and knew that he was as anxious as she was for their daughter.

'Remember what the doctors said about you resting . . .' she reminded.

'I've done nothing but rest since,' Sebastian said grimly. 'Do you think I'm going to sit on my backside and take it easy when Betty might be in trouble? She's our daughter, Lizzie, and I'll do whatever I have to do to find her . . .'

CHAPTER 23

Francie stared at the letter that had arrived that morning. It was from the editor of *Vogue*, the most famous fashion magazine of them all in Francie's opinion, and they wanted to see her to discuss a series of fashions shoots.

You have a fresh new look about you, Miss Winters. We are looking for young models to bring a modern feel to our pages and you have been recommended to us by a photographer we use often. If you are interested, please come to our offices at eleven thirty on Thursday this week for an interview. We apologise for the short notice but we've only just learned that you might be available . . .

Francie put the letter down and picked it up again several times. How could she think of herself and her own career when her parents were both unwell – and worried about her sister?

She was anxious about Betty too. Her mother had told her that Betty had disappeared, but they weren't sure of the details. Aunt Miriam seemed to think she might have gone off with another boyfriend and that made Francie cross. How could Betty be so thoughtless? She must know that Mum and Dad had been out of their minds with worry the first time, so how could she do it again? It was so unfair that this should happen just now! Francie had thought everything would settle down and be all right once Betty was back home, but she'd gone off to live with Aunt Miriam and now she'd disappeared.

Francie still hadn't got over the moment when her father collapsed at her feet and she and Beth had had to rush him to hospital. She'd felt guilt over that, though she knew she hadn't done anything to make it happen – but he'd been angry over those pictures in the magazine, and now she was planning on doing yet more.

She felt consumed with guilt because her father had spent a lot of money on securing a place at the small but prestigious art college in Cambridgeshire for her.

Taking up *Vogue's* invitation would mean confessing to her father, and not only would he be angry, it might mean that she had to make her choice between art and modelling. If she threw up her life here to grab the chance of a career in photographic modelling it would be such a waste of her talent – and yet after her futile attempts at the coursework she'd been set she was uncertain – and she wasn't ready to make that decision yet. She would have to tell Vogue that for the moment she was committed elsewhere and see what happened about her scholarship . . .

Francie wondered if she really could consider herself an artist. Yes, she could paint a bit – and she thought the portraits of Betty and her father were special – but she understood that Miss Honiton would expect her to get good marks on the coursework and Francie knew her work wasn't up to standard. If she sent it in, as she'd been asked to do, she would fail and then all hell would break loose.

Francie had no choice but to send the coursework she'd actually done, though a lot hadn't even been attempted, because she'd been wrapped up in painting the portraits of her sister and father; she would just have to send them and hope they counted for something . . .

In the meantime she might as well go to the interview and hear what they had to say. She felt a surge of guilt as she wondered what had happened to her sister. Had Betty run away again or had something happened to her? A sudden feeling that her sister was in danger sent cold trickles down her spine and she was afraid for her. Something was wrong, she was sure of it. Betty wouldn't have done this to her mother at such a time, Francie knew she was sorry for the trouble she'd already caused, so there must be another reason for her disappearance.

'Oh Betty,' she whispered, and a tear trickled down her cheek. 'Please come home soon. I'm worried about you too and I don't want to upset Mum and Dad – but I can't help it. It might be selfish, but I want to be a model . . .'

Betty lay with her eyes closed. Her head was throbbing and her face felt sore where Pierre had slapped her, cutting her lip and making it bleed. He'd caught her unawares as she got off her bus, just a few yards from Aunt Miriam's and dragged her into his car. She'd fought him for all she was worth, scratching and biting, giving as good as she got, and that's when he'd punched her hard, making her head spin. Unable to resist any longer, she'd hardly been aware of the needle entering her thigh, but after that there was only blackness. Whatever he'd given her had knocked her right out, some kind of strong sedative she supposed.

It was morning now, because the light was filtering through the vertical-slatted blinds, and she felt sick. As the vomit rose in her throat, she rolled over to the side of the bed and vomited on the floor. The smell was vile and the taste bitter. She wiped her mouth and moved cautiously, putting her feet to the floor. Her first attempt to stand sent her crashing back on the bed as the dizziness swept over her, but Betty knew she had to get out of this house, wherever it was, because if she gave into the sickness and the feeling of lethargy the drug had left, she could only guess what Pierre would do to her this time. He meant to punish her for tricking him that night in Paris.

She remembered him calling her all sorts of horrible names when he'd grabbed her and bundled her into his car and she knew he was furious because she'd escaped him once. Unless she was just going to give in, she had to get out of here and fast!

It took Betty several attempts to stand upright and even when she managed it she felt woozy, but finally she was able to take a few steps without stumbling. The light was strengthening and she could see that the bedroom was large and well furnished, and there was a room leading off it with a toilet and a basin. Betty needed to relieve herself urgently, but was afraid that if she ran the water it would make a noise and alert Pierre to the fact that she was awake. She crept into the tiny bathroom but didn't use the flush or the taps, even though she longed to rinse her mouth.

The window in the bathroom was tiny and it would be impossible to get out that way even if she were foolhardy enough to try jumping, because she knew it must be some distance to the ground. In the bedroom the window blinds were fixed so that try as she might, she could not open them, letting in just enough light between the slats for her to guess that it must be at least mid-morning. She stood sideways, squinting through the narrow openings to try and make out where she was. It shocked her to discover that she could see only trees and fields. She must have been taken out of London, driven a long way by the looks of it, and brought to what she now thought might be a large three-storied country house.

A chill of fear went through her as she realised that she was in far more danger than she'd realised. If Pierre had only wanted to teach her a lesson, he would hardly have bothered to bring her out of London – much easier just to give her a good hiding and leave her in a dark alley . . . So why bring her here? Betty's mind worked frantically. Was she going to be forced to work as a prostitute – or worse still sold to someone overseas as a sex slave? No, that was too ridiculous for words. She smiled because she was letting fear take her over and there was no need for that – at least not while she remained in England. She'd outwitted Pierre once and there was no reason why she couldn't do it again – except that he wouldn't hesitate to drug her again . . .

She couldn't fight the powerful drug that he'd injected into her. If Pierre really hated her she would have little chance of escaping him . . . and yet she would rather he beat her to death than give into his threats and bullying.

Tears stung her eyes. If only she'd told someone about her fear of Pierre and what he'd tried to make her do perhaps someone would've looked out for her – prevented him grabbing her. She wished now she'd spoken to Frank or Matt, told them about the threatening phone call . . . A feeling of despair crept over her as she realised that she was trapped and there was very little she could do about it . . .

'Jack, thank you for coming,' Sebastian said, drawing him into his study. 'My daughter Betty is missing – and this time I don't think she went willingly . . .'

'I'm sure she didn't,' Jack said and gripped his shoulder. 'Believe me, I don't like this one bit . . . but the man we spoke of – Pierre Saint-Jacquez . . . I've done a bit more checking, going through our files and he's definitely in with a bad lot. From what I've learned he got into debt when he was in London, gambling out of his depth, and we believe that is when he got mixed up in all this, though he may have known Marcus Samoza previously. Samoza is believed to be of Turkish origin and wanted there for various crimes, but he's the man suspected of being behind the abduction of several young woman. He's part of a gang operating internationally and once they get the girls they disappear for good . . . one was found with her wrists cut in a quiet English country hotel, but we think she probably did that to herself rather than give in to them . . .'

Sebastian blenched. 'You don't hold out much hope then . . .'

'Normally, I would say expect the worst, but one of our agents reported seeing Pierre Saint-Jacquez in London a few days ago . . . if he has taken Betty he will have spirited her out of the city.'

'Have you any idea where?'

Jack shook his head. 'I wish to God I did – our only hope is that one of my agents has spotted him leaving London and followed, which I have to admit is unlikely.'

'Then what can I do?'

'Really, there's nothing you can do except pray,' Jack said. 'Even if I knew their location . . . well, it's going to take a special team to get her back, Seb. They are evil devils and they will have her drugged . . . it may even be too late in terms of what they've done to her . . .'

'It will kill Lizzie if anything like that happens to Betty.'

'You don't look so good yourself, my friend. Believe me when I say I am more sorry than I can tell you . . . we should have rooted these men out long ago, but they're like a rotten canker that spreads insidiously through the blood, their influence penetrating even into high places . . .' He gripped Sebastian's shoulder. 'I swear to you that I'll do everything within my power to find her . . .'

'If I ever find him I'll kill him . . .'

'Just let me know and I'll do it for you,' Jack smiled grimly. 'If I had proof I would take an extermination squad in and shoot the lot of them . . .'

'I just wish I knew where she was . . .'

Betty froze as she heard the sound of a key in the lock. Someone was coming at last and this was her chance. Her fingers tightened around the heavy glass vase that stood on the dressing table. As the door opened slowly, she tensed, ready to spring, and when Pierre walked in she flung herself on him, hitting him with her weapon and cutting his right temple so that the blood trickled down his face. However, her blow merely wounded him, making him react like an injured animal. He grabbed her by the throat, his fingers tightening so that she could scarcely breathe as he lifted her from the ground with his brute strength and what she saw in his eyes filled her with terror. He hated her and there was such viciousness, such evil there that she finally understood that she'd never known this man at all. It dawned on her then that every move he'd made had been calculated to make her fall for him so that when the time came she would do exactly as he chose – only she'd defied him and that had made him angry.

She was gasping for breath as he slammed her back against the wall, his face close to hers as he spat at her. 'You little she-cat,' he hissed. 'If you'd shown as much spirit when we lay together I would have kept you. I'd punish you for that – but you're too valuable to me.' His lips drew back in a sneer. 'He's mad to have you and he'll pay what I want, my little spitfire . . .'

'Who is – what are you talking about?'

'A man I know,' Pierre leered at her, running a finger down between her breasts. 'He'll pay me for you – something that I want more than you can possibly imagine . . .'

'My father would pay you to let me go,' Betty said. 'Why don't you sell me to him rather than that pig – whoever he is?'

'He might pay my gambling debts perhaps, but do you imagine your father could give me a contract that will make me famous and earn me a fortune? My friend is going to build a large complex of luxury apartments in Paris and, if I give him you I get the contract as the architect. After that I'll have them queuing at my door . . . all those businessmen who laughed in my face and wouldn't even grant me an interview . . . they'll be begging me to work for them after I get this contract.' Pierre laughed as he let go of her and watched her slump to her knees. 'If I give him you and any other girl he wants in the future he will look after me, if not . . .' He made a slashing sign across his throat. 'He's ruthless. He would kill me if I crossed him and I owe him money. He owns me just as he'll own you. You'll wish you were dead long before he's finished with you, believe me.'

'Let me go, Pierre, I beg you . . .'

'He'd kill me then. If he were in England, you would already be with him on the way to his home in . . . well, best not to say. Your new owner is away on business so I have to keep you here until he gets back . . .'

Betty lifted her head defiantly. 'I won't let him touch me. I'll fight until the death . . .'

'If he weren't so influential I'd oblige you,' Pierre

said. 'I wouldn't mind making your wait more pleasurable if you wanted to oblige me . . .'

'Go to Hell!' she said, her temper flashing. 'You're evil and you deserve to burn forever . . .'

He laughed in amusement. 'Such a pity you didn't show me this side of you before it was too late, darling. You were so easy, falling into my arms like a ripe peach from the tree.'

'I hate you . . .'

'You will hate me more before he lets you die,' Pierre said, turned and walked to the door before looking back at her. 'Be careful, Betty. I could give you food and drink . . . or I could just let you suffer from thirst. It will be a few days before he gets here. It's up to you how you spend them . . .'

Betty bent her head as the door was locked after him. Tears slipped down her cheeks, because she didn't know what to do. Defiance only made Pierre angry and she didn't have the strength to fight him for long, because he could easily overpower her – and there was always the needle.

Her only escape from an unbearable fate was death.

The man watched the house. He'd waited in the shadows of the dilapidated outbuildings as they day progressed, fretting as he tried to work out his best chance of getting her out of there. Three men had been there earlier. One had opened the door to Pierre and another had come out to put the car away. Two of them had recently left in the car – which by his reckoning meant that only Pierre was still in there.

They were miles away from London. He'd followed them for hours as they drove relentlessly through the night and the early morning. He wasn't sure where they were but he'd seen a sign for Herefordshire and knew they couldn't be too far away. He had family on the borders and it was in his mind that if he could get Betty free from her captors she would be safe there.

It had to be his best chance. He wished for a weapon but had found none lying around. If he'd dared to leave his position he would have telephoned for help, but he knew that to do so might result in the girl being spirited away elsewhere and then they would never find her.

During the early hours he'd scouted round the place, looking for his best chance of entering and getting to the room in which he believed she was being held. And if his reckoning was right the other rogues were entering and leaving without locking the back door of the house – so confident that they'd got away with it that they'd become careless.

He moved silently for a large man, holding his breath as he tried the door and found it opened easily to his touch. So far so good . . . but he needed a weapon because Pierre wasn't going to let him just walk in and take her.

Taking a chance, he snapped on the light and found himself in the kitchen, as he'd expected. He glanced round hoping for a poker or something metal and heavy, but the only thing he could see was a carving knife. It was better than nothing, though he hadn't wanted to kill – but he would rather do that than leave this house without her.

He seized the knife just as the kitchen door opened and the man he sought walked in.

'That you, Rich . . .' Pierre started to say and then swore furiously as he saw and recognised him. 'Damn it! 'Ow the 'ell did you get here?' His eyes narrowed. 'I know you – you attacked me in Paris . . .'

'I should've killed you then . . .'

'Why you no do it?' Pierre taunted, seeming unsure whether to attack or run.

'Because I wasn't sure then – but now I am. I saw you drag Betty into the car and what you did to her, but before I could get near enough to try to help her, you drove off with her.' His eyes glittered with cold anger. 'So I followed you here and I waited. I know you're alone and I intend to take her from you . . .'

Pierre laughed, genuinely amused. 'What can you do? You had your chance with her at the start but she wanted me – and now she's going to pay for defying me.'

'You've got her upstairs, locked in no doubt. Where is the key? I'm asking you nicely – give it to me or I'll take it and you'll be sorry . . .'

'Come and get it . . .' Pierre laughed as he patted his waistcoat. 'Do you really think you can frighten me?'

The man lifted the knife and moved towards him, intent in his every move. He saw doubt in Pierre's eyes for the first time and smiled.

'Wishing you'd got some of that drug you gave Betty to hand?' he mocked, taunting him as he'd sometimes taunted the men he'd fought on the rugby field at college. 'Come on then . . . or aren't you as brave when you're dealing with a man rather than a vulnerable girl?'

Pierre lunged and they wrestled for the knife, which clattered to the floor. Pierre hit out wildly, but he was no match for the strength of the man that faced him and he didn't see the move that had him on his back on the floor, but his hand touched the knife and he scrambled for it desperately, as the man threw himself on top of him and they tumbled over and over, fighting for possession of the weapon. For some seconds the fight was desperate and furious with neither man gaining the advantage, but then Pierre had the knife in his hand and he struck out, but a strong hand gripped his wrist twisting it back until the blade was pointing towards his body rather than his opponent's. Suddenly, the knife touched flesh and one last effort pushed it in . . . deliberately, intentionally, deep into Pierre's side, making him go limp and shudder as he fell back, blood pouring as he slipped into a semi-conscious state.

The man, who had beaten him, searched frantically for the key and found it. One glance at Pierre's body twitching told him that he was probably dying; the blood seeping in a flood from the deep wound to his side. A feeling of horror and shock went through him as he realised he'd killed a man, but then he lifted his head, a look of satisfaction entered his eyes as he left the kitchen, walking through to the hall. Saint-Jacques deserved to die for what he'd done. He could see the stairs and took them two at a time, his athletic prowess making him swift, uncaring of the cuts to his hand where the knife had scored him during his battle to possess it.

He inserted the key and unlocked the door – and then he saw the girl huddled on the bed; she had curled up like a foetus in the womb, looking vulnerable and wretched, and in that moment he hoped with all his heart that the man he'd left bleeding on the floor died of his wounds for what he'd done.

'Betty,' he said softly. 'It's all right, love – you'll be safe now . . .'

She turned and stared at him incredulously, a cry of relief escaping her. 'Oh thank God! Thank God . . . Frank – is that really you? How did you get here? How did you find me?'

'Never mind about that,' he said and smiled at her grimly. 'I've dealt with that devil Saint-Jacquez, but there are two others and they could be back at any moment. We have to get away from here now . . .'

'Yes, he'll kill me if he comes back,' Betty said and rolled over, scrambling off the bed and stumbling towards him. He moved to catch her, holding her steady as she fell into in his arms. Tears were pouring down her face and she was shaking from head to foot. 'Oh, Frank, Frank . . . I'll never be able to thank you enough for this . . .'

He took a firm hold of her arm, supporting her down the stairs, because she was almost in a state of collapse, but taking her straight out of the front door, which he had to unbolt but preferring the short delay to exposing her to the sight of Pierre lying in a pool of his own blood in the kitchen.

There was no sign of Pierre's accomplices returning as Frank hurried her from the grounds and down a narrow country lane to the field gate where he'd parked his car. He opened the door, helped Betty inside and told her to crouch down.

'Just until we get clear of this place,' he said. 'I don't want them following us if they come back.'

Betty ducked her head as they saw a car approaching. The tears had stopped now, as if the seriousness of their situation had just hit her. Frank turned off into a farmyard entrance and stopped, waiting until the other car had disappeared before pulling back into the lane and putting his foot down hard on the accelerator.

'That was them; I think they're probably Turkish, or some kind of Middle-Eastern descent anyway,' he told Betty. 'It won't be long before they discover what's happened and they will have seen the car. I'm going to have to drive fast for a while. You might as well sit up now – and hold on, because it won't be comfortable . . .'

Betty held her breath as Frank's car bumped along the rough country road. The motion made her feel sick and her heart was banging against her ribs in fright, though she tried not to cry out or give way to tears. If they came after her and . . . But she couldn't think about that, because she knew they would kill Frank and her. They had to get away! Oh please God, don't let those men catch up with them! Her heart was racing wildly and she could scarcely breathe in her terror, yet she resisted the urge to look over her shoulder and was relieved when at last they reached a main road. When they came to a crossroads, Frank paused for an instant, but then took the opposite road to the one marked London.

'Where are we going?' she asked him, still a little in awe of the man who had rescued her, because she'd worked out what he'd done. 'You saw Pierre grab me and followed him all the way here, didn't you?'

'Yes,' Frank shot a brief smile at her. 'I'm sorry I wasn't quicker coming in for you, Betty, but I wasn't sure I could handle three of them, because I knew they would be armed – and I was afraid to leave in case they took you somewhere else. I didn't have time to stop and let anyone know what was happening. If I'd lost him God knows if we would ever have found you.'

'You wouldn't . . .' Betty swallowed hard to stop

the tears. She hadn't cried when Pierre hit her, but now she was feeling ridiculously vulnerable and weak. 'He was selling me to someone . . . I would have been taken off to some far-flung place and . . .' She shook her head. 'No, I'm not going to think about it – it didn't happen, because of you, Frank, and I'll never be able to repay you.'

'Why should you? I feel partly responsible for what happened to you, Betty. I'd heard that Saint-Jacquez was mixed up with some pretty nasty people, but I didn't believe it. I tried to keep you away from him, but I should've told you all I knew at the beginning . . .'

'Would I have listened?' Betty asked with a wry smile. 'I wanted excitement and adventure – well, I got more than I bargained for, but I've learned my lesson.'

His gaze was loving and generous and Betty's throat closed with emotion. She didn't know what she felt just now other than relief and gratitude.

'Why had you come round to Aunt Miriam's last night?' she asked. 'It was a chance in a million that you should be there to see what happened. . . .'

'Our dance had been cancelled,' Frank said. 'One of the directors was rushed into hospital and unfortunately died on the operating table. His death was such a shock that it was decided to postpone the evening for a few months. No one wanted to celebrate. I didn't want to just phone about something like that so I came round . . .'

Betty looked at him soberly. Had a man not died

in such tragic circumstances Frank would not have been there when Pierre had taken her and she would still be a prisoner in that house. She could only be thankful that her friend had come to tell her the sad news, but she couldn't rejoice because it was too distressing.

'Mind you,' he said, sensing her mood. 'I might have come anyway, because I like seeing you, and your aunt made me so welcome . . .'

'I can only say I am sorry that a man died, but I'm so glad you were there, Frank – but what made you follow me? Why didn't you just go to the police?'

Frank glanced at her, unsmiling. 'Do you think I would leave your safety to chance, Betty? I wasn't sure if I could get you away from him, but I thought my best opportunity would be to watch and wait . . . I knew I had to get him alone. Perhaps I should've tried to drive him off the road, but you might have been killed in the accident – and if I'd come off worst he would still have you . . .'

Betty nodded, her relief at being rescued had faded and she was aware that she might have died – and so might Frank. She saw the cuts and dried blood on his hands.

'How were you cut?'

'There was a knife . . .' Frank hesitated, then, 'I think I may have killed him, Betty. We struggled for the knife, but I was stronger . . . I was into all kinds of sports, including rugby and wrestling . . . and rowing, of course.'

Betty looked thoughtful. 'Is that why you and Matt were such good friends, because of the rowing?'

'It's how we became friends at college, but we liked each other – and then he took me home and I met you . . .' His gaze was warm now as he glanced her way. 'I shamelessly cultivated his friendship after that, I'm afraid . . .'

'Don't be sorry,' Betty said. 'I owe my freedom and my life to you . . .'

'You owe me nothing,' he said. 'I would have helped any girl in trouble – but when you care about someone you go that little bit further.'

Betty nodded, thoughtful again, but knowing he didn't want excessive thanks or praise for what he'd done. 'Are you taking me home?'

'No, we're going to my grandparents' farm in Herefordshire on the borders between England and Wales,' he said. 'We're already halfway there, because Saint-Jacquez wanted you well away from London. Those thugs will expect us to return to London as fast as we can, so we'll go somewhere they would never think of searching.'

She considered his words and nodded assent. 'I think Pierre hated me and wanted his revenge – but his friend might try again . . .'

'I think Pierre is the main threat, because the others will lie low for a while – especially the fat spiders in their webs of filth, but I'm not sure Saint-Jacquez is dead. While he lives you can't be safe.'

'We'll have to ring my parents and tell them I'm with you . . .' Betty looked thoughtful. 'I don't want them worried again – and Dad knows people . . . he did secret things in the war and I think he still does. As soon as we get the chance we should telephone him.' She looked at Frank in sudden fear. 'Will you be in trouble for what you did, Frank? If Pierre is still alive and tells the police you attacked him . . .'

'As he might,' Frank admitted, because it was partly true. 'I'll face that if it comes, Betty. But I don't regret it – I'd rather go to prison than know I let him take you . . .'

'Oh Frank . . .' Betty said and the tears ran down her cheeks. She was helpless to stop them, because his declaration of love could never have been more powerful. 'I really don't deserve such devotion. I went to Paris with him the first time of my own free will. I slept with him, Frank. I thought I loved him . . . because I was a stupid fool . . .'

Frank pulled into a layby. She saw there was a red phone box, even though it seemed they were miles from anywhere. For a moment he just sat and looked at her, and then he reached out and wiped the tears from her face with his fingertips.

'Don't you know that I care too much to judge you for that?' he asked softly. 'I loved you the first moment I saw you and I thought you perfect – and I still do. I always shall . . .'

Reaching for her, he held her close as she wept against his chest, but then, as the sobs stopped at last, he put her from him and smiled oddly. 'Don't you think we'd better make use of that phone box? There are a few other people that love you too . . .'

'Yes,' Betty gulped and scrubbed the back of her hand across her eyes. 'You tell them what happened, Frank – and then I'll speak to my mother for a moment . . .'

'Come on then,' he said. 'I want you in there with me. I don't think those men will come this way, but just in case . . .'

CHAPTER 24

'Who is this speaking?' Sebastian barked as he snatched up the receiver and heard money being put in to operate the public phone box.

'My name is Frank Hadley and I'm ringing to let you know that Betty is safe now . . .'

'What the hell do you mean by running off with my daughter?' Sebastian exploded furiously. 'I'll have the police on you – she's only eighteen and you don't have my consent to take her or marry her . . .'

'Please listen, Mr Winters,' Frank said patiently. 'Betty was kidnapped by Pierre Saint-Jacquez. I saw it happen and followed. I regret I couldn't let you know sooner but I was afraid of losing them . . .'

'What . . .?' Sebastian was stunned. 'You're the young man who was taking her to a dance . . . how do I know I can trust you?'

'I've just come from the village of Upper Piddlington. It's in Oxfordshire, a tiny hamlet about fifty miles or so from Oxford, and probably not on most maps. There is a large house about three miles outside the village and down a long country lane. You'll know the house when you find it, because there are three stories and it looks a bit run-down . . . and there are black shutters on the upper windows . . .'

'Well, what of it?' Sebastian had calmed down a little, his tone wary now.

'Pierre Saint-Jacquez is lying on the kitchen floor with a carving knife in his side . . . I'm not sure if he's dead. I was in too much of a hurry to get Betty away to check . . .'

'You killed him?'

'Yes, I'm afraid it was the only way . . . otherwise I'd be in his place and Betty wouldn't be free . . .' Frank hesitated. 'Do you think I should make an anonymous call to the police?'

'No! That would be the worst thing you could do – it would put you both at risk of being arrested for murder. You can leave this to me, Frank. I'll take care of it . . .'

'But, you could be in trouble . . .'

'Believe me, I know what to do – just get my daughter home and I'll do the rest . . .'

'I'm taking her to a safe place – somewhere they won't think of looking . . . until we're sure it's safe to bring her home. There are others involved in this business; Betty told me what that rotten devil threatened to do with her . . . and believe me, she can't come home yet.'

'May I speak with her for a moment please?'

'Yes, of course . . .'

Sebastian waited and then Betty's voice came over the line, she sounded contrite and shaken, 'Dad . . . I'm sorry to have caused so much upset . . . can I talk to Mum?'

'She isn't here, Betty, but come home now, please. I promise you'll be safe . . .'

'I can't, not yet. I've made such a mess of everything . . . hurt everyone . . .' she was crying and it tore at his heart.

'It's my fault, Betty. I hurt you and I was wrong – please ask Frank to bring you home to us . . .'

'Not yet, Dad, because there are others who might try to take me,' Betty said. 'Frank says it might not be safe for me in London yet, because they will be afraid I know too much about them and what they do. He's going to take me somewhere I'll be safe for a while . . . but I'll ring you and Mum as soon as I can. We have to go now just in case we're being followed . . .'

'Betty, wait a—' Sebastian frowned as the receiver went down. It was no use trying to get them back, because it was just a phone box and they wouldn't hang around. He'd wanted to tell them she would be safe with him and that he had friends who would make sure of it, but Betty preferred to trust the man who had somehow managed to save her.

He could only thank God for Frank Hadley and pray that he was as reliable as he'd sounded. Of course there was one way to check and that was to discover if there was any sign of Saint-Jacquez lying on the floor of that country house. If Frank had killed for Betty's sake he would need help to avoid the consequences and the only person who could arrange that was Jack.

Sebastian reached for the telephone and rang the number he'd used often in the past. Jack answered and he gave him the details as he'd been given them.

'Not much to go on . . .'

'We'll find it,' Jack said and then, before Sebastian could say it, 'Not you, my friend. You'd best stay out of this . . . she didn't tell you where this Frank was taking her?'

'No, just that it was a place where she would be safe.'

'He sounds like a sound man,' Jack observed wryly. 'Leave it with me, Seb. And be careful with what you tell anyone else . . . the quieter this is kept the better for all of us . . .'

'Yes, I agree,' Sebastian said grimly. 'Don't worry, I'll think of something to tell her mother . . .'

'So Betty was in danger but she isn't now?' Lizzie stared at him and her heart caught with fright. 'Oh, Sebastian, are you sure? Where is she?'

'She's with a man called Frank Hadley. Do you know much about him?'

'He's a good friend of Matt's,' Lizzie said, looking thoughtful. 'Beth said they met at her house in the early days and sometimes they went out as a group, but he took Betty out a few times as a couple . . .

Miriam said he was at hers the other night and she thinks he's serious about Betty . . .'

'That's nonsense,' Sebastian said. 'She hardly knows him – and she's been through too much to want to settle down, even if he did save her life . . .'

'Miriam was positive about his feelings, but she didn't mention Betty's. I personally don't think she's in love with him, and I certainly shan't let her be pushed into marriage out of gratitude – but if he cares about her it means she'll be safe with him, don't you think? She needs a friend and marriage must be a long way from her thoughts just now. I'm sure Frank is sensible enough to know that . . .'

'He'll look after her then. He managed to snatch her while the man who took her wasn't looking and she's going somewhere she'll be safe with him.'

'Who is this man, Sebastian? I need to know the truth.'

'The truth is that Frank has her safe and the rest of it is being taken care of. Believe me, Lizzie; it's best for everyone's sake that you don't know all of it . . .'

'I know there's a lot you haven't told me,' Lizzie said reproachfully. 'In the war I understood because your work was secret and . . .' She broke off, looking at him in suspicion. 'Is this what all this is about? Did Betty see something she wasn't supposed to – is that why she was kidnapped?'

'I have no idea what you mean,' Sebastian looked

314

angry. 'I assure you that I had nothing to do with Betty's abduction . . .'

Lizzie gazed at him and then nodded. 'I'm sorry, but you come and go so mysteriously at times and I've wondered . . .'

Sebastian sighed and took her arm, guiding her to an easy chair and sitting her down. He sat on a stool next to her, looking at her intently.

'I wanted to tell you a long time ago, Lizzie, but it was difficult . . .'

'If there's someone else I'd rather you just tell me . . .'

Sebastian frowned, seeming bewildered. 'What's all that about? You wanted to know about my secret work and I haven't been able to tell you, but it's over now and providing you're discreet I can tell you . . .'

'There isn't anyone else in your life . . . a younger woman?'

'Lizzie?' He stared at her, an odd smile on his lips. 'Where did you get that from . . . did someone see me with Gretchen?'

'Gretchen . . .' Lizzie's heart caught and yet Sebastian's eyes were alight with mischief. He wouldn't look at her like that if he was having an affair. 'It doesn't matter who saw you, I think you'd better tell me the whole story . . .'

'It started again soon after the war ended. I thought it would be just once,' he said and shook his head, 'but I should've known better. Once they get you they don't let go. I was travelling abroad and often for my business – and so they thought I could be of use to them . . . our masters, as Jack calls them. Of course he's one of them really and always has been . . . I've been working for a branch of the Secret Service, Lizzie, and I just broke my oath by telling you that . . . but I think you've always known anyway.'

'I knew it was what you did in the war – but I thought you'd finished with all that . . .'

'Jack got me involved again – and he was a good friend of mine long before the war started . . . I suppose I should've said no, but the things they told me made me feel I wanted to help get people out . . . there isn't a wall in Berlin yet, Lizzie, but the way things are going there will be in the next year or so. The poor devils that are trapped in the Russian sector are desperate to get out; a lot of them make it, but others die in the attempt – either with a shot in the back and an unmarked grave or in a cell forgotten by the world . . . men and women who offend by speaking out simply disappear or are imprisoned . . .'

Lizzie nodded, because she could understand that her husband might feel passionately about such things. He was an honourable man, an honest man, and if he gave his word he kept it . . .

'There really is a Jack then? I went to the address you gave me once during the war. A woman said she was Jack . . . she said there were a lot of them . . .'

'In the war, yes,' Sebastian agreed, 'but you were

meant to see the real Jack, my friend. He got me involved in all this, and I agreed to help them get people they needed out of the Eastern Sector of Germany . . . sometimes important men, sometimes young children, families of people who had defected to us or been lost during the war . . .'

'That must have been dangerous . . .'

'I shan't lie to you, darling. Sometimes it was straightforward; we'd be given passes for them as part of an exchange agreement. But sometimes it wasn't quite like that – and getting Gretchen out was harder than I'd imagined.'

'So she came from East Germany?'

'Yes.' Sebastian hesitated, then, 'I brought someone else out – or at least to the Swiss border. I can't tell you about him, because I don't know – except that we need him here and someone else wants him dead . . .'

'What happened to him?'

'He crossed the border himself. I brought Gretchen through and she's in London with her mother. Marianne was married to Karl, a good friend of mine when I was studying in Germany some years before the war . . .'

Lizzie nodded, because he'd told her a little about that part of his life long ago, but she'd always known there was more he wasn't telling her.

'Karl was tried for war crimes and shot by the Russians soon after the war ended.' Sebastian looked grim. 'He was forced to work by the Nazis to keep his wife and child safe, but Marianne

317

escaped soon after the peace and Karl was to follow with Gretchen, but they came and took her away – and they arrested him . . . her life was in danger, Lizzie. You have to understand why I just went off, leaving Betty stranded the way I did. I put money in an envelope and told her to come home . . . but I know she was hurt . . . and I went back to tie up a few loose ends in Paris because there were things I needed to sort out. I thought Betty might have ignored my letter and still be there . . .'

So that was why he'd rushed back to Paris!

'Yes, she was hurt and I'm finding it difficult to accept that you put Gretchen before our daughter . . .'

'I was told I had to leave immediately or she might disappear for good this time. I didn't want to desert Betty, but I wasn't sure she would even come to the hotel – and I feared that if I delayed Gretchen would be killed . . . can't you accept that it was something I had no choice about?'

'There's always a choice, Sebastian, and if anything had happened to Betty you would never have forgiven yourself – and I don't think I could either . . .'

'Lizzie please, don't do this . . . it's hard enough knowing that I let you all down . . .' His face looked grey and she was suddenly overcome with fear, because he looked so ill.

'I'm so sorry,' Lizzie touched his hand. 'I do understand, Sebastian, and I know you thought you were doing the right thing. Did your friend's wife ask you to look for Gretchen?'

'Yes, when we met by chance. I've been searching for her for three years – but then Jack rang me and told me he might be able to help, but of course he wanted something in return . . . and when he rang me in Paris I'd arranged to meet Betty, but it was urgent that I leave at once and so all I could do was leave money and ask her to come home.'

'I understand,' Lizzie said, because it was all suddenly so clear to her. 'So you fetched Gretchen to join her mother – and you bought her some clothes from the shop of a friend and she kissed you to say thank you . . .' A tear trickled down her cheek as she realised that she'd worried for nothing; it was just Sebastian looking out for others as he always did. 'Thank you for telling me, Sebastian.'

'I always meant to,' he said, 'but it was difficult and then I had that little upset . . .'

Lizzie smiled through the mist of tears. 'Forgive me for doubting you.'

He reached out and took her hand. 'I should've told you before, but the work I've been doing is secret and I wasn't supposed to talk about it . . .'

'You know I shan't tell anyone,' Lizzie said. 'But surely you won't continue now?'

'No, I've given enough; it was almost the finish of me,' Sebastian told her ruefully. 'Jack understands. He won't ask again, but . . .' He shook his head. 'It's possible that I may still be involved even if I don't like it . . .'

'You mustn't let them draw you back in, Sebastian. You're not well enough. And I need you – your family needs you with us . . .'

'Unfortunately, that isn't all the bad news, Lizzie . . .'

'Betty is all right? You promise me?'

'Yes, this isn't anything to do with her – it's business. The factory has been losing money for a while. I should've sold long ago, but I hung on and hoped I could bring it round, because I didn't want to put good men and women out of work. I shall have to sell to cover my debts; there will be some left after the bills are paid, and the shop is holding its own, but . . . I promised Marianne and Gretchen a café of their own. They will need at least a thousand pounds to get them going and see them through the first few months. I asked for a contribution from our masters and Jack finally came up with half of it; I don't know whether he forced them to pay me something for the risks I took for them or if he gave me the money himself, but I took it for Marianne and her daughter's sake – but that means I have to give them five hundred, which is still a lot of money . . . Marianne will pay it all back when she can but that money should be yours and the girls . . .'

'Is that why Gretchen rang the house the other day?'

Sebastian's brows rose. 'She rang you?'

'She wanted to talk to you urgently – I imagine it was her, but she wouldn't tell me why she wanted you . . .'

'I'm sorry she did that,' Sebastian frowned. 'Marianne would never have permitted it had she known, but Gretchen . . . well, she's been through a lot . . .'

'Yes. I'm sure she has, poor girl. I understand better now that you've talked to me – and of course you must honour your promise,' Lizzie said, reaching out for his hand, 'and bring them both here. I'd like to get to know them and I might know some people in the trade who can help them get started. Perhaps it needn't cost quite so much if we use our influence with people we know . . .'

'You don't mind if I give them what they need from the sale of the factory?' Sebastian asked and took her hand, holding it tightly. 'I've got a customer and he's promised to keep the business going, but he will only pay for the stock and the machinery, which amounts to just under three thousand and I have some debts to pay . . .'

'You're sure we can't turn it around if we try?'

'Unfortunately, yes. I've tried everything I know – my customer is going to introduce much cheaper lines, though he says he will still produce a few dozen pairs of the handmade shoes for as long as he can sell them . . .'

'It's a pity, but I know how difficult it is to contend with cheap imports these days,' Lizzie agreed. 'We'll manage, Sebastian. I have my share of Lizzie Larch and you have the shop. We're comfortable and we have so much more . . . our daughters, friends, and now we have another little one to think of . . .' She placed her hands on her bump lovingly. 'It's all I need, Sebastian . . . all I want is for us all to be together . . .'

Francie knew as soon as she entered the house that something had happened. Her mother was singing as she prepared their evening meal and her father was just coming in from the garden, his boots muddy and he looked happy as he bent to unlace them.

'Should you be doing that, Dad?' she asked and knelt to help him off with the boots. 'I thought the doctor told you to rest?'

'Gardening relaxes me,' her father said. 'A spot of physical work never hurt anyone – but I didn't do anything too strenuous.'

'Good . . .' She looked at her mother. 'What's going on?'

'Betty is safe.' Her mother smiled at her. 'We don't know where she is but she's with a friend . . .'

'So she just ran off again?'

'No, it wasn't quite like that,' her father said. 'Betty was in trouble, Francie, but she was lucky. Frank Hadley saw what happened and went after her. He managed to get her away from the man that abducted her – and he's taken her somewhere safe . . .'

Francie sat down, feeling as if the air had been punched out of her. She'd been thinking it might be a good time to tell her parents that she wanted to put her art on hold and take up what looked as if it might be a wonderful career for her, but she couldn't upset them now.

'Betty is all right?' she croaked, her throat tight with emotion. 'He didn't hurt her – this man?'

'Not that we've been told – but your mother and I have been thinking about you, Francie. It isn't likely, but there is a faint possibility that these people might try to take you in retaliation . . .'

'No, why should they?' Francie stared in disbelief. 'How can they even know I exist?'

'Perhaps they don't, but we think you'd be safer back at college,' her mother said and smiled at her. 'Your father has . . . friends and they are trying to sort this mess out, but until then . . .'

Francie swallowed hard. She'd been trying to screw up her courage to tell them about the offer from the magazine but now she realised she might not have to. She could return to college, taking the work she'd done with her – and enter it for her exams. After that there would be a few lectures and then the girls were supposed to work on their own projects . . . no one would wonder where she was if she said she was going away to paint some views by herself, because most of the students did it in the last weeks of term. It wasn't long to the Christmas break and she'd be able to do the shoot *Styled* wanted.

It was wrong to deceive her parents, especially after everything Betty had put them through. She wanted to tell them the news she thought so exciting, but they would get upset and they were still worried about Betty – and her too, it seemed.

'All right, if it's what you both want,' she said but turned away to take some juice from the fridge because she couldn't look into her mother's trusting eyes. 'If you're both well and don't need me . . .'

Francie had packed all her artwork when her mother came up to her bedroom. Clothes for college were easy and she just threw a few pairs of jeans and some tops into the trunk on top of her work. The two portraits were too large to pack but they would be crated and sent with the trunk in the guard's van of the train.

'Almost done, darling?' her mother said and brought a pile of clean undies and a clean skirt to place in the trunk. 'Have you got toiletries, soap, toothbrush and shoes . . .?'

Francie laughed at her mother's priorities. 'I've got everything,' Francie said as she placed a smart pair of slacks on top with her best jumper. She'd want something smart for travelling in when she went on the photo shoot for *Styled*, which had been arranged during the her visit to their offices in London. They were going to use the same photographer.

Her mother sat on the edge of the bed, looking at her oddly. 'Francie, did you and Betty see your father leaving a dress shop with a young woman?'

Francie gasped. 'How did you know – did Betty tell you? We agreed not to . . .'

'I thought you must have,' Mum said and smiled.

'I can't give you details, but your father helped a young woman named Gretchen, and she is the daughter of an old friend of his. It was her you saw leaving that shop with him. She'd been . . . living abroad in dreadful circumstances. Your father rescued her and brought her to London to live with her mother. Because she had nothing, he bought her some new clothes – and she was very grateful and kissed him.'

'He touched her face. We thought . . .' Francie's cheeks burned. 'I feel awful, Mum, but we both thought he was having an affair with her – it's part of the reason Betty was so angry with him. We hated it that he could do that to you . . .'

'I understand, darling, and I thank both of you for caring about my feelings, but your father and I have had a long talk. I too had wondered if there was someone else in his life but it was only the work he's been doing . . . rather important and dangerous work, which he assures me is finished now . . .'

'Is it something to do with what he did in the war?' Francie asked, remembering that she'd heard her parents speak of long separations when her father was working for the War Office.

'Yes, in a way,' Mum said and looked sad. 'I'm proud of him, Francie – and you and Betty should be too. We don't need all the details. Your father is a brave, honest man and he loves us. Never forget that, darling . . .'

'No, I won't,' Francie promised and hugged her.

'I love him, Mum. I was angry with him when I thought he'd hurt you – but I didn't stop loving him.'

'I wish Betty understood . . .'

'She will when you explain. Betty loves both of you but she's never been sure that Dad loves her, because he wasn't her blood father – but I've told her he loves her. I sometimes think he loves her most but I'm not jealous . . . I love her too. She's my beautiful big sister and I miss her when she's not around . . .'

'Perhaps she will telephone you at college. She has agreed to ring us when she can. I'll tell her where you are and she might be able to telephone . . .'

'Miss Honiton doesn't like that, because the girls have to use the telephone in the staff room. Tell her to give me her number in a letter and I'll ring her.'

'If I can I'll get it for you and send it on,' Mum promised. 'Have you finished your packing now, darling? Only, I thought we might all go for a walk to the pub together. We can have a drink and enjoy a little celebration meal now that Betty is safe. Our family is reunited even if Betty can't be with us tonight – and perhaps we shall all be together again at Christmas . . .'

CHAPTER 25

Betty looked at the ancient farmhouse set in the lea of towering hills, at the head of a long valley where it was possible to see for miles, the view of rolling fields dotted with sheep and a few cows. Here on the borders between England and Wales it was wild and bleak, making her imagine what it must have been like in the old days when there were constant raids from each side. A lonely tree braved the winds that could be fierce in winter and had survived the deep snows that often fell in January and February. At the moment wintry sunlight dappled on the white walls of the house and played over the garden where a few roses still straggled and hung on in a sheltered spot, and as Betty got out of the car, it warmed her face, as if to welcome her. She stretched, feeling glad to be out of the car after their long drive. She'd slept some of the way and Frank had stopped several times to take a break and buy them food and hot drinks, but she knew it must have been tiring for him, even though he'd slept in the car during one of their breaks.

'It's magnificent,' she breathed, looking out

across the valley. 'I can only see one house and that's all the way over there . . .' She pointed to a house in the distance.

'That belongs to the Andersons. Their son has the only other house in the valley and you can't see it from here. We don't have many neighbours. The village is just round the bend, so we're not completely out of touch with civilisation, except when it snows for weeks on end. They've got a phone at the Post Office and they took my message to Gran when I rang, because she hasn't got a connection where she is on the hills . . .'

'Did you live here as a child?'

'We came for long holidays in the summer and sometimes at Christmas. One Christmas it snowed so hard that we couldn't get through for nearly a month. I missed school and my father almost lost his job over it . . . so we mostly came in the spring and summer, but I came more often after my father died.'

Betty turned as the door of the farmhouse opened and an elderly woman stood there looking at them. 'Will your grandmother wonder why I'm here?'

'I asked Mrs Jones at the Post office to tell her I was bringing a friend who needed somewhere to stay for a while. She knows you need help, Betty, but not why – and she's perfectly happy for you to stay here . . .'

Betty nodded, lifting her head as she went forward to meet the old lady. The first thing she noticed was how upright and bright-eyed she looked, those almost bird-like eyes studying Betty intently as Frank introduced them.

'This is my special friend, Betty, Gran,' he said and then moved forward to kiss his grandmother's cheek. 'I'm not sure how long she will need to stay here, but I'll be here for a few days . . . if that's all right?'

'I'd say if it wasn't,' she said briskly. 'Come away in the pair of you – that sunshine is misleading. You'll catch your deaths, and especially miss in her thin frock . . .'

'I want to thank you, Mrs Renshaw . . . it's so good of you to have me at short notice . . .' Betty drew a sharp breath as she entered the large room which opened straight off the front door. It had beamed ceilings, but high enough for Frank to stand upright, white-washed walls that looked as if they'd been rough plastered and a huge open fireplace where a log fire blazed. The floor was tiled with bright red and very shiny slabs of some kind of stone, and a large woven rug covered part of the floor where an old-fashioned sofa occupied one wall. There was a large oak desk against another wall with a similar oak-framed elbow chair, a long table under the window on which stood a brass can filled with branches and a few dried flowers, and very little else.

'We only use this room for gatherings,' Frank explained as his grandmother led them through to an inner room which was much larger, perhaps two smaller ones knocked together at some time. At one end was all the paraphernalia of a kitchen, with a black range, a scrubbed pine table, assorted chairs, none of them matching, and a huge oak dresser set with blue and white china and many bits and pieces that all seemed at home on its deep shelves. At the other end were grouped a comfortable sofa and three armchairs, and a large table with dropped ends stood against the wall. The heart of the home, it was warm and welcoming and smelled deliciously of baking and herbs strung from the ceiling.

'Sit yourself down, girl,' Mrs Renshaw said to Betty. 'Are you hungry? I've been baking all afternoon so there will be tea and scones with jam and our own cream – but dinner will be an hour or so yet.'

'Thank you, the scones sound delicious,' Betty said and went to sit in the rocking chair by the fire but a look from Frank stopped her.

'That's my grandfather's chair. No one sits there since he died . . .'

'Oh, I'm sorry,' Betty said and held her hands to the fire. The other end of the room did not look quite as inviting on a cold day when she was wearing only a thin dress, so she chose one of the chairs at the table, smiling at the odd assortment of wheel-back chairs.

'My grandfather used to buy chairs from the markets,' Frank explained. 'When he and Gran first came here he didn't have much money so they furnished it the best they could over the years – the modern chairs at the other end were bought by my uncle Tom when he came to live here with his wife Mary and took over the farm . . .'

Betty nodded, taking in the situation. 'Where is your Aunt Mary?'

'Unfortunately, she was a townie and she couldn't stand the life,' Frank said in low tones. 'Mary became ill after giving birth to a stillborn child. Unfortunately, she never got over it and died soon after. Uncle Tom never married again. Gran held him together through the worst of it and she helped with the sheep, as well as doing housework and cooking – though recently one of our neighbour's girls comes to give her a hand with the heavy work in the house – and we hire extra men when my uncle needs them . . .'

'You said "we" – do you lend a hand?'

'Sometimes,' Frank said. 'This has always been a second home to me . . . hasn't it, Gran?'

'You come and go as suits you,' she acceded. 'Stop withering the girl's ear and let her rest. She looks as if she could do with feeding up . . . too thin by half . . .'

'My mum always says the same thing.' Betty smiled.

'Sensible woman,' Gran grunted. 'You'll call me gran, same as everyone does, girl, and you'll eat what we eat or go hungry while you're here. I haven't time to fuss with picky feeders . . .'

Her words were harsh and yet somehow not

offensive. Frank looked at her and Betty could hardly keep her mirth inside, but she reached for his hand and held it tightly.

The smell coming from Gran's scones was unbelievable. Betty's mother was a good cook, but as she took one of the scones and cut into it, her mouth began to water, and as she spread jam and then the thick buttery cream, she realised she was starving. The first bite was heaven, because she'd never tasted food this good – or perhaps it was the country air. Betty wasn't sure, but the first scone seemed to melt in her mouth and before she knew it she was asking if she could have another.

'Help yourself, girl,' Gran said but her eyes gleamed with satisfaction. 'We've plenty to go round – there's one thing we don't lack here and that's good food. We've none of your fancy goods, televisions and all that rubbish – but there's a wireless that works when it thinks it will and a gramophone my son bought, and you can play that as long as the generator is working – but you'll not be bored if you've no aversion to work. Our guests usually help out in the house or with the sheep . . .'

'Oh . . .' Betty was surprised but pleased, because she'd hoped to be of use. 'I'd love to help you – perhaps you can teach me to cook the way you do . . .'

'Well, as long as you don't get in my way . . .' Gran turned away with a little grunt of satisfaction. 'I dare say you'd only be a hindrance in the fields – but if you're of a mind to help I can find you something to keep you busy . . .'

'Good,' Betty said. 'Unfortunately, I don't have any clothes with me . . .'

'Aye, Frank told me,' Gran said and her knowing eyes assessed her. 'Well, there's a few bits in the trunks in the attics. They'll be a bit out of fashion, but I dare say you won't mind that?'

'Not at all . . .' Betty spied a sewing machine in the corner. It was an old-fashioned treadle machine, but still looked usable. 'I can use your machine to alter them to fit me – if we have any cotton . . .?'

'Aye, you'll find plenty in my workbox,' Gran said, 'and if you're good at sewing there's plenty of mending around . . . it's not my favourite task . . .'

Betty smiled and looked up as the door opened and a man of about fifty entered the room. He'd taken his boots off and his outer coat, but he was wearing old cord trousers and a thick sweater with a rolled neck. His hair was black and he was remarkably good-looking. His dark eyes went to Betty and immediately sparked with interest.

'And who have we here then?' he asked.

Frank introduced them, 'Betty, this is my uncle. Tom . . . this is my friend Betty . . .'

'You'll be the lass our Frank was after then,' Tom said. 'All of last summer he was mooning about and we could hardly get a sensible word out of him . . .'

Betty offered her hand but was instead drawn into a bear-like hug. In size he matched Frank, perhaps even an inch or so taller but of similar stature. Since Gran and Uncle Tom had accepted her, she felt warmed and happy, perhaps happier than she had for a long time. Her parents would be worried, but there was a phone box in the village, and Frank would take her to buy some things she needed and telephone her parents. She had no money with her, because her bag had been lost when she was grabbed, but she would repay him when she could.

When she'd finished her tea, Gran took her up to her room. It too was large but the ceilings were arched and beamed, because there were no attics above this particular room. A fire was burning in the fireplace and very welcoming. The bed looked inviting with its thick patchwork covers, and Betty guessed that the fire was in honour of her as a guest; these hardy people wouldn't light fires up here unless it was bitterly cold.

'Frank will bring the trunk down from the loft,' Gran said. 'Some of the stuff belonged to his mother – but some of it was mine as a girl. Take your pick of it – but there's a cardigan on the bed. It's a new one my son gave me for my birthday. I've had no occasion to use it but it will keep you from shivering to death . . .'

Betty thanked her and went to warm her hands by the fire.

'The toilet is at the end of the hall,' Gran said.

'We've had a bath put in recently, but the men use it at night and the water won't heat up in time if you use it – so wait for the morning, lass.'

'Yes, of course,' Betty said, even though she was dying for a wash.

'I'll get one of the lads to bring up a can of hot water,' Gran said. 'Frank has the room across the hall. I'm next to you – and his uncle at the other end. There's a brush and comb on the dressing table, but nothing to put on your face. I've never used anything but a drop of Pond's face cream . . .'

'It's all right, Frank bought a couple of bits for me on the way here,' Betty said. 'I'd like to use the bathroom just to tidy up – and then I'll come down again. I can bring some hot water up myself later . . .'

'The lads will do it,' Gran said, making Betty smile at the thought of Tom still being called a lad by his mother. 'Take a few moments to refresh yourself, lass. There's no call to hurry . . .'

Betty visited the bathroom and used the toilet, washing her hands but refrained from using hot water. Used to the excellent heating at home, she found the old-fashioned limitations of the farm-house a little strange but accepted them. It was a different way of life – a throwback to the 1930s or even before, when bathrooms and indoor toilets were just coming in, though this was white and quite modern. Clearly Tom had made changes when he took over from his father, but the method of heating didn't run to endless baths . . .

Returning to her bedroom, she discovered that a can of hot water awaited her and she took off her dress, using the soap thoughtfully provided on the washstand. It felt so much better and Betty wished she had clean undies to put on as she redressed in her used ones, but they hadn't passed anywhere that sold women's clothing.

Frank had been in a hurry to reach the farm and Betty knew he was anxious in case those men had managed to follow them, but Betty didn't think they would bother. Pierre had been in charge and with him dead, they would most likely just make themselves scarce in case they were blamed for his death.

A shiver went down her spine as she brushed her hair and used a little of the lipstick Frank had bought for her on the way down. He'd taken such risks for her – killed a man! Betty found that shocking and awesome both at the same time. Frank must care for her very much to have done that for her sake. Tears stung her eyes, because as grateful as she was for his care of her, Betty knew that she wasn't in love with him . . .

CHAPTER 26

Francie handed in her coursework for the end of term exams and then crossed her fingers behind her back. She'd seen some of the work her friends had done, and Jilly's was outstanding. Her modern art looked original and yet in the style of Picasso. Yet Francie seemed to have done more than anyone else, and that surprised her.

'How did you manage those large portraits?' Jilly asked in awe. 'It took me ages to do the course stuff. I only managed one view for my free period . . .'

'Don't tell anyone, but I just sloshed some paint on and scrubbed at it for the modern stuff,' Francie said and pulled a face. 'As for the portraits, they just came. I worked hours without stopping . . . but I know they won't count and I'll probably fail my exams . . .'

'They are fantastic . . . especially the one of the girl,' Averil said. 'I wish I could paint like that, Francie, but I never shall. I'm going into commercial art, which is what I'm good at – but that was real art . . .'

'Even so it probably won't impress the examiners,'

Francie said. 'Well, what have you two been up to while I was away?'

'Missing you,' Jilly said and squeezed her waist. 'What are you planning to do now?'

'Well, there's Christmas coming up soon and I shall enjoy shopping with Mum – and Betty, I hope. I haven't seen her for ages . . .' Francie bit her lip, because she couldn't tell her friends about the things that had been happening to her sister. 'And I've got a photo shoot planned' Francie said cautiously.

'You're not going on with the modelling?'

'*Styled* gave me this contract, but *Vogue* has offered me some work in the future, though I told them I was committed for the moment,' Francie told them. 'I can't believe it but they're paying me so much money . . . just for posing in beautiful clothes . . .'

'Lucky you,' Jilly said. 'I wish I was coming with you. I'll probably get dragged to London shopping with my mother – and shopping with Mum isn't fun, even if it is Christmas, though I like buying my presents . . . I'll probably go and stay with Gran as soon as I can escape.'

'I'll come and visit when I'm not working,' Francie said. 'What are you going to do, Averil?'

'I'm going to work here for a while before I go home. I've got a commission for an engineering firm to design a new logo – and if it is accepted, I'll have a job lined up for when I leave next spring . . .'

'That's wonderful,' her friends exclaimed, and

immediately demanded to know what she'd been asked to do.

Francie joined in the teasing and laughter, but she was busy working out a schedule in her mind. She could take her sketching things with her on the shoot and make some quick drawings while she was waiting for the various changes. There were always long discussions about lighting and locations, and it could be boring just standing around, but she'd used her time successfully before and that was how she'd managed to come up with some of the line drawings she'd put in as part of her coursework.

She'd been given tickets for a chartered flight from Marshall's Airport and the freelance photographer, Michael, she'd met in London on that shoot for *Styled* was flying down with her. His family home was in Cambridge, though his studio was in London. He'd agreed to meet Francie at her college and drive her to the airport on the outskirts of Cambridge so that they could join some of the other crew to fly down to Cornwall. Some of the clothes they were going to model were winter coats and warm boots, but some were for spring and were going to be photographed against a background of cliffs and water settings, which would be chilly but was one of the things models got used to. The scenery would be ideal to sketch roughly and paint later when she had time, because she could take lots of her own photos. If everything worked out well, no one would ever need to know that she was living two lives and deceiving her parents . . .

'Well, that's a wrap I'd say,' Michael came over to where Francie had been sitting working on a sketch for the past ten minutes while he worked with the other models on the shoot. 'We've got all we need for the day, Francie. You can get back to the hotel and warm yourself up now. It's pretty cold out here . . .'

'Is it? I hadn't noticed . . .' Francie put her pencils away and was closing her pad when he reached out to try to tweak it from her hands. 'No, please, don't – they aren't ready for anyone to see . . .'

'You're an artist . . .' Michael had been taking some pictures of her as she worked, clicking away. Then he grabbed her sketchbook, ignoring her pleas to give it back. 'And a damned good one. What are you wasting your time doing this job for?'

Francie blinked away her tears. She snatched the pad back from him, hurt that he'd asked such a question. 'I was offered the contract. Why shouldn't I take it?'

'I didn't mean it that way, Francie,' Michael said, sensing now that he'd upset her. 'Look, you're lovely and the camera adores you – but there are hundreds of girls as beautiful and we get loads of them who only manage to make it for a year or so and then get left behind. Your art is a wonderful gift and it will be yours for a lifetime. I just think it's a waste to neglect it for this . . . hanging about in all weathers just for a few fashion pictures.'

'You do it!' she flashed at him angrily, shrugging away his help as she gathered her things. 'Why is that fine for you but wrong for me – and how do you know that I shan't become famous and go on for years?'

'I don't know,' he said. 'Perhaps you will – but I do know how many fail. Sometimes you're promised a cover shot for a magazine and then they just shove you in at the back somewhere and next time they drop you altogether in favour of the latest sensation . . .'

'I think I hate you,' Francie said crossly as she followed him to the car where her chaperone was waiting patiently to drive her back to the hotel.'

'That's a pity because I've got a few pictures I think some other magazines might like – we might even get you on the front cover of *Vogue*. They asked me to send them something different – and I was thinking of sending some of you sketching . . .'

'On the cover of *Vogue*?' Francie gasped, because that would make her famous overnight. 'You don't mean it?'

'I think you're mad wanting to be a model when you can draw like that,' Michael said with a grin. 'But why not give the girl what she wants . . .'

Francie stared at him. Michael was a mystery, because she knew he had a reputation for flirting, but when he smiled at her . . . well, she couldn't help her heart fluttering a bit, even though she knew she was far too young to think about a man like that . . .

Francie closed her eyes on the train back from London. This time they'd flown back to Heathrow and she'd had to make her own way across town and get back to college under her own steam, because all the others had wanted to be in town.

'You do realise you'll need to be based in London if you're going to take up modelling as a living,' Michael told her on the flight back. 'I agreed that we'd go from Cambridge as I was staying with my parents this week – but I'm mostly based in London and they won't hire a plane just for one unknown model . . .'

'Why are you trying to put me off being a model?' Francie asked, feeling hurt that he would speak to her so harshly.

'Because I don't want to see you get hurt,' he said and his smile took the sting from his words. 'You're pretty, Francie, but you need more than that to make it in this game – you need to be ruthless and I don't think that's in your nature.'

Francie had buried herself in her work, refusing to speak to him again until they parted at the busy airport. He'd stayed with her until she joined the queue for taxis and then given her a brief peck on the cheek.

'Think about what I've said, Francie – either be

here in London so you're available for every job that comes up or do what you do best . . .'

She'd stared after him as he ran to a private car that had just drawn up and climbed in, kissing the cheek of a beautiful woman who was driving. Francie sighed and smiled ruefully. Of course she was far too young to interest a man like that – but it didn't matter, she had a lot of growing up to do before she was ready to fall in love.

She joined the queue for tickets. She knew she had to get back to college and paint like fury if she wanted to get down all the pictures that filled her head. Cornwall, the cliffs, the changing colours of the sea and the birds swooping overhead were swirling in their somewhere. Art was ninety per cent intuition and ten per cent what the artist saw . . .

Francie had been trying to paint a picture of her mother for ages, but she was such a complex subject, and she couldn't make up her mind whether she wanted to paint the woman playing on the beach with Beth and all the kids or the serious and successful milliner . . . or was there someone else in there? Francie was still trying to get it clear in her mind. Perhaps it was because her mother was so special to her that she saw so many facets of her personality . . .

Francie had hardly unpacked her stuff when she got the message to report to Miss Honiton's office. Her heart was beating rapidly as she responded, because the principal had warned her once and she didn't want to be thrown out just yet. Next October she would be sixteen and then it wouldn't matter so much – especially if her last shoot had gone as well as she hoped.

'Well, Francie . . .' she became aware that Miss Honiton was looking at her intently. 'I had the opportunity to look through your coursework this weekend and I must say you produced more quality work than I'd imagined. Those portraits were good, but I am not certain they will gain marks, as I don't recall seeing portraiture on the qualifying list – but the sketches were excellent and the modern art . . . well, I wasn't sure about that personally, but one of the examiners thought it showed excellent freedom of expression. He said that you'd caught the mood of the Modernists in a way that many of the students missed. He thought some students had tried too hard to copy the work of the masters, and of course that isn't what they require . . .'

'It isn't?' Francie was bewildered. She'd done that work in a couple of hours, just literally throwing her loaded paintbrush at the canvas and letting it splodge in pleasing shapes until it formed a pattern. It had looked nothing like Picasso's work or any other of the Modernist painters in her opinion, and was really just her revolt against being asked to do something that went against the grain with her.

'Apparently not.' Miss Honiton gave her a knowing

look. 'I know your work, Francie, and I know when you've given something your time and attention and when you haven't – but my opinion doesn't count for much. I give you marks for your work over the term and they are already in – it's down to the examiners now . . . because this is an expensive course, Francie, and I'm not sure your father will wish to continue paying fees for another two terms for you to waste your time as well as mine and his money . . .'

Francie swallowed hard. 'I did try to do the coursework, Miss Honiton – but the portraits wouldn't be denied. Perhaps I've done enough to scrape through . . .'

'We must hope so,' the principal said, giving her another of those odd looks. 'I should be so disappointed if you were to fail because you had been distracted by other things . . . would you mind showing me what you've been doing this weekend?'

Francie had come prepared with her sketchbook and she passed it across the desk. Miss Honiton took her time looking at the sketches, some finished, some only just attempted, some of Michael that she would rather she had not seen. She closed it and handed it back to Francie.

'I see you were busy,' she said. 'Do you intend to develop this work?'

'I took some photos and I shall use them to paint an oil landscape I think . . .'

'You certainly chose some vibrant settings for

your landscapes – one would almost think you had been to Cornwall quite recently . . .'

Francie felt her cheeks warm and kept her gaze downcast until she was dismissed. As she returned to the dorm she shared with her friends, she felt very uncomfortable. Miss Honiton knew she that she must have been to Cornwall for her free weekend but since it wasn't actually against the college rules, she'd chosen not to say anything. Francie was glad she'd worked for a while on the plane coming home. Because she was quick at sketching and did some of her best work that way, her principal could not know for certain that most of her time had been spent posing for fashion photographs. Francie could only hope that Miss Honiton would keep her suspicions to herself and not communicate them to her parents . . .

CHAPTER 27

'Thanks for meeting me,' Frank said as Matt ordered a beer for them both. 'Let's go over by the window. I want to talk to you in private . . .'

'Sounds serious,' Matt said and sipped his beer. Sitting down, he glanced at headlines in a paper someone had left lying on the chair. 'Terrific about Donald Campbell breaking that speed record isn't it?'

'What? Oh yes,' Frank frowned. 'Matt, for God's sake, listen to me! I have to tell you. I'm going crazy . . .'

'This is about Betty, isn't it? Mum said Aunt Lizzie told her you'd spirited her off somewhere to keep her safe . . .' Matt was all attention now, a nerve flicking in his cheek.

'She's at the farm . . . if anything happens to me . . .'

'What are you talking about?' Matt stared at him, because he sensed Frank was scared. 'Just what happened to Betty this time – and what did you do? I've only heard Mum's version . . .'

'That bugger Saint-Jacquez snatched her and

347

took her off in his car. I followed and waited and when I got the chance I got her back . . .'

'Bloody hell!' Matt whistled and looked at him with respect, then, 'You think Saint-Jacques is going to come after you next?'

'I killed him . . .'

'Killed . . .?' Matt lowered his voice. 'You'd better tell me everything.'

'I had to do it or Betty would've been lost . . .' Frank looked at him a little wildly. 'There were others – if they or the police come after me I could be in a lot of trouble . . .'

'Do the police know?'

Frank shook his head. 'I think it has been taken care of – but that still leaves Saint-Jacques's co-conspirators . . . Anyway, it's not me I'm worried about. I've got a lot of stuff going on. My firm want me to fly out to Amsterdam for a meeting – and I can't get the idea that she might still be in danger out of my head. Can you go down, Matt? Just keep an eye on her . . . and look out for her if the worst happens . . .'

'Look, Betty is special to both of us. You know I will . . .'

'Yes, I thought so,' Frank said and smiled his relief. 'Be careful you're not followed – and don't tell anyone else, even her parents. The less people who know where she is the better – but I know you will take care of her if I can't . . .'

'You have my word on that – and if it helps, I'd

have done the same if I'd had the chance. He was slime, Frank. You did us all a favour . . .'

Frank nodded and seemed to relax. 'I know you care about her,' he said. 'And I think she cares for you . . . perhaps more than either of you realise . . .'

Matt nodded. He'd stayed away from Betty deliberately, leaving the field clear for his friend, but if Frank was walking away . . . it was time Matt made his presence felt. Someone had to look after her . . .

Lizzie took a copy of the fashion magazine from the stall and paid for it. She'd been to see Beth that morning. Beth was busy helping Jenny move into her new home and also knitting baby clothes for her whenever she got the chance. Lizzie made a note to buy some pretty bits and pieces and give them to Beth for her daughter. Perhaps something nice in glass or china for Jenny's home and some clothes for her baby – white would be best, because no one yet knew which sex the child would be.

She'd called in at some of her favourite shops on her way home, browsing the gorgeous baby things now available. She hadn't been able to buy as much as she would have liked for Betty and Francie when they were first born, because of the war and there had been nowhere near the choice there was these days. All sorts of lovely things caught her eyes and she ended up buying several things for her own baby too, though she hadn't intended to, as she was a little afraid it was tempting fate, but she just couldn't resist some of the beautiful clothes on offer. She had her purchases sent to her so that she could wrap the things for Jenny in gift paper and take them to Beth when she was ready. The gorgeous glass vase she could give at once, but the baby things would wait for a while, just in case. It was too easy to lose a child, as Lizzie knew only too well. She smiled as she acknowledged that she felt really well, and her latest visit to the maternity clinic had resulted in smiles all round and a nod of approval.

Sebastian insisted that she rest for an hour in the afternoons, and since he was taking things easily himself, getting up later and spending only an hour or so a day on work she was happy to oblige his whims. They were actually enjoying having more time together, drinking coffee, sharing the papers and just talking – something they hadn't had a great deal of time for in years, and she thought he seemed more relaxed than he had for a long time.

'Once the baby's here and you're feeling well again, I think we should go away for a while – perhaps somewhere a little warmer . . .' he'd said at breakfast that morning.

'That would be lovely,' Lizzie had replied. 'Do you think Betty will come with us . . .?' She looked at him anxiously. 'I hate not knowing where she is and whether she's all right . . .'

'She's fine, Lizzie, really she is. You can talk to her when she rings next time, but she *will* be coming with us. This fuss will all be over soon, I promise you,' Sebastian said with an indulgent smile. 'It must be years since we had a holiday all together . . .'

'I can't remember when,' Lizzie admitted. 'You were usually too busy to spend more than a day or two with us when Beth and I took the children to Cornwall . . .'

'That's why I proposed a holiday for us all,' he said and smiled, 'I want to see you being happy, Lizzie . . . and the girls . . . and I've finished with all that rushing around, believe me.'

Letting herself into the kitchen now, Lizzie placed the magazine on the kitchen table and unpacked her basket. Sebastian entered just as she was putting away some food in the refrigerator. He smiled at her and Lizzie's heart caught, because that smile still had the power to make her feel weak at the knees and long for his arms about her.

'I've had some good news while you were out,' he told her. 'Jack rang me. He believes that the man Pierre Saint-Jacquez was in harness with has been arrested in America for procuring underage girls for sexual purposes. It is possible that he will go to prison for a long time – and if he should wangle his way out of it, he won't be allowed back into this country. Besides, he will have forgotten Betty by then . . . it means she's free of the threat he posed.' He hesitated, then, 'Saint-Jacquez is dead, Lizzie. So I'm going to tell Betty to come home as soon as she's ready . . .'

'Thank God! That is wonderful,' Lizzie cried and went to put her arms about him. Her eyes were wet with tears, because she'd been holding her emotions in check, trying to accept that Betty was safer in her hideout when she desperately wanted her home where she could hold her and touch her. 'The best news we could possibly have . . .

Lizzie stared at him. 'You know where she is – don't you?'

'I've known for a while . . .' He smiled oddly. 'It was easy enough for Jack to trace Frank Hadley's family – but I left her there, because it seemed the best place until things were settled . . .'

'And you didn't tell me!' Lizzie frowned at him. 'I thought we agreed no more secrets. You knew how desperate I was to see her . . .'

'Don't you see, my darling?' Sebastian raised his eyebrows. 'If you'd known, you would have begged me to take you down to see her – and if there was someone watching us it would've led them straight to Betty. Don't you think I wanted to tell you – to fetch her home? It's been just as hard for me, perhaps harder, because I feel to blame for the whole damn thing . . .'

'Yes, I would have asked . . .' she admitted it grudgingly, still a little upset with him. 'But you should have told me, Sebastian. I've had enough of secrets in this family . . .'

The coffee was percolating and the smell was delicious. Lizzie went to the dresser to fetch cups and a cream jug. Sebastian sat down at the table and did something he never did, flicking idly through the pages of *Styled* magazine.

He suddenly gave a snort of disgust and threw it down on the table in front of Lizzie. 'When were you going to tell me about these then?'

Her eye fell on a two-page spread of a young girl wearing some sophisticated evening dresses and she sat down abruptly from the shock. 'Oh no, that's this month's magazine. When did she do that?'

'You mean you didn't know about it?'

'No, I just picked the magazine up as a change from Vogue. I hadn't even looked beyond the cover.'

'How could she?' Sebastian said in a voice of disgust. 'She gave me her word that she wouldn't do any more of this sort of stuff . . .'

Lizzie looked intently at the pictures. 'There's nothing outrageous or suggestive in these, Sebastian. They are just normal fashion photography – perfectly respectable, and the ones at the zoo are rather lovely.'

'She is still my daughter and far too young to be doing this work,' Sebastian said, his mouth was tight with anger. 'She gave me her word – and she has broken it. There is nothing indecent about these but that doesn't alter the fact that she has deceived us – unless you knew about this?'

'I promise you I knew nothing. Had she told me I should have forbidden it . . .' Lizzie frowned. 'These aren't like the other stuff . . .'

'Well, she's still underage and I'm going to speak to my lawyers . . .'

'Sebastian, please don't get angry and do something you may regret,' Lizzie begged. 'If Francie really wants to do this – and it seems to me that she does – I think we should talk to her. I know she deceived us and that is very wrong, but she may have been worried about upsetting us when we were already under enough stress . . .'

'Francie is too young, Lizzie . . .'

'I know she's still a little girl to you, darling – but girls grow up much sooner these days . . .'

'Francie is still too young . . .' Sebastian said but she could see he was thoughtful. He drew the magazine towards him and looked at the pictures again. They were good and Francie looked wonderful, a beautiful girl doing a professional job, and the ones with the animals at the zoo had a charming innocence even he could see and appreciate – but the others were too sophisticated, not as her father saw her, not as his little girl, and Lizzie could see that bothered him. 'I suppose this is a quality magazine . . .'

'It's one of the best,' Lizzie said. 'A lot of young girls would kill for the chance to be in a magazine like this, Sebastian. I know you're so proud of her art – and so am I, but if she wants this chance . . . surely she can always go back to it in time? She's a modern girl, Sebastian, and this is what young girls want these days.'

'You think she is old enough to make up her own mind – that we should let her do what she thinks best?' He shook his head, his eyes still on the glamorous photographs. 'To me she should still be at college for years yet . . . but I suppose if it's what she really wants.' He frowned. 'Yet how can we condone this deceit? She mustn't be allowed to think it is all right to lie to get her own way . . .'

'No, and I doubt she does. If I know Francie she feels guilty. Talk to her when she comes home, Sebastian, but don't lose your temper . . .'

'I learned my lesson with Betty,' he said and a nerve flicked at the corner of his eye. 'I shan't lose my temper – but Francie has disappointed me, Lizzie. If she fails her exams because of this she will lose the chance of that scholarship in Paris . . .'

'Then that will be punishment enough,' Lizzie said. She poured his coffee and passed him the cream jug. 'When will you tell Betty that it's safe for her to come home?'

'Next time she rings, which should be tomorrow morning,' Sebastian said and put two lumps of brown sugar in his cup. 'The people she's staying with don't have their own phone – too far from civilisation . . .' He smiled wryly. 'I should imagine she's heartily sick of it and longing to come home . . .'

'It's perfectly safe now, love,' Sebastian said as Betty asked again if he was sure. 'I've been told the man who paid Saint-Jacquez for you is locked securely in an American prison, and I

355

doubt he'll come out of there for a few years
– if ever . . . and Pierre will never bother you
again, believe me.'

'Oh, Dad . . .' Betty breathed a sigh of relief.
'You don't know how good it is to hear that . . .'

'Your mother and I feel just as relieved as you
do, Betty.'

'Yes, I know. I've caused you a lot of worry . . .
I'm so sorry, Dad.'

'Don't be sorry. Just be happy it's all over, my
darling girl. What happened to you – it was as
much my fault as yours and I'll never forgive
myself for hurting you . . .'

'No, it wasn't your fault,' Betty denied, tears
trickling down her cheeks. She dashed them away
impatiently. 'I'm helping out here with a few jobs
and I can't let them down – but I'll come back at
the weekend. I'll ring you when I know the times
of the trains . . .'

'I could come and fetch you if Frank is too
busy . . .'

'He will be down tomorrow, but Gran has a bit
of a cold and I don't want to leave her with all
the work. She's been so good to me, Dad. I'm fine
here, really, but I miss you and Mum. Give my
love to Mum – and Francie. When I rang the
college she was out with some friends . . . and her
headmistress sounded annoyed so I didn't try to
ring again . . .'

'I'm sure she would've rung you if you were on
the phone there.'

'It's a bit of a nuisance but Frank's family don't have much use for a phone, and I don't like to ask Tom to bring me in too often . . .'

'Well, you'll be home soon.'

'Yes . . .'

Betty put the receiver down just as the pips went. She had more money in her purse but didn't want to talk any more for the moment. Her father's apology had made her feel awful, though it wasn't the first time. He'd told her over and over again that he loved her and it made Betty feel so guilty, because she knew it was partly stress over her that had brought on his heart problems. And of course she did love him, she always had despite their arguments – it was of course her love that had made her so needy towards him. She'd never been sure how important she was to him, but just now his love had seemed to reach out to her as they spoke and she knew she'd been a fool to doubt him.

Mum had explained about Gretchen and the work he'd been doing when she'd telephoned her previously.

'I can't tell you much,' she'd said. 'It's not for discussion, but he brought Gretchen here to have tea with me and we talked. She's had the most terrible time . . . her mother too. I feel so grateful that we've been safe all these years. If things had gone badly in the war . . . who knows what would have happened to any of us . . .'

Walking through the village to where Tom was waiting to take her back to the farm, Betty tried to dismiss her thoughts of the past. It was over now. She could put all that had happened in Paris behind her and get on with her life. She wasn't sure that she would still have a job, but that wasn't the end of the world. Making use of her spare time, Betty had filled a book with ideas for new clothes; many of them had come from redesigning Gran's old-fashioned clothes to something she could happily wear.

When she'd first opened Gran's trunk, she'd thought there was nothing remotely suitable but then she'd begun to realise that a lot of the material was good quality and she started cutting up ankle-length dresses, making them into skirts and shaping offcuts into bodices or separate jackets. She'd mixed pieces from one garment with another, achieving a startling and stylish outfit with a long red dress with a voluminous skirt that had made her a smart suit.

Gran had admired it, hardly believing that her old dance frock had become a modern outfit. 'You ought to do this for a living, girl,' she'd said and Betty laughed, telling her it was her ambition.

'You'll not be wanting to get married yet then,' Gran said and shook her head. 'And there's Frank mooning after you, lass . . .'

Betty had turned away, feeling embarrassed by the old lady's bright stare. Frank had made his feelings clear, and Betty was fond of him – he had rescued her and brought her here, and of course she *was* grateful . . .

As she approached the car, Betty saw that Tom was talking to another man. He turned as if sensing her approach and she gave a cry of pleasure and ran towards him.

'Matt . . .' she said in wonder. 'What are you doing here – how did you know where to find me?'

'Frank told me. I stayed here with him a couple of years back in the summer and I saw Tom as I was on my way to the farm . . .' He grinned at her. 'Frank came to see me. He had to fly out to visit Amsterdam on business unexpectedly and he asked me to look after you . . .'

'Dad has just told me I can go home,' Betty said with a sob in her throat as Matt opened his arms and she went into them, feeling safe and suddenly at home with the man she'd always known and trusted. 'Oh, Matt – can you stay for a couple of days . . . just until Gran is feeling better?'

'Of course I can,' he said and hugged her. He smiled and Betty's heart flipped as she caught the familiar aftershave. He was so handsome and strong. She'd never noticed before how good looking he was, because he was her brother, but of course he wasn't and there was something in the way he looked at her that told her Matt wasn't seeing her as a sister now. Suddenly, a little shy, she moved back. 'I came down to fetch you – but Tom asked if I could give him a hand for a few days . . . we'll stay until the weekend, Betty. It will be good to have a little time with you . . .'

CHAPTER 28

'Is that Sebastian Winters' residence?' the voice asked when Lizzie answered the phone that afternoon. It was a man's voice and cultured but with a slight intonation that made her wonder if he were truly English. 'May I speak to him please?'

'Yes, certainly,' Lizzie said. 'Who may I say is calling please?'

'Just a friend . . .'

'I'm sorry, my husband hasn't been well. I need to know who is calling . . .'

'Tell him Eric would like a few moments of his time – and I'm sorry your husband has been ill, Mrs Winters. I shan't keep him long . . .'

Lizzie frowned as she went through to the sitting room, where Sebastian was relaxing with the papers.

'Someone wants to speak to you,' Lizzie said as he looked up inquiringly. 'He said his name is Eric . . .'

An odd look passed across Sebastian's face. He got up and went past her into the hall, throwing her a smile of reassurance that did nothing to dampen the fear trickling down her spine. Sebastian had promised no secrets, but Lizzie suspected that this phone call wasn't something he would share with her. . She was certain that it was something to do with that secret work he'd kept from her so many years.

Sebastian closed the door of the sitting room after him and that confirmed her fears. He didn't want Lizzie to hear anything she ought not. Her hands curled at her sides but she didn't strain to listen, because if Sebastian wanted to keep it from her he had a good reason.

She sat down and tried to concentrate on her designs but she couldn't think of a single thing, except the sound of that man's voice and the feeling that had come over her. Sebastian was gone for several minutes and when he returned he looked serious.

'I have to go out this evening to meet someone,' he said. 'I'm not going to lie to you, Lizzie – it's to do with the past and I promised you that was all over, but I have to do this one thing.'

'Why – isn't there anyone else?'

'No one he trusts,' Sebastian said. 'The man on the phone is risking his own life to give me something, Lizzie. It's something we need and want – at least I know Jack wants it, but Eric won't meet with anyone but me, and I had to give him my word I would go alone . . .'

'And do you trust this man? How do you know he's telling you the truth – how can you be sure that it won't endanger your life as well as his?'

Sebastian hesitated for a moment, then, 'I can't, of course. I expect it to be dangerous, but I have to go. Eric knows that he only has a short time to deliver his information and get out of England. He isn't safe here – I'm not sure he's safe anywhere – but I have to meet him and I've promised to go alone. I also gave my word not to contact anyone – which is why I want you to ring this number a quarter of an hour after I leave. It can't be before that, Lizzie, because if Eric suspects a trap he'll bolt . . . Jack is only minutes away from the rendez-vous and he'll be there seconds after we arrive, or even slightly before us, but you must wait for the right moment. If Jack gets there too early it could ruin things . . .'

'Are you going to betray Eric?'

'No, of course not, but he doesn't trust Jack. I'm counting on Jack to arrive if there's any trouble. Once I have the stuff, Eric can leave or let Jack help him get away to safety, if he can be brought to accept that Jack is his friend – and I need him there in case it's a trap . . .'

'Why would he want to trap you?'

'I do not think Eric intends anything of the sort, but he may be followed . . . he may have enemies who want the information he's willing to give only to me, because he doesn't know who else to trust.'

'You could be in danger too . . .' Lizzie said. 'How do I ring Jack?'

'I've written it down for you. Once you contact him, destroy it, Lizzie. Put it on the fire and watch it burn . . .'

'Oh, Sebastian . . .' She felt sick inside and her hands trembled as she took the scrap of paper. 'Why don't you let Jack go in your place?'

'Because Eric would just bolt . . . if you ring exactly a quarter of an hour after I leave it will give me time to get there first and talk to him.'

'Supposing he isn't there?'

'In that case I'll have to manage alone. It may be perfectly straightforward, Lizzie – but this is my safety net . . .'

'It's no use my asking you not to go?'

'You know the answer, darling. If there were any other way I wouldn't have told you, but I may need Jack's help – and, besides, I gave my word I would let him know if this happened . . .'

Lizzie nodded; her throat tight with fear, then, 'All right, I'll do what you ask – but this is the last time, Sebastian . . .'

'Thank you, darling.' Sebastian walked towards her and put his arms around her, holding her close for a moment. 'I'm sorry to involve you in all this cloak-and-dagger stuff. Believe me, I wish I didn't have to go – but I gave my word . . .'

Lizzie checked her watch against the mantle clock the moment Sebastian left the house. She had to wait fifteen minutes, because if she panicked and rang too soon it could all go wrong. She decided to sit on the bed. She could use the telephone there and it was something to do, because the waiting was unbearable. Oh why had Sebastian got involved in all this stuff in the first place? Why couldn't he have been content to run his business and stay out of politics or spying or whatever it was?

Her watch hardly seemed to have moved. Just as her hand moved towards the phone to check it was working, it rang loudly, shrilling in her ear and making her jump. She snatched it up.

'Yes, Lizzie here.'

'Lizzie, it's Miriam,' the voice said. 'Betty rang me to tell me she's coming home soon, but she says she's intending to stay with you for a while – see how it goes. She sounded a bit upset – do you know if she's all right?'

'Sebastian took the call last time,' Lizzie said and lifted her arm so that she could see her watch. It was all right, she still had five minutes to go. 'He said she put the phone down abruptly but he thought her money had run out . . . I thought she would be happy to get back to London . . .'

'The thing is I have a letter for her here,' Miriam said. 'I didn't know whether to bring it round or send it on . . .'

'I shouldn't send it on, it might miss her . . .' Lizzie checked the time again . . . seven minutes . . .

'I haven't seen you for ages,' Miriam said. 'Will it be all right if I pop round tomorrow and drop Betty's letter off? Only I don't want to intrude and I know Sebastian is at home more now . . .'

'We shall both be pleased to see you,' Lizzie assured her. 'You know you're always welcome – come to lunch and spend the day with us . . .'

'Yes, I should like that . . .' Aunt Miriam said. 'Did you see those pictures of Francie in that magazine . . . aren't they lovely?'

'Yes . . .' Lizzie saw the clock reach three minutes to the deadline. 'Look, I'm sorry, Miriam. I have to go. I'll ring back if I can, if not I'll see you tomorrow . . .'

She replaced the receiver down and rung the number she'd been given. It was engaged. Lizzie replaced it again and counted to ten. Just as she was about to try for the second time her phone rang. She snatched it off the hook and slammed it down hard and then picked it straight up again and dialled the number she wanted. This time she heard it ringing and then it was picked up.

'Jack . . .' a voice said.

'Sebastian says can you meet him at the place you arranged, right now . . .'

'Who is this?'

'Sebastian's wife. He had a call this evening and asked me to ring you . . .'

'Thanks. All right I'll go . . .'

Lizzie heard the phone go down at the other end. She replaced her receiver and almost immediately her phone rang again and she reached for it, still breathless and trembling. 'Yes, who is it?'

'Mum, is that you?' Francie said. 'I tried to ring just now but it was rather odd; it picked up and whoever it was slammed it down again straight away.'

'How odd, darling, perhaps you got the wrong number,' Lizzie said and leaned back against the pillows. 'Are you all right?'

'Yes, I'm fine, Mum,' Francie said. 'I'm coming home tomorrow . . .'

'Shall I meet your train, darling? What time does it get in?'

'At about three I think. No, don't meet me. I can manage. You don't want to come all the way to the station to fetch me in your condition. I can easily get a taxi . . .'

'Is something the matter, Francie?'

'I've got something to tell you tomorrow and I'd rather tell you and Dad together . . .'

'Can't you tell me now, if it's important?'

'I would rather tell you and Dad tomorrow . . .'

'I'm afraid your Aunt Miriam will be here some of the time,' Lizzie said. 'I've just invited her for lunch . . .'

'Oh – well, I suppose it doesn't matter. I shan't get back until the afternoon anyway. Have you heard from Betty recently? Is she all right? I know she's safe, because Dad told me, and she sent me a pretty card, but I've been worried about her . . .'

'Yes, we all have, love, but she sounds fine. I think she enjoyed her stay with Frank's family, but she's coming home to live soon . . .'

'That makes two of us then . . .' Francie said. 'Bye, Mum. I'll see you sometime tomorrow . . .'

'Look forward to it, darling . . .'

Lizzie replaced the receiver and got up from the bed. Francie's call was intriguing; a little bit ominous. The only reason she would be coming home to live was if she'd failed her exams. At any other time that would have vexed and upset Lizzie, but at the moment all she could think about was Sebastian and whether he was safe. Would Jack arrive in time to help if there was trouble – and just where was the meeting place? It had clearly been pre-arranged, but would their plan – whatever it was – work out as they hoped?

Sebastian approached the safe house. Eric had wanted to meet at a café or somewhere public but he'd overruled him, insisting that they come here.

'If we meet in public it gives your shadow the chance to mingle with the crowd and get near to you, Eric. Do not think yourself safe because there are other people around. The merest scratch of a needle against your hand in a public place and you could be dead within a few hours. The men we're up against are ruthless, believe me. I'm not even sure who their paymasters are – though the Russians are my guess. We know they've infiltrated our own organisation and we're trying to root them out, but they're clever and they use people you would never suspect. Better to meet where I know we'll be safe and we can talk in private . . .'

Eric had been silent for a few seconds, then, 'Very well, I trust you, and only you – give me your word you will not make a phone call to anyone concerning this meeting?'

'I give you my word that I will not betray you,' Sebastian had answered. 'I didn't drive across half of Europe to have you killed here in England, my friend. Even I haven't been briefed about exactly what you have, but I know it's important. I hope it's securely hidden somewhere and not on your person.'

'My information is where no one else could get it – unless I choose to give it . . .' Eric said grimly and Sebastian guessed that most of it was probably in the man's head. He must have a terrific memory to be able to hold names, dates and places, but surely there was more? He would need proof of his claims– photographs, documents. Obviously, Eric wasn't prepared to trust anyone, which meant if he died the information he carried would be lost.

'Do you still have the gun I gave you?'

'Yes.'

'Good. If we need it, use it . . . I'll have one too . . .'

'All right – don't let me down.'

Sebastian approached the deserted warehouse, moving aside the loose boarding he'd told Eric of. He took the strong torch from his pocket and shone it on the ground, making his way further into the huge echoing empty space. It smelled of damp and decay, and the sounds of the river were close. At first he thought he'd arrived first or Eric wasn't coming, but then he sensed something close by.

'Are you here, Eric?' he whispered. For a moment no answer came and then a small scraping noise behind him. Sebastian spun round, fearing a trap. If Eric was being followed, as he suspected, someone could be here, lying in wait for them both.

'Is that you, Sebastian?'

'Yes . . .' He drew a breath of relief. 'Eric – were you followed?'

'For a while, but I think I gave them the slip. I took the underground and jumped off just before the train left, then doubled back and came here on a bus. My shadow will pick me up later when I return to the hotel – at least that is what they think, but this time I don't intend to return.'

'Have you got somewhere to go?'

'I'm trying for the ports. It's too dangerous at the airport. I know they are watched. I can get a working passage on a trawler . . .'

'As long as you have what you need,' Sebastian said. 'I don't have to know the rest . . .'

'Do you have the money?'

'A thousand pounds. If the information is what they want I think you will get more, but for that you'll need to give me a bank account here in London so that we can set the payment up for you . . .'

'Thanks . . .' Eric said and moved forward. He slid his hand into his inside pocket and for a moment Sebastian tensed, his fingers curling round the gun he had in his overcoat, but Eric drew out a bulky envelope and held it out to him. Sebastian took it and gave him the envelope with the money inside. They were about to shake hands when four figures suddenly burst through the doorway. In the sudden light from outside, it was possible to see that they were carrying handguns, which were pointed at Sebastian.

'We'll take that if you please, Mr Winters . . .'

'You swore you wouldn't betray me . . .' Eric said and looked at Sebastian accusingly.

'He didn't,' the cool English voice said. 'You should not assume that because you lose one man you've lost us all . . . you and your information are too important to us . . .'

Sebastian cursed softly. Someone had managed to follow Eric and called reinforcements. So where the hell was Jack? Had Lizzie got the timing wrong? Then he sensed movement behind him and breathed a sigh of relief.

'Look out, Sebastian,' a voice he knew well cried from the shadows. Sebastian dived to the floor, pulling Eric with him and half covering him with his body, as a hail of bullets ripped through the darkness that was suddenly pierced with bright light as several spotlights were beamed on them.

The shots passed over them, though Sebastian heard a moan from Eric, but even as he reached to see if there was blood, the firing stopped. A moment later, he felt hands pulling him up and looking at his hands saw they were covered in blood.

'For God's sake tell me that isn't yours,' Jack said, emerging from behind the blinding lights. 'I'm sorry I couldn't prevent this – but it was always going to come to a showdown . . . and I needed to trap them so I waited until they announced themselves . . .'

Sebastian saw that several men wearing dark green combat dress were examining the men they'd shot, two of whom seemed to be still alive, but bleeding; one had knelt with his hands behind his head and looked unhurt, but another was clearly dead. Sebastian was only interested in the one that still lay at his feet. He heard a moan and bent over Eric, discovering that he was bleeding heavily from a wound to his leg.

'Damn,' Sebastian said. 'I'm sorry I didn't get you down soon enough . . .'

'Are you hit anywhere else, sir?' Jack said and bent over Eric; he took the belt from the dark mackintosh he was wearing to make a tourniquet, working efficiently to stop the flow of blood. 'I'm so sorry you caught a stray shot. 'We've been following you ever since you got to London, protecting your back – but unfortunately this evening, you gave our man the slip, as well as theirs. However, acting on information received, I was able to set this up – but not in time to stop them trying to grab you.'

Eric blinked in the strong lights. 'I might have been killed . . .'

'I can assure you they think you're too valuable for that,' Jack told him with a smile. 'Now, I know you don't know who to trust, but I could've had you killed days ago had I wanted. I could also have pulled you in but I needed to catch the men who betrayed you – and, this was my opportunity. I'm glad to say we are now in a position to root them all out, including the traitor in our own department. As for you, you're going to a special hospital until we can debrief you and set you up with a new identity . . . after that, you'll be free to go where you please . . . although the Americans would love to talk to you about some of the detail you have on Russian intentions towards the West . . .' He took out a flat gold case and offered the contents to Eric, lighting the slim Turkish cigarette he chose as casually as if he were out for a Sunday stroll. 'Rather good this brand I always think . . .'

'Is he really one of your colleagues' Eric demanded of Sebastian, who grinned and nodded. Jack was wearing an evening suit and a shirt with a frill down the front under the mac he'd let fall open when he removed the belt.

'Oh yes, Jack is for real – and you can trust him as much as you trust me. He's never let me down yet . . .'

Jack smiled, lifting his fine brows. 'You can leave this to us now, Seb. You'd better get back to that wife of yours – and tell her I'll be glad to enrol her in the service any time she likes . . .'

'Over my dead body,' Sebastian retorted. 'Lizzie doesn't need any of this – and nor do I . . .'

'I give you my word we shan't be bothering you again . . . unless there's an international emergency, like another war.'

Sebastian sent him a look that would've slayed any other man. Jack merely lifted his brows and started giving orders to his men.

'Good luck in the future,' he said to Eric, who was now on his feet, but leaning heavily on one of the men in combat gear.

'You too,' Eric said. 'Thanks for helping me . . .' he hesitated, then, 'Tell Gretchen I do care about her but I can't afford to get close to anyone . . . marriage isn't for men like me and nothing else is good enough for her. Can you make her understand why? Please . . .'

'I'll talk to her but I'm not sure she'll accept what I have to say . . .'

'Do your best . . .' Eric smiled wryly. 'I'm not much of a catch – she could be a widow before she was a wife. Tell her that . . .'

Sebastian nodded and turned away. He would do what Eric asked for Gretchen's sake, but that was all he could do for Eric. Whatever Jack said, as far as he was concerned all this was a closed book. In another ten days it would be Christmas and he intended to take a long holiday . . .

CHAPTER 29

'You can expect your coursework including the two portraits to be returned in time for Christmas,' Miss Honiton said as she handed Francie the envelope containing her exam results. 'It's a pity about the portraits, but I'm sure you know best what you want to do with them.'

'They were never intended for sale,' Francie said. 'I'm flattered that the gallery wanted to include them in an exhibition of work by young artists but they're meant to be presents.'

'Yes, I perfectly understand . . .' Miss Honiton offered her hand. 'I shall be sorry not to see you here next term, Francie. However, I do wish you all the best with your future work and I hope you have a good life.'

'Thank you, Miss Honiton. I've enjoyed my time here.'

'Very well. You'd better go or you'll miss your train.'

'I have a taxi coming to fetch me,' Francie said. 'I just have to say goodbye to my friends . . .'

She walked back to the room she'd shared with Jilly and Averil. They had their things packed and were ready to leave.

'What was it like?' Jilly asked. 'She congratulated me on getting a B+ – but I know she thinks I'll never get anywhere much with my art. Mum won't care because she thought it was a waste of time, but now she'll have me in a secretarial college as soon as she can sign the forms . . .'

'It's not fair,' Francie said and embraced her. 'Come and stay with us for a while. Your artistic flair could be put to good use in millinery. After all, art comes in many forms, doesn't it?'

'I wish I had the chance to work for your mum,' Jilly said. 'I'd love to be her secretary-cum-assistant . . .'

'I'll ask her,' Francie said but Jilly shook her head. 'Mum will be so cross that I didn't win a scholarship. She'll insist I do a proper job . . .'

'Mothers,' Averil moaned. 'Mine wants me married at the earliest opportunity. She doesn't see the point of a career for women . . . even though I've got my first commission, but I'm determined to resist and my aunt agrees with me.'

'You've done better than any of us to be already working in the art department of a design firm,' Francie said admiringly. 'It's a good job and you can do very well in commercial art.'

'I certainly intend to . . .'

'Lucky you,' Jilly said. 'A nice sensible little job until I'm older and then find a rich man to marry that's Mum's idea of the dutiful daughter . . . especially as I've been told I have no real talent for art . . .'

'You should go and live with your gran,' Francie said, 'but both of you got better marks than I did . . .'

'It's so unfair,' Jilly cried. 'Those portraits were wonderful, Francie. If they'd marked them you would've got an A at least . . . but to just ignore them isn't fair.'

'I knew they didn't fit with the work we were supposed to do, but it doesn't matter,' Francie said and hugged both girls in turn. 'I'll just have to see what my parents say . . .'

'Good luck,' Jilly said and squeezed her round the waist. 'Well, I'd better go if I'm going to catch that train. I'm going to Gran's for Christmas. My mother is abroad with some friends and won't be back until next year so I've got breathing space.'

'You should come and see Mum,' Francie said. 'She really might have a job for you . . .'

'All right, I'll come for a couple of days. I'll telephone and let you know.'

With promises to meet in future, the three girls separated, going outside with their hand luggage. Their trunks had been sent on by train, and Francie's portraits would arrive within a few days. She was thoughtful as she boarded her train half an hour later. She'd hoped she might hear from Michael that *Vogue* had taken one of his freelance photographs of her for the front cover of the magazine, but so far she'd heard nothing. *Styled* hadn't written to her either so it looked as if the work had dried up, at least for the moment.

She'd failed her exams because she'd taken too much time off for the modelling, which now looked as if it might have come to a halt – and what her father would say when he knew, Francie hardly dared to think. She knew he was proud of her talent and he was sure to be angry – but the best thing she could do was to tell him as soon as she got in, because the longer she left it the harder it would become.

'Betty darling,' Lizzie jumped up and opened her arms as her daughter entered the room. 'I'm so glad to see you, my love.' Tears trickled down her cheeks as Betty ran to her and they embraced.

'Mum, I'm so sorry for all I've put you through . . .'

'Not your fault, my love. That awful man taking you off like that . . . thank God for Frank! I don't know what we should have done if he hadn't been so brave.'

'I was very lucky Frank was on his way to see me,' Betty said solemnly, 'but it was my fault, Mum. If I hadn't gone off with Pierre in the first place, none of it need have happened.'

'You were upset and that's our fault for discussing you behind your back.'

'No, it was mine,' Betty said and swiped away her tears. 'Will you forgive me?'

'Of course, I will, my love. Don't you know how much we love you?'

'I think I do now,' Betty said and kissed her cheek.

'You'd better, because I need my daughter here with me, Betty.' Lizzie placed her hands on her bump and sighed. 'I shall be glad when this is all over – and I want you here with your family when your brother is born . . .'

'Of course I shall be here, Mum. I've got some ideas for the future, but I'm not going anywhere yet and when I do I'll talk to you and Dad about it . . .'

'No running off to the Borders or anywhere else?'

'No, I shan't go back there just yet, though I've been invited for a holiday in the summer – in fact we're all invited to go whenever we like . . .' She smiled at a memory of walking the hills with Matt. 'Did you know Matt came down to see me and then brought me home? Frank asked him to look after me . . .' Betty looked around her, feeling happy to be home. 'Where's Francie? I tried phoning her college but she wasn't there.'

'You got here before your sister,' Lizzie said. 'Just in time to have lunch with Aunt Miriam . . .' She led her daughter into the sitting room where her father's aunt was sitting. 'I hope Sebastian will be able to join us for lunch, but he had something he had to attend to this morning. I know he wants to get back, but he said if he isn't here by one we should just go ahead.'

'Betty, darling, come and kiss me,' Aunt Miriam stood up and opened her arms. 'I've been so very worried about you, my love. Let me look at you . . .' She held Betty at arm's length and studied her. 'You look marvellous. Have you put on the tiniest bit of weight?'

'I may have, just a pound or two,' Betty said and laughed, giving her a hug. 'I'm so glad to see you, Miriam – and sorry I put you through all that stress . . .'

'Oh, don't worry about me; it's your mum you need to apologise to.' Miriam frowned at her.

'Mum knows I'm sorry . . .'

'No more apologies,' Lizzie said and smiled at her. 'You're home now and you can take your time deciding what to do next . . .'

'I don't want to return to school . . . and I doubt Mr Walter will take me on now. I tried to speak to him from the village phone box once but his secretary said he was busy and asked me not to bother him again. I think he was offended because in his eyes I didn't bother to show up . . .'

'Well, we could hardly tell him what really happened. Romany said you weren't well, but perhaps he didn't believe her. You can work with her for a while, but there's no rush to do anything, love . . .'

'I was looking forward to working at that fashion house, but . . . It doesn't matter. I'll be happy with Romany or Ed . . .'

'Your father won't try to stop you, though he has a few plans of his own. He hasn't shared them with me yet, but I expect he will when he gets us all together . . .'

'Gosh that dinner smells good, Mum. Frank's

gran is a good cook too, but she doesn't do salmon in white wine or that prawn thing you do – it's all meat puddings and chicken casseroles, food that fills you up and keeps you going in the fields. Sometimes it's bitterly cold there but they still have to count the sheep and make sure the silly creatures haven't hurt themselves. They're always getting into trouble . . .'

'You seem to have enjoyed yourself there, love?'

'Yes, I did,' Betty smiled. 'Frank's grandmother gave me this trunk of old clothes and I made things for myself – and also a dress for her. She couldn't believe how smart it looked. I also helped with some of the chores and went up on the hill with Matt and the dogs . . .' She broke off, looking at her mother. 'That's enough about me – what about you, Mum? How are you?'

'I'm very well, darling,' Lizzie's hand lovingly stroked her stomach. 'Your brother is behaving himself nicely.'

Betty laughed, looking at her mischievously. 'How do you know it's a boy?'

'I just know. I've had two girls and this is – well, it's just different . . .'

'Yes, I agree with Lizzie. I think she's carrying a boy this time . . .' Miriam said and smiled, then, 'I've got a letter for you in my bag, Betty. Don't let me forget, I'll give it to you before I go . . .'

Lizzie reached for Betty's hand and squeezed it tightly. 'It's so good to have you back and safe with us, darling. I was so afraid I might lose you . . .'

'I'm glad to be here, Mum. I'm looking forward to Christmas and helping you and Francie decorate the tree and shopping for presents – and I'm truly sorry I caused you and Dad all this trouble . . .'

'It's over now and we shan't speak of it again, unless you want to, my love. For now I want you to stay here, get ready for a lovely family Christmas and be happy drawing your lovely designs – and then we'll talk about the future . . . so come and have your lunch now . . .'

After lunch, Betty unpacked her clothes in her bedroom. She'd brought the things she'd made while staying with Gran and her family, because she liked some of the ideas she'd put into them and would now have the opportunity to make them and sketch them again with different materials. Her short stay at Gran's had been wonderful, but she was glad to be home. Betty wanted to spend time with her family . . . to put all the things that had hurt her safely behind her . . . and then perhaps she might be ready for a new life.

The peace and serenity of living in the Border countryside with Gran and her family had restored her spirit and she'd particularly enjoyed walking the hills with Matt and the dogs.

They'd laughed and talked, just as they always had, and somehow the shadows of that time in Paris had begun to lift. Matt was still her big brother, the generous protective man she'd known all her life, but Betty knew in her heart something more was happening between them. As yet it was little more than a special friendship. Matt was treating her like a precious piece of china, and she thought he knew or guessed some of what had happened to her so he was being careful not to scare her, but Matt could never do that, because she'd always loved him . . . Betty wasn't sure if that love was changing, becoming something more and it was far too soon to think about a relationship, because there was Frank too and she didn't want to hurt his feelings. He'd done so much for her, but she couldn't give him the kind of love he wanted from her . . .

'Are you coming down, darling?' her mother's voice cut into her reverie. 'Miriam is ready to leave and she has something for you . . .'

Betty smiled at her and followed her from the room. Her aunt had her hat and coat on and was standing in the hall, looking a little anxious. She took a crumpled envelope from her pocket and offered it to Betty.

'This came a week or two ago. I wasn't sure what to do, love – because it's from Paris and I thought . . . I wondered if it was something you would rather not see . . .'

'I don't think Pierre sent it,' Betty said, 'it isn't his writing; I think it's Marie's . . .' She took the envelope from her aunt. Inside were three sheets of paper, and a cheque. The cheque was for a thousand francs and she stared at it for a moment, before turning to the letter. As she read her excitement mounted. 'This is from Marie . . . I worked in her café for a while and made her a dress. She showed it to her cousin and, although I didn't know, she took her one of my sketchbooks. Marie's cousin runs a small fashion house in Paris and she has used four of my designs in her winter collection . . . and this is in payment . . .'

'That's wonderful,' Lizzie said. 'Exactly what you'd hoped for – isn't it?'

Betty nodded, reading on down the page. 'Marie's cousin Hortense wants to meet me and discuss terms for . . .' She looked up at her mother. 'She is willing to give me a job designing and making the designs into samples – or to simply buy the designs she likes from me . . . but she wants me to go to Paris in early spring for a meeting . . .'

'Betty . . .' her mother looked at her doubtfully. 'How do you feel about that, darling?'

'I'm not sure. Of course it would be wonderful . . . but I shouldn't want to go alone and only if Dad agreed . . .'

'If Dad agreed to what?' Sebastian's voice asked from the end of the hall. Three pairs of eyes turned to look at him as he strode towards them. 'Betty, my dearest daughter . . . how good it is to see you . . .' he said and swept her into a bear hug that left Betty laughing and gasping for breath. 'Never run off without telling us where to find you again. I don't think I could stand it . . .'

'I won't; I promise I won't,' Betty vowed as she looked into his eyes and saw the love of the father she'd adored as a little girl. 'I'm so very sorry, Dad. I've wished a thousand times it had never happened . . . I was such a spoiled little fool . . .'

'No. It was all my fault. I spoke hastily and without thinking of the hurt I could inflict. If you'd waited for me to talk to you, Betty, I was going to tell you that your talent lay with clothes not hats . . . though you're good at trimming them, but no one gets close to your mother for designing hats . . .'

'He's biased, but right, you do have a talent for designing clothes,' Lizzie said and laughed. She was looking very happy as she watched their reconciliation. 'Betty has an offer to design for a fashion house in Paris. They want her to go and visit in the spring . . .'

'That's wonderful news, Betty,' Sebastian said, 'but I think you should wait until later in the year before you decide to work there again, although I'll take you over for a couple of days to a meeting if you wish . . .'

'This is a family discussion. I think I should go,' Miriam said, but Sebastian turned to look at her.

'No, please stay. I was saving this until Francie got back . . . but I've arranged to rent a house for us in France for three months next summer – July to the end of September . . . it's quite large so there would be room if you wanted to come, Miriam . . .'

'Sebastian!' Lizzie cried, looking puzzled. 'You haven't said anything about this to me . . .?'

'No, I wanted it to be a surprise. Betty can work with this fashion house if she wishes and it will help her to know we're there if she needs us – and Francie will be on holiday from Art College. So it will just suit everyone . . .'

'Just one thing wrong with that, Dad,' Francie's voice said and they all turned to look at her in the doorway from the kitchen. No one had heard her arrive in the excitement of Sebastian's announcement. 'I'm afraid there isn't going to be a scholarship – I only got a B for my exams and Miss Honiton gave the scholarship to someone else . . .'

'Francie?' Sebastian's face clouded. 'Your teacher was a little harsh but she will realise that you've been worrying over your mother . . .'

'Miss Honiton knows that, Dad,' Francie said, coming forward to join the group. Betty moved to meet her and they hugged. Betty whispered in her ear and Francie smiled and shook her head. 'It's no one's fault but mine. I neglected the coursework to do other stuff. One of the examiner's loved the portraits so much that he asked if he could sell them in his gallery, but I said no. I have other plans for them . . .'

'Your fault, Francie?' Sebastian was looking at her hard and Betty felt her tense. She entwined her fingers with her sister. 'Are you admitting the modelling is to blame for this?'

'Not entirely,' Francie said. 'I've loved it and it's been fun, but I've managed to fit in some work all the way through – I just couldn't make myself do some of the stuff the college wanted. I don't know how far I'll go as a model but I should like to try – if I get the chance. Michael says I may not be offered anything else anyway . . . he says I need to be based in London if I want to grab all the available work, because you have to be ready to fly anywhere at a few hours' notice . . .'

'Who is this Michael?'

'A brilliant freelance photographer. He took some great pictures of me to sell but I don't know if he did . . .'

'So then you can go back to college and settle to your real work,' her father said. 'Your teacher contacted me about this, Francie. We had a long talk and after some persuasion, she's agreed to give you one more chance. You have to return to college after Christmas and finish all the course-work you neglected and if you pass your exams at the end of the summer term, you can go to the Art School in Paris next October when you're sixteen – and perhaps Betty will be working there by then . . .'

'Are you sure, Dad?' Francie asked and her father smiled.

'You have to promise to settle to your work, Francie . . .'

'Yes, Dad . . .' she said and Betty gave her a sympathetic smile.

'That's a wonderful chance for you, Francie,' Aunt Miriam said and kissed her cheek, 'Take notice of your father, like a good girl – and now I really am going, because I'm meeting someone for a game of bridge later . . .'

Sebastian laughed as she shut the front door with a little click. 'Our Miriam has more to her than meets the eye . . .' He looked at Betty and Francie. 'Why don't you girls go upstairs and have a chat – and then I'll take you all out to a nice meal . . . it's almost Christmas and we should celebrate now that we're back together again . . .'

Lizzie looked round as Sebastian entered their bedroom late that night. She'd undressed and was sitting brushing her hair, which had recently been cut into a fashionable bob that suited her and made her look younger. His smile as he saw her made her heart race and she stood up, holding out her hand to him. She felt so lucky to have him back in one piece after what he'd told her about his meeting with Eric and Jack.

'Everything all right, darling?' she asked a little tentatively.

'Yes. I just telephoned Marianne. I wanted to let Gretchen know that Eric is safe. I have to talk to her and give her a message from him. She has gone out with a friend – a woman, not a man. I doubt she'll ever marry after what she went through, but they've signed the lease of the café. She thinks they might just manage to open on Christmas Eve – and she wants us all to go for a meal. Miriam and the girls and friends if they like.

I accepted because she needs to show gratitude and it will be rather nice to have a typical German Christmas meal . . .'

'Of course we'll go. We shall have turkey on Christmas Day as usual. The girls will help so it won't be too hard for me, Sebastian . . . why don't you ask Marianne and Gretchen to come to us on the day?'

'I suggested it but they wanted their first Christmas here on their own – and they will have so much work to do setting up their restaurant. We'll ask them round in the New Year perhaps, and then gradually introduce them to all our friends.'

'Yes, but we must make sure they don't feel neglected. Perhaps I could call on Marianne and take her our presents . . .'

'That would be nice, darling – if you're up to it?'

'I'm really very strong, Sebastian.'

'I know, besides, you look so well.'

'I feel marvellous. Our son seems quite happy where he is for the moment . . .' Lizzie held out her arms to him and nestled into his chest as he kissed her.

It would be Christmas very soon now and she had everything she could ever want right here in her own home. Her daughters were safe and Sebastian loved her. She had never been happier . . .

CHAPTER 30

'Look it's the new *Styled* cover . . .' Francie said as the two sisters paused by the stall selling newspapers and magazines. She picked it up, disappointed to see that her picture hadn't made the front cover. They'd used one of Michael's photos but it was of the more experienced girl who had also been in Cornwall for the shoot. 'Arlene said they might use me on the cover but they haven't . . .'

'Are you inside?' Betty asked, leaning over her shoulder to look. 'We'll buy a copy and have a proper look – let's have a drink and go through it carefully . . .'

Francie followed her sister into the small café and they ordered fizzy drinks and a sticky bun each. Francie flicked through the magazine. She saw several of Michael's pictures, but there was only one small one of her.

'He took loads. I was sure they would use them . . .'

'Never mind, love,' Betty said sympathetically. 'I know you enjoyed the modelling but if you wanted to carry on you wouldn't be able to continue your art – do you really want to give it up. I could talk to Dad; try to make him understand . . .'

'No . . .' Francie's eyes pricked with tears. Her sister was just being sensible and Francie knew in her heart she was right. Modelling was fun, but her true talent was for her art. 'No, it's probably for the best. Michael told me that I would be lucky to get the cover spot. He warned me that lots of girls never really make it.' She raised her head proudly. 'I'd be a fool to throw away my chance of getting a place at the college in Paris for a silly dream, wouldn't I?'

'Let's not worry about it now, Francie. We've got Christmas to look forward to and then we're going to France next summer holidays. You're going to be a successful artist that's all that matters, isn't it?'

Francie nodded, and then a determined look came into her eyes. 'I'll work hard at my art – and forget about modelling. Why don't we buy Mum a nice twinset and some perfume? She always likes things like that . . .'

'Yes, she does,' Betty agreed and smiled. 'I'm going to get Aunt Miriam some new leather gloves and you can get her a scarf. I'm not sure what Dad would like . . .'

'Us home and happy,' Francie told her. 'We'll get him brandy and cigars if you like. But I'm giving him a special present . . . and I've got one for you too . . .'

'I'm not telling what I've got you,' Betty said

and laughed, because the shadows had fled from Francie's face. 'I've got a lot of extra ones to buy this year – Gran needs a nice warm pair of sheepskin slippers and I want to get both Matt and Frank something really nice – though I'm not sure Frank will be here for Christmas.'

'Why not?'

Betty shook her head. 'He rang me earlier this morning. I think he may be going away . . .'

'But why, Frank?' Betty asked later that afternoon when Frank called round to tell her that he was flying to America on one of the new transatlantic flights with BOAC. 'Why must you go away now? You've only just got back from your last trip abroad; I thought you were planning on working in London?'

'My firm changed their minds and asked me to transfer to their office in New York . . .'

'Is that the only reason, Frank? I know what you did for me – but all that awful stuff with Pierre is finished.'

'I know and I'm glad you're safe, more so than you will ever know,' Frank said and his eyes were warm with love. 'I care about you, Betty; so very much – but my firm wants me to leave for America next week. It's important and I can't really refuse. I'll be gone for eighteen months . . . besides, I don't think I'm the right man for you. I think there's someone else who might be, though . . .'

'Is that why you told Matt to come down and bring me back to London?'

'You've always listened to him. I think you care about Matt more than you ever realised, Betty. Pierre was different and he seduced you, but he was never the right man for you, even if he'd loved you . . .'

'Frank . . . I don't know what to say . . . I'm not even sure what I do feel . . .'

'You don't have to say anything. I only did what any friend would do – it was just lucky that I was in the right place at the right time. If Matt had been there he'd have done just the same . . .'

'Matt?'

'Yes . . .' Frank smiled. 'I told him I'd killed Pierre and he said I did just what he might have done in my place.' Frank's voice was husky with emotion. 'That meant a lot to me, Betty . . .'

'Oh, Frank . . .' Betty was close to tears, because she sensed that he'd had a choice about going off to America, but he'd made his decision in order to set her free – free of any sense of duty or obligation. 'You've done so much for me . . . rescuing me and taking me to your family home . . .'

'I wanted to be sure you were safe – because I care what happens to you . . .'

'I'm truly grateful for all you did . . .' the pain in his face stopped her. 'I'm so sorry, Frank . . .'

'Don't be, my darling.' He came forward to take her hands. 'I think I knew after it happened that somehow Pierre's shadow would always lie between us – but you have to move on, put it all behind you now . . .'

'I have, truly, I have,' Betty said and went to kiss him softly on the lips. 'Thank you for making it easy for me, Frank. Believe me when I say that I sincerely wish you happiness in the future.'

'And I hope that you will find love with the kind of man who can care for you and make you happy. I'll never forget you, my special girl . . .'

Betty stood staring at the door as it closed behind him, and her eyelashes were wet with tears. Frank had made the decision she'd found too difficult – he'd walked away and left her free to live her own life.

Francie sat on her bed wrapping her Christmas presents for the family. As a child she'd always been unbearably excited as the day came nearer and secret parcels were hastily tucked out of sight whenever she or Betty entered a room. This Christmas was going to be exciting for her, because she had her special presents to give. The portraits she'd been given no marks for her in her exams and the small oil on canvas she'd done of her mother that no one had seen.

After seeing the contentment in her mother's face after her father had announced that he was taking them all to France next summer, she'd decided on the picture she wanted to paint – and it was one of those halcyon days they'd all spent on the beach one lazy summer in Cornwall. She'd copied the photograph; at least, she'd taken draw-ings of her mother's face then and painted it in the delicate colours that suited her lovely English rose complexion, which had been just kissed by the sun. The photograph was in black and white but in her mind Francie saw her mother as she'd been then and as she worked on the canvas it had come magically to life – and yet when she'd finished she saw that she'd made Mum older than when they were children. All the images she'd been juggling in her head had somehow come together, showing Lizzie Winters as a beautiful, wise and loving woman, which was exactly what she was . . . but there was also a hint of something more there, perhaps sorrow or hurt or just uncertainty. Francie's mind's eye had seen it, even though she couldn't put a name to it.

Francie smiled as she finished all the small gifts with bows of ribbon and sparkly tinsel. She enjoyed making her presents look special and for the moment she had nothing else to do – until her return to college.

She was lucky that her father had managed to persuade Miss Honiton to give her another chance, and she made up her mind that she would work really hard to pass the exams she'd failed. If she didn't manage it this time then she would have to decide what she wanted to do next. Perhaps she could afford to pay for a shorter course in Paris from the money she'd earned from her modelling, though she wanted to pass with flying colours and make everyone proud of her. Modelling had been fun while it lasted, but perhaps Michael had been a better friend than she'd realised by suggesting she would do better to stick to her art.

CHAPTER 31

Lizzie looked round her festive table at her family. Bright, glittering crackers were waiting to be pulled, and the napkins were special ones with Christmas trees embroidered into the corners. Aunt Miriam, Beth, Tony, Tom and Matt as well as her daughters and Sebastian. They were all her family and she loved them all dearly. Beth's daughter had been taken into the maternity hospital the previous evening and they were awaiting the call that would tell them there was another new baby in the family. Beth had gone straight to the ward but been told to go home and wait for a phone call, because it might be hours before Jenny gave birth and her husband was with her.

Sebastian raised a glass of the special wine he'd bought to accompany the turkey and all the trimmings. 'Good health and happiness to you all,' he said and touched his glass to Lizzie's and then to Beth's. Everyone else did the same and then sipped the wine.

'Great stuff, Sebastian,' Matt said and grinned at Betty. 'You won't mind if I come over and stay with you at the chateau for a while in the summer? I'm writing a book and some of it is set in Paris. I'd like to stay for a few weeks to get the flavour . . .'

'The chateau has about twenty rooms,' Sebastian said. 'It belongs to a friend of mine and he's off to America for the next year, and since it is only a few miles outside of Paris I thought it would make an ideal base for us – room for friends, boyfriends, girlfriends and relations . . . as many as you like. Lizzie loves to have her family and friends around her . . .'

'It's going to be lovely for you all,' Beth said. 'I'm not sure if Tony has time, but I'd love to come for a couple of weeks when you go . . .'

'You will both be welcome,' Lizzie said and smiled at her. 'Now tuck in everyone, because I don't want any of this going to waste . . .'

The conversation flowed as easily as the delicious wine; laughter and love and friendship, making it yet another wonderful Christmas, as so many others had been in the past. In the drawing room, which Francie and Betty had decked with holly, paper chains and glittery baubles there was a huge Christmas tree, which almost touched the ceiling in front of the long French windows. It had taken three of them to get it in and most of a morning to decorate it, a shining silver star on top. Several big comfortable chairs were grouped about the room and a huge fire threw out lots of heat so that the big room was warm and cosy. Sebastian had placed a long play stereo record of Christmas music on the new High Fidelity radiogram that he'd bought for Lizzie's present and the words of 'Silent Night' could be heard in the background, though the laughter and chatter almost drowned it out.

Beth and Lizzie had placed gifts for each other and each other's family beneath the tree, and that came after the sumptuous lunch. It was a good thing their drawing room was big enough to accommodate their growing family, Lizzie mused as she looked at Betty. Her eldest daughter looked so happy that Lizzie's heart swelled with love. For a time she'd thought they'd lost the daughter she loved so much, but she was back with them, and that was all she needed to make her happiness complete. Betty hadn't told her about what had happened in Paris yet, but they were becoming close again and Lizzie knew that when she was ready Betty would tell her as much as she could.

Lizzie's gaze moved to her younger daughter. Francie would be sixteen next October, but she already looked seventeen at least. Perhaps it was the experiences of this past year that had made her grow up? She seemed to have accepted that she was going back to college and had to work hard for her exams if she wanted that scholarship for Paris.

Turning her gaze on her husband, Lizzie smiled. For a while she'd feared that she might have lost the love that was so precious to her, but it was there in his eyes as he met her gaze, and she loved him all the more for what he'd done. Lizzie had been thinking of taking on another designer for business now that she had a new baby on the way, and Francie's friend Jilly had given her an idea. When she'd popped up for a couple of days before Christmas Lizzie had asked her if she would like to come and stay with them here in London and go to France with them in the summer.

'I shall need someone to pop back to London and visit the workshops, talk to Romany – and to take any models or samples I make. I need a girl who will be loyal to me and if I train her in my ways will gradually be able to take over from me in years to come . . .'

Jilly had looked at her as if the heavens had opened. 'Will you truly take me on as your assistant, Mrs Winters? You know I only got a B+ in design . . .'

'Francie got just a B,' Lizzie said and smiled.

So it had been agreed that Jilly should work for her and Lizzie was looking forward to gradually passing on the load for *Lizzie Larch Hats*. She was excited about taking the girl on her staff and as a member of her ever growing family.

Lizzie sighed with contentment as she saw all the happy faces around her. It was such a lovely day – and they still had all the present giving to come after lunch and the Queen's speech . . .

Everyone quietened as Sebastian switched on the TV and they saw the setting of Her Majesty at home in Sandringham, watching with pleasure as some footage of the royal children were included for the first time at Christmas. The speech spoke of the importance of family and spiritual values, and for Lizzie it brought home even more how lucky she was to have both her daughters home safe and well . . .

Betty stared at the portrait of her father, hardly believing that it was hers. Francie had told her that the look on his face was when he'd asked if she were home and she'd caught the hope, anguish and hurt so perfectly that it caught at Betty's heart. If Dad felt like that about her she would be an idiot to ever doubt his love again . . . and then she looked at the present he'd given her this year. It was the exact same swan that she'd smashed so wantonly against the wall when she'd been so angry with him. Tears stung her eyes and her gaze strayed to him, as for a moment their eyes met and she felt the warmth of the love that had always been hers. She smiled and got up, went across the room to hug him, feeling her throat close with emotion as he held her tight.

'Thanks, Dad, it's lovely . . .' was all she could manage but she looked up and knew that he understood.

Betty had tried to buy a swan for herself but she'd been told they were unavailable, out of production. Dad must have searched everywhere to find it – or perhaps he'd had it commissioned specially knowing him. He was like that, always going that extra length to please. She turned as Francie came back from trying on the new dress she'd made for her. It was a full-skirted shirtwaist in yellow and white gingham and it suited her well. She was also wearing the yellow ballerina-style leather shoes that Betty had had dyed to match.

'You look lovely, Francie,' she said and hugged her. 'I love your present. Nothing could ever be as wonderful as this . . .'

'I did it for you so that you could never forget how much Dad loves you,' Francie said and kissed her cheek. 'We all love you, Betty. Every one of us . . .'

'I know. I'm very lucky,' Betty said and smiled happily. 'Mum was crying over the picture you did of her when you went to change . . . she loves it and so do I . . .'

'Well, then, Betty,' Matt said, coming up to them with a box of peppermint creams. He'd given Betty an Elvis Presley record she'd been wanting for ages as his present and some Coty perfume. She'd bought him a silk tie, which he'd put on immediately. 'I hear that you've been given a chance to train with a fashion house in Paris. So how long before I see your label in all the fashionable shops?'

'I'm not sure I can take it up,' Betty said. 'Dad's coming to the meeting with me in February, but I'm a bit nervous of living over there again . . . I'll probably take a short course in the workshops when everyone else is there in the summer, but Romany says I can do some evening classes here.'

'If you need to pop over to Paris anytime just ask me,' Matt told her. 'I can always spare a couple of days, or longer, to come with you . . . and I promise you no one is going to hurt you with me around . . .'

'You're my private bodyguard . . .' Betty said laughing and pinched one of his chocolates. 'All right, that's a deal . . . I'll probably need to pop over now and then when I have some designs to show her – and I *should* like to study in her workshops for a while.' And she would be much happier if Matt was around . . .

'Who the hell is that?' Matt said as the doorbell rang. 'I'll go and send them packing unless it's someone we want . . .'

Betty laughed, because he could do it easily with a glare. She couldn't think who would be calling on Christmas afternoon. She sipped her glass of orange juice and ate another peppermint cream from the box he'd left with her. Matt came back looking puzzled. He had something in his hand, but it was just a rather large envelope, so not a late present.

'Who was it? Surely not the postman?'

'I've no idea,' Matt said. 'He wouldn't give me his name . . . just handed me this for Francie . . .'

Francie frowned as she took the huge envelope. Opening it, she withdrew the magazine inside and saw the picture Michael had taken of her smiling at him as the wind blew her hair. She'd been wearing a coat over her glamorous dress and bent

402

over her sketch pad, a thoughtful look on her face. She read the title and saw it was a photography magazine. Turning to the title page, she read out aloud the dedication, which said that the cover was of a young model named Francie Winters taken by Michael – and it had won a prestigious photography competition.

She saw that a brief message had been slipped inside the pages.

Sorry, it was the best I could do. I tried Vogue, because I thought they might use it for a cover as I said, but they refused it so I thought this was the next best thing. Happy Christmas Francie and hope to see you around . . .

Francie handed the magazine and the note to Betty. She frowned over it and returned it with a lift of her brows.

'It's a wonderful cover, Francie – not what you wanted but a nice gesture on his part . . .'

'Yes . . .' Francie's smile was beautiful and Betty felt her sister's happiness reach out to touch her. 'It doesn't matter now, Betty. I've made up my mind. Modelling was fun for a while and I enjoyed doing it – but Michael was right, it isn't really the life I want. He's an artist in his own field and he recognised my talent – art is what I do best and I'm going to work hard and try to learn all that I can so that perhaps one day I'll have my own shows in London, Paris and even New York.

'I'm sure you will,' Betty told her lovingly. 'If these portraits are a taste of what is to come, you'll be a real talent one day, love. I can see your pictures selling for thousands of pounds and all the rich people in the world will want to own one. I'll be offered a fortune for my painting, but I'll never sell even if I'm starving in a garret . . .'

'You'll probably be rich and famous long before that,' Francie said. 'I'll be known as the sister of that famous fashion designer . . .'

'What are you two girls giggling over?' Lizzie asked, smiling at them indulgently as they both fell about laughing.

'Francie's picture has won a prestigious prize for the photographer,' Betty said and took it to her.

'It's lovely, Francie,' their mother said and passed it on to Beth and then Sebastian took it. He looked at it for ages and then smiled his approval.

'I'd like to meet this gentleman,' he said. 'I'd like a copy of this blown up to portrait size so that I can frame it . . . and perhaps he'd take photos of the family . . .'

'I think he's too busy, Dad,' Francie said. 'He's a famous freelance fashion photographer, based in London, but he's hardly ever here, because he's in such demand . . .'

'In that case he might care to come to Paris while we're there next summer,' Sebastian replied, his eyes never leaving her face. 'I want a copy of this, Francie – and then I'll have both my beautiful girls on the wall of my study . . .' He looked proudly at the painting Francie had done of her sister.

Betty and Francie looked at each other and started giggling and clutching each other.

'And what is so funny about that?' Sebastian asked with a straight face, even though his eyes were laughing with them. 'One of these days, when I'm old and grey and all my children have grown up and flown the nest, I'll need something to remind me of my lovely daughters.'

'We'll never leave you alone for long,' Betty promised. 'We might be married or famous, we might even be living miles and miles away, but we'll always be in touch . . . won't we, Francie?'

'Of course you will,' Lizzie said and her smile embraced them all. 'You're our daughters and your father wants you to be happy and make your own lives and families. That is what having children is all about . . . the start of more families that go on and on until you are just a fond memory in the distant past . . .'

'That's very profound, Lizzie,' Miriam said. 'I didn't realise you were such a deep thinker . . .'

'I'm not,' Lizzie disclaimed, 'but I know that my family is what makes me happy. Success in business is good and it means you can afford the nice things in life . . . but loving and giving and enjoying your family is the important bit . . .'

'Yes, I agree with you,' Tony said surprising them all. 'I wanted Matt to come into the business with me, but I've realised that he has his own talents and it's only fair he has his chance to make them work . . . so I'll be training up a younger man to help me – and you can do what makes you happy, son . . .'

'Dad . . .' Matt looked at him in surprise. 'Thanks, that's big of you to say it in front of everyone.'

'Well, it is Christmas,' Tony said gruffly. 'And I've probably had too much of Sebastian's wine and brandy . . .'

'Have another glass,' Sebastian said and lifted the decanter. 'To the family . . . all of us, because each and every one of us is a part of Lizzie's family and mine . . .'

'To Beth and Tony and Matt . . .' Lizzie raised her glass just as the telephone shrilled. Beth jumped up and ran to answer it. They could hear her voice chattering excitedly and when she returned a few minutes later she was beaming all over her face.

'Jenny has a daughter and they're both doing well,' she said. 'She's having a rest now but we can go and see her later this evening . . .'

'Oh, Beth, that's wonderful,' Lizzie said and got up to embrace her friend. 'You must be so excited and happy for her.'

'I can't quite believe it,' Beth said and looked at Tony. 'We're grandparents . . .'

'This calls for a celebration,' Sebastian said and produced the bottle of champagne he'd had cooling in the fridge.

'Oh, I couldn't . . .' Beth looked at Tony. 'Well,

perhaps just one, although we've both had rather a lot to drink already . . .'

'You can't go without celebrating something like that,' Sebastian insisted, pouring drinks into fragile crystal glasses. 'I kept this back specially to toast the baby's head.'

'Yes, we'll stay for the champagne,' Tony said and Matt grinned at his mother.

'Don't worry, Mum. I'm driving because I've only had one glass of wine,' he said and grinned, 'and I'll be taking you to the hospital this evening so just relax and enjoy the moment. It isn't every day you become a grandparent for the first time . . . and I'm an uncle . . .'

'No, it isn't . . .' Beth giggled and sat on the arm of Lizzie's comfortable chair. 'I'm so excited I don't know whether I'm on my head or my heels . . .'

'That's too much of Sebastian's wine or something . . .' Matt teased and a look in his eyes made Betty go into a fit of giggles. He raised his brows at her, winked and then turned to Miriam. 'Can we give you a lift home? I can assure you that I'm quite sober . . .'

'That's kind of you, Matt . . . yes, why not, but I'd rather have a cup of tea than champagne if you don't mind, Sebastian.'

'I'll make it, Dad,' Betty said and jumped up from her seat on the soft rug in front of the fire. Matt got up and followed her into the kitchen, saying that he would help her.

'Dad's generosity means I could come to Paris

with you, Betty,' he said. 'I can write there as well as anywhere so we'll get to spend time together that way . . .'

'Yes, that would be nice,' Betty said and closed the door behind them.

It was more than an hour later when Sebastian finally saw all their guests to the door and then came back to the sitting room and looked at his daughters.

'Washing up time, you two! We'll do it between us – and you will sit where you are, Lizzie.'

'I can help . . .'

'Do as Dad says, Mum,' Betty said. 'You were cooking all morning and we're full of energy, aren't we, Francie?'

'Yep,' Francie said and bounced up. 'Most of it was done earlier; it's only glasses and small plates – oh, and the trifle dishes. We made pigs of ourselves, Mum, and ate the lot . . .'

She ran after her sister and father and Lizzie heard them laughing and giggling in the kitchen as they worked. The sound was sweet music to her ears. They sounded so happy and she knew that as a family and individually they were all happy at this moment in time. Yes, her daughters would have bad days to come as well as good ones, because that happened to everyone, but for now they were happy, just as she and Sebastian were.

Her lovely daughters were showing their true natures by looking after her and she knew how lucky she was to have such a generous family. Not just Sebastian and her daughters, but Beth and her family, Aunt Miriam – and others who had not been there today but were not forgotten. Romany was spending Christmas with her latest man and Ed had found a widow he was enjoying spending time with. She'd asked him round for Christmas Day and it was the first Christmas for years that he'd not come to Lizzie for his dinner. She was glad he was content, though he'd never remarried.

In the summer they would do as Sebastian had suggested and take a house in France. Betty could send designs to her friends in Paris and meet up with them in a few months, when she was surer of what she wanted to do with her life, and Francie could work hard at college and try to pass the exam for the French art school.

It was a new adventure, another stage of their lives, and Lizzie was looking forward to it, just as she was to the birth of her son. Her daughters stood at a threshold and both of them were about to embark on the journey of a lifetime that would bring excitement, happiness, some sadness of course, and perhaps fame – but she would have a new life, a new child to care for.

Lizzie smiled with contentment. Happy just to sit back and watch them – her daughters. It was time to let them spread their wings and fly . . .